ONE

A man surged out of s[...] at Murdock, swinging a baseball bat. . . . Murdock pulled his KA-BAR, and was about to challenge him when he saw a second man come from directly in front of him with a knife. He ducked the charge, threw up his left arm, and felt the knife hit it, but the blade didn't cut through. He whirled and found a third man charging toward him.

Murdock grabbed the speargun and fired for his legs. The steel ten-inch dart dug into the man's right thigh and put him down. Murdock swung around and caught the man with the knife bearing in again. Murdock's knife came up and sliced the attacker's bare arm. Then he spun around and slashed again, drawing blood across the man's chest. The attacker screamed and ran into the darkness.

The man with the baseball bat knelt on the ground holding his right wrist.

"Bastard, you broke my wrist," he shrilled. Then he stood, holding his wrist, and ran toward the street. Murdock moved up to the man with the spear in his thigh. The man held up both hands.

"No more," he said. "Christ, but that hurts. Damn speargun? You some kind of one-man army?"

"Something like that."

SEAL TEAM SEVEN
PAYBACK

KEITH DOUGLASS

BERKLEY BOOKS, NEW YORK

Special thanks to Chet Cunningham for his contributions to this book.

SEAL TEAM SEVEN: PAYBACK

A Berkley Book / published by arrangement with
the author

PRINTING HISTORY
Berkley edition / July 2002

Copyright © 2002 by The Berkley Publishing Group.
SEAL TEAM SEVEN logo illustration by Michael Racz.
Cover art by Cliff Miller.

Visit our website at
www.penguinputnam.com

ISBN: 0-425-18544-3

BERKLEY®
Berkley Books are published by The Berkley Publishing Group,
a division of Penguin Putnam Inc.,
375 Hudson Street, New York, New York 10014.
BERKLEY and the "B" design
are trademarks belonging to Penguin Putnam Inc.

PRINTED IN THE UNITED STATES OF AMERICA

10 9 8 7 6 5 4 3 2 1

Dedicated to those U.S. Navy SEALs

*who have died in the service
of their country in some
dirty little war in a
strange land far from home,
or in some covert
operation that
only a few
will ever know about.
Ave, hail and farewell.
We salute you.*

Dear Reader,

Hey, wanted to thank you for your fine response to my plea for mail in book number sixteen. A plea made due to an unfortunate wager I made with an erstwhile friend. No, I didn't get the thousand letters, but he backed off and we had an arm-wrestling contest instead for the small inheritance, and now he owes me two hundred dollars. I said the inheritance was small.

A note of caution. Men, more and more mail is coming to me from women readers. Yes! A lot of the fair sex like the shenanigans and combat of our SEAL Team Seven. The loudest protest against having my favorite girl-type nuclear weapons expert along on the two missions came from a woman, an ex-Navy lady at that.

So, it might be a good idea to hide this copy of *Payback* under a pillow or slip it in with the magazines so your wife, or lady friend, doesn't find it. I'm warning you now. I won't be responsible if some female discovers your copy and you never get a chance to finish reading it.

Oh, yes, keep those cards and letters coming. If I goof, yell at me. If you like these books, you can say that too. I'll pitch your letters at my new editor. Every little bit helps. Send your letters to:

SEAL TEAM SEVEN
Keith Douglass,
8431 Beaver Lake Drive
San Diego, CA 92119

Take care and, please, read more (of my) books.

Keith Douglass

SEAL TEAM SEVEN

THIRD PLATOON*
CORONADO, CALIFORNIA

Rear Admiral (L) Richard Kenner. Commander of all SEALs. Based in Little Creek, Virginia.

Captain Harry L. Arjarack. 51, Commanding Officer of NAVSPECWARGRUP ONE, in Coronado, California, including SEAL Teams One, Three, Five and Seven.

Commander Dean Masciareli. 47, 5' 11", 220 pounds. Annapolis graduate. Commanding officer of Seal Team Seven in Coronado.

Master Chief Petty Officer Gordon MacKenzie. 47, 5' 10", 180 pounds. Administrator and head enlisted man of all of SEAL Team Seven.

Lieutenant Commander Blake Murdock. Platoon Leader, Third Platoon. 32, 6' 2", 210 pounds. Annapolis graduate. Six years in SEALs. Father important congressman from Virginia. Murdock recently promoted. Apartment in Coronado. Has a car and a motorcycle, loves to fish. Weapon: Alliant Bull Pup duo 5.56mm & 20mm explosive round. Alternate: H & K MP-5SD submachine gun.

ALPHA SQUAD

Timothy F. Sadler. Senior Chief Petty Officer. Top EM in Third Platoon. Third in command. 32, 6' 2", 220 pounds. Married to

---

*Third Platoon assigned exclusively to the Central Intelligence Agency to perform any needed tasks on a covert basis anywhere in the world. All are top-secret assignments. Goes around Navy chain of command. Direct orders from the CIA.

Sylvia, no children. Been in the Navy for fifteen years, a SEAL for last eight. Expert fisherman. Plays trumpet in any Dixieland combo he can find. Weapon: Alliant Bull Pup duo 5.56mm & 20mm explosive round. Good with the men.

David "Jaybird" Sterling. Machinist's Mate First Class. Lead petty officer. 24, 5' 10", 170 pounds. Quick mind, fine tactician. Single. Drinks too much sometimes. Crack shot with all arms. Grew up in Oregon. Helps plan attack operations. Weapon: H & K MP-5SD submachine gun.

Luke "Mountain" Howard. Gunner's Mate Second Class. 28, 6' 4", 250 pounds. Black man. Football at Oregon State. Tryout with Oakland Raiders six years ago. In Navy six years. SEAL for four. Single. Rides a motorcycle. A skiing and wind-surfing nut. Squad sniper. Weapon: H & K PSG1 7.62 NATO sniper rifle.

Bill Bradford. Quartermaster's Mate First Class. 24, 6' 2", 215 pounds. An artist in his spare time. Paints oils. He sells his marine paintings. Single. Quiet. Reads a lot. Has two years of college. Platoon radio operator. Carries a SATCOM on most missions. Weapon: Alliant Bull Pup duo 5.56mm & 20mm explosive round.

Joe "Ricochet" Lampedusa. Operations Specialist Second Class. 21, 5' 11", 175 pounds. Good tracker, quick thinker. Had a year of college. Loves motorcycles. Wants a Hog. Pot smoker on the sly. Picks up plain girls. Platoon scout. Weapon: Colt M-4A1 with grenade launcher. Alternate: Bull Pup duo 5.56mm & 20mm explosive round.

Kenneth Ching. Quartermaster's Mate First Class. 25, 6' even, 180 pounds. Full-blooded Chinese. Platoon translator. Speaks Mandarin Chinese, Japanese, Russian, and Spanish. Bicycling nut. Paid $1,200 for off-road bike. Is trying for Officer Candidate School. Weapon: Colt M-4A1 rifle with grenade launcher.

Vincent "Vinnie" Van Dyke. Electrician's Mate Second Class. 24, 6' 2", 220 pounds. Enlisted out of high school. Played varsity basketball. Wants to be a commercial fisherman after his current hitch. Good with his hands. Squad machine gunner. Weapon: H & K 21-E 7.62 NATO round machine gun.

Bravo Squad

Lieutenant Ed DeWitt. Leader Bravo Squad. Second in command of the platoon. 30, 6' 1", 175 pounds. From Seattle. Wiry. Married to Milly. No kids. Annapolis graduate. A career man. Plays a good game of chess on traveling board. Weapon: Alliant Bull Pup duo 5.56mm & 20mm explosive round. Alternate: H & K G-11 submachine gun.

George "Petard" Canzoneri. Torpedoman's Mate First Class. 27, 5' 11", 190 pounds. Married to Navy wife, Phyllis. No kids. Nine years in Navy. Expert on explosives. Nicknamed "Petard" for almost hoisting himself one time. Top pick in platoon for explosives work. Weapon: Alliant Bull Pup duo 5.56mm & 20mm explosive round.

Miguel Fernandez. Gunner's Mate First Class. 26, 6' 1", 180 pounds. Wife, Maria, daughter, Linda, 7, in Coronado. Spends his off time with them. Highly family-oriented. He has family in San Diego. Speaks Spanish and Portuguese. Squad sniper. Weapon: H & K PSG1 7.62 NATO sniper rifle.

Colt "Guns" Franklin. Yeoman Second Class. 24, 5' 10", 175 pounds. A former gymnast. Powerful arms and shoulders. Expert mountain climber. Has a motorcycle, and does hang gliding. Speaks Farsi and Arabic. Weapon: Colt M-4A1 with grenade launcher.

Tracy Donegan. Signalman Second Class. 24, 6' even, 185 pounds. Former Navy boxer. Tough. Single. Expert tracker and expert on camouflage and ground warfare. Expert marksman. Platoon driver, mechanic. Frantic Chargers football fan. Speaks Italian and Swahili. Weapon: H & K G-11 with caseless rounds.

Jack Mahanani. Hospital Corpsman First Class. 25, 6' 4", 240 pounds. Platoon medic. Tahitian/Hawaiian. Expert swimmer. Bench-presses four hundred pounds. Divorced. Top surfer. Wants the .50 sniper rifle. Weapon: Alliant Bull Pup duo 5.56mm & 20mm explosive round. Alternate: Colt M-4A1 with grenade launcher.

Frank Victor. Gunner's Mate Second Class. 23, 6' even, 185 pounds. Two years in SEALs. Radio, computer expert. Can program, repair, and build computers. Shoots small-bore rifle competitively. Married. Wife, June, a computer programmer/specialist. No children. Lives in Coronado. Weapon: Alliant Bull Pup duo with 5.56mm & 20mm explosive round.

Paul "Jeff" Jefferson. Engineman Second Class. Black man. 23, 6' 1", 200 pounds. Expert in small arms. Can tear apart most weapons and reassemble, repair, and innovate them. A chess player to match Ed DeWitt. Weapon: Alliant Bull Pup duo 5.56mm & 20mm explosive round.

1

Caribbean Sea
Off Puerto Rico

Lieutenant Ed DeWitt kept one eye on the radar screen in the sleek cabin of the Pegasus as it slammed through the azure Caribbean Sea at thirty knots. He could just make out the trace of the pirate cruiser slashing through the water five miles ahead of them. The boatmen had done nothing illegal yet, but the Navy spotter in an aircraft high overhead had been shadowing the power cruiser for two hours and had called in the Pegasus for assistance. The same boat had been chased before by the plane, but it had become hidden and then lost in a maze of small inlets, narrow waterways, and tangled growth on an uninhabited stretch of the southern coast of Puerto Rico east of Punta Petrona. Now the spotter kept DeWitt up to date through his ear speaker on his Motorola personal-commo radio.

"Yes, I'd say the pirates are definitely aiming at that sailboat," the spotter went on. "The target is about five miles ahead of the pirate, but he's dead on course to overtake her shortly. Our hope was that you could charge up there and intercept the pirates before they hit the sail ship. But not a chance. I didn't call you in soon enough."

"We can kick this boat up to forty-five knots. Wouldn't that be enough to cut him off?" DeWitt asked. He watched his seven-man team in the slender Navy powerboat.

"Negative. He's got too much lead on you. My fault. We protect these sail craft whenever we can, but this bastard pirate came out of that damn fog bank and surprised everybody. We didn't think he was out hunting today." The spotter's voice came through showing his frustration. The Navy coxswain at the controls of the Pegasus heard the exchange on his Motorola and nodded.

"Watch and wait," DeWitt told his Bravo Squad of Third Platoon, SEAL Team Seven, home-based in Coronado, California. His squad was on special duty with the Coast Guard and the Navy to cut down on the pirating of small vessels in the Caribbean area.

The Pegasus is the Navy version of a "cigar" boat, eighty-two feet long and only seventeen feet wide. Officially it's the Pegasus Class MKV (SOC/PBF). It was designed specifically to insert and withdraw Navy SEALs from unfriendly territory. Eight of the boats went into service in 1997, with twenty more added to the fleet in 1999. It's powered by two 12V 396 TE94 diesels that turn out 4,500 horsepower.

DeWitt checked his men. All were ready. They had specific instructions to do as little harm as possible to the pirates, and were ordered not to use the Bull Pup exploding 20mm rounds on the pirates unless they had to, if it turned into a running gun battle.

Three minutes later the Motorola spoke again. "Yes, yes, we have the pirate ship within hailing distance of the sailing vessel. You can't get there in time," the spotter in the Navy plane said with a touch of guilt.

On board the charging powerboat, Sancho waved at the man steering the forty-two-foot sailboat only thirty feet away. Then he angled in closer and from twenty feet pointed to his best shot, Hernando, who blasted ten rounds from a Colt Commando on full automatic. The man at the yacht's wheel didn't even have time to look up as the sound of the shots and the 5.56mm lead messengers jolted into his body at the same time. He screamed once; then another round caught him in the throat and angled upward into his brain, dumping him on the deck, where he sprawled in sudden death.

Sancho eased his forty-foot powerboat up to the sailboat. Two of his men tied the crafts together, and at once six men leaped on board the pleasure craft. Each of the Puerto Rican pirates carried a submachine gun. Two had Ingrams, two had

Beretta 3's, and the rest CZ Model 25's from Czechoslovakia.

A man rushed up from the cabin. He yelled at the first gunman he saw, and was rewarded with four rounds of parabellums to his chest. The shooter stripped out the dead man's wallet from his shorts, and pulled off rings and his watch. Three pirates stormed below. They found four women and two more men in the saloon.

The pirate's submachine guns stuttered out instant death as all three men fired. They killed two of the women where they sat. One of the men tried to charge forward, but was stopped in mid-stride when six rounds hit his chest and shoulders and two more punched deadly holes in his brain.

One blond woman in a bikini still held a drink in her hand where she sat on a couch. She looked up in terror as Sancho walked up to her and fondled her breasts. "Hey, pretty lady, I really hate to do this, but you know, it just got to be done." He smiled at her and winked, then shot her once in the heart. Sancho laughed. "Hey, dead lady, I lied."

The men belowdeck split up. One took wallets, rings, and jewelry from the women. Another one darted into the rear cabin, found the safe, and blew it open with a small controlled charge. He then quickly looted everything of value in the safe.

In the small forward cabin the boat's navigation equipment, radios, depth gauges, and other instruments were stripped off the fittings, and rushed to the pirate ship.

Sancho stood by the wheel of his powerboat, Ingram in hand, watching the men work, and checking his watch.

"Sixty seconds," he bellowed into the silence of the sea. "You have one minute to finish. Quickly now. The damn Navy plane is getting interested again. We need to race out of here."

Sancho heard another controlled explosion. Good, they had found the second safe. There was always one hidden, but he and his men had seen plans of most of the yachts and he knew where to look. Moments later men began jumping back on board the motor launch. "All on board," one of the pirates, wearing a bandanna over his head, called.

Sancho motioned for them to untie the sailboat, and then

he counted his men. Everyone had returned. He took a small black case from his pocket and gunned the launch away from the sailboat. He opened the lid on the case and pushed one red button; then when they were a hundred yards from the sailboat, he pushed the second red button. A blast echoed across the water, splinters flew over the *Marylue,* and smoke gushed from two blown-out portholes. A moment later fire billowed up the stairwell and the ship began listing to port.

Sancho grinned, turned the launch toward shore, and pushed the throttles forward all the way. Now it would be a race between him and whoever the Navy and Coast Guard tried to throw at him this time. He laughed softly, fingering the scar tissue across his right cheek. Sometimes he enjoyed the chase as much as he did the attack. He coaxed one more knot of speed out of the big engines belowdeck and charged across the water.

The Pegasus had been slamming through the waves at its full forty-five-knot speed, making the SEALs hang on to keep from being bounded overboard as the long craft skipped from one wave top to the next.

DeWitt pulled down his mike from where it rested out of the way against his floppy hat brim. "These guys work as quick as expert car strippers. Everyone with a specific job to get done fast. We play it by ear when we get there."

Two minutes later the radios came on. "The pirates have pushed away from the sailboat," the spotter said. "The sails are down and she's drifting; now she's showing smoke and starting to list to port. The pirate ship is gunning for land."

"Moving as fast as we can," DeWitt said.

Two minutes later, the Pegasus nosed up to the danger-ously listing sailboat. Her port rail was almost in the water. DeWitt had used his binoculars and seen one dead man on the deck. The man had slid almost into the water. The mo-ment the Navy craft touched the sailboat they lashed both craft together. DeWitt pointed to Mahanani and Fernandez.

"You two, on board with me, the rest hold here. Get ready to cut loose the second you think this sailboat is going down."

They jumped onto the slanted deck and hurried to the steps

going down to the cabin. Inside, they paused.

"My God, a slaughterhouse," Jack Mahanani, hospital corpsman first class, said.

"Check them," DeWitt ordered.

Mahanani moved from one body to the next quickly. The whole boat gave a lunge to the left as it listed farther to port. The corpsman touched the throat of the last woman victim and looked up. "All dead, Lieutenant."

The boat slued to port again.

"Out of here, she's going down," DeWitt barked, and the three raced up the steps to the canted deck. All but one of the ties had been undone, and they worked up the deck to the edge of the Pegasus and stepped on board. The last tie was cut and the Pegasus drifted a dozen feet to the left.

Ten seconds later the craft with the name *Marylue* on the bow tipped the rest of the way on her side, slowly took on water, and sank below the light chop of the blue sea.

Then they heard the spotter plane race overhead.

"We have it, SEALs. Videotaped the sinking and your getaway. You have the name of the craft?"

"Affirmative. The *Marylue*. Eight dead. No time for ID on any of them. We're going after the pirates. Can you give us a heading?"

The northwest heading came through, and the Pegasus gunned through the waters heading toward Puerto Rico.

Five minutes later the spotter plane came on the air again.

"We've reported the attack and the sinking. Also have a new heading for you on the pirate. We estimate his speed at about thirty-five knots. He's twelve miles ahead of you and looks to be heading for the coast of Puerto Rico. He's got a nest there that we can't find. It's an elaborate complex of shallow waterways and tangled growth and canals and all sorts of places to hide and set up camp. The locals have been chasing this guy for years. We know about where he heads, but we've never been able to watch him go ashore. There are a hundred spots along here he could slip in and we'd never spot him from the air."

"Busting our asses to get to him, spotter. No way we can catch him even at our forty-five knots. Best we can do is get a firm radar fix on him where he vanishes into the maze."

"Better than we've had from the air, Pegasus. Once when we had a shot at him, we were on a hundred-twenty-foot cutter and no chance to follow him up those narrow little ditches he used. When you get the radar fix on his entrance, tell us and we'll get ground units in there as close as we can. Use your second radio to contact them on TAC Two. Good luck."

The three SEALs who came back from the sunken sailboat were subdued. Miguel Fernandez, gunner's mate first class, stared at his hands and shook his head. He closed his eyes and held his sniper rifle close to his chest. "Worst damn slaughter I've ever seen," he said. "They just mowed the tourists down where they sat like they were targets in a shooting gallery."

Mahanani wiped the victims' blood off his hands. He washed them with alcohol from his medic kit and took a long deep breath. "Like a damn close-combat kill house in there, only these were real people who bled a lot. Most of them were in their fifties. Retired, I'd bet, out to see the world. Those fucking pirates are worse than animals. I'll be damn glad to find them."

DeWitt stared straight ahead at the sea and the radar. He wouldn't let his emotions get control. He had beaten down nausea twice since he came out of the sailboat's cabin. He had wanted to throw up and then cry and scream to the heavens. But he didn't. Officers don't cry. He had to maintain.

He scanned the water ahead. No sign of the pirate ship yet. They were on the right heading. The plane had moved forward and tracked the pirate ship, but they had only a general idea where the boat would hit land.

Ten minutes later the longer-range radar picked up the powerboat, and less than two minutes after that it vanished off the screen, to be replaced by the solid land mass of southern Puerto Rico.

"Save that heading," DeWitt said, and the ship's driver nodded. On this angle they could come within a hundred feet of the spot where the pirate ship vanished into the maze of trees and waterways.

Ten minutes later, the Pegasus nosed up to the uninviting Puerto Rican coastline. It was mostly uninhabited along here, covered with jungle. They probed along a hundred yards each direction, and found several half-clogged narrow waterways. Which was the right one? Canzoneri sat on the bow watching the vegetation. He held up his hand, and DeWitt had the coxswain stop the boat.

"Look over there," DeWitt said. Some vines and tree limbs had been stripped of their leaves, and a few branches hung almost touching the water.

"Could be it," Lam said. "How about nosing into that same spot and see what we can see."

DeWitt looked at young Ensign Swartz, who commanded the boat. Swartz scowled and planted both fists on his hips.

"I told you when we started that the open sea is fine, but this running up channels and dodging vines is something else," Swartz said. He paused. "I know our mission. I also know that as skipper of this boat I'm responsible for her. If anything gets damaged or broken or if we get grounded, I'm the one on the hot seat."

DeWitt stepped toward him. "Hey, Swartz, understood. I've got carte blanche on this mission. The CNO himself authorized it. If we scrape up this Pegasus or total it, you won't be given a statement of charges. I guarantee you that. Let's nose in there and take a gander."

Ensign Swartz looked at his coxswain.

"Sir, looks deep enough, good quantity of water coming out, check that current. We can nudge those vines apart and if we don't hit the bank, we should be home free. Let's try it."

"Ahead, slow," Swartz said. The coxswain moved the throttle and wheel and headed for the spot with the sheared-off branches. DeWitt, Swartz, and Lam stood on the bow of the sleek boat and watched the vegetation come closer. When they touched it, Lam brushed it aside and the craft edged inward. A moment later they were past the curtain of green growth and in a channel thirty feet wide that extended forward into the gloom.

"Yeah, looks good to me," DeWitt said. Swartz took a deep breath and signaled the coxswain to motor forward slowly.

Ensign Swartz scowled. "We move inland only to the point where it could endanger my boat. Then we back off."

"Agreed," DeWitt said. "Looks from here like we have a clear way a long way ahead."

The driver nudged the long, thin boat through the channel, and the officers retreated into the cabin as the brush trailed almost to the water on both sides. It was a slow-moving stream that angled to the left, and they went with it. Trees and brush and vines grew on both sides, sometimes bridging over the top, turning the small waterway into a tunnel.

Ahead fifty yards the stream turned right. Inland, on the left, they saw an open space with a shack of a house, a rowboat tied to the small one-plank dock, and a half-dozen chickens scratching in the moist soil. No people showed.

"Hold it," DeWitt said. The coxswain cut the motors. "Get us to that bank," DeWitt said, pointing to the side where the shack stood. "Franklin, Victor. Go check out that place. Capture or waste anybody you see. Silenced weapons."

The two men waited until the Pegasus nosed into the bank. Then they jumped off the bow to solid ground, parted, and came up on both sides of the shack. There was no window facing the water, only a door half open.

Franklin signaled to Victor he'd go first. He charged up to the cabin, pressed himself against the outer wall three feet from the door, and waited. No movement or noise from inside. He edged to the door and jolted through it, his MP-5 pointing the way. He swept the single room and grinned.

A few seconds later, Victor charged into the same room. They both snorted. The downriver lookout had slumped over a wreck of a table. One hand held a nearly empty bottle of rum, the other a sandwich with only one bite gone. A small two-way radio lay beside the sandwich. His Uzi submachine gun lay on the floor at his feet.

Victor grabbed the man and dropped him to the floor on his belly, then bound his hands behind him. The man grunted and frowned, but remained unconscious. Franklin bound his ankles together with the plastic cuffs.

"Skipper, we've got one lookout, drunk as a skunk, and a sandwich. He's bound up. I'll bring his weapon."

"Roger that," DeWitt said. "Return quickly."

In less than a minute the two SEALs were on board, and the Pegasus moved slowly forward. The throb of its engine was low and guttural, but mostly eaten up by the sound-absorbing jungle.

"Let's stay alert, people," DeWitt said softly into the Motorola. "Locked and loaded."

The stream narrowed. Ensign Swartz bit his lip and kept watching the banks. At least they didn't have to worry about the screws hitting bottom. The craft was propelled with twin water jets.

Anther small turn, and the coxswain idled the engines so the Pegasus stood still in the gentle current. Ahead fifty yards DeWitt saw two buildings, both built facing the river on the left-hand side. He guessed they were for storage.

"We've got to clear those buildings," DeWitt said. "Canzoneri, Franklin, and Jefferson, on me. The rest of you set up a perimeter around the sides of the boat. Coxswain, move us over to that little sandbar and we'll jump to it."

The driver motored twenty feet upstream and to the left until the bow nudged the sandbar. The SEALs jumped off the bow onto the sand, stayed dry, and ran into the fringe of brush between them and the buildings.

They lay belly-down in the grass and weeds looking at the two structures forty yards ahead. Frame, one-story, maybe twenty feet square. No doors or windows in the back or on this side.

"On me, ten yards," DeWitt said, and lifted up and ran through the brush crouched over until he could see the other side of the closer building. The three SEALs trailed him at ten-yard intervals. When all were around and down in the grass, they saw that there was a door and a window.

DeWitt pointed to Canzoneri, waved him forward, and then pointed to the building. They lifted up at the same time and sprinted for the side of the structure. DeWitt expected to hear the stutter of submachine guns at any time, but he made it there with no gunfire. Canzoneri hit the wall on the other side of the window. He lifted up and tried to look through the glass. He dropped down, moved his hand in front of his eyes, and shook his head.

So, the door. DeWitt moved silently to the door and tried

the knob. It was unlocked. He pulled it gently forward fearing a squeak. Nothing. He edged it out an inch and looked inside. At first he couldn't see a thing. Then, at the far side, he saw two chairs and a card table with a single lightbulb burning above them. Two men sat in the chairs, and a submachine gun and a small two-way radio lay on the table.

DeWitt took a breath, motioned Canzoneri over, and let him look through the inch-wide slot. He motioned to the SEAL to jerk the door open. DeWitt would be in first. He held a silenced MP-5 set on three-round bursts.

DeWitt took one more look. The men were playing cards. He nodded. Canzoneri jerked the door open and DeWitt charged forward across the wooden floor, his boots sounding like thunderclaps as he brought up the sub gun.

"Don't try for it or you're dead," DeWitt brayed. One man grabbed the submachine gun and dove to the floor. DeWitt tracked him with the MP-5 and sprayed six rounds into him before he could get the weapon around to fire. The second man froze in his chair, and then silently lifted his hands high over his head.

Canzoneri was right behind DeWitt. He checked the throat on the man on the floor. He shook his head. The man in the chair mumbled something, and DeWitt pushed the MP-5 into his belly.

"What did you say?"

"Hablo español. Hablo español."

Canzoneri waved at DeWitt. "I'll go get Fernandez."

Five minutes later the Spanish-speaking Fernandez had all the information the downriver guard knew. They were hired to stay there and guard the river. Nobody ever came up there. It was an easy job. He didn't even think his gun was loaded. Yes, the radio connected them with the first guard in the shack. If he said somebody was coming upstream, they were alerted.

DeWitt checked the live guard's weapon. It was loaded with a full magazine, and a round was in the chamber with the safety off.

"That's about it, Lieutenant," said Fernandez. "He said the boat went upstream about half an hour ago and they all waved. Most of the men on the boat were drunk. He said the camp is upstream another mile, but the motorboat can go only half that distance."

"Tie up this one and bring his sub gun," DeWitt said. He used the Motorola. "Ensign Swartz, tie up the Peg there. We'll move on up by foot. SEALs, get your asses up here to the buildings. This one is clear. Canzoneri and Fernandez, clear that other building. Then we'll be ready to haul ass out of here." The two SEALs rushed out the door and approached the other structure. There was no light inside. They crept up to the door that sagged on one hinge and looked inside. One room, some boxes, and a large rat that scurried away. Nobody else in the place.

Five minutes later the SEALs had assembled, checked weapons, and moved up the left-hand side of the stream. The prisoner had said that was the side the camp was on, a mile ahead. The SEALs left the lookout tied hand and foot on the floor.

"There will be someone with the boat, so we take them down silently," DeWitt said. He sent Colt Franklin out in front as point, and they moved out ten yards apart.

Franklin had always wanted to be scout, and now was his chance. He moved as silently as he knew how, keeping a hundred yards ahead of the main body. The closer he came to where the boat should be, the slower, more deliberate, and more careful his movements. He faded from one tree to the next, skirted a spot of brush, and always kept near the river so its gurgling and bouncing down rocks would cover any sounds he made.

Ten minutes later he edged up to a clearing, parted some heavy grass, and stared at a dock on the river. It was solid, made of four-by-sixes and built to last. The floating pier would rise and fall with the water level. Tied to the pier was the boat they had chased. Two men worked on it. One was scrubbing it down with fresh water and a sudsy brush. Franklin saw a second man working inside. Both men had sub guns slung over their backs.

"Lieutenant, you need to take a look," Franklin whispered into his Motorola mike. A few moments later, DeWitt bellied up to where Franklin lay.

"Oh, yeah. Just two. We take them out, then move on up.

Fernandez, get up here with that sniper. We need you."

When all of the SEALs had lined up along the edge of the brush facing the boat, DeWitt gave Fernandez the go. He sighted in on the man washing down the boat, who was on the dock now with a swab and a bucket of soapy water. Just as he started the next swipe with the swab, Fernandez nailed him in the middle of the back with a silenced 7.62 NATO round. The pirate crumpled without a sound and didn't move.

They heard the other man call out. Then when he had no response, he came out of the cabin to the rail looking for his buddy. Fernandez let him lean over the rail, then shot him in the chest with one round. He added a second one, and the inside man tumbled over the rail and hit hard on the wooden dock. He never moved again.

Three silenced shots, like a huff or a puff, and it was over. They left the dead men where they had fallen and moved up the river. There was a good trail here, much used. Franklin kept a fifty-yard interval now in front of the troops. Things were tightening up. He'd seen Lam do it a dozen times. Move and watch, all eyes and ears. Every bit of him. Observe and work ahead if it was clear.

Franklin stopped after a quarter of a mile and asked DeWitt to come up for a look. Not a lot to see except trees and brush and vines and a few wildflowers. Green on green. Then DeWitt found it. Thirty yards ahead along this open stretch of trail a lone lookout leaned against a thick tree trunk smoking. He wore jungle fatigues to blend in with the foliage, and held a radio in one hand and the end of a smoke in the other.

"Can't risk a silenced shot," DeWitt said. "Too damn close to where there must be others. Keep the rest of our guys here. I'll go up and shake hands with him."

"How about Lam?" Then Franklin realized. "Oh, yeah, he ain't here. Lieutenant, you be careful. I'll be up about half-way with my MP-5 if you get in trouble."

DeWitt slung his MP-5 across his back, and a moment later had vanished into the thick brush. Time to shit or get off the pot. Never ask one of the men to do something that he wouldn't do. Yeah, now was the time. DeWitt moved with more caution than he had ever done, working slowly, never putting weight on one foot until he was sure nothing would go swish or snap. He angled slightly toward the river. At the higher elevation it was much shallower now, and the gurgle and splash as it came down mini rapids gave him some sound cover.

He worked forward for five minutes, then took a break and relaxed all the muscles in his body a pair at a time. The process took two minutes; then he was on his feet and moving again. He drew his KA-BAR fighting knife. He'd honed the blade last night so it was far, far sharper than it ever had been. He bent back to the left toward the trail. Yes. There it was. The smoker?

The sentry had put out the cigarette, and held a sub gun in both hands as he looked up the trail toward the camp. Why was he looking that way? Then he turned and stared down the trail, then relaxed against the large trunk of his favorite tree.

Twenty feet.

Almost no cover.

How would he do it? The old distraction trick? A rock the other way to make the sentry look that way? Could he take a half-dozen steps silently, then charge toward the man before he realized someone was coming? Maybe. How about a knife throw? DeWitt vetoed that one at once. He could throw a knife and hit a target, but he wasn't going to bet his life on it. He came back to the rock.

Twice more the sentry turned and looked toward the camp. Maybe a replacement was coming. Wait for the next turn. It took two or three minutes. As soon as the sentry turned again, DeWitt came upright and took six running, almost silent steps toward the man. Just as the guard was due to look down the trail, the lieutenant threw a fist-sized rock beyond where the guard had been looking. The pirate jolted his gaze that way for another two seconds.

It was long enough. DeWitt kept up his charge at the sentry, holding the knife straight in front of him like a lance, gaining four feet of distance and precious tenths of a second.

The sentry never even started to turn. Instead he pulled up his weapon and aimed it at the rock sound. DeWitt's KA-BAR sliced through the man's shirt on the side, missed his ribs, and slanted through half a lung and stabbed two inches into his heart, killing him instantly. DeWitt caught him before he fell, pressed the sub gun against his chest, and dragged him off the trail into the brush.

By the time DeWitt had returned to the trail, Franklin knelt there looking upstream. He flashed the officer a grin and gave him a thumbs-up, then waved his arm forward and the rest of the SEALs moved silently up the trail with five-yard intervals.

"Out twenty yards, Franklin," DeWitt whispered, and the scout moved forward with caution. DeWitt and the rest of the squad followed. Franklin found no more guards, and five minutes later he and the rest of the SEALs stared at the group of buildings ahead from a fringe of brush that bordered a cleared area. DeWitt scanned the structures and decided there were three houses, a large garage, and two outbuildings that could be used for storage. It was still daylight, and he could see electric wires strung around, so they had power.

"Could be thirty guns in there, Lieutenant," Franklin said. "We got any help coming land side?"

"Supposed to be. The spotter plane man said as soon as our boat vanished into the woods, they would get land troops out and cover all roads, buildings, and houses in our general area. Let's hope that they do."

"Hey, Cap. How about a small diversion?" It was Mahanani.

"Like what?"

"I was thinking maybe one of them outbuildings could catch on fire. One twenty-mike-mike WP into that far one should make it burn like a torch."

"Too much noise. They'd know we were here."

"Right, Lieutenant," Franklin said. "But what if I was to slip up on the back side of that shack and drop in a couple of Willy Peter grenades. They don't make much more than a pop."

"Good. Get in position, but don't drop the WP until I give the word. We're supposed to have help out front. They gave me a radio, and I hope to hell it works. Donegan, you still have that GPS to pinpoint our location?"

"Sure do, Cap. You want the coordinates?"

"Work them out. I'll see if I can raise anybody on this tin box."

He turned on the second radio he took from his vest and lifted a two-foot antenna.

"Skyhook, this is Grounded. Do you read me?"

There was no response. He tried again. "Skyhook, this is Grounded off the Pegasus. Do you read me?"

"Yes, Grounded. Skyhook here with the land troops. We have fifty men on roads leading into the area where you vanished. What have you found?"

DeWitt told him the setup. "Can't see any cars from here, but there must be some in front. Here is the GPS coordinates." He read them off, and the Coast Guard man repeated them.

"Yes, we have men near there. We'll move forty men to the one lane leading into those three houses. The old Bamford place. Sold recently. We'll be on station in about fifteen minutes."

"Let us know when you're ready. You bring your men in from the front on an attack, and we'll bottle them up if they try to come down the river. We have their boat."

"Good. Talk to you in fourteen."

Five minutes later, Franklin said he was ready. He was against the side of the building. It looked like it once had been a barn with hay and stalls, he said. "Even has a window with the glass out," Franklin said. "I'll toss in the WP and haul ass on your command."

"Make it in ten minutes, Franklin."

"Roger that."

DeWitt started the timer on his wristwatch, and then told the rest of his men what was going down. "We spread out along here as a blocking force. We'll wait until we see if they are armed, then give them a chance to surrender. If they don't, we'll blow their asses all the way into San Juan."

The SEALs spread out, found cover, settled in, and waited. Then DeWitt gave Franklin the go, and they heard the WPs pop. A short time later smoke gushed from a broken window on the side of the old barn, and there were shouts from the houses.

Quickly a dozen men, women, and children ran out of the

houses and stared at the fire. It was beyond a bucket brigade, and the one garden hose had no pressure.

While they watched the barn burn, a submachine gun chattered off a dozen rounds in front of the houses.

"Men in the three houses," a powerful bullhorn blasted. "This is the FBI. You are surrounded. Come out the front doors of your homes with your hands in the air and we won't fire. Don't endanger the lives of your women and children. You have three minutes to move."

The people around the fire raced back into their houses. A short time later the bullhorn sounded again.

"No, we don't want your women and children to come out. We want the men to show themselves with their hands in the air."

Just then a dozen men ran out the back of the houses heading for the river trail. Each man had at least two weapons.

"I'll do warning shots," DeWitt said into the Motorola. "Hold fire." He fired three three-round bursts from his MP-5. "Hold it right there and drop your weapons," DeWitt bellowed.

Three of the pirates fired at the woods in front of them.

"Open season on pirates," DeWitt said, and the SEALs opened fire with eight guns. Five of the pirates went down. Two tried to keep firing as they crawled away. Five more dropped their weapons and held their hands in the air.

DeWitt called a cease-fire and used the special radio. "Skyhook, looks like it's time for you to come through the houses and collect the garbage. We have five pirates down and wounded, five with their hands in the air, and two trying to crawl away. Happy hunting. As soon as you collect this filth, we're heading back to San Diego."

2

NAVSPECWARGRUP-ONE
Coronado, California

Lieutenant Commander Blake Murdock leaned back in the chair at his small desk in the Third Platoon's tiny office and waved at Ed DeWitt, who angled through the door.

"Well, DeWitt. I hear you had a great vacation down there in the Caribbean."

"We kicked butt and asked for more, but they sent us home. No casualties, no wounds, all fit for duty." He dropped into the only other chair in the office and sprawled long legs halfway across the room. "Anything cooking?"

"Not so you could notice. Your buddy and mine, Masciareli, wants us to participate in an all-Seven exercise next week."

"All ten platoons? Why?"

"Unity, cohesiveness, and the American way. He's still pissed you got to hit the Carib and he didn't get to go along."

"Maybe Don Stroh will rescue us."

"Not a word from him or the CIA for a month now. He must be on vacation or maybe found a new girl."

"Thought he was married."

"He never has said one way or the other."

"So how are the three wounded coming along?" DeWitt asked.

"You had Franklin with you. He said he was fit for duty."

"Franklin worked as scout, did a good job. I don't think that bullet in and out in his left thigh bothered him a bit."

"Watch him on training for the next week. Not too sure about Bradford. He was in the hospital for a week, then out

17

on limited duty, and so he didn't report back here until last week. I kept him on an easy training sked. Doctors said that round missed his kidney by an inch and grazed one intestine. So when the infection is gone, he should be back in good shape. But I'm still worried about a torso wound."

"What about Lam?"

"He's sucking it up and gutting it out. Had a slug through his lower right leg and a ricochet on his right arm. Both healing well and he keeps up with everybody else on our training marches."

"So, it's training time. You have it set for next week?"

"This is Friday, Ed. Who is ready for next week? Unless you want to work Saturday instead of taking your four-day leave."

DeWitt sighed and crossed his ankles way out on the floor. "Yeah, I'm with you. I'm taking the four days, rest up a little. All that killing pirates makes a guy tired."

"All I need is your after-action report and you're out of here."

"Done in ten minutes." He pulled out his laptop computer and began pounding away. After a few minutes he looked up. "Oh, keep tabs on Mahanani for me. He's been acting a little weird lately. Nothing I can pin down. I asked him about it, and he said not to worry, he'd take care of any problems he had."

"That doesn't sound like our happy Hawaiian," Murdock said. "I'll watch him. Now finish that report and get out of here. Milly know you're home yet?"

"She's still at work."

Meanwhile, Alpha Squad rolled into the equipment room after its ten-mile hike and found Bravo there.

"Vacation over for you guys," Jaybird yelled. "Now you can get back to real work."

Paul Jefferson picked up Jaybird and hung him upside down until he bellowed in fury, then tipped him over and sat him on a bench. "Never tease a man when he's tired, little bird, otherwise you might get your feathers plucked out."

"Easy on the merchandise, chess player. I don't want to disappoint a certain little lady bird tonight in the nest."

"Didn't know we had buzzards around here," Bradford

jabbed, and Jaybird threw his sweaty T-shirt at him.

Jack Mahanani sat by himself getting dressed after his shower. Usually he was a big part of the high jinks and the drinking parties, but not today. He dressed and cast off as quickly as he could. He had on his civilian clothes when he went over the Quarter Deck, past Master Chief Petty Officer Gordon MacKenzie, and out to his car.

He drove by rote, hardly thinking where he was going. Tonight had to be better, his luck had to change. It hadn't helped him the last time. He drove steadily for twenty minutes out U.S. Interstate 8 toward a bustling little town, went just past it to the Indian reservation and the sprawling Casa Grande Casino. Mahanani parked and walked in the front door, and at once a man went into step beside him. Mahanani knew him; he was what the casino called a "counselor."

"Hey Jack, how's it going, man?"

"In and out, same-oh, same-oh."

"How are you treating our car?"

"Yeah, the Buick is riding good. I'm keeping up the tire pressure and getting ready for an oil change. I appreciate the lease you gave me on it, Harley, for a dollar a year." Harley was five ten, all Mesa Grande Indian, with stylish cut black hair, a sparse little beard, and a slight 140-pound body. His main job seemed to be to help people who spent too much at the casino.

"Let me buy you a drink, Jack. We need to talk. Hey, if you weren't a SEAL, I'd have dusted you out of here weeks ago. Yeah, you had a string of bad luck, but what can I say? I got a five-thousand-dollar credit for you now, which is on my tab, and that's as far as it's going."

They went into one of the bars in the casino, and Jack felt the sweat begin on his forehead. His armpits were already wet. Damn, he just needed a little luck. Twenty-one, the blackjack table, was the best way a player could beat the house. All the rest of the games and the machines were fixed with a definite house advantage. If he could just read the cards a little better.

"Jack, you aren't listening to me. You're into us for five thousand, we have the pink slip to your Buick, and can claim it at any time. If you want to put that five thousand on your MasterCard, I can get you back to the tables."

"You know I don't have a credit card." He hesitated, then pulled out his wallet. "But I do have three hundred dollars. You have any objection to a man spending his own money?"

"Hell, man, I should take it on account. If my boss knew you had that scratch, I'd be in a whole pot of trouble."

"The Buick is worth twice what I owe you. You want to sell it and give me the extra cash?"

"Hey, man, no worry there. We want to keep you happy. So go ahead. Try the table. Maybe it'll be good to you tonight."

"No lie? I can just go and play?"

"That's the business we're in, Jack. Go on. Have a blast."

Mahanani finished the drink, bought three hundred in chips, and went to his favorite blackjack table. He watched the play, mentally bet three times, and won each time. A player left the horseshoe and he moved in.

A familiar calm settled over him. Yeah, this was it, the thinking man's way to gamble. If you played the odds right and could remember just a few cards. He saw the four decks the dealer was using and frowned. Nobody could count cards with four decks. He'd go with logic and the odds. Yes.

The first round he had a jack for a hole card, and came up with an eight. He stayed. The dealer knew he had eighteen or nineteen. The dealer showed seventeen. Two players blew over the twenty-one limit, and two stayed. The dealer checked the cards, then drew a card. He had to hit seventeen. He pulled out a three of diamonds.

"Pay twenty-one, who has twenty-one?" he asked in a singsong voice that Mahanani tried not to let irritate him. He paid one player and dealt the cards again. It was only a ten-dollar chip. He had deliberately bought only tens to help him conserve.

The second round he won, and was even. Then he lost four times in a row. After a half hour of playing, he was down a hundred dollars. He should quit and leave. Have a good dinner down in San Diego and take in that action movie he'd heard a lot about.

He kept playing. Logic, damnit, he told himself. You don't

hit seventeen when the house shows a max of sixteen. Stupid.
He drew a five and broke. Get with it.

An hour later he was cleaned out. He saw Harley talk to
the dealer and give him a green slip of paper. The dealer
pushed the paper across the table toward Mahanani. He knew
what it was. A credit slip. He looked at the amount. A thousand dollars. That would put him into the casino for six thousand. How much was the Buick worth? Nine thousand tops.
Nowhere near the fifteen he paid for it. He looked at the
green slip. The dealer closed the game and he wasn't in it.
Harley came up and touched his shoulder.

"Yeah, some bad luck. Three hundred ain't no stake for
this table. With a thou you can drop a few hundred and come
back."

"Can't do it, Harley. I'm in too deep now. You know what
I make a month? I can't afford to sell the Buick. Got to have
wheels."

"You get healthy tonight and get your pink back. Give it
a try. Hell, it's only money."

Mahanani stared at the green slip with his name on it and
the printed figure of a thousand dollars. This was getting
serious. He told himself he could stop anytime he wanted to.
Now he wasn't so sure. The green slip or his Buick. What
would he do without wheels?

Hell, why not? His luck had to change. Logic. He had to
think his way into each round. Logic. Yeah, he could do that.
He took the pen beside the slip, signed it, and pushed it over
to the dealer, who counted out a thousand dollars for him
mostly in hundreds. Mahanani pushed the hundred-dollar
chips back and asked for tens.

He took his first two cards. A seven in the hole and a jack
showing. Good bluffing count, only these dealers never
bluffed. Dealer showed sixteen. He watched two players
break, saw the next one hold with a nine showing. Probably
a nineteen. He looked at the dealer, who had to hit sixteen.
The last two cards played out were under five. Bad odds. He
put his two ten-dollar chips on top of his cards and waved
the dealer off.

The next woman stayed with an eight showing. The dealer
checked the hands still alive, then dealt himself a card. A

damn four. It would have been *his* damn four if he'd taken it. The dealer closed out with twenty. He paid one player.

One of those damned nights.

By eleven-thirty that night, Mahanani was down to his last four ten-dollar chips. He shrugged and played all four. He came up with twenty on the deal and stayed. The dealer hit seventeen and pulled a five to break. The house paid.

Mahanani felt a lucky streak coming. Should he let the eighty dollars ride? Hell, no. He grabbed the eight chips, went to the cashier, exchanged them for money, and got out of the casino before he saw Harley.

Six thousand fucking dollars in the red to the Indians. He could stop anytime he wanted to. Sure he could. He sat behind the wheel of the Buick that he owned less than half of, and swore for ten minutes. Then he backed out slowly and took the freeway downhill to his apartment in Coronado. He had to work tomorrow. He was a SEAL. He frowned. No, they just came back from the Caribbean. He was on a four-day leave. What the hell was he going to do for four days? Surf. He'd hit Wind and Sea Beach and surf his balls off.

He wouldn't gamble anymore. Never again. He laughed. Sure, never again until tomorrow night, because he was off duty and they didn't have a night maneuver or training. He was a shitty gambler, didn't have the knack for it. But he knew he couldn't quit. Not until they refused to let him in the door without a wad of cash. Where would he get a stash of cash? In two or three days his Buick would be gone. The casino's dollar-a-year lease price would be jumped to four hundred a month and he'd have to bow out. Then how in hell did he get to the casino? How did he get to work? How did he get anywhere?

He parked at his apartment and went up the steps two at a time the way he always did. How was he going to do anything after he lost the Buick? Fuck it. He'd think of something. Fuck it.

Murdock had called a Saturday training session for Alpha Squad. He was there when the SEALs arrived at 0730 looking sleepy and ready to eat nails.

"Good morning to you too, SEALs. Yesterday was our

easy day. Today we go up to the mountain and learn again how to fire our weapons. We'll do fire and move and cover. Then do it again and again until we can do it in our sleep. I won't lose a man on our next little party because some fucking SEAL in my squad doesn't know how to fire, cover, and move."

He looked around, but not even Jaybird had a comment.

"Bring some cash with you because we'll stop up in Pine Valley for some chow on our way home. No MREs. We load the truck in twenty minutes. I want every man to carry three times normal ammo. We won't be taking the usual 20mm rounds, but plenty of 5.56. I'll take some twenties in case we need them. Any questions?"

He looked around. Nobody said a word. Yeah, he decided. It was going to be one of those days.

Timothy Sadler, senior chief petty officer and top EM in the platoon, came into the office a few minutes later when Murdock assembled his gear.

"Do we supply our own driver?" the chief asked.

"Howard gets that assignment. The truck should be out front in less than five. You ready?"

Murdock rode in the cab with Howard. There wasn't much conversation. Murdock felt grumpy. No reason. He was almost thirty-three years old, unmarried, and still playing kid games with lethal weapons and roaming the world getting shot at by all sorts of unhappy campers. He'd been promoted to lieutenant commander, the fourth step up the officers' ladder, and could have a career shot at making captain some day before he retired. Of course he couldn't do that in the SEALs. Too few spots, too many candidates. So he was back to playing with lethal toys hoping he didn't get too many of his men killed.

His father kept trying to get him to resign and run for Congress. A real opportunity there, and then when the next opening came, he could go for Senator from the Great State of Virginia. Yeah, just what would make him, happy kissing babies and lying to everyone he met so he could get elected.

Then last night Ardith Jane Manchester had called. They'd talked for almost an hour and she'd said she was considering a job in the San Diego area. She was almost certain that she would be leaving Washington, D.C., and government service. So, with Ardith in town all the time, it would mean a better apartment and then the pressure to get married. He had enough troubles already.

It was a three-hour truck ride in the updated version of the trusty old six-by-six basic military truck. They turned off Interstate 8 somewhere the other side of Boulder Oaks, just outside the boundary of the Cleveland National Forest, where they had a loose arrangement with the landowner that they could use his mountains for target practice as long as they closed any gates they came to and policed up their brass and any trash. They always did.

They drove five miles on a dirt track to the left of the highway into sharp-rising hills and mountains. Howard had done this route before, and he came to a stop at a windblown live oak tree that had managed to stay alive through the last four droughts.

Five minutes later Senior Chief Sadler had the squad in a diamond formation and looked over at Murdock.

"Move them into a wide V formation so they don't kill everyone in sight," he said. "You and I will be at the center observing. Do a radio check."

He listened as Sadler had each man chime in on the personal Motorola radios.

"All working, sir."

"Move them out, Sadler. Keep five yards separation. No firing until my orders."

The sun was out, tempering the five-thousand-foot altitude, as the SEALs worked up the first slope toward a pair of twin peaks about eight miles distant.

"Hit the dirt," Murdock called in the radio. "Okay, we're going to fire and move. I want the squad to move into a line of skirmishers on the senior chief. Ten yards apart. Move it now." Murdock watched as the men at the end of the V ran back to line up with Saddler. Murdock moved up to the left end of the line.

"Teamwork is the key. I want you to count off by twos from the left. Count." He barked out the first "one," the next man called out "two," the next called out "one," and so on along the line.

"Number-one men, I want you to fire twelve rounds on my command, straight ahead. As you fire, number-two men will be charging ten yards straight ahead. Check your field of fire. When number-one man finishes firing, the number-two man will hit the dirt and cover for him as he runs up ten yards past where his cover man is firing. Check your fields of fire. We don't want anyone getting killed out here. It would mess up the whole weekend. Each man will fire and move three times. Any questions?"

There were none. "Yes, I know, we've done this a hundred times, but this is a refresher. Time out your cover fire so you can shoot your last shot when your partner hits the dirt ahead of you. Number-two men charge forward first, number-ones support him with live fire. Ready. Start running and firing."

Murdock hit the dirt and fired straight ahead. He timed his rounds, and quit when his number-two hit the dirt. Then he ran straight ahead past his support man ten yards, before he dropped into the dirt and rocks. The firing behind him stopped. He looked back and saw Jaybird lift up and run forward. He had twenty yards to go. Murdock timed his firing to last until Jaybird dropped down in a prone position ready to fire.

After Murdock had run forward three times, he stood and watched the rest of the men. Only one more man had to complete his run and get covering fire.

"All right," Murdock said into the Motorola. "Anybody get killed?" He waited a moment. "Good, now let's move up into a line of skirmishers and see what we can do about the nest of snipers up there in that old oak snag out about two hundred yards."

Murdock took one end of the line of six men, and Senior Chief Sadler manned the far end.

"Walking fire, every ten seconds. No twenties. Keep the damn line straight. Let's move."

They worked ahead with assault fire, blasting the old snag. Twice Murdock had to yell to keep the line straight. When they were within fifty yards of the snag, Murdock called a cease-fire.

"Hold it right here. We're going to work a new wrinkle. Been a while since we've played horse. Now and then we get into a situation where we have to carry out one of our men. Tough, and we can do some training on it.

"Right now I want you to pair up by weight. That's Jaybird and Lam, Ching and Sadler, Bradford and Van Dyke. I've got the small one, Howard. We'll be working downhill, so that may help. I want you to take the other man on your back and pack him for two hundred yards. Then we switch. We're going to do that five times if our legs hold out. Let's do it."

Murdock motioned for Howard to get on his back. Howard weighed in at 250 to Murdock's 210.

"You're giving away forty pounds, Skipper," Jaybird said.

"So, you want to take him?" Bradford snapped.

Murdock lifted the big man, gritted his teeth, and started downhill, holding on to Howard's legs with Howard's huge arms draped over Murdock's shoulders. He took the steps deliberately, not sure how far he could go. He was in good shape, but this was a real test.

He worked well the first hundred yards. There were some yells and screeches from the other men. Murdock concentrated on getting his feet in front of each other and down the hill. By the time he made it to the last twenty yards, his legs were feeling rubbery, as if they might collapse.

Howard thumped him on the shoulder. "Far enough, Skipper," he said, and Murdock let him down, then dropped to the ground rubbing his legs.

The others arrived, and the carriers looked spent. Murdock gave everyone a moment, then stood. "Let's move out another two hundred. Change riders and carriers."

Howard picked up Murdock as if he was an inflated toy and marched down the hill. He looked over his shoulder at Murdock. "Hey, sometimes I have trouble with distances. We might get closer to three hundred than two. Won't hurt nothing. Know I'm a load. I'm gonna be damn sure not to get shot up bad."

Howard did work down almost three hundred before they changed places and caught up with the other men. Murdock's legs were hurting again, and when everyone was at the six-hundred-yard mark, Murdock called it off.

"Enough for this time. We'll try to keep the weight class

more even when we have Bravo with us. Now, take ten and let my legs get back to normal."

"Hey, one thing," Jaybird chirped. "I'm gonna write a law that says Howard can't get bad shot up on a mission."

"Yeah, and I'll sign that bill into law," Murdock said.

Murdock gave himself and the rest fifteen minutes to get their breath back and legs rested. Then he pointed to the tallest peak in the range. "See Bald Cap over there? How far do you think the top of it is from us?"

"Ten miles," Bradford said.

"No way," Lam said. "Look at those ridges in front of it. Got to be twenty-five at least."

"That's our target for tonight," Murdock said.

"Twenty-five out and twenty-five back?" Ching asked.

"No, we fly back," Jaybird said.

"Not going all the way," Murdock said. "We'll do ten miles due north and then turn around."

"Only ten?" Van Dyke asked. "Hey, we're getting a break."

"Then back to the bus?" Jaybird asked.

"About the size of it," Murdock said.

"Good," Jaybird said. "That's where the food has to be. Even an MRE will look good by the time we get back."

Murdock put Howard in the lead with Bradford and Lam right behind him. They hiked in a column five yards apart. Murdock was behind Lam watching the two men who'd been wounded on the last mission. Any trouble and he'd drop them out for pickup on the return leg.

Everyone made the ten miles. Then Murdock turned them around at once and led out at a stronger pace for the bus.

"Oh, yes, big bad food-laden bus, here we come," Jaybird sang out.

Bradford straggled a little on the return hike. Murdock gave the lead to Jaybird and hung back with Bradford. They were a quarter of a mile behind when the others hit the bus.

"Sorry, Skipper, just not as strong yet as I'm gonna be. Another two weeks and I'll be shit-kicking guys all over the place."

The men had a big cardboard box out of the bus when Murdock got there, but they hadn't opened it.

Murdock slit the tape with his KA-BAR and handed out the box lunches he had conned out of the mess hall early that morning. They each had two two-slices-of-bread sandwiches, raw carrots, a big dill pickle, a candy bar, and a small can of mixed fruit with a snap top.

"Hey, anybody want to trade his mixed fruit for one of my sandwiches?" Vinnie Van Dyke asked. Nobody did.

After the meal, Murdock gave them fifteen minutes more to relax, then sent Jaybird and Lam out to the target range. He had them unfold the cardboard boxes they carried. They were two feet square, and the SEALs anchored them with a few rocks so they wouldn't blow away. They put a box at four, five, and six hundred yards, then jogged back to the bus.

"Going to see exactly how far we can use the EAR weapon," Murdock said. "Bradford, try one shot at the box at four hundred yards."

Bradford went prone, sighted in on the box, and fired. There was the usual whooshing sound as the Enhanced Audio Rifle fired and the blast of air out the back kicked up a dust devil.

The box at four hundred yards slammed backward, collapsed, and rolled thirty yards along the side of the hill.

"Works at four," Murdock said. "Sadler, try the five-hundred-yard target."

He did, and the box flattened and jolted backward ten yards.

"Acceptable," Murdock said. "Ching, take a shot with the EAR at the six-hundred-yard box."

He did, and there was no movement of the box or the ground on either side of it. Fifty yards this side of the box, there was a minor disturbance and some dust kicked up.

"So, we have a working range of five hundred for the EAR. Who hasn't fired one of the twenties in a while?"

Three men lifted hands, and Sadler, Howard, and Jaybird each put three rounds through the twenty at a huge rock out about a thousand yards.

When they finished, Murdock told the men to load up, then police the area. He thought about the brass they had left on the assault fire going up the hill. Tough. They'd done enough today. They would police up that part next time out.

On the bus ride back to Coronado, Murdock could think only of a nice hot shower and a good dinner out somewhere. The men had voted not to stop in Alpine for a store-bought meal. Murdock wondered if he could figure out how to set up a chat room with Ardith so they could talk back and forth on the Internet. It could be done. He'd just have to work it out.

Lam had made the hike and workout with no problem. Bradford was still a little weak, but if they had two or three weeks before any serious assignment, he should round into shape with no problem. Now the only question was, would the CNO, Don Stroh of the CIA, and the President give them the three weeks they needed?

3

The Channel
Off Santa Barbara, California

Arnie Gifford watched the big clamps grab the next section of pipe and slowly lower it into the test well they were drilling in the edge of the Santa Barbara Channel. It was far enough offshore not to infuriate the conservationists. Still, they'd had their share of Greenpeace trouble. Arnie chewed on the unlit cigar and eyed the oil-drilling platform a quarter of a mile farther away from the coast. It was in deeper water, too deep he figured, and there had been no good reports coming from it.

He had been an oil driller most of his forty-seven years. His face and arms were burned brown by the sun, and his blue eyes these days always held sunglasses to cut the glare and the damage of the sun. He was in good shape, swam and dove a lot in the ocean. He had done weight lifting in his youth, and still had a well-developed upper body. He squinted slightly as he stared at the rig known as Wentworth Petroleum Number 4. He wondered where the others were. What puzzled Arnie was the unusual activity around the rig. For the past six months he had seen large cargo ships anchor near the platform. The next day the ships seemed to ride much higher in the water. What in hell were they doing there? They couldn't discharge that much cargo on that small drilling platform.

He had seen a couple of the men he knew who worked on the rig in a bar just last week, and he'd asked them about the ships. They'd laughed and said he was seeing things.

"What the hell would a cargo ship be doing around our

rig?" they'd said. "Maybe they were bringing out our payday cash." The two men had laughed it off and headed for the door.

He'd seen the federal inspection boat head out to the rig, and heard that Number 4 had passed the safety and environmental tests with no problems. There was no oil on the rig or in its hole, so the test was a little premature.

As Arnie watched, another freighter flying a Panamanian flag eased to a stop forty yards off the oil rig and put out anchors. Maybe sea anchors at that depth, he figured.

He wiped one hand across his face and decided. Tonight was the night. He was going to swim out there and see what the hell they were doing. They had to be up to something fishy. Still, the inspectors had given them a go. He had his wet suit on the rig. He used it from time to time to go down and check the sea legs that extended down to solid footing on the channel seabed. A quarter of a mile wouldn't even be a warm-up for him. Yeah, he'd go out tonight as soon as it got dark. He wouldn't use his tanks, too damn heavy. He'd use a snorkel and stay just under the water. He'd done it a thousand times.

Arnie waited five minutes after midnight before he entered the water. It was an easy swim, and he used the snorkel. When he came up to the rig, he circled it once, then swam up to one of the steel legs and held on to it taking a rest. He could see nothing in the water that indicated anything strange going on. It had to be topside. It wasn't one of the huge platforms, just an exploratory one, but still had a night crew and a hundred glowing lights. He could hear the machinery clanging away.

He pushed away from the steel ready to swim around to the surface platform and the ladders that extended up to the first level of the platform. For a moment he didn't understand what he saw in front of him. Then he threw up his arms to try to protect himself.

The next morning Santa Barbara County Coroner Warren Watts shook his head as he looked at the body tangled in wire three feet underwater and against one of the legs of Oso Platform 27.

"How in hell did he get fouled up in wire like that? I didn't think you guys were supposed to throw any solid trash into the water." He looked at the body again. It was pinned against the steel legs of the tower with one arm sloshing back and forth with the swells.

"The damn-fool wet suit doesn't seem to be damaged, and he's still got the face mask around his neck," the coroner said. The face with open eyes looked out at Watts through three feet of the clear Pacific Ocean. Two Santa Barbara County sheriff's deputies stared at the body over Watts's back.

Pete Rumford, the platform boss of 27, sat in the sheriff's boat and shook his head as he looked at his worker. "Arnie Gifford is his name. He liked to scuba and free-dive. He was good at it. We used him to check our legs underwater. Nobody on board last night knew he was going to go diving. What would he be looking for at night? It just doesn't make sense."

The coroner scowled. "Probably drowned, but we can't be sure until I do some work. Can you get a couple of men down here with bolt cutters and cut him loose so we can get him in the boat? This is the damnedest thing I've seen in a long time." He looked at the older deputy sheriff. "You checked with the Coast Guard? They like to know when things like this happen. They'll want to do a search for another body in the water if we think there might be one."

"Didn't even call them. Sheriff says it's our jurisdiction on a felony. They'd just turn it over to us anyway. So why bother them? The sheriff is on another case. Said he'd come out later and talk."

Ten minutes later they had the body in the boat. The coroner frowned. "You say he worked for you here at Platform 27?"

"Right, my best foreman. Why in hell was he diving at night? Nobody saw him get in the water."

"I'll let you know what the autopsy shows."

The deputy sheriff at the tiller moved the boat up to the small water-level dock so the platform boss could step off; then he pushed the throttles forward and the twenty-two-footer raced toward the Santa Barbara harbor and the Sheriff and Lifeguard Dock.

An hour later Santa Barbara County Sheriff Hal Kirkendol leaned on the first level rail of Platform 27 and stared out where the platform boss pointed.

"Hell, Hal, you've known me for ten years. All I can say is the last thing Arnie told me last night before I went ashore was that he didn't like what was going on out on Rig Number 4, right out there. We've all seen the big ships that anchor just off the platform. Nobody can figure out why freighters would stop there. The platform has its own resupply ship that makes daily runs. Why in hell those big freighters? Arnie was getting worked up about it, but I said not our business, nothing we can do about it anyway."

"You telling me that Arnie's drowning has something to do with that other platform?"

"Not saying that, Hal. That just the only thing I can think of that might be connected to Arnie dying. Hell, the men liked to work for him. He was good at his job. Got a good day's work out of everyone including himself, and I can guarantee not a man on board would try to kill him."

"Hey, nobody said anything about Arnie getting killed. He was diving, he got tangled up in that wire, and couldn't get any air. I've seen a hundred reasons why people drown."

"True, Sheriff. But I know Arnie. He was on a championship college swim team, almost went to the Olympics in the freestyle. He teaches scuba at the Y here in town. He takes a herd of kids free-diving every Saturday. Arnie is the last guy in the world who would drown, especially caught in a bunch of wire right around one of our platform legs. Part of his job was to dive down those legs once a week, all the way to the bottom, and remove any debris that might have hung up there. I can assure you that yesterday there was no mess of wire on the leg that held Arnie underwater. If he drowned, it's because somebody surprised him and killed him. There's no other way to look at his death. Arnie was murdered. That I'm sure of. Now I'm trying to figure out why."

Sheriff Kirkendol rubbed his chin the way he had been doing lately when he had a case he couldn't figure out. At last he nodded at the oil driller. "Okay, Pete. I've known you long enough to believe what you say. I didn't know the swimming background on the dead man. You say he was murdered. That puts a whole new spin on the case. Why? Why was he killed? That's the next thing we have to find out."

"Maybe the answer is out there on Number 4."

"Now you're making a lot of assumptions, Hal. First you're saying Platform Number 4 out there has something to hide. Next you indicate that it's so secret that they will kill anyone who tries to find out about it, even a late-night swimmer around their platform. They would also have to use some kind of a security system that would warn them when any unauthorized boat or swimmer entered the protected zone around their tower. In the water that would have to be highly sophisticated. Then you're saying that they have the killer or killers on the platform who could do the job. Those are a whole shitpot full of assumptions. Proving any or all of them is going to be one hell of a tough job."

"Right, Sheriff, and that's why you get the big bucks to do that work."

Sheriff Kirkendol rubbed his chin a moment, then the back of his neck with his right hand. As soon as he realized he was doing it, he stopped. One of his women detectives had told him that the repeated gesture was a dead giveaway that he was worried, troubled, or stumped.

"So I take two men and go visit Platform Number 4."

"You have jurisdiction?"

"Damn right. It's in my front yard. So it's wet. It's still my own front yard. I've got a murder to solve and I'll do what I have to and let the lawyers yell about it later. You want to come along?"

"Not a chance. I've got a rig to run. Besides, I don't even want to talk to those guys. I might shoot off my mouth about my suspicions. You can do it with a much cooler touch."

"Flattery . . ."

"Yeah, still works."

Two hours later, Sheriff Kirkendol headed for Platform Number 4. He'd had a talk with the coroner, who'd put a rush on his cutting. He'd found two serious head wounds made by a blunt instrument. Neither severe enough to cause death. There was plenty of seawater in the dead man's lungs, so technically he had drowned. But the man had had a lot of help.

"He must have been clubbed, then held underwater until he drowned. How he got back to his own drill rig is your job, Sheriff. I'm putting the death as a murder by person or persons unknown."

"Don't release that information yet," the sheriff had said. "I have a courtesy call to make first."

The sheriff had brought with him Nevin Irwin, a former SEAL who had been with him for almost two years handling all of the water-related problems including crimes on boats, drownings, and even one case of piracy. Irwin had blown out a knee on a heavily laden parachute jump somewhere over Europe, and had been eased out of the SEALs. If he couldn't be in an action platoon, he didn't want to stay in the service. He did another year on his enlistment in the support units at Coronado, then found his spot with the Santa Barbara Sheriff's Department.

The third man was a longtime deputy who handled the boats for the department. The sheriff had radioed the tower indicating he needed to visit the platform for a routine safety inspection. He asked for the safety engineer to be on hand, and was invited to come out at his convenience.

That turned out to be slightly after eleven o'clock that morning. The twenty-four-footer eased up to the water-level dock at Rig Number 4 where a man in a white shirt and tie met it.

"Preston," the man said, holding out his hand to the sheriff. "Good to see you. Safety around here is one of our primary concerns. So far we have a hundred and eighty-two days without a lost-time accident. We want to keep that record going. Any suggestions you can make will help."

"Just routine, Preston. We'll try not to trip over anything. This is Deputy Irwin, who will go with us." He waved for the boat driver to stay on the boat, and the three men climbed the steel steps that took them to the first level.

"As you can see, we're a small platform," said Preston. "None of those giants you may have seen. We have five levels, with the driller's cabin in the top level. We have basic steel-pipe tendons with direct tendon-pile connections on the bed of the strait. We do work twenty-four hours a day, and we are so far a test hole that we hope will produce. Many of our crewmen are foreigners. We try to get the best men we can regardless of their country of origin. Do you have any questions?"

The noise of the drilling and the various motors running on the level above them set up a clatter and roar that made talking a little hard.

"Do you ever have any security problems? Like boats stopping by, fishermen, paddleboard guys, maybe sea lions crawling up on your little water-level dock down there?" Irwin asked.

"Not a problem. The sea lions get frightened off by the motors and the vibrations before they get anywhere near the platform. Then we do have a fisherman stopping by now and then just out of curiosity. Usually they just want to stare up at the platform and ask a few questions. We don't exactly give them a guided tour, if you know what I mean."

Sheriff Kirkendol listened to the reply critically. He couldn't detect any reluctance or any hint that it wasn't the truth. The man didn't seem to be hiding anything.

They took a quick look at levels two and three, and twenty minutes later they were back in the boat heading for shore.

Deputy Irwin looked at his boss and shook his head. "Didn't play right for me, Chief. Sounded like the guy was trying to hide something. And why is he wearing a white shirt and a tie on a greasy, oily, smelly place like a drilling platform? I just don't trust the guy."

Sheriff Kirkendol frowned. "I didn't get that feeling, Nevin. He was smooth, maybe like he had worked over what he was going to tell us. But he answered your question off the top of his head and I bought it."

"Maybe I'm just suspicious. I have a hard time accepting that a scuba man, snorkeling instructor, and college swimmer is going to drown in an accident like that. What bugs me is that somebody went to a lot of work with that wire to make it look natural. Still, it held the man three feet underwater. Besides, the dead man complained to his boss about that other platform. He may have been the kind of guy who decided he'd swim out there and take a look for himself. Do it at night when they wouldn't see him. Can't be more than five hundred yards, a warm-up for him."

The head man in the Santa Barbara County Sheriff's Department lifted his brows and shook his head. "Hell, right now your doubts are the only thing we have to go on. We've got a murdered man on our hands, and so far not a hope of finding out who did it. How many men on the 27 platform where the man worked?"

"I saw a report that said it had about thirty men," Irwin said.

"Okay, tomorrow we'll send out three of our detectives and they will interview every man. We might turn up somebody who had a grudge against Gifford strong enough to kill him. Whoever murdered Gifford must also have been a diver, or at least a good swimmer. Something to watch for."

"I'd like to go along."

"Negative, Irwin. Interviewing is not your strong suit. I have three men who are experts at it. They'll go out tomorrow and do a good job."

"So that leaves me to do what?"

"You watch for any signs of activity or problems in the water around that tower. Large boats coming there and anchoring. Next time one does that, we get the Coast Guard and we go out and inspect the ship on some pretext. You keep in touch with Pete Rumford, that platform boss on 27. Whenever he spots a freighter dropping anchor near that Platform 4, have him give you a ring."

"Yes, sir," Irwin said, reverting to his SEAL training. He could take orders even if he didn't like them. He spent the rest of the day on routine calls, and just after dark, drove his two-year-old SUV to his favorite parking spot when he went diving. He put on his wet suit, cap, and boots and took out the new Draegr III. It was the latest underwater rebreathing device, and didn't leave a string of bubbles. This one was programmed to mix the right amount of chemicals with the oxygen so a diver could go as deep as he wanted to and still get the right mix of air. It was the same type he had used in the SEALs. He locked the SUV, put the key in the small flap pocket on the wet suit, and walked into the water off Goleta Point.

Nevin swam toward the lighted oil-drilling rig. He figured it was about two miles, not even a warm-up. He went down ten feet and stroked toward the tower the way he used to in the SEALs. His blown-out knee had been replaced and worked fine in the water. It was the parachute drops hitting the ground at twenty-one feet per second with two hundred pounds of equipment and ammo that his new knee couldn't take. He loved the water. Sometimes he felt more at home in the ocean than he did on land. He surfaced with just his face out of the water. He was dead on course. A small moon gave off its feeble light, but he didn't need it. The required marine lights were on the tower, plus a few hundred more bulbs to make sure no wandering tanker or freighter crashed into the rig.

Nevin went back down to ten feet and stroked toward the tower. He had no idea what he would find once he got there. He had looked at the steel pipes that extended downward into the depths when he had been there that morning. He could see about ten feet, and nothing had looked unusual.

At least he could do a good scouting job, and if he did find anything out of the ordinary, he'd go back out with the sheriff and make a thorough inspection. What could you hide around an oil-drilling rig? It didn't make a lot of sense. But then neither did the murder of a man who the platform boss on 27 thought had had suspicions about Oil Rig 4.

The next time Nevin surfaced, he was fifty feet from the tower. He dove then, working down to fifty feet and sensing change in the air/chemical mix that would keep his body functioning despite the added depth pressure. He came on the first tendon and touched it. He circled it and looked upward. No huge mass obstructed his view of the surface where the half-moon and the rig's lightbulbs gave off a faint glow. He dove down, checking the pipe all the way to the bottom. Nevin had no idea how deep the water was here, but well beyond what the old Draegr would tolerate.

Nothing. He found nothing. That troubled him. There had to be something here or nearby. What in the hell was going on? He worked his way back up. At forty feet he saw a

swimmer above him, moving slowly back and forth from one
steel tendon to the next. Hunting him, or patrolling? Either
way it was bad news and good news. It could mean they
knew he was there. The good news was if they had a swimmer out at night, they did have something to hide.

He worked up cautiously, trying to stay away from the
swimmer above, confident that the one on top could not see
him in the gloom of the deeper water. Then the swimmer
above turned and came directly toward him. Nevin's hand
flashed to the KA-BAR knife in its leg scabbard. He had it
out and ready when some sixth sense made him turn his head
and look behind him. Another swimmer was there within
arm's reach and Nevin saw the blade in his hand. Nevin tried
to power away, but he was too late. He hadn't watched his
back the way every good SEAL always did. The thrust of
the blade missed his back, but cut a slit across the wet suit's
side, letting in a surge of cold water.

Nevin spun around to face the fighter just as the second
diver above reached him and drove his own knife into the
Draegr, disabling it and ripping off the mouthpiece. Nevin
kicked and powered for the surface. He figured he had about
ninety seconds. That was as long as he could hold his breath,
and he was getting no air from the torn-apart Draegr. The
second diver followed him, slashing at his kicking feet. Then
he was closer to Nevin and the knife went into his side,
daggering through the tough wet suit and bringing a gush of
water into his screaming mouth.

His beating legs slowed and then stopped. Nevin had never
felt pain like that. It overwhelmed him. It burned in his side;
it exploded in his brain. He mouth refused to close and more
water surged in. He tried to find the attackers. They had
pulled back and he could barely make them out. They had
attacked. Now they rested and let the sea claim one of her
own. His arms went limp. He had no control over them or
his legs. The lights from above fuzzed out, came back, then
went almost black. He didn't know if he was floating upward
or sinking. He hadn't thought about dying since leaving the
SEALs. Now the idea came into his fogged brain and he
rejected it. Spewed it out with the water in his mouth and
held his breath. Another few strokes and he would be on the

surface and find plenty of air. But his arms wouldn't work. His side hurt like fire. For a moment his whole body shook, and then a strange calm settled over him. He looked up at the lights, but they faded more and more to a dusty gray, and then to full black. He let out the last breath in his burning lungs and let the Pacific Ocean stream into his mouth and nose. He couldn't fight it anymore. He felt his whole body relax, and he knew then that he was sinking. There was no light or dark, there was only the cool, serene waters of the ocean. Now at last he had returned to the ocean from which life had begun so many millions of years ago. He was one with the sea. Then a total, inescapable, deadly deep darkness engulfed him and he sank deeper and deeper into the Santa Barbara Channel.

4

NAVSPECWARGRUP-ONE
Coronado, California

Murdock stared at the news story in the San Diego *Union-Tribune*. It had made the front page. "Former Coronado SEAL Murdered in Santa Barbara." He read the item quickly.

"Santa Barbara Deputy Sheriff Nevin Irwin . . ."

"Damn, it's Irwin, he's dead," Murdock blurted out. Lieutenant Ed DeWitt looked up from the training chart he was writing. "Irwin? Nevin Irwin, who used to be in Team Five?"

"Yeah. I interviewed him a couple of times to come to our platoon. Then he blew out a knee. I knew he was up at Santa Barbara with the Sheriff's Department." He read the article aloud.

"The body of missing former Navy SEAL Nevin Irwin, a county deputy sheriff, washed up on Goleta Beach this morning. The county coroner said the body had been in the water for up to a week. Irwin had been reported missing at the Sheriff's Department six days ago when he failed to report to work.

"His vehicle, a late-model SUV, was found near Goleta Point, where many surfers and divers often park. Irwin wore a full wet suit and an underwater breathing device. The coroner said death was due to a deep knife wound through the side that penetrated the wet suit. There was also seawater in the victim's lungs.

"Irwin had been with the Sheriff's Department for almost two years, had as his special assignment all water-related problems, and did whatever diving the sheriff needed doing.

"Sheriff Kirkendol expressed regrets at the death, and

praised Irwin as an ideal deputy. He said Irwin had not been on any specific assignment involving the beach or the channel and that he did little recreational diving. Sheriff Kirkendol said the murder of the deputy would be investigated thoroughly and the perpetrator would be brought to justice."

Murdock passed the paper to DeWitt, who read it and looked up. "Most SEALs don't lose underwater knife fights."

"Unless he was outnumbered three or four to one." Murdock stared at the paper. A former SEAL killed in the water. That was unusual. Who would be skillful enough to do that? Another SEAL or some other highly trained diver. Who and from where? He looked at DeWitt. "You have the training sked worked out for the rest of the week?"

"Nearly done, Commander."

"Good, you've got the con. I'm going to take three days leave and I'll see you next Monday."

Ed looked up, then nodded. "My guess is you're going up to Santa Barbara."

"Thought I might, but you don't need to tell anyone. I'll tell the master chief. He can reach me on my cell phone if we get an alert."

Ed stood. "My guess is you'll be needing your full wet suit and a Draegr."

"Might just need them at that, Ed. Thanks. You take care of the store."

Santa Barbara, California

Just after noon that same day, Blake Murdock sat across the desk from Sheriff Kirkendol. He wore civilian clothes and had just shown the sheriff his military ID and his SEAL Special Duty Card.

"Sheriff, I knew Nevin Irwin. He wasn't in my platoon, but I had interviewed him twice. If he hadn't blown out his knee he would have been one of my men. It bothers me that a former SEAL was killed in a knife fight in the channel. Our men are highly trained in knife fighting in and out of the water. In the water there are few men in the world who can beat us."

"We can't say for sure he was killed in the water, Commander. He might have been drowned first, then stabbed, or the other way around."

"Still, it would take an extremely skilled and trained man to do it to Irwin. If that's so, you may be dealing here with something more than a shiv fight at a tavern."

The sheriff shifted in his seat, took a sip of his coffee, and stared at Murdock over the rim of the cup.

"Commander, I don't know just how much to tell you. Irwin wasn't on a water assignment the night he was killed, but we had been talking about another water death of an oil-rig worker. The man had been snorkeling and became entangled in wire around one leg of his diving platform three feet underwater. He drowned. The wire hadn't been there the day before."

"You have any suspects?"

"Not for sure. The platform boss where the man died said the worker had been curious about another drilling platform. Said curious things were going on out there. Gifford, the drowned man, was a scuba instructor and led kids on free-diving tours. He was an expert in the water. The coroner's report says he was clubbed on the head and then drowned."

"So, Irwin wanted to check out that other oil platform?" Murdock asked.

"We did. Went on a safety inspection. Everything seemed normal. She was drilling, nothing out of order."

"But Irwin wasn't satisfied. You guess that he parked his car on the point and swam out to the other platform."

The sheriff frowned. "I'm not sure of anything. But that is a strong possibility. Irwin wasn't easy to get off a project once he got a sniff of something rotten. I'd bet my last twenty he swam out there the night he was killed."

"What could they be doing illegal on that drilling rig?" Murdock asked. "It's too small to store drugs on there that they took off some ship. They could be smuggling diamonds, but that would be a lot of extra trouble. What could be going on?"

"We've had reports of merchant freighters stopping at the platform," the sheriff said. "Some stay a few hours, some overnight. Makes no sense to me."

"A question. If they killed the first man and tried to make

it look like an accident, why didn't they do the same with Irwin? If they couldn't, why would they let the body wash up on shore when it would be obvious he was murdered?"

"Bothered us here too. Our best ideas are that in the fight the other man might have been wounded and had to go for aid, or maybe he simply lost the body. It would sink right after being killed, and at night at even a hundred feet a black-clad body would be tough to find."

"Makes sense, Sheriff. This is sounding more and more like something highly sensitive is happening on or near that tower. The ships stopping is puzzling. Were there many Orientals on that platform?"

"Yes, now that you mention it. The man who toured us around said they had a lot of foreign workers. They didn't care what nationality they were if they were good at their jobs."

"Orientals? Chinese?"

"I'm no expert telling Chinese from Japanese from Koreans, but I'd guess there were ten or fifteen Orientals out there who I saw."

"Have you made a report to any other agency?"

"Just the Coast Guard. I reminded them that I have jurisdiction on the platforms, but they might want to keep an eye on them."

"I was thinking more like the U.S. Attorney General's office or the FBI."

"Oh, hell, no. Why would they be interested?"

"I don't know, just wondered."

The two men looked at each other for a moment. Then the sheriff shook his head. "I can't let you go out there, Commander. I lost one good man to whatever it is out there. I don't want you on my conscience too."

"Thanks for the warning, Sheriff. But I'm just a private citizen going for a nighttime swim."

"You don't know what's out there, Commander."

"No, but I know they are deadly, and knowing that, I'll be ready for whoever shows up. I'd like to bring back one of those live divers they must have. There had to be more than one to get the drop on Irwin that way. He had to have been surprised and attacked from the side or the back while facing another fighter."

"Are you better in the water than Irwin was?"

"Sheriff, I've killed at least a dozen divers in the water in my career. So far I've been better than the man facing me."

"A dozen?"

"Sheriff, we're SEALs. We work in places and on big and little jobs you never hear about. So don't let me be a worry to you. If I find out anything, I'll tell you, or the FBI or the CIA or the President. If I don't, nothing is lost. If I don't come back, I've met the man who's better than I am at underwater fighting."

Two hours later, Murdock found the spot he wanted on Goleta Point to park his Ford Explorer. It was another two hours until dark. He had a burger and a milk shake and took a quick combat nap in the cab of his SUV. At dusk he put on his full wet suit, boots, and cap and then shrugged into his Dracgr. It was the new type that mixed nitrogen and oxygen according to the depth you were diving. At a hundred feet it was a 32% mixture. If you went deeper it changed. It meant you didn't have to set the depth mixture you wanted as you did on the older Draegrs.

He'd had special Velcro flaps put on the wet suit on each thigh. One held an ultra-short speargun. It was powered by CO_2 cartridges and fired a steel shaft that looked like a ten-inch dart. It had three shots. Accuracy was good up to twenty feet. Beyond that it was plain luck. On his left thigh he positioned an old reliable Colt Detective Special .38-caliber with a two-inch barrel and six rounds. He checked the loads and put rounds in all six holes. Firing a pistol underwater wasn't the smartest move. It was a last-ditch defense. He checked his KA-BAR to be sure it was in place. He put in earplugs and carried his flippers to the edge of the water. The point was deserted. He slipped into the channel just as complete darkness fell.

As he waded out, he spotted the lights of the two drill rigs in the immediate area. The one they called 27 was to the left, and farther out to the right would be the mystery tower, 4. The lights on both towers glowed in the darkness of the channel and the faint islands beyond. He figured it at two miles at the most.

For the first mile, Murdock swam on the surface. It was faster and there was no way his splash would be noticed. He had just passed the first platform when he went underwater to his normal fifteen feet and powered forward toward the second tower. He had no idea what he would find there, but he would start out deep and check around. He would constantly keep watching his back, and if any divers showed up, he'd be ready for them.

He came up once more to check his course, changed it slightly to the right. He was two hundred yards from the tower. It looked benign enough. Lights everywhere. He could see men working, hear the clang and roar of motors and steel hitting steel. Nowhere could he see any security lights bathing the channel waters around the tower legs. To detect any movement in the water around the tower would take a series of sonars, and he doubted if this outfit had them. But how else would they know there was a swimmer in the water near the tower? He gave his silent mind a point. All right, they had sonar, and highly sophisticated so it could tell the difference between a shark and a man swimming.

When he could see the lights through the fifteen feet of water, he surfaced once more and checked the oil rig. He was so close now he couldn't see the top two levels. He could spot nobody on the first story. One more long look around, then he swam down and worked toward the depths. He leveled off at what he guessed was eighty feet and did a slow circle, watching every way around the compass. He spotted no swimmers, but his visibility was no more than five feet down this deep. He could still see the lights of the tower above, although now they were faint and wavering.

Time to start up. The sonar should have picked him up by now. Where did they have the sonar setup? How powerful was it? He leveled off at fifty feet. No swimmers, no spearguns, no bang sticks. He wondered if a bang stick would disable a man as well as a shark? He knew it would. The CO_2 set off by a shotgun shell would slam through a wet suit and gush inside the body cavity, expanding rapidly. It probably would collapse both lungs and balloon the body, sending it floating quickly to the surface. He should have a few for the SEALs.

At thirty feet he paused again, then swam around the square legs of the tower. No enemy divers. Why? If they had regular scuba gear they could easily go to thirty feet. The old Draegrs were set to work at a maximum of thirty-five feet. He looked upward watching for any shadows crossing the pattern of light from the hundreds of bare bulbs burning on the platform. Nothing. The third time he swept the area he found a swimmer. High up, maybe at fifteen feet.

Could the ones running the sonar communicate with a swimmer in the water? He didn't know. If they had sonar, they might have a way to use voice through the water to a swimmer. He'd have to check that out. Upstairs. They were watching for him up there. They? He watched for another fifteen minutes and saw three swimmers. They came together for a conference evidently, then parted. Two went out of sight and the third one stayed on Murdock's side of the platform.

He knew now the swimmers were there. Time for more surveillance. He swam down to the bottom. He wasn't sure of the depth as he began to swim around the tower in ever-widening circles. Out about fifty yards on the west side of the tower, he found a strange structure on the sea floor. It was a dark blob, but definitely man-made. He didn't want to use the one waterproof light he had. Up close he estimated the concrete-looking dome of a building was fifty feet square and fifteen feet high. There were no pipes, tubes, or wires extending from the structure on any side he could see, and no entryway on the sides or top. He pulled away from it and swam toward the tower and upward.

At fifty feet he paused again and watched for the shadow divers above him. Once more they gathered, probably exchanging notes on write boards, flashing small lights. Then they parted. Murdock drew his KA-BAR and powered upward at the lone diver on his side of the tower. The guard swimmer moved slowly back and forth as if walking a post. Murdock came up beneath him and touched his foot. The man reacted at once, drawing a knife and turning to face Murdock. The Navy SEAL powered straight at the surprised

diver, batted away his knife hand, feinted one way, then
drove in the other way, his KA-BAR slashing and tearing at
the diver's face mask and air tube. The man wore air tanks
and was clumsy in his turns. Murdock dodged one way,
surged upward as the airless diver clawed his way toward
the surface. Murdock caught him and drove his blade deeply
into the man's stomach, then jerked it out.

He saw a second diver coming from his left, and pivoted
around in the water. Murdock pulled the speargun from his
leg, and when the diver was ten feet away and waving his
fighting knife, Murdock fired the first ten-inch steel shaft. It
hit the attacking diver just under his clavicle, missing his
heart and lung. The diver soared upward out of the fight.
Murdock waited, but no third diver appeared. He had no
prisoner. He swam down to fifty feet and moved away from
the tower. After a hundred yards he surfaced to get his bearings, angled more to the southeast, and began stroking for
the shore.

Twice he came to the surface from his familiar fifteen feet,
and adjusted his course to hit the point. It was easy to see
from the water, being just up a ways from the Goleta campground where there were a dozen beach fires blazing brightly.

He stopped just offshore and checked the landing area. His
Explorer was where he had left it. Nobody seemed to be
around it. No one on the beach. He swam the rest of the way,
walked out of the water, pulled off his fins, and carried them.

A man surged out of some shadows to his left straight at
Murdock, swinging a baseball bat. Murdock spotted him at
once and threw his swim fins at the man, knocking the bat
out of his hands. Murdock pulled his KA-BAR, and was
about to challenge him when he saw a second man come
from directly in front of him with a knife. He ducked the
charge, threw up his left arm, and felt the knife hit it, but
the blade didn't cut through. He whirled and found a third
man charging toward him.

Murdock grabbed the speargun and fired for his legs. The
steel ten-inch dart dug into the man's right thigh and put him
down. Murdock swung around and caught the man with the
knife bearing in again. Murdock's knife came up and sliced
the attacker's bare arm. Then he spun around and slashed

again, drawing blood across the man's chest. The attacker screamed and ran into the darkness.

The man with the baseball bat knelt on the ground holding his right wrist.

"Bastard, you broke my wrist," he shrilled. Then he stood, holding his wrist, and ran toward the street. Murdock moved up to the man with the spear in his thigh. The man held up both hands.

"No more," he said. "Christ, but that hurts. Damn speargun? You some kind of one-man army?"

"Something like that. Right now you've got a date with the local sheriff."

"Hell, no, take me to the hospital, I'm bleeding."

"You'll bleed more if you give me any trouble. Get in the rig and shut your face."

The man with the dart in his leg looked at Murdock's stern expression and the KA-BAR knife he waved around. He nodded and crawled in the Explorer.

Fifteen minutes later at the Sheriff's Department headquarters, Murdock, two detectives, and the sheriff questioned the man.

"Three of you came after me," Murdock said. "Why?"

"Hell, we figured you'd have a wallet and some cash and maybe steal your car. We needed some loot to make a score."

"You waited for me when there were twenty guys in the campground you could have rolled. I don't buy it."

The sheriff moved up. "Your ID shows you're J. J. Martin. Look, Martin, we can get you to the hospital just as soon as you tell us who hired you to beat up Murdock. We found the brand-new hundred-dollar bill hidden in your wallet. A bum like you couldn't hold on to a C note for ten minutes. Who hired you?"

"Just waiting for this dude to come back to his—"

One of the deputies slapped Martin with his open hand and knocked him off his chair. He wailed in pain. They sat him back on the chair.

Sheriff Kirkendol grinned. "Did you like that, J. J.? We've got lots more where that came from. Now. Nice and slow. Who paid you the hundred clams to beat up on the diver coming out of the water on Goleta Point?"

J. J. looked at the sheriff, then at the big deputy, who was opening his fist and closing it.

"Aw, hell, not worth getting beat up for. Don't know a name. Some guy in The Pelican, that dark little bar on Fourth Street. He paid us a hundred each to find this diver and smash him up. Never saw the guy before."

"Would you recognize him if you saw him again?"

"Oh, hell, no. He had a hat on pulled down low and shades on in the bar. Could have been almost anybody. Now can I get to see a doctor?"

"You want to press charges of assault and battery with a lethal weapon?" the sheriff asked Murdock.

"Too much bother."

The sheriff turned to a deputy. "Take him to the emergency room and dump him off. No charges. And be sure that hundred-dollar bill is still in his billfold."

When the wounded man had left, Murdock and the sheriff sat alone in the interrogation room.

"So, did you get to the tower?" the sheriff asked.

"Oh, yes. I'm sure they have some kind of sonar protection around the tower so they can spot boats or swimmers coming in. I don't know how they do it. They put three armed divers in the water to greet me. One of them is going to be sleeping with the fishes tonight, another one has a speargun dart in his upper chest, and the third one swam away."

"Thirteen," Sheriff Kirkendol said.

"What?"

"That must be the thirteenth man you've killed. Glad that's out of my jurisdiction. Did you find anything out there?"

"I can't tell you, not until I tell some other people. But I thank you for your help. I'm heading back to San Diego."

"Just like that?"

"It's a federal case, Sheriff. I've got to report it. If we can give you any help on your case, we will. Right now I'm due back in the squad room down in Coronado. Thanks for your help. Don't worry, I'll clean up the blood that good old J. J. got on my Explorer."

"Federal? Murdock, I don't understand."

"You don't have to. Just don't talk about that other oil rig out there. Something should be happening soon. You take care now."

It was almost midnight when Murdock gassed his Explorer and headed out for home. Three hours, maybe three-and-a-half drive time to get down to Coronado. Shouldn't be any traffic this time of night, and if he pushed it a little, he might get in some sleep tonight before calling Don Stroh at 0600. If he was lucky the spook would be in his office by 0900 Washington, D.C., time. Murdock pictured the solid structure built on the bottom of the Santa Barbara Channel about two miles offshore. What in hell was it? Who put it down there? What could it possibly be used for? Why would the protectors kill anyone snooping around? He wanted some answers, and he knew Don Stroh would too.

5

NAVSPECWARGRUP-ONE
Coronado, California

At 0615 Murdock stormed through the Quarter Deck, waved at the night watch still on duty, and hurried to his small office in SEAL Team Seven, Third Platoon. He picked up the unsecure phone and dialed the number of Don Stroh at his CIA office in Arlington, Virginia. The spook answered on the fourth ring.

"Yeah, I'm here but I'm not awake. Haven't even had my coffee yet. What's up?"

"Good morning to you too, Super Spook. You know my voice. This is not a secure line. Get your SATCOM out and warmed up. I'll be calling you in ten minutes on something important."

"Murdock, you're drunk again, right? What the hell is this? A secure line. When do we use a secure line?"

"Almost always, like when I catch more eatable fish than you do. Get somebody who can run a SATCOM for you and get it tuned in and turned on. Fifteen minutes. Be there. I've got to find my SATCOM."

"You're not joking."

"I never joke when I have to get up after three hours of sleep. Now get cracking." Murdock hung up, went to the equipment storage closets, and took out one of three SAT-COMs they used. He set it up in his office with the dish antenna pointing out the window. He had to open the window to get it to give off the beep to show it was properly aligned with one of the satellites. Then he checked his watch. His stopwatch dial showed eight minutes had elapsed since he'd talked with Stroh. At twelve minutes he turned on the set, heard the beep again, and pushed the send button on the handset.

"Don Stroh in D.C. Murdock calling."

He waited a moment, and then a voice came back that wasn't Don Stroh.

"Yes, Don Stroh's office here. We're just set up and working. Here's Mr. Stroh."

"Don, record this, you'll want to refer to it. Have your recorder ready?"

"Yes, go ahead. What in hell do you have?"

Murdock sketched in his long day in Santa Barbara, including his fight with the three divers. He told about finding the structure on the channel floor.

"Somebody with a lot of resources is doing something off that oil platform besides drilling. Figured you'd want to know. I'm telling my boss here as soon as he gets on board. You didn't hear this from me. Let's see what happens going up the chain of command."

"Sounds ominous. They killed two men who tried to check on the underwater, including one ex-SEAL?"

"Right. That's why I went to take a look. It's in your hands now. I want to write up a report for Masciareli. You've got it on your end."

"Good enough. We'll get something on it, then contact the chain and see where we go. I'm out of here."

Murdock signed off and made the coffee. He ate two bear claws he'd picked up on the way to the base. Then he tackled the report. He had it on the screen within a half hour. Then he went back over it and rewrote it until he had it the way he wanted it. He spell-checked it on the computer, thanked the grammar unit for catching a small goof, and then printed out four copies. He gave it a file name and left it on his hard disk. Then all he had to do was wait for SEAL Team Seven's commander to get into his office.

Murdock tried to do some paperwork he was behind on, but couldn't get with it. He kept thinking about that domelike structure he had seen fifty yards from the oil rig. What the hell was it and who had put it there?

At 0700 Master Chief Petty Officer Gordon MacKenzie phoned.

"Commander, lad, you're up early this morning, it being a Friday and all."

"Master Chief, remember I told you I was going to Santa Barbara? I did. Want to read something interesting before I show it to the commander?"

"Indeed I do. I have some fresh-brewed and a few donuts if you would care to honor me with your selfness."

Murdock grinned. "Be right there, Master Chief."

The old Scotsman frowned as he read the two-page report.

"Two men dead including Irwin. I remember him well. You even think they have some kind of sonar protection around the tower and this building?"

"The way it looks, Master Chief. I'd like to know what's inside that building down there on the bottom of the channel."

"Of course, Don Stroh hasn't seen this report," MacKenzie said.

"Absolutely not. I just wrote it. No time for him to see it."

"And you didn't call him this morning at 0613 on your regular phone?"

Murdock laughed. "Can't get ahead of you, Master Chief, can I? That call will be our little secret. I figured that the CIA should get on this and get cracking in case the chain of command upward didn't work well."

MacKenzie's green eyes sparkled. "Aye, laddie, and a good move it was. I know nothing. The good commander said he would be in his office this morning to make some early morning calls, but I haven't seen him yet. When he comes in . . ." The chief stopped. "His Lincoln just pulled into the parking lot, lad. You're in luck. You can deliver your missive yourself."

Ten minutes later Commander Dean Masciareli frowned at the two sheets of paper and then looked up at Murdock.

"Somebody up there killed these two men including an ex-SEAL, and you say they have a building on the bottom of the channel?"

"Yes, sir. I'd really like to know what's inside that concrete-looking structure."

The commander paused for a moment, then he nodded. "All right, I'm faxing this to Admiral Kenner immediately. Then I'll call him. This is something somebody needs to look into and it should be us. Sonar that can pick up men swimming and let the sharks go by. Amazing." He pushed a buzzer, and his yeoman came in, took the two sheets, and got his instructions. The two officers waited a few minutes until the faxes went through. Then the yeoman came back.

"The two pages are sent, confirmed," he said.

Commander Masciareli reached for his phone and dialed the long-distance number. It rang four times.

"This is Commander Masciareli in Coronado. I need to speak with the admiral at the first possible moment." He waited. Less than a minute later he lifted one hand and nodded at Murdock.

"Richard, did you get the two-page fax I just sent you? Something strange going on up by Santa Barbara I think you'll be interested in."

The commander put his hand over the mouthpiece. "He's getting the fax. He's a fast reader."

Masciareli grinned when he listened. "Yes, sir, I agree it's something that could be tremendously important, especially if the Chinese or North Koreans are involved. Would it be FBI or CIA jurisdiction?"

He listened. "Yes, sir, Murdock is right here." Masciareli frowned as he held out the phone to Blake.

"Yes, sir, Lieutenant Commander Murdock, sir."

"Murdock, yes. Good scouting mission. How deep is the water there?"

"From eighty to a hundred feet."

"The structure on the bottom of the channel, it looks like concrete?"

"Yes, sir. But no lines or tubes or wires leading away from it."

"Antennas?"

"Didn't see any, but it was dark down there, and I didn't use any lights."

"I'll fax this to the CNO. I'll suggest the CIA do the investigation here. They should dig into the owners of that platform. In the meantime I'm suggesting to the CNO that we do a training exercise off Santa Barbara in the channel, with a dozen warships and landing craft as a cover for your platoon to dive and get all the specs you can on that structure. They won't dare use their sonar or we will pick it up. Look for antennas especially. I'll suggest we get this mounted for tomorrow afternoon. If the CNO goes for it, and I think he will, we should know something before nightfall tomorrow. Get your platoon ready, Commander. Let me have Masciareli again."

"Yes, sir."

He gave the phone back to his boss and watched. The man's eyes lit up and he began to breathe faster. He grinned. "Yes, sir. I'll start getting ready on this end. We'll use just the one platoon. Can the Navy get the ships ready to move that quickly?"

He listened for a moment. "Yes, sir. I understand. Yes, sir. Good-bye."

Masciareli turned to Murdock smiling. "Well, it looks like we have lit a fire under the admiral, and he expects the CNO to act as soon as he gets the fax. He said if the Navy can't get enough ships up there, we'll go with whatever they can move, destroyers, some cruisers, at least one amphibious landing ship with their landing craft, even some surface-effect ships. All we need is a good display to shield what you guys do downstairs." He paused. "Good work, Murdock. I'm sorry about Irwin. I remember him. Blew out his knee over in Europe somewhere on a parachute drop." He stood. Murdock stood. "That will be all, Commander."

Murdock hurried to his office. Ten minutes later Don Stroh called him.

"Boy, you set off a whirlwind back here. I've got my boss and the CNO and the President yelling at me. So far I've dug up the owner of that platform. Some outfit in Texas, but it has six North Koreans on the board of directors. Also the President of the outfit has made twenty-four long-distance calls to Pyongyang within the past three weeks. His passport also shows four stamps to North Korea."

"Stroh, could this be a nasty payback for the trouncing we gave North Korea when it tried to invade the South the last time?"

"Could be. Those Orientals have long memories."

"So what do we do now?"

"We wait to see how the CNO reacts to your chief's suggestion that we do a recon over the spot tomorrow with a dozen or so Navy ships and your platoon."

Think the brass will go for it?"

"It's either that or blow up the thing without knowing what's inside of it. They'll go for the recon. How far is it from San Diego to Santa Barbara?"

"A little over two hundred miles by highway. Probably not quite that far as the ships could cut across the arc the land mass makes along here."

"At flank speed it would take eight or nine hours to get up there from San Diego," Stroh said.

"We wait and we see. Let's hope we get to fly up and land on a cruiser instead of a ride on a boat."

Don started to say good-bye.

"Oh, Stroh. You told the CNO about the North Korean tie-in to that oil-drilling tower."

"You betcha, Red Ryder. Oh, you're too young to know about Red Ryder and his faithful Indian kid, Little Beaver. Yeah, everyone knows. I blabbed it all over town."

"Take care."

The same night that Murdock drove four hours to get home from Santa Barbara, Jack Mahanani braved the Casa Grande Casino east of San Diego. He got in the door and halfway to the cashier to buy chips before Harley caught up with him.

"Hey, Jack, how is it hanging tonight?"

"Straight down, man, not a good day. Your Buick is doing fine, not even a scratch."

"You can't play tonight, Jack," Harley said. "Word just came down. Sorry." He waited for Mahanani to react. The big Hawaiian's shoulders slumped. Then he slammed his fist into his hand.

"You want the Buick too?"

"No, but there may be a way out."

Mahanani looked up. "Oh, sure, on my knees in front of some bare-assed prick."

Harley laughed. "Hey, nothing like that. Come on, have a

talk with a guy called Martillo. He can sometimes come up with plans to help when a friend gets in the hole with too much gambling."

Mahanani snorted. He had heard stories about the fringes of the gambling world. This definitely would be the fringe. He frowned. "The guy is here in the casino?"

"Yeah."

"He works for you guys?"

"Well, he's part of the larger picture. He's a kind of a consultant. Talk with him. If you don't want to work your way out of trouble, hell, you've only wasted a half hour."

"Okay, but I don't make any promises."

Harley led him through one section of the casino into a door marked "Employees Only," and through a hallway with offices on both sides. Mahanani decided it must take a lot of behind-the-scenes business operations to run a large casino. They stopped at a door with no name on it and Harley knocked, then opened it. He went in first and waved Mahanani in. It was an office that looked more like a den or a living room. A seventy-two-inch television set hovered in one corner. A full-sized sofa took up one wall. On the other side was a large desk that had a clean top, with the exception of one picture in a silver frame. Behind the desk sat Martillo. He was Mexican, with bushy black hair, a full beard, and mustache all kept tightly trimmed. His eyes were so dark brown they were almost black, and now his face looked up and he nearly smiled.

"You must be Mahanani, the Navy SEAL, right?"

"Yes."

"Sit down and rest yourself. Harley, bring us both a drink." He looked back at the SEAL and his smile vanished. "Mahanani, you now owe us six thousand, six hundred dollars. We're holding the pink slip on your Buick."

"Not sixty-six hundred. Just six thousand."

"Young man, you didn't read the agreement you signed. The loan of six thousand is at a rate of ten percent per month. This is the second month, so you owe us another six hundred."

"That's illegal."

"So sue us." The black eyes blazed at Mahanani and Martillo leaned back in the chair.

"You owe us a lot of money. We could simply collect your car and sell it for maybe eight thousand and give you the balance. But then you would have no wheels. A man isn't a man in Southern California without his wheels." He stared at the SEAL for fifteen seconds. Then the touch of a smile came back. "Because you've been a good customer, we have a plan for you to pay off your debt. You can start tonight. Before you say anything, let me go through the plan. We loan you a car, not new and not in the best body condition, but it runs well. You drive to Tijuana, to a garage on Presidente Avenue. Friends will meet you there. You go to the restaurant just around the corner and have a meal but no alcohol. When you come back, you will get in the car and drive back to San Ysidro, just across the border where you picked up the car. You leave the car there and we deduct four hundred dollars off your loan. Simple, easy, no harm, no foul."

Mahanani laughed. "Sure. You use me for a mule and if I get caught, I spend ten years in a federal pen for drug smuggling. I know about those garages. I've heard stories and seen articles in the paper. Do I look like an idiot?" He stood.

"I'll take your keys to the Buick now," Martillo said, his voice with a snap to it.

"So that's it. I either bring in drugs for you, or you take my Buick and give me a thousand in change."

The dark Mexican shrugged. "Amigo, it is your car. Do as you wish. Take your time. No rush at all. You have two minutes to decide."

"Shit. How much extra weight would be on the car? It couldn't be tilted or riding too low or it would be pulled into secondary inspection for sure."

"My friend. We have been doing this for years. We know how, we know how much. There is never more than a hundred pounds in any one car. That's less than another passenger, and makes no change in the springing of the car or how it rides or how low it hangs on the frame. Believe me, we'd be out of business soon if we started losing half of our mules."

"How many do you lose?"

"Last year, only three. That was out of more than two hundred trips."

"How many trips could I make before they became suspicious?" Mahanani asked.

"You would go in a different car each time, with different clothes. Once a week, maximum. For you it would have to be on a weekend. But that's when traffic is heaviest and the investigations are fewest. Ten trips and you would have four thousand paid off on your debt."

"Ten trips. Fifteen to pay you guys off. Not counting the interest."

"You make the runs, we'll forget the interest," Martillo said. "Hey, we're the good guys. We'd like to work with you to get you out of debt. We don't want to take your car. We have the pink slip just for our own protection. Collateral. Now, what do you think about making your first run tonight? I'll go to San Yisdro with you to get your first car. After this you just report to Jose down there and he'll work you from there."

Mahanani squeezed his eyes shut. He'd never so much as stolen a pencil or shoplifted a magazine. Now he was considering smuggling in dope, probably heroin or cocaine. He could get ten years easy. But if he didn't, he could be without his car. Yeah, not in jail, but bumming rides from the other guys and trying to explain how he lost his damn Buick. Fuck this whole thing. How did he get trapped into gambling in the first place?

"Hey kid, I ain't got all night. You want to take a run down to Mexico or not? Your call."

"Let's go."

A little over an hour later a new Cadillac pulled up to a decrepit-looking garage and used-car lot in San Ysidro, a run-down section of San Diego less than two miles from the international border with Mexico. Martillo honked the horn three times, and a garage door opened and a man came out wiping his greasy hands on a rag.

"Yes sir, Martillo. We doing business?"

Martillo chattered with him in Spanish, then pointed at Mahanani and then pointed out the passenger's-side door. "When you get to the garage in TJ, honk three short ones, like I did. They will get you turned around in about an hour. Don't watch. Go to the café and have something to eat."

As Mahanani got out of the car, he saw his Buick pull into the same lot and stop. A man got out of it, tossed the keys to Mahanani, and slid into the Cadillac, which promptly left.

"Hey, kid, come in here and I'll introduce you to your new wheels," said the man from the garage. "You drive like Martillo told you to. No detours, no shortcuts. It's an easy place to find. I'll give you directions. Stop at the garage, go get a taco, and go to the garage, then drive back here. Beep your horn twice and I'll open up and you drive into the garage. Got that? You better. I can't hold your hand no more. Come on."

The two miles to the border went fine in the old Chevy. Then when the Mexican border man waved him through into Mexico without a word or a glance, Mahanani felt better. The route was easy, down the main street that led off the freeway to Presidente, then down it three blocks to the garage, which he could see. There were no lights on. It was nearly ten o'clock. He beeped the horn three times, and a door opened up and he drove inside.

Four Mexicans stood there waiting for him. One took him by the arm. "Tacos around corner," he said. It may have been the only English he knew. Mahanani felt strange as he walked out the door and around the corner to a small café. Inside he ate a taco, then had a second one. It took about half an hour. He retraced his steps and found the door he had come out locked. He knocked three times. A small panel in the door opened, and then the door unlocked.

"Early," Jose said. They put him in a small office with a chair. Ten minutes later he backed the 1985 Chevy out of the garage. He could feel no difference in the handling. He retraced his route, and suddenly he was at U.S. Customs. A bored inspector looked at his car and scowled.

"Where were you born?"

"Honolulu, Hawaii."

"How long you been in Mexico?" he asked.

"Just tonight, playing tourist."

"Anything to declare, booze, fur coats?"

"Nothing."

"Okay, move on."

He was through, and trying not to feel the thrill of getting away with something. For a mile he kept watching in his rearview mirror, but no flashing lights came racing toward him. Yes, he'd done it, earned four hundred dollars, and he hadn't been caught. Of course, now he was a drug smuggler. He was shaking by the time he drove the two miles into San Ysidro to the garage. There he beeped twice and the door opened. Mahanani drove inside.

Jose grinned at him. "No trouble, *no problema. Sí.* Is easy, no? Your car's just outside."

Mahanani nodded and hurried toward his car. He wasn't sure he could walk that far. He'd never committed a crime before in his life. Now he was a fucking dope smuggler. He sat inside the Buick for five minutes before he started it. By then he figured he could drive home on the freeway without wrecking the car. He was so hyped up he couldn't believe it.

He tried to calm down. He'd done it, and would do it again, and maybe he could get out of his IOU with the casino. But fourteen more trips? He didn't know. There had to be a better way. He could investigate. He would think on it. Gradually he calmed down. He eased off on the throttle, realizing he was passing everyone on the freeway. He was doing almost ninety miles an hour down U.S. 805. He slowed to sixty and moved into the right-hand lane. Better. Yes. He drove with the utmost caution to his apartment in Coronado. It had been a tough evening. How in hell was he going to get out of this one?

6

Lieutenant Commander Blake Murdock leaned back in his office chair and tried to relax. It had been a pounding twelve hours. He went over his talk with Admiral Kenner, who'd been in his office back in Little Creek, Virginia. Yes, he'd done everything right. He'd lit the fuse, and it would explode sometime tomorrow. Now all he had to do was get through this day. The three hours of sleep were getting to him. Strange, when he was twenty-one he could stay up all night and be fit and fighting the next morning. Maybe he was getting older.

He watched Ed DeWitt come in, and briefed him on what had happened. Then he gave him a copy of his report.

"Holy shit, Murdock. You ran into a rattlesnake nest up there. Any idea what it's about?"

Murdock told him the current theory about the North Koreans.

"Yeah, they're still pissed how we blasted them a year ago," said DeWitt. "So is the operation on for sure?"

"Nothing is for sure until we hear it from the CNO, but I'd say it's about ninety-nine-percent go."

"Regular training session today?"

"Let's keep it light, a five-mile run and a five-mile swim. While you're gone, I'm going to take a nap. I'm played out."

"You earned it. We tell the troops about tomorrow?"

"Not until it's official. It could get stalled somewhere along the long chain of command."

"Yeah, but it's a better bet when we start at the top." Ed went out to meet the men as they filtered in. Murdock heard them groan when they heard about the five-mile run at 1000.

He stared at his computer until the screen went fuzzy. Then he turned it off, leaned back in his chair, and before he realized it, went to sleep.

Ed woke him when he came back in the small office grumbling. Murdock came up in the chair blinking.

"Sorry, Cap, didn't mean to wake you. We've got two men out with the flu. Both called in this morning and could hardly talk. We'll be short-handed tomorrow if we go."

"We'll go, I'm sure of it. The idea of some foreign power having a secret facility on our coast really shook up the brass and the CIA. We'll be doing recon only, but there could be some opposition. Wouldn't be smart with all of the assets we're going to have prowling around the area. I'd guess we won't see anybody down there, just the damn dome. We'll need some underwater lights. Can you get us about four to take down? Some strong ones. I don't know where we'd requisition them."

"Supply will know. I'll get them on it right now."

"You about ready for your run?"

DeWitt grinned. "Cap, we just got back. You've been out of it for two hours."

Murdock stretched and stood. "Then about time I get to work."

"Yeah, lunchtime," DeWitt said. "You up for that?"

They both laughed.

That afternoon Murdock went with the platoon on the five-mile swim. They did it on the surface without flippers or Draegrs. It was harder that way, a purely conditioning exercise. Jaybird led the way, and brought them in four minutes late, but close enough for a timed routine.

Back in the office, Murdock found a call waiting for him.

"Yes, Master Chief, what's cooking?"

"A call came through channels from the CNO. It's a go tomorrow. He's lined up two destroyers, two missile cruisers, and an amphibious assault ship as well as two air-cushion landing craft. They will pull out of San Diego tonight and steam north, and be on station just off Santa Barbara in the channel at 0800. Your platoon will be airlifted from North Island in a CH-46 and land on the command cruiser. Then deployed via an air-cushion craft when ready. The ships will be working a mock attack and maneuvers just off the tower. Aircraft from the amphibious assault ship will be working the area, and both towers will be included in the maneuvers so as not to attract attention to one."

"When do we leave from North Island?"

"I talked to the Forty-Six pilot assigned to the run. You'll need an hour and fifteen minutes for the flight. If you take off at 0700, you'll get up there just after 0815 when they are ready to rumble."

"We're out of here at 0630. Any restrictions?"

"No, full combat-ready. Don Stroh sends his regrets. He's on another assignment."

"We'll struggle along without him."

"All your men ready to go?"

"We'll see about the two who are out today with the flu. It might get better in a rush when they know we have an operation."

"Let me know before you push off."

Murdock went into the assembly room to tell the platoon. The men were getting on their civvies ready for the road.

"So that's the skinny, guys. Report here at 0500 and we'll get suited up and move out. We'll go in full wet suits and Draegrs, and half our ammo load. Doubt if we'll need our weapons, but we'll be ready in case. Any questions?"

"Yeah, you say it might be the damn North Koreans?" Howard asked.

"Speculation, but we don't think the Chinese would be that stupid. Anything else?" There wasn't. "Senior Chief, get in touch with Fernandez and Lam and see if they will be coming along on the ride, or if they still have the flu. That's all."

Ten minutes later Jack Mahanani drove his Buick away from the Special Warfare section and into Coronado. He kept going, heading for the bridge into San Diego, then on toward East County. He was going back to the Casa Grande Casino. He wanted another run into TJ. If he was going to do it, he'd better get it done. Or if he was going to try to outwit them, he'd better figure out how.

He'd been thinking about a hundred pounds of cocaine. What would that bring on the wholesale level? He'd heard the price of drugs was down, but a hundred pounds should still be worth well over a half-million dollars. He'd heard coke was going for twenty thousand a kilo. What he could do with that kind of money. Yeah, and how quickly he would be dead in a lonely stretch of the Borego Desert. Must be some way. What could they do, go to the police? No, they had their own way of dealing with thieves. He shivered. Hell, he had to figure something.

He just made it in the door at the casino when Harley nailed him. It was as if he had been waiting.

"How'd your ride go last night?"

"Good, except the tacos gave me heartburn." They both grinned. "I want another ride tonight. Have one scheduled?"

"We don't schedule. We go whenever we get a driver. You want to go, you got a ride. You have different clothes on, good. Why not wear a hat too. Every little bit helps."

"I'll get one. I go back down to San Ysidro?"

"Right. You're not packing a hideout, are you?" Harley moved in close to Mahanani and patted him down. If he'd had a wire-recording device on, Harley would have found it.

"Okay, Jack. I'll call Jose and tell him you're coming. Give it three hours before you come back this time. They can check by computer to see how long your license-numbered car was gone. They don't like twenty-minute stays in the country and then a drive out. The car will be clean and hasn't been driven across for six months. They check on that too. Just be casual. Don't act drunk or they'll pull you over and hold you. Just nice and easy."

"Sure, yeah, and me looking at ten years if I get caught. I must be nuts. But it's a try. Hell, I can only die once, right?"

"Yeah, right. But you sure as hell better not blow our operation while you're getting dead."

"No sweat. I'm gone to Tijuana."

He drove to San Ysidro the same way he had the previous night, and found the garage with Jose there. The second time around, it seemed routine. Hell, he was a dope smuggler, a candidate for the big house. Jose checked him out and handed him the keys. His wheels for this trip was a 1992 Ford Taurus. The paint job was still good, and it only had one dinged rear fender. It had some junk in it, including some stuffed toys and a kid's game. After the short drive to the border, he went through the Tijuana gate, and the Mexican guard waved him on through without stopping. They liked the American dollar the tourists brought with them.

He made the turn on Presidente Avenue and pulled up to the same garage. Three beeps with his horn, and the garage door rolled upward and he drove inside. The same Mexican came over as he stepped out of the car.

"*Hola.*"

"Yeah, hi, where is there a better restaurant than the café?"

"Better eats?"

"Right."

"Two blocks down. Good eats."

"I'm supposed to wait three hours this time." The Mexican nodded, and Mahanani waved and headed for his dinner. He hadn't been a fan of Mexico, almost never came down here. He'd gotten drunk here once a year ago, and had nearly never made it home. That cured him of TJ. He walked to the restaurant, tried to read the Spanish menu in the window, but gave up and went inside. He had a steak with all the side dishes and two bottled Cokes. He couldn't even risk drinking a beer, and he wanted something bottled so he didn't get food poisoning. The steak was good, and he meandered back to the garage. The Taurus sat outside, so he knocked on the door and the Mexican man nodded.

"Car ready, but wait two hours."

Mahanani had no trouble with that. He crawled in, pushed the seat back as far as it would go, and reclined it. He could stand a two-hour nap.

It was almost three hours before one leg cramped and woke him. The sleep had left him groggy and bleary-eyed. He walked around the car a dozen times; then he was ready. He drove carefully, but had trouble keeping his mind on the road. His stomach growled and he quickly felt ill, but he didn't know why. Maybe the flu bug the other guys had. He shook his head. It was only three or four miles; then he'd be back in his own country and in his own set of wheels.

It took all of his concentration to find the border. He drove up to the tenth open inspection gate, and waited ten minutes to get up to the man. The border guard started to wave him through, then stopped and came up to the window.

"Sir, are you all right? You look a little strange."

"Got the flu coming on, I think, but I can drive."

"You could pull over into secondary inspection and have a half-hour nap. Would that help?"

"No, I had some coffee, I should be okay. I don't have far to go, just into Imperial Beach."

Mahanani blinked and stared wide-eyed at the border guard. "Yeah, I'm doing better now. Just some gas, I think. Thanks for the help." He let his foot off the brake, and the car rolled ahead. The guard hesitated, then waved him on through. Mahanani was sweating like a marathon runner in July. That had been so close. If they'd pulled him into secondary inspection, the drug-sniffing dog would have roamed around his car automatically, and he'd have been busted and on his way to Chino State Prison for ten to fifteen. Shit, what a fucking close call.

He was still sweating, his stomach growled, and his whole gut felt like it was going to explode. A mile down the road there was a little turnout, and Mahanani pulled off the freeway and opened the door quickly. He vomited out the door before he could get his feet on the ground. He retched three times, then shook his head. Maybe it was the steak. He wiped his mouth and wished he had some water. But he did feel better. It had been a bug of some kind. He closed the door, sat there for five minutes while his stomach settled down, then started the engine and drove away into the traffic with no trouble.

Ten minutes later he delivered the car to Jose, and received a receipt for four hundred dollars. Jose looked at him sharply. "Why did you take so long to drive six miles?"

"What do you mean? I came right here. Oh, I had to pull over and throw up. I guess I had some bad food. There's still some of the vomit on the edge of the door. Take a look."

Jose did. "So, be careful what you eat down there. Take a few McDonald burgers with you the next time. Don't ever stop once you leave the garage. We have you on a clock. Just a warning."

Mahanani climbed into his Buick, found the can of Coke he always kept in the tray, and drank half of it. Then he drove back to Coronado with no trouble. Damn, there had to be some way to beat them at their own game. Just thinking about that half-million-dollar cargo he had transported made him ready to invent all sorts of plans. Something had to work. Now he knew they had him on a clock from the time he left the garage until he beeped for Jose. They would know how long the wait time was at the border. One TV news channel gave the wait time every ten minutes. Not even a long holdup at the border would get him off the hook. No time to stop on this side and stash the goods. Oh, sure, if he tried that, he'd be dead before he could get back into his Buick.

But he kept thinking about it. How in hell did he get out of this mess, stop being a fucking mule, get his Buick pink slip back, and pay out his IOU at the casino? A thought crept into his mind, but didn't seem to make sense. Did the casino management know that these two men were working a drug-smuggling operation? He shrugged. How could they not know? They were making millions off the gambling, but a few hundred thousand on the side from drugs wouldn't hurt. Top management over there had to know.

7

The Channel
Off Santa Barbara, California

The trusty CH-46 landed on the command cruiser *Vicksburg*, CG 59, at 0820, and the SEALs jumped off and assembled on the fantail. Ed DeWitt waited with the other SEALs as Murdock went to talk to the cruiser's captain, Commander Roth.

Roth was a short, heavily muscled redhead, and he grinned when he saw Murdock.

"So, I just wanted to take a look at the guy who has shaken up the brass and the CIA. I've never had an order directly from the CNO before, probably never will again. Can you tell me what this is all about?"

"Commander, I'd be glad to if we knew. That's why we're going on a recon down about a hundred feet. Want to come along?"

The captain chuckled. "Not about to get down that deep. Hell, it's been so long since I've been in the water I don't even know if I remember how to swim. Oh, the CNO says my ship is your ship, you've got the whole damn fleet we brought up here. Whatever you want, you get.

"He said we are on maneuvers, we do some simulated attacks, some circles around the two towers, and a general charging back and forth to cover our dropping you and your men into the water. Might as well get something started. You can board the surface-effect boat whenever you're ready. You need one or two, Commander?"

"One will be good for our men, but send the other one along to play tag with us and maybe shield us when we drop into the water. Appreciate it if you have somebody watch for us to surface. We'll shoot up a red flare when we're ready for a pickup."

"Sounds good to me. Let's get this circus started."

Murdock nodded, and left the cabin and headed back to his men. Two of the air-cushion landing craft hovered around the stern of the cruiser. Murdock signaled to the closest one, and it backed into the cruiser's squared-off stern. The big ship was making less than five knots, so there was no trouble tying up. Sailors put down a ladder from the deck to the air-cushion craft, and the SEALs went down it quickly and sat down on both sides of the deck against the large machinery pods. Murdock came down last. They had four battery-powered stream lights, which would light up the ocean floor for fifty feet. Four of the SEALs each carried one of the lights in a heavy-duty shoulder bag.

Murdock talked with the boat driver, and moments later the craft backed away from the cruiser and angled toward the closest oil rig. The ships had collected on the island side of the tower and a mile away, and now they began to move. The destroyers charged north, then cut back, slashed past the 27 tower, and circled back toward the islands to the west.

The Santa Barbara Channel Islands lay almost twenty-five miles off the mainland opposite Santa Barbara. The largest one, Santa Cruz Island, is over twenty miles long and part of the Channel Islands National Park system, which contains three large islands and several smaller ones.

Murdock slowed the air cushion boat and waved the second one on toward the tower closest to shore. The big ships put on a good display for anyone watching, and he was sure that the men on both towers were watching it all with interest.

Now Murdock moved his air boat closer to Tower 4, and when they were a quarter of a mile west of it, he signaled the second air boat to ease between them and the tower. Then he and his men dropped off the boat as quickly as they could. They went to fifteen feet at once, and Murdock swam around locating them and getting them all in a group. Then he motioned for a move, and they headed toward the tower using a bearing on Murdock's handheld compass board.

After what Murdock figured was four hundred yards, he

came up and took a peek by putting just his face out of a Pacific swell. He saw the tower a hundred yards dead ahead. Back down with the men, he angled on east and slanted down as they began working their way toward the bottom. Another five minutes and they came to what Murdock had seen before, the concrete blockhouse resting on the channel floor. He checked a depth gauge on his wrist: 110 feet.

The concrete dome looked more ominous now in the half-light from above. Each squad had two of the lights; Murdock motioned for them to be turned on. He positioned one man on each corner of the dome, and then all the SEALs began swimming around the structure, examining it, looking for an entrance, or wires or cables or tubes coming out of it.

Murdock completed a circle and found nothing. He moved to the top of the dome, and again there was no hint of an opening. If there was one there, it was cleverly concealed. They worked the recon for another ten minutes; then word went around the unit that they were done and should head back the way they had come. The heavy lights were passed on to new men, who shouldered the added weight, and they kicked to the west, in a gradual upward slant toward the surface.

Murdock broke to the fresh air first. Yes, they were at least a quarter mile west of the suspect tower. They swam on the surface for another quarter mile west, and then Jaybird fired a red flare and one of the air-cushion boats headed toward them. It sent up a furious spray of water as the powerful fans directed a cushion of air directly down on the water, while other fans pushed the craft forward just above the surface of the water. The spray of water was fifty feet long and half that high, which meant the air-cushioned craft were not for slipping up on anyone. They were eighty-eight feet long and forty-three feet on the beam, and could travel over water, desert, or a highway at forty miles an hour.

The closest one powered down as it neared them and settled into the water. The SEALs used a rope ladder, and climbed up over the blunt bow of the craft and flaked out on the deck. Murdock went to find the driver and use his radio.

"Is it scrambled?"

"Afraid not, Commander."

"Figures. Tell the captain we're coming back to his cruiser. Ask him if he has a SATCOM. Let's move."

Fifteen minutes later on board the *Vicksburg*, the radio room got through to Admiral Kenner in his Virginia office with a military scrambled signal. Murdock had been instructed to report his findings directly to the head of all the SEAL teams.

"Yes, sir, Admiral. Measurements were about the same, probably on some metric scale, but about forty by fifty feet oblong with a fifteen-foot-high roof slightly domed."

"How in hell did anybody get that thing down there, and right under our noses?"

"Sir, the freighters must have brought it in one piece at a time, and they sunk them and fastened them together, then pumped out the water."

"Why?"

"We've been considering that, sir. If it is North Korea, they have a big loss of face from when we smashed that invasion attempt last year, and they'd want to get even with us for it. We were wondering why they didn't just put a submarine offshore and send a few missiles into our cities, but then we discovered they don't have any missile subs."

"Is the structure set up so they could fire missiles from it?" Kenner asked.

"No, sir, too small."

"Does North Korea have missiles capable of hitting our cities from some platform offshore?"

"They do, Admiral. The Taepo Dong-1 has an extended range of four thousand kilometers with its third stage. They have rockets similar to the SCUD with a three-hundred-kilometer range. The Nodong missile reaches out a thousand kilometers."

"So why do they want a facility in close to shore?"

"Maybe for recon, for intelligence gathering, maybe even as a forward direction control for something coming over the ocean."

"Is there any easy way to get into that thing?"

"No, sir. It's solid as a rock. We found no indications of windows, doors, openings of any kind."

"We could blast it open."

"Probably about the only way, which would really mess up whatever they were trying to do down there."

"Is there a tie-in with the oil platform?" the admiral asked.

"My guess is that there must be, but I have no idea what it might be. Perhaps a control station of some kind. Intelligence gathering for sure. That oil rig could hold a dozen antennas to gather all sort of electronic data, phone calls, e-mail, faxes, anything that has an electronic base. The same way we get electronic intel around the world."

There were a few moments of silence; then the admiral came back on the air.

"Thanks, Commander Murdock. Well done. I'll be reporting immediately to the CNO, the President, the heads of the CIA and FBI. They will work out any continuing action. You and your men are released to return to your normal duties in Coronado. Well done, Commander Murdock. Now, get Captain Roth on that mike."

"Aye, aye, Admiral. Right away."

A chief heard the conversation, and bolted out the door to bring in Commander Roth. He was there in thirty seconds. Murdock waved and left the radio room.

Murdock found his men in an assembly room where they had cleaned and oiled their weapons, changed out of their wet suits into cammies, and tried to look busy.

DeWitt caught Murdock at the door and asked him how it went. Murdock gave him a quick rundown. "What's with the men?" Murdock asked. "The admiral has released us to get back to quarters."

"The XO told me we could take the men to the regular mess at 1130. It's almost that now."

The Navy chief who had handled their embarking and landing on the air-cushion landing craft came in the door and walked up to the officers.

"Sirs, the captain tells me that you're released and to arrange for the CH-46 to transport you back to Coronado. The bird will be ready to board at 1300. That way we all get to go to chow."

"Thanks, Chief. We'll be on the fantail at 1300."

NAVSPECWARGRUP-ONE
Coronado, California

By 1430 the SEALs had stowed their equipment. Jaybird had taken the lights back to Team Supply, and Murdock and DeWitt had eyed the training schedule.

"Let's do the O course for time," DeWitt said. "I'm trying to cut down my personal best."

Murdock studied the schedule again, then nodded. "Everyone but Bradford. I don't want him tearing anything loose."

"Right, he can keep the time tally."

The Coronado O course, O short for obstacle, was said by some to be the toughest in the country. Murdock had cursed and praised it depending on his exhaustion factor. It had the usual walls and logs and jumps, and several with nearly impossible challenges.

Each man was timed going through, with the average about six minutes. The all-time verified record was a little over four minutes. DeWitt warmed them up with a two-mile run in the sand down the beach toward the Navy communication towers. They had ten minutes to cool out, then Jaybird led off.

"Want to get through the course before all you guys with your sweaty hands get everything out there all slippery wet," he said. The men hooted him down, some with envy. Jaybird had one of the fastest times in the platoon for the O course. Today's times were not for publication. Bradford would tell each man his time, but not record it.

Mahanani sat quietly as he waited for his turn on the devices. Usually he was good at them, but he didn't know how he would do today. The casino/mule situation still bugged him. How in hell had he been so stupid as to get into debt gambling? Okay, he admitted that he had a problem with gambling, but he could kick it—if he could get out of his current situation without getting killed and without getting kicked out of the Navy. He'd heard about one Marine who got a dishonorable discharge and reduction in rate because of his gambling. The Marine had finally sold his car and started robbing his friends where they lived out at Camp

Pendleton just to have enough money to gamble with. So it could happen.

He had to come up with a plan. It all depended on whether or not the casino owners and operators knew about the drug running. If they knew about it, he was in deep shit. If they didn't, there was a chance he could turn in Martillo, and Harley, and maybe get the stateside connection busted in San Ysidro. Maybe. All he had to do was figure out how to do it and when. The sooner the better. Each time he ran the border with half to three quarters of a million dollars worth of cocaine, he was risking his neck and prison time. Wouldn't that go over big with the family!

Mahanani stared at the sand. If he had forty-five kilos in the car, and a kilo went for fifteen to twenty thousand dollars, that meant one load could be worth up to nine hundred thousand dollars. He shook his head. He couldn't even imagine what that kind of money was. They must have a massive distribution system if they moved that much coke every week or so. Maybe it was in a huge pipeline that funneled it back East and to the South. He shivered. He was in about a mile over his head. How in hell . . . He knew how. Now what did he do about getting out?

The whole idea of drug money repulsed him. He could just imagine the hundreds of thousands of addicts who were cheating and lying and stealing to feed their habit. He wouldn't touch that money. Not even if he had a guaranteed way he could hijack his load and turn in the druggers at the same time. No way. Not a chance. He just wanted out clean and with his Buick and no damned debt to the casino.

As he waited his turn on the O course, he tried out various scenarios. He could go straight to the president of the tribe, the head of the casino, and tell them what Harley and Martillo had done to him. Sure, and if they were in on it, he'd be just another nameless corpse found half buried somewhere out in the dry hills of the East County backcountry.

Maybe he could call in an anonymous tip to the narc squad at the San Diego Police Department. He could tell them where the garage in San Ysidro was and how Harley and Martillo got their mules. No, then the cops would set up a watch and raid the place when they thought a mule was coming in. If he had to keep running, it might be him. That was out. If he was going to get it done, he'd have to contact the cops, tell them when he was making a run, and then let them raid the place just as he arrived with the cargo. They would have to give him immunity from any prosecution for turning in the place. At the same time they would have to arrest Martillo and Harley. No way. Then he'd have to testify. Oh, yeah, and then he'd have to quit the SEALs because he'd have to go into the witness protection program and get shipped off to Idaho or Montana or Georgia. Not a chance.

"Hey, Mahanani, you got water in your ears?"

He stood up, vaguely aware that it was the second or third time that Bradford had called him to take his turn on the O course. He'd attack each part of the course as if it were Martillo himself. Martillo was Spanish for "hammer." He'd looked it up after the first run.

When he was through with the course, Bradford gave him his time. It was a full thirty seconds under his personal best on the big hairy O course.

Murdock cut the men loose about four that afternoon and told them to stay loose. Something could break on this sea-dome thing at any time. It was payday, so Mahanani stopped by the administration office for the team and signed for his paycheck. Most of the men had the cash sent directly to their banks electronically. But he'd never had a bank account. He liked to feel the cash in his hand. In his one-bedroom apartment in Coronado he stared at the cash. He could buy a lot of chips with that at one of the other casinos. They wouldn't know him, and there were four or five more Indian casinos less than twenty miles away.

For a moment he could see the cards turning over. Hear the shouts of glee from the slots when someone won. It stirred him as little else did these days. But he squashed it in a second. He put most of the cash away and some in his billfold. Then he made supper. He was a good cook, and he ate well. It would give him something to do.

The rest of the evening he didn't watch TV. He kept his pen busy on a pad of paper working on one plan after another to get out from under the Hammer and his damned mule operation. By eleven o'clock he had nothing that would work. He stacked the sheets of paper and saved them. He'd dig into it the next night, and the next, until he figured out a way to turn in the smuggling operation and to nail Harley and the Hammer and not get himself killed, jailed, or thrown out of the SEALs.

8

San Francisco, California

Harry Towner sat in his eighth-floor office and watched his secretary come in, close the door, and snap on the lock. She had on a tight sweater and a short skirt, and had put her hair high on her head the way he liked it. She was twenty-three. He was thirty-seven and feeling it.

"You said you had some dictation, Mr. Towner?" she asked, walking toward him, swaying her hips, and smiling. She had neither pen nor pad.

Harry grinned. "We've got to stop doing this, kitten," he said, rolling out his executive chair so she could sit in his lap. She did, and turned her face to be kissed. Harry kissed her. She reached out and turned over the framed picture of Harry's wife and three kids that stood on his desk.

She slipped out of the sweater, and Harry grinned seeing that she wore nothing under it. He reached out and kissed her firm young breasts and licked the nipples. Then Harry's head snapped up. He thought he saw a flash somewhere out in the bay. A few seconds later the sound of an explosion pounded through the windows. He frowned.

Harry never saw what killed him. The missile came almost straight down, and its 434 pounds of high explosives hit the roof of his building just over his head. It penetrated through two stories before it detonated, turning the eight-story Towner Building into a one-story pile of rubble and killing twenty-seven people.

Jonas Sanchez had sat in his twelve-foot boat all morning on San Francisco Bay near a shoal where he had caught fish before. It was ten A.M., and so far he hadn't even had a nibble. He was seventy-three, on Social Security, and had enough cash in the bank so he could do just about what he wanted to. This morning it was fishing. Fridays and Tuesdays it was bowling in a seniors' league. He watched the line closely. The fish here were tricky. They might be any kind that came in with the morning tide.

He was about to lift his line, with seven hooks on it baited with dead anchovies, when he heard something to the north. A second later a tremendous roar shattered the peaceful morning and a quarter of a mile away a huge geyser of water jolted upward where some kind of a bomb must have exploded. Jonas forgot his line, dropped his pole in the bottom of the boat, and jerked the starter on his motor. Five seconds later he was churning across the bay toward the landing ramp on the western bank where he had left his car and boat trailer. As he raced across the water, he saw more explosions in San Francisco just to the north. What in hell was going on? Somebody starting another war? He'd had his fill of wars and killing. He just wanted to fish and bowl.

Dorothy Johnson had just strapped her one-year-old daughter Marci in the rear seat of her car, and took the purse off her shoulder as she opened the driver's-side door ready to get into her two-year-old Volvo sedan. She was late for a dental appointment, but she would tell them that she was the customer, they were the sellers. She'd spent enough hours waiting in that same dentist's office. Let them wait ten minutes, wouldn't hurt them. She'd still probably have to wait when she got there, and then one of the nurses would complain about having to watch Marci while Dorothy had her crown fitted.

Dorothy heard nothing as the pavement in front of her car shattered into a million pieces and a thundering explosion ripped through the quiet street. Hundreds of the shards of rock and blacktop slammed toward her with tornadolike force as a missile struck ten feet ahead of her car on Filbert Street. The blast shattered twelve cars, blew out windows for ten blocks around, and killed Dorothy and Marci Johnson outright, along with ten more people.

From 0814 to 0822, nine missiles fell on San Francisco or in the bay. Those in the bay caused no damage. Six struck various parts of the city, and the death toll would not be known for several days as rubble and debris would have to be cleared away.

In City Hall, the mayor screamed at his police chief. The chief was trying to get the Presidio. The few military at the Presidio were calling Washington.

The news wire services and TV networks had the story at 0829. One of TV-8's crews was on a story when a missile hit less than half a mile away. The station sent the network a warning, and had a special report on the air seven minutes after the last missile hit.

The news alerted the military. The closest military airfield to San Francisco is Lemoore Naval Air Station south of Fresno. The large Alameda Naval Air Station across the bay from San Francisco had been closed for some time.

Military telephone and radio messages slashed back and forth, and twelve minutes after the first news report on national TV, six F-18 fighter/bombers lifted off the long runway at Lemoore Naval Air Station. They angled for San Francisco with orders to hunt for any invaders, any submarines prowling coastal waters, and any platforms that could fire the relatively small missiles. The F-18's blasted up to Mach 1.8, and were traveling at a little better than 1,200 mph at twenty thousand feet. It took them only fifteen minutes to drop down and flash over San Francisco. They were combat-loaded with 570 20mm rounds for their Vulcan six-barrel rotary cannon, along with seventeen thousand pounds of missiles, free-fall bombs, and cluster bombs.

The pilots talked to each other. "This is Hunter Leader. I see five blast points, two fires which are being worked, and a general traffic jam. Hunter Four, Five, and Six, take a south course and check out everything along the coast out twenty miles and down to Los Angeles. The rest of us will patrol to the north same distances. Remember to look for long dark shadows near shore. There could be enemy submarines, so watch for them as well. Go. Over."

The six planes did graceful banks, and half went in each direction. The aircraft maintained their speed and worked the area at twenty miles a minute, or a mile every three seconds.

"Hunter Leader, this is Hunter Four. I have a freighter,

maybe four hundred feet long, moving north about twenty miles off the coast about opposite Santa Cruz thirty or forty miles south of San Francisco. Nothing on the ship looks unusual. I'll slow down for another pass and see what else I can see."

"Roger that, Four. Anybody else have any prospects?"

"Hunter Leader, This is Six. I have a medium-sized oil tanker loading somewhere off Oxnard and Port Hueneme. Not much of a candidate for a shooter. Over."

"Roger, Three. Copy."

"Hunter Leader. This is Four. That freighter is flying a Panamanian Flag and there's some activity on deck, but nothing frantic. My guess she's making about twenty knots on a generally north course. Over."

"Hunter Leader. There has to be something out here. From the looks of the blast sites, those had to be fairly small, short-range missiles, say up to three hundred miles. Hunter Leader to Homeplate. Should we extend our search out to three hundred miles? Over."

"This is Homeplate. If you find nothing more, extend, Hunter Leader. Over."

"You heard the man, Hunters. Let's do it. Same pattern, work a hundred miles north, south each half and out to three hundred. Move it. Over."

In San Francisco veterans of the Gulf War quickly labeled the missile hits as being made by Scuds, the missiles used extensively in the Gulf War by Iraq. They had a payload of 434 pounds of TNT, which would make a nice bang, but nothing like the longer-range missiles with much larger payloads that most nations in the world had available.

San Francisco went into a state of shock. Public services kept working remarkably well. Hospitals and clinics were overloaded with the wounded. Every man in the police force was called to duty, and protection was put around the mayor, City Hall, and all federal buildings in the city. As the day wore on, the first panic passed and the shock began to wear off. In the blast-effect areas, neighbors were helping neighbors who hadn't even known their names before.

In San Diego, Commander Masciareli received a message directly from the CNO to put Third Platoon of SEAL Team

Seven on standby alert. They were not to leave the base until released. There would be a CH-46 fully fueled on standby. It would have machine guns mounted in both side doors. The two gunners and pilots would be on standby at North Island Naval Air Station until further notice. Canzoneri was on an emergency leave due to a death in the family in San Diego. He was recalled, and the platoon was at full strength. Murdock and DeWitt continued with their light workouts and training schedule for the platoon.

"This alert could last for days," DeWitt said. "We can't just sit around and wait for the phone to ring."

At six P.M. the President made a statement to the nation and the world, decrying the atrocity of the sneak missile attack and vowing that the perpetrators would be found and severely punished.

The entire West Coast military establishment and all federal offices had gone on stage-three alert an hour after the attack. Navy and Air Force planes flew search missions along the entire coast, interconnecting to be sure every inch of the coastal Pacific was covered. All federal buildings had total security, with armed guards on each door and two photo IDs needed to enter.

Patrol planes out of San Diego reported six freighters en route, some incoming, some outgoing. The Panamanian freighter first sighted had continued its northerly course.

For the first time in memory, the SEALs posted guards along the six-mile strip of the Pacific Ocean connecting Coronado and the base with Imperial Beach to the south. The men walked two-hour tours, were off four hours, and on for another two hours. They would be on duty for twenty-four hours, and then a new guard would take over. The sentries all carried M-4A1 rifles with full magazines of live ammunition.

The individual SEALs reacted to the full alert in various fashions. Ed DeWitt and Paul Jefferson held a marathon chess series. At the end of the first day, Jefferson was ahead five games to three. Jaybird and Howard went to work on sit-ups and pull-ups, challenging each other who could do the most. Howard won, and they moved on to push-ups. Jaybird won with 214.

Murdock kept in close touch with Commander Masciareli, his boss, but no request had come for their services.

The day after the bombing, San Francisco settled down and continued to clean up the debris and repair the damage. The final death count was 132. No nation or organization had claimed responsibility for the missile attack.

Military specialists were searching for pieces of the missiles. They already had several hundred fragments that would be analyzed to find out exactly what type they were, the source, the type and make, and who those particular missiles had been sold to.

Portland International Airport
Portland, Oregon

United World Flight 434 rolled along the taxi strip, waited its turn, then swung onto the main runway and gunned the big jet engines. The three-jet aircraft leaped ahead, rapidly gaining speed, and lifted off on schedule heading toward the end of the runway with the waters of the Columbia River just ahead.

Before he was fifty feet off the ground and well before the end of the runway, Pilot Jan Jenkins saw a curious trail of smoke come from below and ahead of the big jet. The former F-14 Navy combat pilot had seen them before, and it made him scream. "Missile incoming," he bellowed, and the co-pilot snapped her head around just as the smoke trail and the aircraft met. The explosion ripped into the left wing, igniting the full fuel tank in a huge ball of fire as the big jet slowly slewed to the left and dove into the Columbia River before the pilot could pull the throttles back. The furious splash the jet created sprayed water two hundred feet in every direction. The silver bird hung on the slowly flowing Columbia for a moment, then slid beneath the water before anyone could escape. Moments later there was only a roiling splotch on the serene Columbia's surface before that faded and there was no sign of United World Flight 434 out of Portland, bound for San Francisco and Los Angeles.

Portland broke the news first with a network bulletin about a plane crash. The network didn't interrupt normal program-

ming, but put it on their sheets, and it would play on the first
network newscast.

An hour after the crash, TV-7 in Portland received an envelope with a videotape. It came by a bicycle messenger who
vanished quickly. It went to the desk of Rolland Hemphil,
the news editor, who let it sit on his desk for twenty minutes
before he screened it. Then he pushed it into his player and
sat in front of his monitor. Less than a minute into the tape
he began screaming for a reporter.

He played the short tape, rewound it, and had twenty curious staffers watching as he played it again.

The tape started with a shot over the shoulder of a man in
a baseball cap. Then it went in close on a shoulder-mounted
rocket-propelled grenade. It showed the man lifting the
weapon to his shoulder. The camera panned up and it viewed
an airliner starting its takeoff on the familiar Portland Airport
runway. The camera followed the plane, then pulled back to
include both the plane and the gunman. When the plane was
a hundred feet away and not fifty feet off the concrete, the
gunman fired.

The video plainly showed the shot and the smoke trail as
the rocket jolted upward directly into the path of the jetliner
and exploded on the left wing. The resulting blast ignited the
jet fuel in the left wing tank and a huge ball of fire blossomed. The jet screamed overhead.

The camera panned with it. The plane gained altitude for
another ten seconds, then turned to the left, where the burning wing couldn't provide lift, and then the jet passenger liner
quickly crashed into the Columbia River.

Hemphil pulled the tape out and gave it to an editor. "Get
this ready to broadcast. I'm calling the network right now."
Two minutes later Hemphil had the go-ahead and a local
announcer broke into network broadcasting.

"This is a special news bulletin. A terrorist has just shot
down a scheduled airliner taking off from the Portland,
Oregon, International Airport. The terrorists took this uned-
ited tape and sent it to our office. There is no indication who
these men are, or even their nationality. We warn you that
this is graphic and young children shouldn't be allowed to
view it. Here is the videotape just as we received it."

The network ran the tape exactly as it had come into the station. When it was over, the announcer went back on. "We repeat, the jetliner went down into the Columbia River and it is doubtful if there are any survivors. We have learned from the airport that the plane was United World Flight 434 bound for San Francisco and Los Angeles. We will have a list of the passengers, but the names will not be made public. The airport reports that there were one hundred forty-eight passengers on the plane and a crew of nine. There has been no indication who the gunmen were who shot down the plane. Nothing on the videotape indicated this. There has been no public notice claiming the terrorist act. We return you now to your regularly scheduled programming."

9

Pacific Ocean
Off Point Arguello, California

Susie Jamison relaxed in the chaise longue on the promenade deck of the *Princess Royal,* one of the new limited-sized luxury cruise ships on its maiden voyage heading around the world. She was Dutch-registered and crewed by a majority of Filipinos and Italians. She carried only 1200 passengers, and every cabin was in the luxury class. The staterooms were fifty percent larger than anything else on the water, and with amenities found only in the highest-priced spas and five-star hotels.

The *Princess Royal* had sailed only the day before out of San Diego, and was working her way up the coast. Then she would stop in Seattle for a two-day port call. From there she would ply the inland passage to Alaska, making stops at Ketchikan, Sitka, Skagway, and Juneau along the way. When she was in port at Seward, there would be three days of excursions through Anchorage to see even more of Alaska. The *Princess Royal* was in no rush in making her way around the world.

Susie Jamison and her husband Allegro were on their first world cruise, and she was determined to make the best of it. Susie had married her husband when he was stationed in Korea well after the Korean War, and had come to the States with him and watched him get in on the floor of the computer-chip world and quickly surge to the top of the industry. His company had expanded again and again. Just before the big financial shakedown of the computer industry in late 2000, he had sold out for over twelve billion dollars.

Allegro, known to the world as Chip Al, was celebrated for having had the insight to know which way the market and the chip industry would be going. Not so, Al would tell anyone who would listen. His wife had wanted him to quit working and do some traveling. She'd said they had too much money already. She'd wanted to go back to Korea and look up some of her family whom she hadn't seen in thirty years. She'd wanted him to sell, so he'd sold.

Now he had money in a hundred different industries. He had become such a widespread player in the international market that he lost less than three percent during the bust of 2001, when some firms skidded by sixty percent.

Susie was a small woman, slender, with light brown skin and definite Korean features. Her three children looked more like their blond father, but they had the slightly tipped Oriental eyes, giving them an exotic look that fascinated photographers. The two girls were both models, and her son had taken to the chip industry, and now had a large chip firm of his own that he had spun off from one of his father's firms.

That morning Susie had been the first to go to the spa, where she was in the middle of a facial to be followed by a full body mud bath. She luxuriated in the attention and the consideration the staff gave to each of the passengers.

Al sat in the salon, pumping gold Sacajawea dollars into the slot machine. The big ship sailed along at sixteen knots, not in a rush to get anywhere. Al looked out the broad window, and saw a school of more than a hundred small Pacific dolphins skipping through the water, the whole pack moving close to the big ship, then angling away, satisfying their curiosity and giving the passengers a seldom-seen sight.

Al tired of the machine. Slots were fun only if you could win, and these were set so tight they squealed when they paid out ten dollars. He went to the fantail, bought a bucket of golf balls, and set up on the driving turf. It was real grass, and would have to be resodded every six weeks. He set up the first ball. The balls were real. He took out a power driver with the slightly larger head, and slammed a dozen straight down the ship's wake. On a good solid course that was a little dry, the drives would carry at least 260 feet. Not bad for a guy in his early sixties.

He switched to a five iron, and drove four straight and true, then pretended he had to slice around a tree in the edge of the course to get to the pin behind a short dogleg. The slices were tougher to control. At last he gave up and sent the last ball in the bucket straight and true. One of his small goals was to play golf in every nation in the world.

Ten miles behind the luxury liner and two miles seaward, a Panamanian freighter picked up speed and slashed through the water at twenty-four knots. On board, her skipper looked at the radar report of the location of the luxury liner and smiled. He wore the uniform of a captain in the North Korean Navy, and he watched his crack Navy crew at work in the ship's combat control center. The ship had not changed from its camouflage as a freighter. Before long the main antennas would be lifted from their bent-down positions. The radars would be raised and the fake wooden sides of the "freighter" would be pushed overboard to reveal the North Korean Navy Frigate *Najin 531*. It had fired all nine of the Scud missiles it had mounted on board. Now it had only its six SSM-1 missiles left in the tubes and ready to fire. But they were defensive hardware for homing on enemy ships with a range up to twenty-five miles.

It had two one-hundred-millimeter guns with a range of eight miles, and four fifty-seven-millimeter guns that would reach out two and a half miles. Scattered around the deck were sixteen quad-.50-caliber machine guns for close-in work.

Captain Kim Seng Ho was thirty-seven years old, young to be a full captain, and eager to get his stars. He had volunteered for this raid, even though he knew it could well be a suicide mission. He'd decided that he never would surrender. He would fight until every man on board was killed and he would go down with his ship. His name would live in Korean history for centuries, showing honor and bravery and the ability to slap a powerful enemy in the face and then fight to the death.

"How far now from the big ship?" he asked his radar man from his position on the bridge.

"Eight miles and closing. We should be within range a little under an hour."

"Sound general quarters. Prepare for the attack. Have the boarding party ready with ropes and grappling hooks to go up the side of the liner if we need to."

Captain Kim watched ahead as they came up on the luxury liner. His major mission was accomplished. He had started the attack on the hated America. His orders after that were a bit unclear. In essence they said he was to "return to home port at the first opportunity when all pursuit has ended." His senior admiral had bowed deeply when he gave the orders. Both knew that there would be no return. His craft would be discovered and it would be blown out of the water by American missiles. So he was on his own. If he captured the American cruise ship, and put all his men on board, the United States would not be able to attack her. He would have three thousand hostages. Perhaps he could sail the cruise ship all the way to North Korea. Perhaps. It was the only chance he saw. The camouflage of his ship as a merchantman had worked well. That phase was over. He was surprised he had not been discovered before now.

"Sir, we are within range of our guns," the radar man said.

"Continue on course. We want to come within five hundred meters of her. Then we will fire."

He would use the 57mm guns. He decided eight rounds into the cabin areas would be sufficient to bring the big ship to a standstill. He didn't want to harm her sailing ability.

"Stand by on the 57mm weapons," Captain Kim said in the public speaker system. "You will have the honor of firing two rounds each into the cabin areas. Space your shots along the entire length of the big ship. Fire on my command."

The captain watched as the big white ship came into view, and then soon they were closing on her. He felt his heart racing, his eyes widening as he watched the luxury liner *Royal Princess* continue to steam along at a leisurely sixteen knots.

"Range one thousand meters, Captain," the radar officer said.

"Stand by."

The huge white ship seemed to grow in size as they came closer.

"Range five hundred meters, Captain."

"All four guns two rounds each. Fire."

He heard the immediate reports as his weapons fired. He had out his big binoculars watching the white ship. The first round hit near the bow about halfway up the side and exploded with a muffled roar. Then, in rapid succession, the seven other rounds slammed into the side of the big ship. She cut power at once and coasted through the azure sea, letting the sixteen knots of forward motion reduce slowly until she was dead in the water.

The North Korean Navy Frigate *Najin 531* had pushed most of the shielding and camouflage overboard, and now cruised up close to the *Royal Princess*. Captain Kim used a bullhorn from the bridge wing and called to the liner.

"Captain of the *Royal Princess,* you are to consider yourself captured by the People's Democratic Republic of Korea Naval Forces. You will not resist our boarding party. You will treat your wounded and keep all activities on as normal a course as possible. We are coming alongside and will put a boarding party in the water. Open your dockside hatch so my men may board. Any resistance will be treated with the utmost severity. If you hear and understand my orders, respond through an amplified horn."

Moments later the men on the frigate heard a reply.

"We hear you and for the moment will allow you to board if you guarantee the safety of the rest of my passengers and crew. We are in a turmoil from your savage attack. Already we have found twelve passengers and four crewmen dead. We don't understand your sudden and vicious attack."

Captain Kim signaled, and four small boats pulled away from his frigate and angled toward the dockside hatch that had just opened on the port side of the big ship. It was barely three feet off the Pacific swells. He smiled as sixty men came off the small boats and surged into the big pleasure craft. He would join the men shortly. His XO would be in command of the frigate and would complete the conversion from freighter to man-of-war.

He wasn't exactly sure what he would do next. The frigate

would shadow the big boat, staying within two hundred meters of it as a form of protection. He was sure that the ship's radio had sent out a Mayday call for help as soon as the first round hit. By now the U.S. military would have figured out where the missiles came from and would have aircraft on the way. He moved his ship closer to the big liner, nudging up to within fifty yards of her side. Then he transferred to the luxury cruise ship and went directly to see the captain.

The cruise liner's captain was Wilhein Van Derhorn, 57, at the top of his trade and furious at the wanton attack on his ship. His face was still red from screeching at his workers to locate all of the injured and dead and get help for the dying. He had blood on his pure white uniform from helping lift two elderly women out of their shattered cabin and putting them down on a mattress in the corridor.

He had seen the armed men on board, but ignored them as he rushed around trying to save as many of the wounded as he and the two doctors on board could.

When Captain Kim found Captain Van Derhorn, he was kneeling on the carpet next to the elevators where six wounded lay. He had just watched a woman in her forties die. He closed her eyelids and turned to a man who had shrapnel wounds on his neck and head. The captain didn't know if he was alive or dead. Beside the man sat a small Korean woman whose face was smudged with tears and blood from the man. She looked around in fury.

"Who did this? Who has killed my wonderful husband? Whoever ordered those shots fired is a madman. I'll gladly tear his eyes out if I can find him." She looked up at the strange uniform in front of the cruise ship's captain.

"You," she shrilled. "You are the bastard, and you're Korean. You bastard!" She leaped up, ducked under Captain Van Derhorn's outstretched arms, and sprang on the startled Captain Kim. His guards were slow reacting and her fingernails clawed at his eyes, missed, and two fingernails dug deep furrows down his right cheek, bringing a trickle of blood. Kim jumped back, pushed the woman to the floor, and his guards grabbed her.

"You bastard, no-good fucking bastard. You killed my Al, you shot him with a big gun. You are a coward and a demon.

You don't deserve to be called a Korean. You are a dishonor to your mother and your grandparents. May your shriveled-up soul forever roam the planets of the universe searching for a resting place."

Kim held a white handkerchief to his bloody cheek and scowled at Susie Jamison. He was surprised to see she was Korean, and stunned when she tried to put a curse on him against his ancestors. He recovered his wits quickly. "Madam, I am sorry for your loss, but in war people are killed. We are at war with the United States."

One of his officers just behind him spoke. "Captain, do you want me to lock this troublemaker in a cabin?"

Captain Kim thought for a moment, rubbed his chin, then shook his head. "She will calm down. Have one of our doctors give her a sedative."

He turned to the luxury liner's captain. "Now, Captain, we need to talk. There are several changes that must be made in your routines. Get the damage cleaned up as quickly as you can. I would suggest a quick burial at sea for the dead. My two doctors will come and help with your wounded."

Captain Van Derhorn stared at the man in front of him in a strange naval uniform. Then he stood, and his bloody hands reached out toward Captain Kim. "Blood. Look what you have done. There was no reason to fire on us. We would have had to surrender after a shot across our bow. Are you an animal? No, you're worse than an animal. Look at the dead and dying. How can you call yourself an officer?" Two North Korean guards stepped in front of their captain, holding rifles and blocking the cruise ship captain's way. "Why have you killed all of these innocent people?" he shouted.

Captain Kim pushed the guards in front of him aside. "I have declared war on the United States. Your ship is a prize of war and I claim it. You will get your vessel under way at once and steer a westerly course."

"Impossible, you idiot. We would run out of fuel in mid-Pacific. We have fuel enough only to reach Seattle. We have food enough to feed our guests and crew only until we reach Seattle. If we sail west you will have a dead ship in four days."

Captain Kim frowned. He had not considered the fuel

problem. He had a tanker positioned four thousand miles from his home port where he had refueled on the way east. He would stop there on his return trip. He couldn't refuel two ships.

"For now, continue north on your regular course. Cut speed to ten knots. Now take me to your bridge. We have more matters to discuss." Captain Kim took out a handheld radio. He spoke in Korean so few could understand him. He ordered his ship's medical staff of doctors and corpsmen to get a small boat, report to the cruise ship at once, and aid in any way possible the civilian wounded. Then he and Captain Van Derhorn went to the bridge.

The liner captain saw several uniformed Korean sailors with submachine guns on the way, but he didn't comment. He was surprised to find two Korean officers with automatic weapons guarding the bridge.

"All ahead fifty percent," Captain Van Derhorn said. "Adjust the speed to ten knots, steer the regular course for Seattle." The Korean officers looked at their captain, who nodded. The big ship began to stir and slowly to move forward.

Captain Kim sat in the captain's chair and smiled. "This is much more comfortable than my chair on the frigate."

"So your ship sent the Scud missiles on San Francisco," Captain Van Derhorn said.

"Yes, and no one knew. Now they will. Did you send out a Mayday call just after we shelled you?"

"Our radioman did. He contacted the local Coast Guard and our headquarters. Everyone knows that you attacked an unarmed ship and that you are not a freighter. We watched you come out of your merchantman shell. We realized that no freighter could make twenty-four knots. Your speed gave you away. We had reported your transformation before you fired on us."

"Then we should be seeing some visiting aircraft within a few minutes," Captain Kim said. "When they arrive, my ship will come within a few paint thicknesses of this fine vessel. The aircraft will not be able to fire their missiles for fear of striking your ship. Or if our frigate explodes from their missiles, it also will severely damage the *Royal Princess*."

"I was worried about that."

"Captain, sir. I have six blips on the radar coming from the east at a high rate of speed. Estimated at twelve hundred miles an hour."

"The glorious U.S. Air Force has arrived," Captain Kim said. "Can you get their frequency so we can talk to them?"

Captain Van Derhorn picked up the phone, called his communications center, and gave the order. A moment later the radio chatter by the pilots came through a loudspeaker in the Bridge. The radar officer handed Captain Van Derhorn a microphone on a long cord. The pilot's voices sounded clearly.

"This is Blue Leader. We do a flyover first and inform Senora about the situation."

"Roger that, Blue Leader. This is Blue Four. How low are we going?"

"This is Blue Leader. We drop down to five hundred for the flyover. Don't want to upset any china down there."

"You sure we have two ships below, Blue Leader? This is Blue Six and I have only one blip on my radar."

"We're still ten miles off," Blue Leader said. "Could be he's hiding behind the cruise ship."

"We have confirm that it's a frigate?" Blue Six asked.

"The report from the liner said it was disguised as a freighter. The same ship we saw earlier. They did some fancy concealment."

"Coming up on the target, Blue Leader. Less than a mile off."

"Blue second half, after the flyover, do a turnaround to the left, we'll take the right. We come back low and slow for a better look," Blue Leader said. "Here we go."

The men in the bridge ducked instinctively as the blasting roar of the six F-18's slammed overhead and vanished into the blue sky.

Captain Kim took the mike, keyed the talk button. "Blue Leader, this is Captain Kim of the North Korean Frigate *Najin 531*. You will not engage my craft. If there is any hostile military action, I will personally kill ten passengers on board this liner. Do I make myself perfectly clear?"

"What the hell. . . ."

"Who is that bitch on the air . . ."

"Captain Kim. This is Blue Leader. We can blow your frigate out of the water and not touch the *Royal Princess*. Then what would you do?"

Before the Korean captain could answer, another voice came on the air.

"Blue Leader, this is Senora. You are restricted to observation only. You do not have guns free. I repeat, you do not have guns free. Confirmation?"

"This is Blue Leader coming in low and slow. The frigate is about forty yards from the luxury liner. We could take her out."

"Blue Leader, this is Senora. You do not have guns free. Do another flyby, obtain any data possible, and return to base."

"Senora, that's a Roger. Negative on free guns. Making flyover now. Returning to base."

The roaring, grinding, thundering sound of six F-18's in a tight formation made the men in the bridge duck again, even though they knew the planes were coming.

When the sound died, the cruise ship's captain looked at the modern pirate in uniform.

"Captain Kim. What are you going to do now?"

"First you are going to order up captain's dinners for me and my two men here. Then I'll go on the promenade deck and pick at random the first ten victims I will kill. Your men will use your digital cameras and take pictures of the faces of the ten, and you will then transmit them on the Internet and explain what fate awaits them if there is any action against this ship."

10

Coronado, California

The CNO, the President, the CIA chief, and the FBI director all heard about the ultimatum from the frigate commander at about the same time, 1640. Radio messages flew back and forth, secure phone calls were made, and at 1740 it was determined that there should be a night assault on the ship by two platoons of SEALs. Murdock's platoon would take down the luxury liner, roping down from a CH-46 chopper to the fantail of the big luxury liner, which was usually used for driving golf balls and trapshooting.

The second platoon would drop into the water behind the luxury liner, swim to the Korean frigate, and blow off her rudders and otherwise disable her. Both ships would be dead in the water for the night.

Word came to the SEALs through channels, and Masciareli bellowed over the phone for an immediate scramble to get to the chopper at North Island. They would take two birds and land in a baseball field in the small town of Guadalupe, just west of Santa Maria. The SEALs had ten minutes to get their gear ready and in the truck to go the six miles to the North Island Naval Air Station where the CH-46's were waiting.

From takeoff to landing would take an hour and forty-five minutes, the pilot told Masciareli. First Platoon of Team Seven would also be on the mission, with Lieutenant Joe Socha, the platoon leader. He had fifteen men fit for duty. Murdock used all sixteen of his men. On the flight one of the door gunners motioned for Murdock to go up to the pilot.

They put a headset on him, and he heard Admiral Kenner's voice.

"Commander, any suggestions for this party?"

"Yes, sir. We can't get on board silently, so we'll need a diversion. If Lemoore could send over four or five choppers to make a fake attack some two hundred yards from the bow of the liner, it would be a big help. They could buzz the area, throw out flares, and fire door guns into the Pacific. Create a lot of noise. Then if two or three F-18's could buzz the ship, it would be another help. All coordinated for the exact time that we come in and touch down."

"Sounds good, Murdock. I'll contact the CNO. Has any attack time been set?"

"Sometime after dark. We can go in at midnight or 0200. Whenever the other assets are ready. One more thing. One squad can disable that frigate. I could use the other eight men from Platoon One with me on our chopper to take down the liner. Somebody said there were fifty armed North Korean sailors on board."

"I'll talk to the CNO on that too. Hang in there, Murdock. I'll get back to you on this frequency."

Murdock went back to the men and yelled out what the admiral had said.

"Help we can use," Jaybird shouted. They settled down for the rest of the hour-and-forty-five-minute ride.

They came into the field marked by four red flares ten minutes early, and settled down on the lighted city recreation baseball field. They were five miles from the beach, and the two ships were about three miles offshore. As soon as they landed, the pilot motioned for Murdock and handed him an earphone and mike.

"Commander, this is Admiral Kenner. We have some support for your idea of a diversion. The birds will drop some depth charges as well and cause all sorts of racket three hundred yards off the bow. The choppers will fire door guns, shoot flares, and try not to run into each other. We'll have six F-18's making passes over the area, not the ship. The commander at Lemoore said he could have his chopper people assemble at the ball field where you are and coordinate everything. He'll put up his Eighteens when we have the time set. He'll have the six choppers on your site within thirty minutes. Want to establish an attack time?"

"Set the diversion for 0115," Murdock said. "We'll bring in the SEAL choppers at 0120. In that five minutes the deck guards should be all running to the bow to see what's happening."

"Sounds good from here. I'll check with Lemoore. Oh, tell Platoon One to loan you eight men. Give you a little more power."

"Any weapons restrictions, sir? We'd planned on using MP-5's with suppressors to cut down on sound and bullet travel."

"On that basis you have weapons free."

"Thank you, sir."

"Commander, good luck."

They broke the connection.

Murdock went to talk to Lieutenant Socha, First Platoon leader. He had his men outside their bird checking equipment.

"Joe, you ready for this?" Murdock asked.

Socha stood up and towered over Murdock by four inches. He was heavily muscled and looked like an overgrown grizzly bear.

"Hell, yes, been waiting. What am I going to do with fifteen swimmers around that frigate?"

"Admiral Kenner just talked to me, and said you might loan eight of them to me to take down the big ship. Be a help."

"You've got them. Want them with suppressed MP-5's?"

"Right. Pick them out and send them over. We'll integrate. Thanks for the loan." They shook hands, and Murdock felt the pain of the big man's grip.

A half hour later, Murdock had his twenty-four men teamed up. Each of the twelve pairs had specific assignments. Murdock and Jaybird would get to the bridge. Others would fan out and capture any North Korean sailors they saw as they took down engineering, communications, the engine room, and the guards on all of the ten decks.

"Every team knows its assignment. We don't know the names of the decks. Those assigned to clear any deck guards work by the numbers. One is the top deck, down one is number two, and so on. When you have secured a facility, report in. Use your weapons with discretion. There are twelve hundred passengers on board and probably six or seven hundred in the crew. Let a terr get away rather than risking a shot that might hurt a civilian. It's the middle of the night, so there shouldn't be a lot of vacationers running round the decks. Questions?"

"Do we take prisoners?"

"Absolutely. We don't have to transport them anywhere. Use your plastic riot cuffs and check them for hideouts. If you find one with a radio, give me a call. We should listen in. Does anybody speak Korean?"

"Skoshi," Franklin said.

"That's Japanese," Mahanani said.

"Oh, yeah. Damn."

"Okay, flake out, you guys. We have three hours until we shove off. You men from First, you all have on your cammies, right? You won't be needing any wet suits?"

"Yes, sir," they chorused.

"Good. Double-check your weapons and ammo. Your combat vests should be filled with regular ammo loads. If not, try to bum some off the Third guys. See you all in about two and a half."

Murdock heard the other choppers coming. He went to the edge of the baseball field lights and waited. The first bird slanted in and landed. The motor shut down, the rotors stopped, and a short, slightly heavy man crawled out of the Forty-Six and looked around. When he saw Murdock he came over.

"Who's running this cattle call?" the man asked. He held out his hand. "I'm Phillips. This is the most fun my crew has had in months. We get to shoot up a spot on the Pacific Ocean."

"Murdock," he said, taking the man's firm grip. "Yeah, and if you do it right, my boys won't get their asses shot off by some trigger-happy North Korean slants."

"Best of luck on board."

"Thanks, and don't run into each other out there."

"We won't. We worked it out. We'll come in single file

and stay a hundred apart, with our landing lights on. Plenty of firepower and flares all over the place. Should be a good show. This will be a carbon copy of an exhibition we put on during the daylight for some VIPs a couple of months ago. This time we won't have a shack to blow apart, just some ocean."

The five other choppers came in one by one and landed. Lieutenant Phillips went to brief his crews.

Murdock went over, sat in his Forty-Six, and tried to think of anything they hadn't planned. It was all on paper. Now all they had to do was make it work in practice. They had taken down a ship or two before. The bridge, engineering, the engine room, and communications were the prime areas they needed to nail quickly.

He had forgotten to tell the men about guides. He'd tell them later. When the SEALs spotted any workers on the ship, stewards, cooks, anybody, they should be used as guides to show the SEALs how to get quickly to each team's assigned area.

By 0030 there had been no return call from the admiral. Murdock woke up the chopper pilot and asked him if he could get in touch with Lemoore. The pilot made two tries, then got somebody. He handed the headset and mike to Murdock.

"Lemoore, this is Murdock on the beach. Did your Eighteens get the timetable on our little party?"

"We did. This is the OD. We have the birds on the flight line and ready. They only need fifteen minutes to get to the coast. They'll be off and over your area on time. As soon as they see the flares from the choppers, they'll make their runs."

"Thanks, just checking. Murdock out."

The next time Murdock looked at his watch it was five minutes to takeoff. He rousted out his men and stuffed them into the bird, and saw the six Lemoore field choppers warming up. He made a quick check with Lieutenant Socha.

"We'll lift off five minutes after your two sixes leave," he said. "Give them time to get to the target. By the time we get there it should be lit up out front with lots of racket and firing."

"What about pickup of my men from the water?" Socha asked.

"Stay cool around the liner. We'll have the dock-level hatch open so your guys can climb in that way and won't have to worry about a chopper pickup. Tell your pilot that on your way in. If everything goes right, we can get a chopper liftoff after daylight. First we'll want to see the ship get under way just far enough so the Eighteens can take care of that frigate. After you do your job, he won't be able to follow the white ship. But we don't want him using his big guns either."

Murdock went back, stepped into the Forty-Six, and watched the other choppers lift off and head west. He touched his stopwatch button. In five minutes they would be on their way.

The two U.S. Navy CH-46 helicopters took off precisely on time, and choppered their way across the five miles to the beach, and then slightly to the north, where they could see the hundreds of lightbulbs outlining the luxury cruise ship.

The SEALs stood in two lines along the sides of the bird. At each door lay a thirty-foot coil of rope, one end fastened to the bar over the side opening. The door snipers watched the fantail of the big luxury liner as they came up from the stern.

In front of the ship they saw flares, heard rapid-fire machine guns, and heard depth charges boom as the six choppers fought a war all their own. The snipers scanned the fantail as the first bird approached. It edged across the stern of the big ship. One sniper saw a gunman alongside a panel and drilled him with three silenced shots. He crumpled and lay still. The big chopper hovered over the fantail fifteen feet off the deck.

"Drop now," Murdock thundered, and the first two men at each door kicked out the coils of rope and fast-dropped to the deck, then left the rope and scurried to assigned locations facing outward to cover the other men coming down.

In twenty seconds all twenty-four SEALs had hit the deck and run to their assigned positions. Only one more Korean was seen, and he ran for a stairway, but two silenced rounds dropped him before he got up two steps.

All the SEALs had the new Motorolas on. The new radios had the same belt pack and wires up to the ear, but now a new earpiece had a swing-away mike that hovered in front of the mouth or could be rotated up to the forehead or down to the chin.

"Move to assigned areas," Murdock ordered on the Motorola, and the men charged to ladders and vanished into the big ship. Murdock and three men ran up the metal steps to the next deck, and ran forward around the pool and deck tennis court to the highest section of the ship, where the bridge should be. They hit another set of steps and went up quietly. Then they found a door that was marked in English: "Restricted to Ship Personnel Only." It had to be the bridge.

Murdock tested the door. Unlocked. He motioned to Jaybird, who was right beside him, to take the left. He'd take the right, the way they had cleared rooms a hundred times. Jaybird jerked the door open and charged in, diving to the left. He came up with his MP-5 aimed at two Koreans who sat at a table eating. A three-round burst of silent slugs drilled into them, putting both down on the floor behind the table. One drew a pistol, and Jaybird sent three rounds into him before he could fire. There was no one else in the room.

Murdock had charged in right behind Jaybird and darted to the only other door in the room straight ahead. He tried the handle. Unlocked. He heard Lam and Ching surge into the room behind him. He motioned Jaybird up beside the next door, and he jerked it open and they charged through. The door opened on a set of ten steps that went up to another door that was marked: "Bridge, No Admittance." The English wording had to be for the convenience of the mostly English-speaking passengers.

Murdock and Jaybird went up the steps silently and paused at the door. Jaybird tried the knob and found it unlocked. He changed positions with Murdock and jerked the door open, and the pair charged into the room, covering the four men they found on the bridge. Two were tall and brown-haired and wore the all-white uniform of officers of the ship, with mortarboards on their shirt shoulders. The other two were Korean, in jungle-print cammies. One tried to draw a pistol, but Jaybird put one round into his chest and he went down pawing at it and screaming.

One of the ship's officers kicked the gun out of his hand and put his foot on the smaller man's throat.

"I should kill you right now, you little bastard," the officer said. He looked up at Murdock. "Thank God you're here. They've been making our lives a living hell. Where did you come from?"

The second Korean charged Murdock, who shot him three times in the chest, and he sagged to the floor, his face smashing into Murdock's boots. He was dead before he hit the deck.

"Where is their leader?" Murdock asked.

"Probably sleeping in the captain's quarters," the second Dutch officer said. "He made me take him down there just before midnight."

"We'll get to him later. Can you men move the ship if you get the engine room and engineering under control?"

"Yes," the taller man said. "I'm Van Dyke, first officer. We could do it, but it would take a half hour at least, and pulling up the sea anchor would make a lot of noise and the sentries on the frigate would hear. They said if we tried to move, they would shoot us in the waterline with their one-hundred-millimeter guns."

"Which way is the current running here, to the south?" Murdock asked.

"Yes, and the frigate is anchored just to the north of us but not more than fifty yards away."

"Could you drop the anchor chain and drift away from them without starting the engines, with no noise whatsoever?"

"Could, but we'd need to power up quickly so we could gain control. Drifting isn't good for a ship this size."

"We may need to try it," Murdock said. "We have men disabling the frigate, but it could still shoot. We don't want that. If we can get you far enough away from the frigate, we can send in aircraft to sink it before it can fire on you."

"They have a watch out on the frigate, I'm sure," Van Dyke said. "If they see us start to move, they'll alert their commander on board."

"So we have to gain control of the ship and their captain.

We have other men working on capturing the vital centers so we can get your ship back. Where is this Korean captain you said is in command?"

"I can show you," the shorter Dutchman said. "I'm Larry Verbort. I can take you to the captain's cabin." He hesitated. "Would you have another weapon? I was in the Navy for six years. I can handle a pistol."

Murdock reached to his ankle and took out a .32 revolver. "It has six rounds in the chambers, so be careful. Let's move. Van Dyke, when we leave, lock the bridge doors. We'll leave Lam here for protection. Don't let anybody inside unless Lam's radio says it's all right."

Van Dyke nodded. Murdock, Jaybird, and Ching followed Verbort out a door on the other side of the bridge, and went down eight steps.

"What happened to your captain?" Murdock asked.

"We don't know. The last we saw of him he was hand-cuffed with his hands behind him and Captain Kim was leading him away."

"Did you notice our little demonstration out front of your ship, the planes and choppers?" Murdock asked.

"Yes, most of the Koreans went forward to watch it. They had no idea what has happening."

They came to a door a short time later and the officer pointed. "The captain's cabin. It's three rooms and a bath. Usually the door is locked. I have a key."

"Knock," Murdock ordered.

"The Dutch officer rapped on the door five times. There was no response. He looked at Murdock, who nodded, and Verbort knocked again. They waited but no one came.

"Open it," Murdock said.

Murdock jerked the unlocked door open and went in fast with his MP-5 up and the safety off. No one was in any of the three rooms.

Outside, Murdock used his radio. "Report on engineering and communications. Are they secure?"

"Engineering, Skipper. DeWitt here. We have a small problem. The Koreans saw us coming and have barricaded themselves inside. We're working on the situation."

"We need engineering and the sooner the better," Murdock said.

11

Lieutenant Joe Socha and his six men dropped out both sides of the CH-46 at the same time Murdock's men roped down to the luxury liner. They fell ten feet into the water in their wet suits and drag bags. All wore Draegr breathing gear, and at once went underwater fifteen feet and swam toward the Korean frigate a hundred yards away. They wanted enough separation from the man-of-war so the lookouts wouldn't know they were aiming at their ship.

Socha angled the men to the stern of the 334-foot frigate, and missed it by only a dozen feet. He checked carefully and made sure the big ship's twin screws were still. The craft was sea-anchored.

He motioned the two men who would attach small limpet mines to the two propellers. Four other men floated the larger, heavier limpets to the sides of the stern, where the magnets clamped them to the ship's hull two feet under the waterline. When all was ready, the men surfaced so close to the frigate that no lookout could see them.

Socha signaled for the men to set the timers for two minutes; then they would swim north ten feet underwater for a minute before they surfaced to avoid the killing concussion that would rip through the water. Socha went with the men to the screws, and saw them set the timers and then dart away, swim fins thrashing the water as they hurried away as fast as they could swim. A minute later, they surfaced and met the other four men. They swam away from the ship as the timer ticked down.

For a moment Socha feared that the timers might not have worked; then he felt a pounding surge of water catch him and drive him forward. Almost at the same time two blasts sounded as the water-level limpets exploded, sending water spraying out a hundred feet and flashing a bright light into the darkness on each side of the big ship. Another underwater blast came, and the SEALs began a surface swim away from the man-of-war south toward the brightly lit luxury liner. Socha figured the *Royal Princess* was about a hundred yards from the stricken frigate. The SEALs turned and watched the activity on board the Korean Naval vessel. A siren shrilled, and whistles blew, but even as they did, the stern of the big ship began to drop lower in the water. Watertight compartments inside the blasted area would prevent it from sinking, but it would not be moving anywhere unless it was towed.

The seven SEALs from First Platoon of SEAL Team Seven grinned around their face masks and stroked toward the luxury liner. If the side hatch wasn't open, they would simply turn and swim the three miles to the beach. Socha shrugged as he swam. Three miles in the Pacific Ocean wouldn't even be a warm-up for his in-condition SEALs.

On board the *Royal Princess,* Lieutenant Ed DeWitt heard the blasts from the north where the Korean ship was anchored. Socha had done his job. Now DeWitt had to finish his. He peered around the corner of the passageway where the engineering section was located. A Korean guard still stood at the door. DeWitt pushed his MP-5 around the corner, aimed carefully on single-shot, and drove a 5.56 slug through the Korean's skull. The dead sailor slammed to the left away from the door.

"C-5," DeWitt said. Franklin and Fernandez were close behind him. Both dug into pockets on their combat vests and pulled out quarter-pound sticks of the highly powerful plastic explosive.

"About an inch square on the door lock," DeWitt said. "Set the timer for ten seconds and get back here."

Franklin ran ahead with a chunk of C-5, pushing the detonator/timer into the puttylike explosive as he ran. He stopped at the door, ducked down, and moved forward to press the explosive against the door lock near the handle. He set the timer for fifteen seconds, pushed it to the "on" position, and scurried back around the corner. A moment later

the blast shattered the silence and pounded into the ears of
the SEALs. All had covered their ears with their hands, and
they could still hear when the sound jolted down the corridor
each way. They charged the door and found it blown inward.
Two Koreans lay on the floor holding their heads. One tried
to lift a pistol. Fernandez shot him twice with silenced
rounds, and the other man saw them and lifted his hands.
Franklin quickly bound his wrists and feet with plastic riot
cuffs.

"Where's the operators?" DeWitt asked. They found them
in a small adjoining room tied hand and foot. Fernandez cut
them loose, and they talked rapidly in Dutch. None of the
SEALs could understand them. DeWitt pointed to the equipment, the computers and screens.

"Okay?" he asked.

The most universal word in the world worked.

"Okay," one said after he checked over the equipment.
Fernandez dragged the dead man and the tied-up sailor into
the small room where the others had been, and left them.
DeWitt used the Motorola.

"DeWitt here. We have engineering. The two operators
here say all of the equipment is A-okay."

"Roger that, DeWitt. Leave one man there and see if you
can find out what's going on in the engine room."

DeWitt had no idea where it was. He made motions and
signs to one of the crew, until the man understood where
they wanted to go.

"Okay," he said, and motioned for them to follow him.

At the communications center, First Platoon SEALs Parson
and Underhill checked out the situation. There were two
armed men inside and the door was locked. Parson told Underhill to wait, and he ran back down the corridor until he
found a crewman. The Filipino said he was a steward and
knew nothing about the communications room.

"Hey, man, I want you to knock on the door and ask these
guys if they want any food to eat. Make motions, get them
to understand. You speak English. One of them might. Give
it a try. You won't get hurt, we promise. Look, we're trying

to take back your ship and get rid of these murdering bastards."

The steward had been surprised to see the armed men who were not Korean. Now he thought it over. He shrugged. "Might as well. Got to get them out of there. Let me get a tray with some stuff on it under a napkin. Fool the fuckers."

He came back a moment later with a tray and walked up to the door. He knocked, then knocked again. The SEALs couldn't see the Koreans through the glass in the door, but they could see the steward. He motioned to the tray and then made motions as if he was eating. He nodded and started away, then came back. He made more motions to the men inside and then to the tray.

The steward said something the SEALs couldn't understand, then started away again. The door opened a crack, then more. Parson had been crawling along the side of the corridor out of sight of the Koreans. As soon as the door cracked open, the steward pushed it farther open so he could hand in the tray, Parson came to his feet, jolted forward the last six feet, and sent a dozen rounds into the belly of the Korean reaching for the tray. He went down to the left and gave Parson a clear shot at the second Korean, who had brought up a submachine gun. Parson's three-round burst hit the hijacker in the throat and drove him backward into a set of monitor screens before he slid to the floor dead on impact.

The steward had turned and raced away as soon as he heard the gunfire. Underhill stormed into the room, saw it was under control, and reached for his Motorola.

"Lieutenant, Underhill in communications. We have captured this section, but haven't found any civilian operators. Will hold it until we get further orders."

"Well done, Underhill," Murdock said. "Lock the door and hold the fort." Murdock stared around the captain's cabin. "Where could they have taken your captain?"

"The cap was a coffee nut," the officer said. "Maybe they went to the kitchen for some late-night latte."

"Wasn't Captain Kim upset about the fireworks off his bow?"

"He said he couldn't figure it out. We had a good view of the whole thing. Looks like it's about over now."

"So where is Captain Kim and the rest of his hijackers?"

Two Koreans came around the corner of the companionway and stared in surprise at Murdock. Before they could swing up their submachine guns, Murdock and Jaybird drilled them with six rounds each. They flopped onto the deck. One tried to fire, but Jaybird shot him with three more rounds and he died on the floor.

Verbort stared down at the Koreans.

He shook his head. "You guys don't fool around, do you? Damn, I have seen four men killed in the past fifteen minutes."

"Our job," Murdock said. "Now where could the captain be?"

Verbort nodded. "Oh, yeah, he could be down at the doctor's office. He was concerned about the wounded. The medical area now looks like a battlefield hospital. Down this way."

Murdock, Lam, and Ching followed the ship's officer to an elevator, and down several decks. They got off and Murdock cleared the area, saw no Koreans, and let Verbort leave the car and head down a corridor.

Six people sat in the doctor's office. Murdock and his men went through a door into a small clinic that was now filled wall to wall with wounded. Twelve victims lay in the beds. Some were sleeping, others crying. One man moaned with every breath he took.

A harried-looking man in a white lab coat came in, stared around, and lifted his brows.

"Dr. Hanson, have you seen Captain Van Derhorn?" Verbort asked.

"Not for an hour. He's recruiting passengers who are doctors or nurses. So far we have five helping. We could use a dozen more. I've taken over the next four storage areas and need more room. If you see him, get him back down here. We've had two more pass away. I hate this. I had enough of this in Vietnam."

Murdock set his jaw. "Doctor, I promise you we won't leave you any wounded Koreans to tend to." He turned and walked out with his men. Verbort followed.

"I have no idea where either of the two captains are, Lieutenant," Verbort said.

"We'll find them eventually." He used the Motorola. "Engine room, any report?"

"Cap, we've got a situation here. There are four crew in there working on the machinery, doing something. There are six armed Koreans watching them. They're all too close together to get off good shots. They don't know we're here yet."

Murdock recognized Mahanani's voice.

"You have access through a door?"

"Affirmative."

"How many flashbangs with your team?"

There was a pause.

"Yeah, Cap. Good thinking. We have four. I'd say we put two in the bunch, let them play out, then do it again. We have a go?"

"Just don't hurt any of the crew. Single shot on the Fives when you get through the door. How many men you have?"

"We picked up a couple from First. Now we have five."

"Get them all in as fast as you can after the last flashbangs go off. Nail the bad guys with gun butts, or kicks to the head. Try not to shoot while the crew is mixed in."

"That's a roger, Cap. We're working on it. Report in about ten."

"Cap, you still got your ears on?" another voice asked.

"Yes, Canzoneri, what's happening?"

"That frigate is lit up like a spring dance. You heard the explosions. I think our boys used some claymores on it. She's dipping her stern rail in the briny deep. Must be down eight feet at least. Her screws must be off, but she could still shoot. Don't know if she could depress those big guns enough, but she's got quad-fifties that could do the job. Suggest we call in some air before they start mowing us down with the fifties."

Verbort was looking pale. "They could do it, Lieutenant. How can you call in an air strike?"

"We can't, unless you can use your radio to contact the fighters overhead."

"They did it this afternoon when the fighters first flew

over. I used to do the radio. I'll run up to communications and see if we can contact them. Are the fighters still up there?"

"I haven't heard them lately, but I'd guess they are flying CAP on us. Let's get to communications."

They ran to the door and rushed to the elevators. A few minutes later they came into the communications room. No crewman was there. Verbort started turning on equipment, and soon he made a call.

"F-18's, this is the *Royal Princess* calling. We could use some help. Are you still with us?"

"*Royal*, this is High Fly Leader. Just cruising around up above you."

Murdock took the mike. "High Fly Leader. This is Murdock. Can you get weapons free on the frigate? She's down in the stern from some mines. We think she may fire on the cruise ship with her quad-fifties. Can you ask your field for guns free?"

"This is Home Base. Murdock. The admiral called us. We understand your situation. If you think more gunfire is imminent from the frigate, I can give High Fly guns free."

"Home Base, this is Murdock. I'd say the frigate is past due to fire on us with his three-inchers and his quads. The frigate is now almost a hundred yards from the liner. If the eighteens make their runs from south to north, any debris should not hit the liner. Yes, please, guns free."

"Splash one frigate, High Fly. You have guns free on the frigate. The south-to-north run might be a good idea."

"Roger that, Home Base. Going around now to make a south-to-north run. A forty-five-degree angle to target would be best. We'll use that heading. High Fly One and Two, you have guns free on the frigate. Use the Harpoon missiles. Make the run now. High Fly Two, make the first run. I'll be right behind you."

Murdock looked at Jaybird.

"Cap, the Harpoon is an air-to-ship missile. A five-hundred-pound warhead that will put down a good-sized ship. Two of them will blow it right out of the water and all the way to San Bernardino."

"Let's go watch."

The men all ran to the rail, then toward the stern. Two Koreans lifted up from around a lifeboat and fired. One round clipped Murdock in the left arm, and Jaybird nailed both the shooters with two bursts of three rounds. Murdock and his men moved back farther, and saw the frigate behind them a hundred yards. Jaybird saw blood on Murdock's arm, and made him stop while he examined it.

"It's an in-and-out, but it might have grazed the bone. We'll check later." He tied up the wound to stop the bleeding as they all watched the planes.

"Hope they target the right ship," Jaybird said. "One of those Harpoon missiles would put this luxury liner on the bottom of the mother-loving Pacific."

They watched. They knew there wouldn't be any warning. Jaybird explained: "A jet coming straight at you doesn't make any sound out front. It's when it slams overhead and goes away that the sound comes. By then you're either dead or they missed you."

Jaybird saw a touch of exhaust out the back of the first jet, and pointed. A moment later the big bird screamed overhead, and they saw a burst of smoke as the sea-skimming missile angled straight for the Korean frigate. The fourteen-hundred-pound missile hit the frigate just off mid-ship, and blasted ten feet into the craft before the five hundred pounds of explosives detonated. The 334-foot-long Korean frigate jolted upward twenty feet when the missile exploded. Then it heeled over to port, and smoke poured from a massive fire that had ruptured the ship's fuel tanks.

The fire outlined the ship at once. A creaking and groaning came from the massive steel structure of the ship, and then a ripping and tearing as the stern broke off and sank immediately. The bow and most of the middle of the ship floated, held in place by the anchor line. The fires grew and explosions racked the ship as one after another blossomed into the dark sky.

Less than two minutes after the missile hit the ship, it slipped under the water, the anchor still holding, bringing it straight down to the bottom.

A siren sounded on board the *Royal Princess*.

Then the public-address system came on. "This is Captain

Van Derhorn speaking. All available crew members are to report to the lifeboats. Man boats and launch at once to search for survivors of the frigate. There were a hundred and thirty men on board. Search now and continue searching. I repeat, all available crew members trained in lifeboat launching report to the davits now for launching."

Verbort ran back toward the lifeboats and began lowering the nearest to the water. Three crewmen stepped into the boat, and it pulled away toward the stern of the big ship and the place where the frigate had sunk.

Crewmen came out of their bunks, dressed quickly, and ran to the lifeboats. Soon they had twenty in the water, scouring the area that now showed as black as death, as they worked through the few items that had floated from the sinking frigate. Many of the passengers were awake and watching from the rails.

The PA system came on again. "Is there anyone on board who speaks Korean? We need to inform all the Korean sailors on board that they should turn in their weapons and give themselves up. They will not be harmed and will be turned over to representatives of their government when we reach port."

Murdock called on his radio net. "All SEALs report in the usual rotation. First Platoon go first."

He listened as the men checked in and told where they were and what they were doing. When the reports were done, Murdock knew that they had captured all of the vital control areas of the big ship. They had put down an estimated fourteen of the Koreans and captured six more. That still left at least thirty on the ship, including the frigate captain, Kim.

Five minutes later the PA system came on again with a woman speaking Korean. She pleaded with the men in their own language to lay down their arms and turn themselves in. Murdock headed for the bridge. The last he knew, the luxury-ship captain had been a prisoner of Captain Kim. Evidently he'd escaped. He might know where the Korean was.

On the bridge, Captain Van Derhorn shook his head. "I don't know what happened to him. Three of us overpowered Kim, and took his weapon away from him, but he ran down a corridor and vanished."

"He still has at least thirty armed men on board and could do a lot of damage. Could you get all passengers back in their cabins?"

The captain said he could, and made the announcement.

"All passengers are requested to return to their cabins and lock the doors. There are still hijackers on board who are armed and dangerous. Please return to your cabins at once."

Murdock, Jaybird, and Ching huddled on the bridge.

"Where the hell can he be?" Ching asked.

"He's lost his power base, no frigate," Jaybird said. "So he's on his own with his remaining troops. If he can find them. He could always swim to shore and fade into Korean Town in San Francisco or Los Angeles."

"Or jump a South Korean flagship out of San Pedro and get back to Korea," Murdock said. "More likely he'll try fighting to the end on the ship. How do we find him?"

"Call him out for a one-on-one shoot-out on the fantail, like the old Westerns," Ching said.

"Maybe not exactly that, but that's an idea. We use the PA system for sure."

The Motorolas sounded and the three listened. "Skipper, Jefferson. We've got a situation down here on the promenade deck that you need to be in on. Some wild-eyed Korean with a sub gun has six passengers in nightclothes pasted against a bulkhead and is threatening to shoot them. Too damn many civvies around for Donegan or me to get off a good shot."

"Hold the fort, Jefferson. We're on our way," Murdock said, and the three SEALs took off running.

12

Murdock, Ching, and Jaybird darted out of the bridge, flew down two flights of steps, and came to the promenade deck. Standing in front of them were three North Koreans with their hands in the air. Their submachine guns lay on the deck at their feet.

"Tie them," Murdock called to Ching, and he and Jaybird ran on to the center of the long and mostly dark promenade where they say a group of people. The SEALs slowed and came up behind a dozen middle-aged men and women in pajamas and robes. Murdock slouched so he wouldn't tower over the others, and stared between them. Six men and women in their robes were lined up against the bulkhead. A man stood in front of them wearing the off-blue uniform of the North Korean Navy. Then Murdock saw the submachine gun he carried and aimed at the six. The Korean shouted something in English, but Murdock couldn't understand it. He worked through the crowd to get closer.

"I told you once," the Korean shouted. "I want a motor launch out the dockside hatch and I want guaranteed free passage to the boat and on to shore. Otherwise these six die here and right now."

There was no ship's officer there. The man talked to the crowd. He turned looking at the people behind him.

"I'll shoot them down, believe it," he shouted. "I am Captain Kim, and I'm used to being obeyed. Who can speak for the boat captain?"

A small woman with a long robe stepped from the group of people ten feet behind Kim.

"I can help you," she said.

116

He turned to look at her. "Little woman of Korea, I remember you from before. Don't bother me. I spoke with you already and you were not polite. Go away." He shrugged and turned from her. Before Murdock could make a move, the small Korean woman lifted a heavy .45 pistol from the folds of her dress.

"This is for killing my husband," she shouted, and at once fired the heavy gun. It kicked high. The bullet slammed into Kim's right shoulder and spun him around. Before he could bring up the submachine gun, she brought the pistol down and fired again. This round jolted into his chest just over his heart and knocked him down, the sub gun skittering away from him on the deck.

The small Korean woman stepped up near him. Murdock pushed people aside and rushed toward the woman.

"You're not dead yet, Kim," the woman screamed. "You should be." Before Murdock got to her, she fired four times more from point-blank range above where he lay on the deck. All the rounds hit him in the chest.

Murdock lunged the last three feet and grabbed the weapon before she could fire again. "He's dead," Murdock said.

Susie Jamison nodded, stepped closer to the body, and kicked it three times. "May your soul wander for all eternity in the nether regions of the unforgiven and may your ancestors deride you and scream at you for a thousand centuries for disgracing them and making them lose face." Mrs. Jamison turned and walked away through the gawking vacationers.

Murdock used his drill-field command voice. "All of you passengers. This has been a shocking sight. Now please clear this area. Return to your cabins and lock the doors. There are still more than two dozen armed and dangerous North Korean Navy killers on board who could strike at any time. Go now and stay in your cabins until Captain Van Derhorn gives you an all-clear." He watched as the people took a last look at the dead man, then slowly filtered into the inside of the ship. The six people against the wall surged out and gathered around Murdock, thanking him, glancing with fright at the man who had almost killed them. Murdock urged the six to hurry to their cabins.

Murdock and Jaybird went back to the bridge. The captain reported that fifteen of the hostiles had surrendered.

"We're getting survivors from the frigate at the dockside hatch. So far we've brought twenty on board. I've called the nearest Coast Guard station to send out two rescue choppers to transport some of our most seriously injured passengers and crew to a hospital. They say twenty minutes. They also will send three cutters to come and take the North Koreans off our hands. They can have the wounded ones too. Not sure how many survived the sinking."

"Good work, Captain. The Coast Guard should take the bodies too. As soon as we get the ship cleared of all the Korean live ones, we'll gather up the corpses and take them down to the hatch level. The North Korean government will want the bodies returned, I'm sure."

Murdock talked to the Motorola. "Okay, team. Maintain one guard at each of the vital areas. The rest of you report to the top deck and we'll start a sweep of the decks to find any reluctant North Koreans. May be some trouble, may not."

They made the sweep. On the top deck they found no one. Two Koreans came out of a closet-type room on the second level and surrendered. Then it went faster, and they found only six more Koreans, and none offered any resistance.

When they finished the last passenger-area sweep, Murdock checked his watch. Almost 0300. He didn't think it had taken that long to cleanse the big ship.

His Motorola sounded in his earpiece.

"Murdock, this is Socha. The dockside hatch wasn't open when we finished our exercise, so we swam for shore. We're all present and accounted for. How is the job there moving?"

Murdock told him. "About ready to call in our Forty-Sixes. You want a pickup?"

"Roger that, Murdock. Let us know when our chopper is coming and we'll use some red flares to mark our beach. We're almost due east of the ship. Nice and quiet over here. Understand that frigate is bottomed out somewhere out there."

"Affirmative, Socha. An F-86 christened it with a Harpoon missile. The old tub broke in half and went down."

"Good. Let me know when our pickup is."

At 0420 the Coast Guard choppers arrived and transported the six critical passengers to the closest hospital. Cutters came soon after that and swallowed up sixty-nine North Koreans, alive and dead. The cutters would transport them to shore to be turned over to the county sheriff to be jailed awaiting possible prosecution, or pickup by federal authorities. The other two cutters began a systematic search of the still-dark waters for survivors. They estimated there could be as many as fifty or sixty more North Korean sailors out there in the water.

Murdock asked Verbort to contact the fly guys again. The plan had been for the two Forty-Six choppers to wait at the ballpark until they were needed. They set up an 0530 pickup off the fantail of the big luxury liner. The captain was anxious to get under way. He pulled in his sea anchor, and had been instructed by his company to return to San Diego, where the passengers would be released and given vouchers good for another trip. The ship would go in for repairs, which the captain estimated would take at least four months.

At 0530 one Forty-Six landed on the golf tee on the stern of the *Royal Princess,* and the other one stopped by at the beach. The chopper crews were refreshed after four hours of sleep, and turned their craft toward San Diego and Coronado. They had just passed Oceanside, and it was daylight, when the chopper pilot called Murdock up front.

"Not sure what is going on, Commander. Suddenly my radio reception went dead. Now I'm getting one transmission from a SATCOM my CO is using outside his office. He told me that the whole base and San Diego is blacked out. It's not a rolling blackout. The whole county is black. My CO said he's getting SATCOM traffic from Los Angeles and San Francisco. From what they say, the whole damn West Coast is running without the aid of electrical power. Everything electrical except battery power is shut down."

"Terrorists or a nuke explosion in the atmosphere that blanked out all electrical?" Murdock asked.

"Can't be the nuke, or my whole electrical system would be down regardless of the battery.

"Sounds like a power grid went down. That would flash through huge surges on the rest of the West Coast power grids and they all could blow. Remember when five or six of them went down in Northern California and Oregon when a transformer island blew up a few years ago?"

"Heard about it. So far nobody is reporting any enemy action."

"We just might not have heard of it yet. I'd guess the satellites are still up if we can talk through them. At least the SATCOM satellite is still there."

The pilot shrugged. "My skipper says to come home. We should land in about twenty minutes. Plenty of fuel. I'm going to stay over the ocean all the way down instead of cutting across. All of the commercial flights must be down. Good thing it's light enough for them to land."

Murdock went back to the troops and shouted the news to them. Sadler scowled. "Who the hell did it?" he asked.

"Could have been a power grid accident, explosion, almost anything to put down the whole West Coast grid," Lam said.

"Who has our SATCOM?" Murdock asked.

"Back at the base," Sadler said. "Didn't think we'd need it."

"Looks like we do, Senior Chief. But I don't know if we could use it inside this bird or not. From here on out, I want that SATCOM glued to somebody's back. Wherever we go, training or an operation. We have waterproofing for it?"

"No, sir," Jaybird said.

"Everything except training swims and wet operations, we take the set. Senior Chief, get it waterproofed as soon as possible. Must be some gear that will do the job."

"Copy that, Commander."

DeWitt slid in beside Murdock. "Suppose this is some more of the North Korean attack?"

"Hadn't thought about it, but sure as hell could be. Doesn't take much to throw the whole grid into a blackout. All they would have to do is pick the right relay stations and a few major transmission lines."

"How long was the power out before?" DeWitt asked.

"Don't remember exactly. They found the problem almost at once and fixed it. As I recall, ten or twelve hours. Caused a horrendous mess."

"Yeah, and now with the Internet and e-mail, think of the trouble it will cause. All business is shut down at the git-go. Can't run a store without lights and cash registers. Oh, little places can get by, but not the big ones. Any on-line outfits are dead for the day or the week, and the stock market is deader than last year's Super Bowl tickets."

"Thanks, and the market was just starting on an upward trend," DeWitt said.

Murdock went back to the pilot. "Check to see if there will be a bus or trucks waiting for us at your field."

"My commander told me that the bus is there waiting. Has been since you took off. It can drive through Coronado, but there's a huge traffic jam there with folks coming to work at North Island. No traffic lights. He says there are two radio stations still on using emergency generators. They keep telling people that when they come to an intersection to treat it like a four-way stop. Coronado has cops at the major intersections, but the whole thing is one huge mess. You might get back to your quarters faster if you hiked."

"Thanks, Lieutenant. We'll see the lay of the land when we get there."

A few minutes later, the twenty-four SEALs stepped out of the CH-46 after it had landed at North Island Naval Air Station, six miles from the SEALs headquarters. Murdock looked around. It was a little after 0745. He didn't see the usual activity around the big base. The SEALs trooped fifty yards to the Navy bus waiting for them, and boarded with all their gear.

"Can you get us through the traffic?" Murdock asked. The Navy second class driving the bus shrugged. "Don't have the faintest. The station sent most of the civilian workers home as soon as they got here, and that's caused a reverse traffic jam. We'll work it out and go around the ocean side. Might work."

A half hour later the bus stopped in the NAVSPEC-WARGRUP-ONE parking area, and the SEALs traipsed over the Quarter Deck and into their quarters. Murdock and

DeWitt stopped to talk with Master Chief Petty Officer Gordon MacKenzie. They had known each other for over six years.

"Well, Commander, lad, sir. A fine mess you've got us in this time. No juice at all, up the whole damn coast. Nobody has a shot glass of an idea what caused it, and evidently no idea about how to fix it."

"You using your SATCOM?"

"Aye. Picking up lots of transmissions on all frequencies. Most are just short of panic calls."

"Anything official?"

MacKenzie pulled out a small radio and turned it on.

"So, this is KFMB, one of two radio stations in San Diego still functioning. Our big turbine is spinning away driving the large generator and providing our station with power. So far we have received little information from the network. We have some receivers on covering many bands and frequencies. Up to now this is all we know for sure.

"Power is out all along the coast from the top of Washington State to San Ysidro. Most stores and businesses are closed. Traffic is snarled. No TV stations in town are on the air. Television takes a tremendous lot of power. We're trying to get our sister TV station up, but so far no luck.

"What caused it? Nobody knows. Some emergency government agencies are swinging into action. We understand the county emergency radio system overlooking El Cajon has been staffed and will soon be operational. Power is out in what is called the Pacific Electrical Grid, which covers the coast states and most of Idaho, part of Montana, and all of Nevada, Utah, and Arizona. It could be a long day and a horrendous night if they don't figure out the problem.

"I have just received a call from a ham radio operator. All of you hams out there get your sets into operation and see what you can find out. This is a transmission from a woman north of Redding who says she witnessed a gigantic explosion in a huge electrical substation near her home. Redding is in the Central Valley about a hundred and ninety miles north of San Francisco. It's a center where high-voltage power lines come in and power goes out in several directions. She said she's seen a transformer explode on a pole.

"She assured my contact that it was a hundred times that big and loud. The whole area was covered with sparking wires and snapping and smoking for a half hour before it calmed down.

"Now, the question is, was there just one explosion like this one? Was it done deliberately or was it an accident? Could one large power substation blow out the entire electrical grid to seven-and-a-half states? I don't know.

"A small update for you. Yes, most telephones are working. However, if you have a cell phone, it probably won't. The cell phone repeater antennas need electricity to function. If you have a cordless phone that plugs into a socket and transmits your voice from handset to base, it probably won't work. Ordinary phones use a very small amount of electrical power and are not connected to the electrical lines. So, you can call, but most circuits are so jammed that you can't get through. Just sit tight, hang on, welcome your day of vacation, and hope they put the grids back on line soon. By the same logic, most long-distance calls won't go through since they are often sent through microwave relay stations. Those stations here in the affected area are also down and out, so no long-distance calls."

Murdock and DeWitt listened to the radio. Murdock shrugged. "Hey, I have an after-action report to do. I can write it on my battery-powered laptop, but won't be able to print it. So I'll print it out later."

Murdock had just sat down in his small office at Platoon Three when his phone rang. It startled him. He grabbed it. "Murdock here sir," he said.

"Good, you're back." It was Commander Masciareli, Murdock's immediate superior. "I have my SATCOM on and just received a mission-well-done from the CNO. He also said nobody knows much about the power blackout. He suggested that your platoon be on standby. He had just come from a meeting with several federal agencies and they were concerned with the power blackout. By now they concede that it is sabotage, probably by the same North Korean elements who attacked San Francisco and shot down the jet passenger liner."

"Yes, sir. I'd say that's a good assumption," Murdock said.

"He said one of the large power stations blasted is in the desert north of Palm Springs near Yucca Valley. Two witnesses saw the huge power substation there blow up; then two cars full of men drove off into the desert south toward the Little San Bernardino Mountains. So far nobody has tried to chase them down. He wants your men to get airlifted up there and use your choppers to locate them and capture them if possible. The report said six to eight men in two vehicles."

"Sir, we just got back."

"At ease, mister. I know where you've been. You'll have two hours of prep time, then lift off North Island at 1000 in two Forty-Sixes. Take all the ammo and weapons you can carry. The choppers will be your horses. Each will have a door gunner. That's a go, Commander. You better get cracking."

13

Murdock stepped into the assembly room where the SEALs were stowing gear in lockers, cleaning and oiling weapons, and filling their combat vests with the usual gear.

"Listen up," Murdock said with more force than usual. "We're on the button again. The CNO wants us to check out some men who blew up a power substation up by Palm Springs. We take off in two hours, so let's pack up and get ready to move."

"This is gunna ruin my love life," Jaybird yelped.

"Hey, that redhead you dated last week said your love life had been ruined years ago," Howard gibed. They all laughed, and it helped relieve some of the tension.

"These guys North Ks?" Lam asked.

"Nobody knows," Murdock said. "We'll go up and track them from the chopper, find, and engage. The boss wants a prisoner. We'll have two birds with one squad in each."

"Weapons mix?" Senior Chief Sadler asked.

"DeWitt, your call," Murdock said.

"Take all seven Bull Pups, one EAR, one MG per squad, one sniper rifle per squad, and the rest MP 5's. Let's get working, people."

Murdock repacked his combat vest along with the rest of them, and cleaned his Bull Pup. Then he slipped a standard-band battery-operated radio into one of the pockets. They might learn something from a radio station if he could find one. He made certain that the SATCOM had a fresh battery and that it was glued to Bradford when they stepped on the chopper.

• • •

The two CH-46's flew on a straight line from North Island Air Station to Indio, jumped over the Little San Bernardino mountain range, and began a low-level search for tire tracks working north.

"We're in the edge of the Joshua Tree National Park," Murdock told the men in his bird. "Don't know what we'll find."

The choppers were down to a hundred feet, roving along the edge of the mountains in a search pattern that moved slowly to the north. They passed Key's View, and swung west with the curve of the mountain ridges, and were almost to the Black Rock canyon area before they found the twin tracks of two wheeled rigs entering the desert terrain.

"Got them," DeWitt called on the Motorola. "Let's swing around and follow them south. Don't see where the hell they could hide in this wide-open desert kind of country."

"Maybe back in one of the canyons leading into the mountains," Murdock said. "Keep a sharp look."

Lam went to one of the open side doors and sat there watching the terrain a hundred feet below. Sand, cactus, stunted desert growth. Not the Sahara, but not much plant life here either, with only three inches or less of rainfall a year. Here and there a gully showed where runoff came after a hard, quick rainfall. Along these watercourses, now long dry, there were smatterings of brush. Nothing large enough to hide a car.

They kept looking.

"There," Franklin called. "I've got one rig turning off into that small watercourse moving into the hills."

"We'll take the turnoff," Murdock shouted. "DeWitt, stay with the other one." The commander went forward to tell the pilot to follow the turned tracks. Ahead they could see no sight of a car or anywhere it might hide. The arroyo became deeper, now ten feet below the level of the desert floor and twenty feet wide. It made a slow turn to the left, and ended suddenly a hundred yards ahead where a sheer rock wall a hundred feet high blocked the gully.

"What the hell?" Murdock asked no one. He had stayed in the small cabin.

The pilot looked at him. "Want me to lift up and see what's above the rock wall?"

"No use, the car can't go up there. Put us down back here about fifty yards from the wall and we'll do some exploring.

"DeWitt," Murdock said on the Motorola.

"Copy that," DeWitt responded.

"We've found a dead end on the tracks against a stone wall. We're landing and taking a look. This one car has to be here somewhere. You stay with the other tracks."

"Got, it Commander. Will do. We're still moving generally south, but have seen no car."

Murdock touched the pilot's shoulder. "As soon as we get off, you lift away and wait for us out of range. Could be some weapons down there and an RPG or two. We'll use a red flare when we want to be picked up."

The chopper slowed and lowered gently to the ground. Murdock stepped into the big cargo area.

"We don't know what might be out there, so we take it slow and easy. I want a line of skirmishers and we'll work up this side of the gully. I saw the car tracks back there about a hundred yards, so it has to be here somewhere."

Murdock took the end of the line next to the gully, and looked at it carefully. Patches of soft sand showed the tire tracks. Where the hell could that vehicle be? They walked slowly forward, weapons with rounds in the chambers and safeties off.

Forty yards from the end of the gully, Murdock halted the men. Something wasn't quite right about the bottom of the rock wall. If this gully had been gouged out after hard rains when the water had no place to soak in and came down this way, the water would have had to come from high in the mountains and spill over the sheer wall. A waterfall that high would carve out a serious hole in the sand in front of the wall. It could be ten or twelve feet below the level of the arroyo. There was no such hole here.

"Hit the dirt, men, and get behind any cover you can find. I'm going to shoot the wall at the end of the gully with a twenty and see what reaction we get."

Alpha Squad dove to the ground, some men rolling into small depressions, or moving behind a handy rock. Murdock went prone, aimed at the center of the wall where the water should be coming from, and fired. The contact fuse detonated on impact, and when the smoke cleared, showed a two-foot-wide hole punched through a non-rock wall.

"Twenties, two rounds each at that wall. It has to be a cave in there. Fire when ready."

The first three rounds shattered what turned out to be a wood wall built into the side of the granite slab. The next rounds slammed deep into the tunnel and exploded. When the fourteen rounds finished their killing ways in the cave, Murdock and the men sprinted for the side of the wall next to the opening. Smoke and dust filtered out of the cave.

"DeWitt. We've found a cave and it looks like one of the cars ran right into it. Do you have anything on the other rig?"

"Not yet, but we're getting closer. We can see a dust trail ahead from the tires. Keep us informed."

From what Murdock could see, the blasted opening was about eight feet high and ten feet wide. "Lam, take a look. Don't go inside."

Lam edged around the side of the cave and past a blown-apart stud wall, and peered inside from ground level.

"Can't see much, Cap. Looks like one dead body about three feet back. He has a weapon. Still smoky in there."

"No sign of the car?"

"Not a trace. It could have been driven back in there. The place is plenty big enough."

"You sense any air currents coming out of the opening?"

"Yeah, now I do. Yes. Something is blowing the smoke out of the place. So it must have an air inlet somewhere."

"Maybe a chimney or another entrance," Murdock said. "Let's give it five minutes to clear out and then we'll work our way inside. Who brought flashlights?" The two-cell lights were standard on missions, but many times the men didn't carry them. Murdock received ayes from five of his seven men. "Good, we'll need them. Patrol order when we go in. Remember to hold the lights at arm's length from your body. Lam, edge into the place ten feet and hold, let me know what you can see."

"Copy that, Skipper."

Lam squirmed around the jagged piece of the wall and

into the cave. At once he felt a temperature change from hot to less than hot, but not yet cool. He used the ambient light to stare into the cave, but could see little. The dead man's head was turned away from him, so he couldn't tell if he was Korean. He gave up and turned on the Maglite, holding it in his left outstretched hand. He scanned the floor just ahead of him checking for trip wires or pressure plates for mines. Nothing. He sectioned the rock floor and eased forward. When he was ten feet inside the opening, he had found nothing but rock walls, rock ceiling, and rock floor. It didn't even look like it could be the channel of an underground river.

"Nada, Skipper. Just the one body and a whole potful of rock. No car, no tracks, no trip wires. Clear and benign."

"Roger, Lam, we're moving in. Take it easy and go out another twenty feet, but slowly and clearing the terrain as you go. Keep up a running commentary to us as you move."

"Copy that, Skipper. Yeah, now I see where one of our twenties must have hit. Shattered some rock and dropped it on an otherwise clean rock floor. Might have been water that washed this rock clean of dust and dirt, I don't know. Can't figure it. Where the hell can it go? Can't tell if it's a manmade tunnel carved out of the rock, or if it was some kind of a volcanic tube. Don't see how it could have been cut by this small volume of water coming through. This is solid damn granite."

Lam kept moving. When he was twenty feet inside the cave he spotted a booby trap. "I've got a trip wire, Skipper. Not sure what the hell to do with it. Oh, yeah, followed the wire up the wall to a claymore. Looks like one of our own. Can Canzoneri get up here and disarm this thing?"

"No sweat, Chicken Lam," Canzoneri said. "Hell, that's the easiest kind to deactivate. Be there in about three if you guarantee there are no trip wires between you and me."

"Guarantee. Bet your life on it. Move."

Canzoneri arrived a minute later and moved his flashlight beam along the wire and up to the claymore. The blue mine was about four inches high, eight inches wide, and two inches thick. It had been taped to the rock wall and aimed toward the cave mouth. Inside, it was little more than a slab of C4 explosive behind up to two hundred steel pellets that formed a killing field sixty yards in front of it. Canzoneri was the platoon explosives maven. He checked the mine itself, then adjusted a lever on the back and eased the claymore off the wall. He pointed it away from the entrance and then snipped off the trigger wire. It didn't explode.

"Not sure if any of these have a delay mechanism on them, but would be a great idea for the future. Then you get it disarmed, which is really a second way to arm it, and in ten or twenty seconds it goes off." He paused. "Okay, the twenty seconds are up. I'd say we're home free." He put the claymore down on the side of the cave with the face of it on the rock.

"I'm moving forward," Lam said. He continued to scope every foot of the cave floor as he walked. For fifteen feet he found nothing unusual. Then another body. This one was definitely Korean. He'd taken a dozen pieces of shrapnel in his chest. He still cradled a submachine gun. Lam reported it and continued. Ahead twenty more feet, the cave became smaller, but still large enough to drive a car through. It took a turn to the left. Lam went to the left side of the cave wall and edged up to where he could see around it. He shone his light down the cave, and took a burst of three rounds from a submachine gun. They missed his light and his arm. He jerked both back.

"Heard it," Murdock said on the radio. "Sub gun. Hold there."

Two minutes later Murdock was beside Lam. "We could use some more twenties, but the brass wants one alive. Who has the EAR? Get your ass up front now."

Frank Victor came up behind them. "Ho, Cap. The EAR is here."

Murdock moved back. "Ease the barrel around the wall and send one shot down there. Then after ten seconds give them one more. When you're ready."

The first whooshing sound came from the weapon, and Murdock realized there was something of a rear blast of air as well, but not as concentrated as the front one. He counted down the ten seconds with elephant-one, elephant-two. Then Victor fired the second round.

"We three," Murdock said. "We move down quickly, watching for trip wires. They're like rattlesnakes, always travel in pairs."

They worked ahead faster than before. Twenty yards down they found a shooter. He had a sub gun and was prone facing toward them. He was breathing and unconscious. They bound his hands and feet and moved on. Another twenty yards ahead and the size of the cave shrank again, but it was still seven feet high and eight feet wide.

"The damned vehicle could still get through here," Lam said. "Where the hell is it going?"

Around another small bend in the cave they found three men down and out. All had weapons. It looked like they had been eating a meal. A blown-down mantle gas lantern lay to one side.

"Base camp," Murdock said. "But where is the car?" They tied up the unconscious North Koreans and continued. They found the car a dozen feet down the cave. Inside were explosives, mines, weapons, and lots of ammunition.

"They came to fight a war," Murdock said. He checked the arms, and all of them looked shockingly familiar. "This is all U.S.-made weapons and ammo," he said. "Where did they get it?"

"Not too hard these days with some connections," Lam said.

"We've accounted for six men so far," Murdock said. "The caller said six or eight. Where are the other two?"

Lam had worked ahead of the car. "Might be a clue up here. We've got some dirt and dust on the rocks now. I see two sets of boot prints moving away from us."

"Let's go get them," Murdock said, and the three charged up the cave at a jog, using the lights just enough to stay on track, not worried now about trip wires. The two men ahead were running for their lives.

Around another bend, the tunnel became sharply smaller. It was still high enough to stand in, but now was only six feet wide. The boot prints showed the men were running. Lam stopped and lifted his hand. He licked a finger and held it up.

"Oh, yeah, fresh air coming in from ahead. Have we been going uphill or downhill?"

"I'd say slight uphill," Victor said. "Got to be an old lava tube or a damn powerful underwater river."

They ran again. This time, far ahead they could see a faint light. The tunnel took a steep slant upward, and they walked instead of ran. Now there were moist spots on the rocks.

Murdock didn't know if it was from condensation, or if there had once been a furious river flowing through here. The tunnel kept getting smaller and smaller, and soon they had to bend over to move ahead. But the light was coming closer.

"There's an opening ahead for damn sure," Lam said. "From here on we're going to have to crawl to get to it. Hands and knees should do it."

Lam led the trio. He moved quickly, and for a moment the light ahead cut off and Victor yelped. Then it came on strong and Lam was gone.

Victor crawled up to the opening and pushed his head out. "Be damned, Skipper. We're back in the open halfway up the mountain and at the end of a good-sized arroyo." He pushed out and let Murdock crawl out.

The three stared at the runoff scene. "The water must come down the slope; part of it goes into this hole and down through the tunnel, and the rest of the water goes on down this gully," Murdock said. "So where are the other two Koreans?"

Lam did a quick scan of the country ahead of them, the mountains. He spent five minutes on it, then came back to one spot a third time.

"There, on the side of the slope maybe a half mile over. See those two figures moving?"

"Oh, yeah," Murdock said. He lasered the figures and pulled the trigger. Seconds later the SEALs saw the flash, and then the sound came drifting over.

"They still moving?" Murdock asked.

"Not that I can see. But a small tree that was nearby just lost all of its leaves and a lot of branches." He kept watching. "Not a sign of movement. Either they are good at playing dead, or they got the real roles."

Murdock used the Motorola. "DeWitt, what's with you guys?"

The sound came back faint. "Almost out of range. About six miles south of you. Found the car. The men scattered when they heard us coming. My guess is there are just three of them, but could be more. We're tracking them. One is a KIA, one a POW, and the third one is still running. Jefferson is on him with a Bull Pup, so I'd put a bundle down that Jefferson wins this one."

"We found the first car. Tell you about it later." Murdock pushed the mike back up to his floppy hat. "Let's find the mouth to that cave and see what we can take back for show-and-tell."

Six miles south, Jefferson struggled through a sea of huge boulders. They were everywhere, and from house size to basketball size. He moved up the side of one, stared ahead over the devil's marble yard of huge rocks, and tried to find the running Korean. The man didn't have a weapon; at least Jefferson didn't think he did. Jefferson jumped off the rock just as he felt splinters of granite fly as a bullet missed him by a foot. He reconsidered.

This time he moved more cautiously. He had an idea where the Korean was, but getting to him was another problem. If Jefferson could pinpoint him well enough, the laser and an airburst should do the trick. The SEAL found a point where he had cover, and fired six rounds of 5.56 at the area forty yards ahead of where he thought the Korean had picked for his defensive position. A moment later the man fired a round from just to the left of where Jefferson had targeted. Jefferson moved to the 20mm, lasered a spot on the rocks to the left of his former target, and fired. Then he fired a second lasered round.

The sharp report of the airbursts came through the clear air with a deadly crack, and Jefferson watched and listened. He heard a low moaning sound that rose in pitch until it was a high keening, and it put Jefferson on his feet running around and over the boulders to the spot where he had fired.

He peered around the last boulder and saw the man lying on his back, one hand over his eyes, the same high-pitched wail coming again and again. There was no weapon in sight.

Jefferson charged the position, and kept the Korean under his gun until he searched him and threw away an ankle hideout revolver. The Korean's second hand held his chest, where he was vainly trying to hold in his blood. It coursed through his fingers and pooled under him in the rocky ground.

A moment later the Korean tried to sit up. He screamed and fell back to the ground, his head turning slowly to the side so his unseeing dead eyes seemed to stare directly at Jefferson. It took the SEAL a few minutes, but he found the rifle the Korean had used. He put it beside the man, and looked around for three rocks he could lift. He found them and piled them on the nearest large boulder. The three-rock stack would serve as a marker, because he knew he was going to have to lead some officials out here to pick up the body. He took the rifle and made his way back to the out-of-gas car where the rest of Bravo Squad waited.

By the time Jefferson came to the car, the chopper had already landed and they were waiting for him.

"Damn, but you're getting slower and slower killing these damn Koreans, Jefferson," Donegan chided.

"Would have been faster but the sonofabitch actually took a shot at me. Slowed me down some."

"He's dead?" Fernandez asked.

"Hey, a man don't give up his rifle when he's alive and kicking," Jefferson said.

"Murdock told us to meet him back at the turnoff to the cave," DeWitt said. "Let's get loaded up."

Back by the cave entrance, the two officers conferred.

"What the hell county are we in?" DeWitt asked. "The county coroner is going to be interested in all these dead bodies."

"The county sheriff too, unless we can shortstop them. With the coast still blacked out and no military around, our best bet is to call Stroh and let him sort it out. Bradford, front and center with the SATCOM."

"Right there, Skipper."

It took four tries before they made contact with Don Stroh in his office in Virginia across from Washington, D.C.

"Heard about you boys on an outing," Stroh said. "What happened?"

"Tracked them down. One may have got away. We have the rest. Five of them are still alive, and six more cashed in. We can't contact anybody locally to take care of those who perished."

"Call your CO and have him contact the Riverside County authorities. I'm sure that's the county you're in. He should be able to get them by phone or through some emergency ham operators. Best to sit right there until the sheriff gets there. Yeah, I know, a hassle, but the locals have certain rights too."

"Since when did you get to be such a going-through-channels guy? A change of spots for you, Stroh. Hell, might as well call Masciareli. Take care, Stroh. Out."

The top frog in San Diego said he'd take care of it, and yes, they should stay put until the sheriff's chopper arrived. Shouldn't be long.

By the time the sheriff and three deputies arrived, they had been well briefed by the military that this was a highly classified mission and that it was a matter of national defense. The SEALs could be questioned, but not quoted. The military would arrive as quickly as possible to take charge of the live Koreans for questioning. The dead ones were to be referred to the United Nations.

Sheriff Windy Wheeler stepped out of his chopper two hours after Murdock's call. He had on khaki pants and shirt and a .45 on his hip. The SEALs had carried the dead out of the cave, and walked out the live ones, then retied their feet.

It was nearly dark before the sheriff's vans had loaded up the dead and the prisoners and left the area. Sheriff Wheeler shook hands with Murdock and DeWitt and grinned.

"Be damned. You got the bastards that helped turn the coast into a black hole. I don't know what kind of a report I'll make, but you gentlemen won't ever be mentioned. We'll send out a search party tomorrow to scour that hill you showed me to see if you did nail the other three North Korean bombers up there. You say a 20mm rifle? Damn, I thought that was a cannon the jet fighters use." He shrugged.

"Whatever, it worked damn good. I think I can release you boys so you can scoot back to Coronado. Of course, I never have met you or seen you and these deaths are by person or persons unknown. Oh, yeah! You boys have a safe trip now."

It was a quick flight back to Coronado. Some of the men slept, some relived the chase of the bombers. Murdock tried to remember when he'd had a good night's sleep. Maybe tonight, if he could drive through the two traffic lights he had to pass to get to his condo. He hoped traffic tie-ups were smoothed out by now. Sleep, yeah, maybe tonight.

14

Casa Grande Casino
Near San Diego, California

Jack Mahanani parked in the lot outside the luxurious casino and drummed his fingers on the steering wheel. He had remembered correctly. The Indian management at the casino had been worried about rolling blackouts during the electrical energy shortage, so they'd bought and installed a large commercial turbine to power their huge generators. They could provide enough electrical power themselves to run the whole casino and the rest of the tribal reservation. He had heard them talking about it several times.

Once the SEALs hit their home base that afternoon, they had cleaned up equipment and weapons and been cut loose for the day. Nothing to do until 0730 the next morning. Mahanani had stewed around in his condo for two hours, cursing the coastwide blackout that still held. His portable radio said the big shots were working on it. Some of Washington state was powered up, and some areas of Los Angeles.

No traffic lights, no house lights. Then he remembered that the casino would be up and running. This might be a good time to take another trip to Tijuana. The electronic stuff at the border would be off. Or would it? No matter. He could chisel another four hundred dollars off his IOU. Yeah, and bet that against ten years in Chino State Prison. At last he talked himself into it, and drove to the casino east of San Diego.

Now he kicked out of the car and locked it. Wouldn't matter. The Hammer had a key to it, along with the pink slip, the ownership certificate. If they wanted it, they would take it.

He saw the lot had only half as many cars as usual. A lot of people had forgotten that the casino would be running, blackout or no. Mahanani strode toward the big front door, and was halfway to the tellers to buy some chips when Harley pulled up in front of him and held out his hand.

"Hey, buddy, haven't seen you for a couple of days. Business?"

"Yeah, Harley, I have to work for a living, remember?"

"You sure aren't a good enough gambler to make a living off us, Mahanani. Doesn't matter much, because you're blacklisted now until you work off your IOU and get your Buick back. No more gambling for you."

"Not even twenty bucks for the slots?"

"Not even that. You want to talk to the Hammer?"

"Will he want me to make a run tonight?"

"No way. With the blackout you could be crashed into, or held up somewhere. Besides, we don't have a full load ready to go. Tijuana is having some trouble with the cops over there. The damned cops get bought off and then steal half a load and sell it themselves. Nothing crooked-er than a crooked Tijuana cop."

"So what am I supposed to do? I can't play and I can't drive."

"Suck your thumb or anything else you can reach, buddy. That's up to you. Just thought I'd save you some embarrassment at the window, that's all."

"Thanks a load of shit, Harley. Get out of my face or I might just lose my temper and throw your ass across the room."

Harley stepped back. Mahanani outweighed the small Indian man almost two to one.

"Don't get nasty. Nobody made you come here and play. Remember that. Now, probably be better if you just headed for the door and drove away."

"Yeah, a lot better." Mahanani gave him a scowl and walked toward the door. He was outside the casino and one row from his car when a man came up in front of him and asked about the time. Mahanani looked down at his watch and the big guy slugged him in the gut, doubling him over. A knee pumped upward, met the big Hawaiian's chin, and dumped all 240 pounds of him on the blacktop. He gagged and turned to get up. Then another man came from behind a car and kicked him in the side just over his kidney. Mahanani shrilled in surprise and pain and rolled to the side away from his attackers.

They were ready. A third man kicked him in the other side and he slid onto his back, one arm over his face. The pain was worse than he had ever known before, even when he was shot in the left arm. He tried to get up. Surprisingly, somebody lifted him from behind so he could sit up. He tried to look around as a jolting fist crashed into his jaw and spun him sideways. Somebody behind held him now in a choke hold around his throat. The fist came again, and then a third time, and Mahanani tried to shake the cobwebs out of his brain, but it wouldn't clear. The man behind let loose of him, and a fourth blow hit him on the side of the cheek, and he flopped to the parking lot's freshly striped blacktop. He wanted to pass out, but he couldn't. The parking lot lights were fuzzy balls.

Somebody dropped beside him and picked up his head. Mahanani didn't recognize the face that jammed in an inch from his. "Look, Mahanani, I thought we had a deal. You drive for us and be nice to the help. You just keep doing that and we're all friendly again. You threaten Harley or don't drive, and we find you and my boys will really put the fear of the tribe into you. You dig, Hawaiian beach bum?"

Mahanani blinked and tried to see who it was. Then he knew. The Hammer. "Yeah, I dig," he said through cut-up lips and with blood running down his chin.

The Hammer let his head fall the eight inches to where it hit hard on the blacktop, causing some blue stars to go off in Mahanani's head. The other men turned and walked away.

It was ten minutes before Mahanani could sit up. He had to hold himself up with both hands. His car, where in hell did he park? He couldn't remember. His vision cleared and he stared at the rows of vehicles. One car was only six feet away. He crawled to it and tried to stand. On the first three tries, he couldn't get his legs under him. On the fourth, he made it only when a guy with a teamster's hat and a month of body odor helped him up.

"Hey, pardner, looks like you had some trouble," the teamster said. "Know where your car is?"

Mahanani shook his head.

"What make and color?"

The SEAL told the man.

"Yeah, shouldn't be too hard to find. Lean right there on this Cadillac and I'll do a quick recon."

He was back three minutes later. "Got her, right over here about twenty feet. Can you walk, or you want some help?"

Mahanani held out his hand for help, and five minutes later he was inside his car with the window rolled down.

"Thanks," he said to the trucker through cut-up lips and cheeks.

"Hey, no problem. Had me a fight or two myself and didn't always win. You sure you can drive?"

"Yeah, I'll take a break, then drive." The trucker waved and went on to his big eighteen-wheeler parked at the far end of the lot. Mahanani sat there trying to figure it out. He'd been beaten up just because he'd made a small threat to Harley?

After sitting there for a half hour and trying to think it through, Mahanani knew what he was going to do. These guys were going down, one way or the other. He would risk two more runs to TJ for them and bring back the drugs. Then, on the third one, he would bring in the DEA, the Drug Enforcement Agency, agents. The more he thought of it, the more certain he was that the tribal council and the people who ran the huge Casa Grande Casino did not know about the strong-arm tactics and the drug smuggling. They had too much at stake to risk it all. Now, all he had to do was figure out how to bring the DEA in on it without getting charged himself.

He started the engine and headed for the exit. He was almost there before he realized it had grown dark and he hadn't turned on his headlights. He stopped, turned them on, and put on his seat belt, then checked both ways and made sure his vision was acceptable. Yeah, okay. He pulled through the parking lot and back on the freeway driving at fifty-five mph in the right-hand lane. He didn't want to have to make any quick decisions that fast driving might call for.

The big SEAL tried to figure out how to do it with the DEA. He would say this was his first run for them. They'd threatened him, and were going to turn him in to his commanding officer for gambling, which could get him thrown out of the Navy. Yeah. Good start. He wouldn't agree to wear a wire. The DEA would have to trail him. He'd make it easy. They could hang back when the car went into the garage in TJ. Yeah, and then tail him back to San Ysidro and the garage and take them down. Then go to the casino and arrest Harley and the Hammer and their wrecking crew. That is, if they could get to the casino without the San Ysidro men warning the Hammer.

Mahanani settled down to drive carefully. He knew he was driving so safely a cop might think he was steady-drunk. He hadn't had a drop, no problem there. He speeded up to sixty miles an hour and moved into the second lane. Yeah, he could do that. Now all he wanted to do was get home through the blacked-out four-way-stop intersections and across the bridge into Coronado and his condo. It was spooky driving with no house lights anywhere and no freeway signs lit. You really had to know where you were going.

He tried to relax. Oh, yes, he'd give somebody half a month's pay just to magically zap him into his own bathroom. Then he could start repairing the damage to his face and lips. For sure he'd have a black eye, and maybe a broken nose. He was going to look terrible by tomorrow morning. Maybe a little makeup would help, or some camo paint.

He had stopped the car twice on the way home to vomit from the aftereffects of the kidney kicks. At last he cruised into his parking spot at the condo and sat there thinking. Or was he stalling, wondering if he could walk up the steps to his condo? He stepped from the car and threw up again. He wiped his mouth, and hurried up the stairs and inside so he could rinse out his mouth. His face was a mess. He washed it tenderly, then patted down the cut-open areas with alcohol swabs, and decided to let it be until morning. Then he'd have to decide what to do. Call in sick? Not an option unless he was half dead. He wasn't even a quarter dead. He'd be there bruises, Band-Aids, and all.

NAVSPECWARGRUP-ONE
Coronado, California

For the tenth time that morning, Murdock realized how much he missed the use of the Internet and e-mail. The damn lights were still out. A newsman on his battery-powered radio said it might be two more days before all sections of the San Diego area were powered up. Strange how he had come to rely on the Internet for several aspects of his job and his communications with Ardith in Washington, D.C. He looked at the sheaf of papers that the master chief had given him when he arrived that morning. Most of them were routine. MacKenzie had copied them down from SATCOM transmissions. It was still their only communications off base.

The telephone still worked for local calls, but the military radio net had been vital to the whole operation. Murdock had worked through most of the stack of material when Master Chief MacKenzie rushed into the office about 0930 that morning. DeWitt and the platoon were at the O course running it again for time.

The usually calm old salt MacKenzie had a sheen of sweat on his brow and his eyes were spiked open with alarm.

"This just came in, Lad sir. It's bad news." He thrust a paper at Murdock who read it.

"From Don Stroh. To Lieutenant Commander Blake Murdock, Third Squad, SEAL Team Seven. We've had tight security about the fact that the President and Vice President and his top planning staff have been at a secret retreat for the past two days. The President has kept on top of the attack on San Francisco and the hijacking of the cruise ship and has issued the required orders to deal with the matters. Communications had been with his usual travel group of high performance radios. When the power grid went down yesterday morning just after daylight on the Pacific Grid, it also blacked out the President's radio communications from his retreat. He's up in the Sierra Nevada Mountains.

"Their only communications is by SATCOM, and their last report was four hours ago. It said that they were being attacked by an armed group of men operating like soldiers.

They were having to scatter so they wouldn't be captured. That was the last report we had from him. Something must have happened to the SATCOM.

"One of the last messages reported that the three helicopters at the site were destroyed with what looked like RPG's. So they couldn't fly out. The SATCOM report said they were under a heavy military attack and were on the run. Then the transmissions stopped.

"A rescue force is now being put together by the FBI and the military. It has been suggested that two Army Ranger platoons and one platoon of Navy SEALs be included in the package.

"I have made a strong pitch that Platoon Three from SEAL Team Seven be assigned to the rescue force. Will keep you informed. If this plans flies, the forces will be activated almost at once today. Stroh out."

"The President," Murdock whispered. He held up his left arm and looked at the homemade bandage. "I guess I should have had the medics take another look at this arm and get it ready for some action. Yes, it bothers me some, but my buddy ibuprofen is a real help. Show this paper to DeWitt when he comes back. Tell nobody else and ask DeWitt to keep mum on it until I get back. I've got to see the medics. I'm gone."

Ten minutes later, Master Chief MacKenzie called to Lieutenant Ed DeWitt as he came back from the O course.

"Lieutenant, sir. Something for you to read here, if you have a moment."

DeWitt looked up, sensing a note of urgency and shock in the master chief's tone and demeanor that he hadn't seen before.

"Right, Master Chief," DeWitt said, and reached for the sheet of paper.

He read it, his frown turning into a scowl. "The damn North Koreans knew the President was up there and are making a play for him. What a coup it would be if they could kill him. The bastards."

"This is not to be spread around. It's for you and Murdock and me right now. If we get orders, they will come through channels. I'll keep the paper. Commander Murdock went to the medics for them to look at his in-and-out gunshot wound to his left arm."

"I didn't know he was hit." DeWitt shook his head. "This could be a damn big problem. The North Ks must already be on the ground, and we're just starting to get into action. We could be there in two hours if we had firm GPS coordinates."

DeWitt stood there a moment and his shoulders sagged; then he straightened them and stood taller. "Master Chief, I'm going to get the men ready for a call. If you hear anything about our going, yell at us. We'll probably need the time." DeWitt began running on his way to the small office of Third Platoon.

He went to his equipment locker and checked his traveling gear. His Bull Pup was ready, the magazines loaded for both the twenty and the 5.56. He had filled his combat vest that morning. He set out his favorite floppy hat and gloves with the fingers cut out, and boots. He was ready.

In the small office he looked over the roster. Everyone was fit and ready to fight. Mahanani looked like he had been in a fight, but he was on duty. He had done the O course in good time. The CIA would tell the FBI about Third Platoon. Don Stroh would get his oar in and the CNO would have some input. All they had to do was wait for the call through channels.

His only worry was Mahanani. He had been acting just a little off center lately. Not like the happy-go-lucky island boy he usually was. Something was going on with him, but there was nothing DeWitt could do until the man wanted to talk about it.

DeWitt paced the assembly room. Jaybird spoke up, and stared at the officer walking up and down.

"Troubles, Lieutenant?" he asked.

"Huh, oh, no, just thinking how to make the training sked tougher." He sat down in the chair and stared at the telephone. No long distance, but something should be happening. It was the President and his top advisors up there under the North Korean guns. The Secret Service would have their Ingrams, for short-range stuff. But that wouldn't be much of a fighting force against, say, a platoon of North Ks.

When DeWitt looked into the assembly room the next time, he called the men around. DeWitt looked at Mahanani's beat-up face and frowned.

"Who did you pick a fight with?"

"A little old grandmother in a big Cadillac who was seriously confused about which one was the brake and which the gas pedal and just what right-of-way means. I took a fender bender in the Buick. Bumper got dinged, but I had a close encounter with my steering wheel. Lucky I didn't lose any teeth. Figure I'll heal up without any need for more than six or eight pints of O positive."

"What does the Cadillac look like?"

"No serious damage. Mostly just hurt feelings. I said some rather unflattering things, and threatened to report her to the Coronado cops so they could yank her license."

"Well, take it easy and medicate those cuts. You're the corpsman around here."

"Yes, sir."

DeWitt told the platoon to check their traveling gear. They could get another mission at any time. He wondered if he should say anything. Before he had to decide, Murdock came striding in the room. One arm had a white bandage around it, and the other hand waved a piece of paper. "Gather round, Froggies. We've got a job to do, and we can leave our wet suits at home."

15

Saddle Mountain Ranch
Sierra Nevada Mountains, California

President Milford Dunnington hunched over the polished redwood plank table in the luxuriously Western-rustic-style conference room at the ranch of his boyhood friend, and studied his top team. He could always trust his right hand and Chief of Staff, Walt Eddings. Eddings had been with him since his days as a State Senator in California. Walt was short and a little pudgy, but had a mind like a computer and a memory better than the best computer chip. The National Security Advisor, Major General Beth Arnold, was a wonder and exactly the right choice. She was still slender at fifty-one, tall, with dark hair, a perfect complexion, and a solid military mind that Dunnington needed. Vice President Grover Paulson sat in as head of the Special Presidential Social Security Task Force. The VP was tall and gaunt, looked older than his forty-six years, and was being groomed to run in two years when Dunnington's second term expired.

Maria Alvarez, the Secretary of Health and Human Services, was on hand. She was tiny, with dark, flashing black eyes, slender, and with an iron will to fight for every child in America. She was a Mexican American and proud of it. Social Security Administrator Leonard Gilstrap was the last one around the mirrorlike table. He had come up through the House and Senate, had been governor of Maine for a while, then been tapped as the man to save Social Security. He was sixty-one, had dark hair, and wore a full beard kept trimmed to a half inch. He had been a Recon Marine and his favorite expression was "Semper fi."

The President cleared his throat, and everyone stopped talking and looked at him.

"Looks like we're at a point where we need an hour break to think things over. We need to get together on one concentrated plan that will work for everyone. We must come up with a solution to this Social Security problem. Be back here in an hour."

President Dunnington watched them leave. Even though the lights had suddenly shut down yesterday morning, they had made do. The SATCOM kept working with its batteries. They heard that the electricity was out all along the coast. The right people would work out the problem. He had his own here. Two days and almost no progress. He had to have a bill to send to Congress when they went back in two more days. The President stood and looked out the large windows at a spread of gentle green timbered slopes that ran down to a ridgeline a mile away. He loved the mountains. They were magnificent, and always gave him strength, resolve, and a new sense of purpose.

He frowned as he saw movement in the sky to the west. Two dots that became quickly larger, and soon he knew they were helicopters. Strange. This had been designated a no-fly zone for the length of his stay. He looked a hundred yards from the ranch house at a parking lot usually used for cars, but now holding three Presidential Super Stallion helicopters. When the President looked back at the choppers flying toward the ranch, he saw that they were not going to just fly past, they were heading directly for the ranch house.

A moment later they were fifty yards away and three plumes of smoke came from them. "Rockets," he said. "My God, somebody is firing RPGs at us." As he said it two of the smoke trails ended in the parking lot striking two of the Super Stallions. Both exploded in large balls of flames as the fuel tanks erupted and detonated like two bombs. The flaming fuel immediately engulfed the third Super Stallion, and all three burned furiously in seconds.

Two Secret Service agents rushed into the big conference room, grabbed the President, and ran him out the side door and down a long sidewalk that extended to the stables and a heavily wooded area just to the side of the front pasture.

"This way, Mr. President," Larry Sanborn said. He was the head of the Presidential Secret Service detachment. "We've been attacked and we think that they have troops in the choppers. We have set up a defensive perimeter here, but we have no heavy weapons. It will take them some time to find us. It's only nine A.M. Soon we'll move into better cover and get away from the ranch house. There is no way we can defend the house with the weapons we have. We must work our prepared emergency plan to disperse into the woods and hills."

The two men led the President into the timber for a quarter of a mile along a faint trail. Then they came to a clearing in front of a small log house. Behind it a sheer cliff rose fifty feet, and to one side a small stream chattered down the incline.

"Inside, Mr. President. We have some necessities including a SATCOM radio. As soon as it's safe, we'll tell Washington we've been attacked and lost all three of our choppers. We're stranded here until some help arrives."

"Who did this?" the President asked as he entered the small cabin. It was rustic, but adequate. A bed sat in one corner, a small propane heater and cooking stove in the other. There were no windows, and firing slots had been bored through the foot-thick logs that made up the walls. It was part of a set for an Indian battle demonstration put on by the rancher's staff for guests at the end of the tourist week.

"What about the others?" the President asked.

"I have two men with the Vice President. He's in another secure location. One man was assigned to each of the others, but I'm not sure if they could find them or defend them before any men landed from the choppers."

"Who did this?"

"We don't know. We suspect the same ones who attacked the cruise ship and attacked San Francisco. North Korea."

"What do they hope to gain?"

"Our only guess at a motive would be face saving. They were devastated by their defeat recently by the U.S. and South Korea and having to accept massive food supplies from the world to feed their starving people."

"We feed them so they repay us with sound Oriental logic

by attacking and killing us," the President said. "Not a good trade-off. How many men could they have in the two helicopters?"

"The birds were small, eight men at the most. They used rocket-propelled grenades against our choppers. Now we wait and see what they do." Sanborn paused and listened to his earpiece, then nodded. "I have reports that the Vice President is safe, and that three of the Cabinet are with their guardians. We have no report from the sixth member of our group. We're not sure who the three are. I'll get their names just as soon as their guardians feel they are safe."

"What about the staff here at the ranch?"

"We don't have enough men to provide protection for them. They know the territory. As soon as they heard the helicopters explode, it's my guess that they all ran to some safe haven."

"Not Barney. He'd grab that forty-five pistol and charge out to defend his property. Known Barney since Nam and he was one gung-ho Marine. Never saw a man who took to the nasty war the way he did. Oh, yeah, Barney would not cower behind a wall somewhere and pray for help. He'd be right in there battling, and this time, probably getting his balls shot off."

Sanborn touched the speaker in his ear and listened. He looked up at the President. "We've established that Maria Alvarez is the one member of our group we can't account for. General Arnold said she saw her go into the rest room just before the attack."

Two explosions sounded and Sanborn looked up. "Hand grenades. They may be trying to flush out anyone in the main house before going in."

"They could have sixteen men?" the President asked.

"That's an estimate, Mr. President. We'll try to get some sightings of them when we can." Sanborn moved to the side of the cabin and used his lip mike. "Net call. Can anyone see any of the attackers? Are they on the ground yet? Where are they?"

"Six here. I saw them land at the far end of the parking lot. Two small birds. Ten men came out one of them, and eight out the other one. If we had the ordnance, I'd suggest we splash the choppers."

"We don't have the right weapons. Everyone hold with your charges. Has anyone seen Mara Alvarez?" The net remained quiet. "Who had Mrs. Alvarez as his charge?"

"Five here. That was number Seven. Williams was assigned to Alvarez. I haven't seen him or heard from him either."

"Thanks, Five. A chance he's been taken and they may have his radio, so watch what you say on air. Has anyone seen the troops go into the main ranch house?"

"Four here. I saw six of them go in from the north door. All wore cammy uniforms and they had long guns and sub guns."

"Copy that, Four. Has anyone seen members of the staff? There are still twelve workers on duty this week, down from the usual twenty-four. Any reports on them?"

"Three here. I saw four of the staff running into the brush and woods above the house. They were waiters and cooks, I think."

"Any more?" He waited. "Okay. Keep the principals scattered as well as you can. Our weapons can't match theirs. As soon as it looks safe we filter deeper into the wilderness away from the house. Don't move more than three miles from the house so we can keep in radio contact. Don't worry about food or water. It takes nineteen days to starve to death. You can go without water for three days. But there are small streams all over the place. Don't worry about the quality of the water. Up here it's all good, so drink it. I want a net check every hour on the hour. Sign off net."

Sanborn listened as his men signed off in order, except for number seven. Williams was still missing. The rest were all up and doing their jobs.

"Larry?"

Sanborn looked at the President, who had sat down on the bed and was looking wrung out.

"How long will this last?"

"We don't know, Mr. President. We have used the SAT-COM on several chanels asking for help, and try for some nearby military. We'll put out a Mayday call on rotating channels until we get somebody." The President nodded and lay back on the bed with his feet still on the floor.

Sanborn motioned to his partner, Phil, who took the SAT-COM outside, sat up the antenna, zeroed it in, and made the calls on one channel after the next. Five minutes later he had reported to the Secret Service in Washington, D.C., and to two military posts.

The two Secret Service men with the Vice President had planned what to do in an emergency the first day at the ranch. They did that on every location, in every situation. Seldom did they have to follow through on the plan. This time they did. They rushed the Vice President out the back door, followed a trail past the stables, and cut left directly up the slope.

"We get as far away as quickly as we can without being seen," Dirk Elwell said. After five minutes, they paused in their run/walk and looked back. They could barely see the top of the ranch house through the trees. They saw no men in military uniforms.

"Another half mile and we come to that little ridge we can use as a lookout and as a fort," Dirk said. They both carried the short-range Uzi submachine guns, belt .38's in the middle of their backs, and hideouts on their left ankles. All short-range weapons.

"Who are these guys?" Vice President Paulson asked.

"Best guess is they are North Koreans and are a part of the attack they made on us in several places. Small, slashing attacks, guerillalike, but deadly. What worries me is how they knew you and your party were up here. It was supposed to be a top-secret getaway."

"In Washington it's hard to keep a secret," Paulson said. "Somebody told me that in Washington even the ears have ears."

Ten minutes later they made it to the ridge and sat down behind it. Looking over the top, they had a perfect view of the ranch house. Trees obscured the rear of it, but they could see the burned-out hulks of the choppers. They saw the two smaller birds at the far end of the parking lot. As far as he could tell, Dirk decided there were no guards around the enemy helicopters.

Below in the cabin, Sanborn nudged the President of the United States. "Sir, it's time we move on. We're too close to the ranch house here. We need another mile at least."

President Dunnington put his feet on the floor and sat up. "Yes, more distance. You're right. At least I had a short rest. Old bones don't work as well as they did when I was fifty."

They left by the side door and moved upward. Sanborn led the way, crashing brush, holding branches, making the walk as easy as he could for the President. There was no trail here. They moved at a slant up the hill, then angled back the other way, always working upward.

Ten minutes into the hike the President called a halt.

"Sorry, guys. I need to take ten. Heard anything new on your radios?"

"Nothing, sir. All of our people are moving away from the ranch house on predetermined courses. We had a plan. So far it seems to be working."

"Hear anything on the SATCOM?"

"No, sir."

"Get it started up and call AT&T. That thing will hook up with telephones, right?"

"Yes, sir."

"Try it. Any area code, then five-five-five, and one-two, one-two. See what happens. It could work. Then you get the number of the nearest military base here in California."

Phil, the other Secret Service man, set up the small dish antenna and aimed it toward where the satellite should be. He moved it slightly until he received an on-line beep from the set. Then he studied the radio a minute, flipped some switches, adjusted a dial, and then used the handset. "Never tried this before. Hey, it works."

"AT&T information. What city, please?"

"Operator, this is the Secret Service on a satellite phone. I need the phone number of the closest military air base to Sacramento, California."

"Just a moment."

"Dead air. I guess she's looking it up."

"Sir, that would be Lemoore Naval Air Station just south of Fresno."

"Would you ring the commanding officer, please?" Phil

said. He grinned and handed the mike to Sanborn.

"Yes, sir, ringing."

"Captain Johnson's office, sir. How may I assist you?"

"This is Secret Service Agent Sanborn. I have an extreme emergency and need to speak to your CO."

"Sorry, sir, he's not on the base. Would the OD do?"

"Yes. Get him."

A moment later a ring and an answer.

"Officer of the Day."

"Hello, this is Secret Service Agent Sanborn with President Dunnington's party in the Sierra Nevadas. We have a problem."

"Yes, sir. How can I confirm your identity?"

"You can't. What's your name?"

"Lieutenant Commander Richard Jones, sir."

"Good, Commander. We're in the Sierras west of Sacramento with President Dunnington and some of his top advisors. We've been attacked by an armed force and our three HU-53's have been destroyed. We're at the Saddle Mountain Ranch resort south of Saddle Mountain peak about three miles. We need help. An armed force from two choppers has captured the ranch house and we're in the brush. You can contact us on SATCOM channel two. Do you have any Marine Recon on your base?"

"No, sir. Not exactly an infantry-type outfit."

"Any SEALs?"

"No, sir, they're in San Diego."

"Well, get somebody in here fast, before dark if you can. We're in big trouble and it's on your head, Commander. My name is Sanborn, with the Secret Service. Now get cracking and report back to us on SATCOM channel two within twenty minutes."

"Yes, sir. Out."

Sanborn made some adjustments on the dials and called his home office in Washington, D.C. There was an immediate response. The SATCOM transmissions were scrambled, and thus perfectly secure.

"Secret Service, Presidential Detail."

"Joe, this is Sanborn with the President. We've been attacked by a foreign military unit and lost our three birds.

We're scattered in the brush and woods around the ranch we came to. We need help and we need it now. We contacted Lemoore Air Station, but they don't have much help. Get us some Marine Recon or SEALs or Airborne Rangers. Get some armed forces here as quickly as you can."

"This for real, Sanborn?"

"Absolutely. Get us some help or I'll personally tear your balls off. Now move something."

"I'll tell the chief and we're on it."

They signed off and Sanborn nodded. "Now we'll see who can get somebody here first."

Before they could move on, an amplified voice boomed over the mountainside.

"Secret Service agents. This is a warning to you. We know that you and President Dunnington and his top aides are here. We are asking you to come back to the ranch house and be comfortable. Tonight it will be dark and then cold, miserable, and perhaps wet out there."

The English had a decided accent to it.

"We encourage you to come in because we have captured a pretty lady named Maria Alvarez. We also have six members of the staff of workers. We simply require all of you to report in within an hour, or we will start executing one of the captives for every half hour you are late. Is that clear? We would start with the owner, Mr. Bronson, but unfortunately he challenged us with a pistol and was shot to death. So, the first hostage to be shot precisely at one-thirty P.M. will be Mrs. Alvarez."

16

Bill Bradford shook his head at the commander's announcement. "No wet suits, you said, so that means we have another land-slogger assignment."

"More like a mountain-climbing event," Murdock said. "Now listen up, we don't have a lot of time. We fly out of North Island in a little less than an hour. The trip could last a couple of days, so take an extra set of cammies. The usual mix of weapons, with the snipers on both squads to use the new Knight Mk 11. We haven't had much work on that new weapon yet, so this will be its test under fire.

"Now to the particulars. We'll be going out of North Island in the luxury flight on the Gulfstream directly into Sacramento. From there we will move by CH-46 to a road three miles from the Saddle Mountain Ranch. It's a working cattle ranch, which also has luxury accommodations for city slickers who want to be cowboys for a week. From our drop-off point we will move with two platoons of Army Rangers toward the ranch, with the hope that we can find the North Koreans who have attacked the President and his party, take them down, and rescue the civilians."

There was a yell and lots of loud talk.

"You mean somebody tried to hit the President?" Luke Howard asked.

"Correct. He was on a secret conference with his top aides, and two choppers bored in and blew up three CH-53's and we don't know what else. They are hurting and need help.

The hit took place just about 9 A.M. It's now 1115. We fly out at 1200, so let's get moving.

"That's a huge wilderness area up there in the Sierra Nevada Mountains. We'll be around the five-thousand-foot level and near Saddle Mountain. That's somewhere near the South Fork of the American River. Questions?"

"Cold-weather gear?" Franklin asked.

"Snow should be long gone up there by now. We might wind up wearing both sets of cammies. No special cold gear."

Murdock looked around. No more questions. "All right, let's get our gear ready. Double on the ammo. We'll all take drag bags for additional ammo. We won't have any friendly local supplier. We take what we'll need including six MREs per man. Senior Chief, see if you can get some of those good ones with the heating pouches. That's it. Let's move."

The sleek Gulfstream II, which the Navy called the VC-11, rolled off North Island using only handheld blinkers from the tower for control. Because of the blackout the tower was down. The bird was usually reserved for VIPs for fast trips. Lately the SEALs had been in the fast-trip category and had used the business jet several times. It was made by Grumman, now called Gulfstream Aerospace, held a crew of three, and could carry nineteen passengers in the best airliner recliner seats.

The Gulfstream has a wingspan of sixty-nine feet and is eighty feet long. It uses two Rolls Royce MK 511-8 turbofan engines that push her along at 505 miles an hour with a ceiling of 43,000 feet. Range was no problem getting to Sacramento. The bird would do 4,275 miles without gulping any new fuel.

They landed VFR at the Sacramento airport, working through a series of blinker signals and filtering in with hardly any air traffic. Flight time was a little over an hour and a half. More than twenty airliners sat on the ground, not able to take off due to the blackout that had shut down all air-control facilities. The Gulfstream pilots did a lot of looking around the sky before they brought the ship into Sacramento airport, to be sure that there were no other aircraft in the same area at the same time.

They taxied to the transient plane hangar and were met by an airport safety jeep. The driver talked to Murdock. Then the SEALs picked up their drag bags and gear and headed past the business jet fifty yards to where a CH-46 sat with two armed guards around it. The time was slightly after 1335.

Jaybird couldn't let it pass. "Hey, guys, we in a hot LZ here or what? Why the cannons?"

A second class glared at him. "Loudmouth, they just lost three CH-53's over there where we're going. We don't want to lose this one. Any objections?"

"None at all," Bradford said as he walked past the guard and into the bird. The rest of the SEALs climbed on board and sat down where they could find a spot on the floor. This wouldn't be a luxury flight. Murdock and DeWitt talked with the pilot outside, and then all came in and the two guards moved to the side doors and hooked up their machine guns on swivel mounts.

"How many civilians are we hunting up there in cold country?" Canzoneri asked.

Murdock looked up from a map he was studying. "Our orders didn't say. Just the Presidential party. Could be ten or twelve, maybe with six or eight Secret Service agents along."

"Those guys still carry the Ingrams under their coats?" Jefferson asked. "Think for an outing like this they'd get some long guns to take along."

Murdock pulled down his lip mike on the Motorola. "Listen up. The pilot gave me a message from Don Stroh. There were supposed to be two Army Ranger platoons waiting for us here with their choppers going along on this ride. They got hung up at an airport and the locals wouldn't let them take off. They were up the coast somewhere that's still blacked out, and the local sheriff clamped down and blocked the runways with fire-fighting trucks. So for the first phase, we're on our own."

"Shit, they don't get to come to the party," Jaybird said. "Bet they are pissed."

"We've got six hours of daylight left. Take us maybe half an hour to get up to the PD. From the Point of Departure, we'll work up hill toward the ranch. We'll go cross-country, and we don't know where the sneaky North Koreans are, or if they're still even in the area."

"Wilderness, you said, up in there," DeWitt said. "Where could they go?"

"From the sound of things, the Ks have been planning this thing for some time," Lam said. "They could have come in as civilians, hired a pair of choppers, and moved in forty men, made their hit, and gone out the same way they choppered in."

The engines on the big chopper started and revved up, and soon they lifted off and flew northeast.

"We'll be about ten miles north of Placerville," Murdock shouted to DeWitt, who sat beside him. "Damn rugged country. I don't know how the owner gets to his ranch. Probably made his own road into the place."

"This dude ranch. Do they have guests there while the President is there?" DeWitt called.

Murdock shook his head. "Last radio message said no guests, just the President and his team and Secret Service."

"No recon, no data, we're really going in blind."

"That's why you earn the big bucks, DeWitt. Our first job is to find the ranch and see if anyone is there. Depending on what we find, we figure out what to do next."

"We have the SATCOM," DeWitt said.

"The pilot says he's to stay in the general area. If we want him we should use our Motorolas, or fire a red flare. He'll jump ahead if we're getting out of the five-mile radio range."

"He can talk to his home base?"

"Right, Lemoore Naval Air Station down below Fresno."

They were quiet then, watching the country out the side doors. The chopper had moved up to a thousand feet over the terrain, and had to keep climbing as the ground rose into the foothills, then into the Sierra Nevadas themselves.

The crew chief came back and hollered at Murdock. "Ten minutes to our LZ. The lieutenant says he'll let you off, then move back three miles and shut down."

"Tell him to keep his Motorola on too," Murdock said. The sailor nodded and went back to the cockpit.

Five minutes later the chopper pilot found a road through

the wilderness, and followed it to a spot where a small bridge spanned a stream. He put the bird down just past the bridge and the SEALs poured out each door, setting up an immediate perimeter around the CH-46.

When the SEALs had cleared the ship, the pilot lifted off, showering the men with dust, dirt, and a few stray pebbles from the downward wash of the rotor blades. Then it was up and away. The SEALs formed up in twin diamonds and began to move on a compass bearing due west. The immediate area had an open space near the creek and extending a quarter of a mile to the start of the timbered slope that lifted upward.

They established a pace of about three miles to the hour, due to the altitude and the drag bags. The idea of the bags was that by pulling them along, most of the weight rested on the ground and the man didn't have to carry it, just drag it.

The timber was mostly pine and some fir, with clumps of oak and cedar. They moved through it with Lam fifty yards out front watching, checking out any problems he could see.

They had covered a mile and a half up the slopes when they came to a fence. It was new, with steel posts set in concrete and four strands of bright new barbed wire. The SEALs stepped between the middle two strands, and then pulled the drag bags under the bottom one.

On the point, Lam hit the dirt when he heard something to his left. He lifted up and looked, then dropped down. A moment later a pair of steers walked past some brush, grazing as they moved slowly toward the men. Neither animal looked up. Lam grinned and reported his find to the troops, then kept moving forward.

A mile later they came to the top of a sharp little ridge, and Lam eased up so he could look over it without skylining himself and becoming an easy target. He peered under the brim of his floppy hat and just over the ridgeline. Ahead a thousand yards on a broad mesa, he could see the ranch buildings. He called up Murdock, who took a look at them with his binoculars.

"Okay, we've got the buildings. Looks like they're set on a flat area. I can't see any movement or any bodies. How about you?"

"Saw one man run from the ranch house out to the next building to the left. Only action. So there are troops in there."

"So where is the President and his people?"

"What would we do in the same situation?" Lam asked. "If we had this spot and overwhelming firepower moved in, we wouldn't be able to hold the buildings, right? So where would we go?"

"Scatter and make a lot of trails for the bad guys to try to follow," Murdock said.

"Makes sense. About what I'd do. So, the President and his advisors and the Secret Service shields probably aren't in the ranch house or the other buildings."

"Roger that, but there could still be some of the staff. You don't run a place like this with Mom and Pop."

"True, so we can't hit them with the twenties."

They stared at the setup again. Murdock moved his view to the left and grunted. "See to the left of the buildings, that flat area just below the level of the ranch house?"

"Oh, yeah, Skipper. Looks like three burned-out Fifty-Threes."

"Agree, and next to them are?"

"Two smaller choppers, maybe the ones the bad guys arrived in."

The two SEALs looked at each other and grinned.

"Oh, yeah, what do you make the range, Skipper?"

"Eight hundred yards," Murdock said, and pumped a 20mm round into the chamber on the Bull Pup, then sighted in the laser on the chopper nearest him. When he had the target he squeezed the trigger. Seconds later the airburst ripped through the pristine-pure high Sierra air right over the first chopper. Shrapnel rained down on it, and some hit the second chopper nearby. Murdock didn't use the laser on the second round. He sighted in and fired. The contact round jolted into the engine compartment of the bird, and it exploded in a gush of flames, soon involving the second helicopter.

"Two men just ran out of the ranch house," Lam said. "They are looking at their transportation out of there. Now they are zigzagging back to the house like they expected to be shot at."

"So, they know we're here," Murdock said. "Let's get the troops up here and move forward." He flipped his lip mike down from where it rested against his floppy hat.

"You men heard two shots. We just splashed two enemy choppers. There are terrorists at the ranch house. Let's chogie that way and figure out what the hell to do."

Ed Dewitt came up with Jaybird and Senior Chief Sadler.

"How many men?" Jaybird asked.

Murdock rubbed his jaw. "Chopper that size could pack in maybe eight men. So we're looking at sixteen, maybe eighteen tops."

"The fucking odds don't seem fair," Sadler said. "I mean, those poor sods up there don't have a tinker's damn chance in hell."

Murdock put down his glasses. "DeWitt, take Bravo up that gully over there and position at the left side of the buildings. My squad will work the right end and when we get within three hundred yards, we'll take a look and see what we have. Move out."

Murdock held his Alpha Squad until DeWitt had traversed the hundred yards to the left side of the complex and the ravine. Then Murdock moved his men over the ridge in the cover of the trees and down the far side. Eight hundred yards to the ranch house. He wondered if those inside would realize that a much better armed force was coming against them and that they couldn't hold the buildings. Would they flee into the brush and trees as well and try to get lost? It depended what they had done so far. If they had captured and murdered the President and his staff, their job would be done and they would exfiltrate out of the area, and try to reach a Korean settlement in San Francisco or Los Angeles where they would blend in.

Lam led the squad as scout. He moved from tree to tree and hurried through brushy areas, then went flat as he saw something ahead he didn't understand.

"Come take a look, Skipper."

Murdock moved up, bellied down in the grass next to Lam, and pulled out his glasses.

"Off about three fingers from that big pine out there, looks like a red splotch. Could it be a red shirt or a dress?"

They concentrated with their binoculars. "Moving," Murdock said. "Oh, yes, that's a dress. Must be part of the President's party or staff. Get up there without getting shot by the Secret Service and let them know we're coming."

"Roger that," Lam said, stowed his field glasses, and eased to his feet. A moment later he vanished into the brush and trees. The red dress was less than a hundred yards ahead. Well away from the ranch house but within sight of it. They must have seen the Korean helicopters destroyed. Murdock knew the general route Lam would take to approach the friendlies. Try as he might, he couldn't detect the scout as he moved through the trees and undergrowth.

Murdock used his mike and told the rest of the SEALs what they had found. He told the squad to come up to his position. The other men spread out five yards apart near Murdock waiting to see what happened.

The Motorola earpieces spoke.

"Skipper, I'm at about twenty yards from them. I have four civilians. One definitely Secret Service with his Uzi with stock extended. Another is an older woman. The other two are young women, who might be on the staff at the ranch. I'm moving in softly."

Lam pushed up the mike so it touched his floppy hat, and edged around the pine tree and then angled into some heavy brush. He worked ahead slowly now, not moving a branch, not stepping on a dead branch or pile of leaf mold. He put weight on his foot only when he knew it would not make any noise.

Ahead was a six-foot-wide open space. To go around it would take twenty minutes. He watched the four people. All could see the opening if they looked his way. Two faced away from him. A third sat on a log staring straight ahead. The Secret Service man moved back and forth watching mostly uphill through the trees toward the ranch house.

Lam waited until the man turned and headed away from him, then darted across the opening and faded into the brush. One of the women staring straight ahead turned and looked at the opening, but Lam had gone across it. She shrugged.

Lam moved again, slowly, cautiously. He came within ten feet of the group, and waited until the Secret Service man paced away from him. Lam surged forward silently and walked beside the government security man.

"You must be Secret Service," Lam said.

The man jolted around, started to swing the Uzi upward, but Lam caught it and kept it aimed away from him.

"Hey, I'm a friend. Easy with the sub gun. I'm Lampedusa, a Navy SEAL. We've come to help you."

The Secret Service man stepped back, his eyes still wide, sweat popping out on his forehead. He shook his head in wonder. "How in hell did you do that, slip up on me that way? I've been watching for anything." The Secret Service man shook his head again and grinned. "Damn, but I'm glad to see you. I'm Horowitz. How many SEALs are there?"

"Sixteen of us, sir. Let me call up my boss." He flipped down the mike. "Skipper, all clear to come forward. Four here are A-OK."

"You on a radio net with the other Secret Service people?" Lam asked.

"Yes. We check in every hour."

"You lose anybody on the attack?"

"One of our men is missing, doesn't report on the net. We don't know what happened to him."

"So your net may be compromised. The North Koreans could have one of your radios listening. Are all of the civilians safe?"

"Not sure. The commander of the North Koreans said they would execute prisoners every half hour. We're not sure if they did or not. I watched the first one. They said they would kill Secretary Alvarez. I saw the shot and saw her fall, but they might have faked it. They did it again a half hour later. I heard the shot. I don't know if anybody was killed."

"So don't tell your net that we're here. They only know that somebody blew up their choppers. We like to surprise the North Ks."

"You took out their helicopters?"

"Yeah, with a twenty-mike-mike rifle."

"You kidding. A round that big from a rifle?"

"New. Show you one when they get here. Where are the rest of the party and the President?"

"Our plan was to scatter if anything happened," Horowitz

said. "The Koreans came in suddenly and burned our birds, and we knew we couldn't hold the ranch house so we all split. The plan was for two men to take the President and two more to take the Vice President generally to the north. I know they made it out of the house and to their first holding point. Beyond that we haven't heard much except the net checks."

A booming voice came through the air. It was an amplified voice on a bullhorn.

"Secret Service men, it is time to come in and give up your weapons. We have captured the President and killed the two men trying to protect him. I repeat. We have captured President Dunnington."

17

"Is he bluffing?" Lam asked.

"One way to find out," Horowitz said. He took out a small radio and pushed a button. "This is Five. Mr. President, are you safe?"

They waited, but nothing came over the air. After a twenty-second pause a voice responded.

"This is Four. I've had no transmission from the President in a little more than an hour."

"Four, on the net checks, did you hear everyone?"

"All but the missing man."

"Then something may have happened to the President. I'm calling for a radio check by the numbers," Horowitz said.

Lam listened as four Secret Service men checked in.

Horowitz scowled. He looked at Lam. "We could be in a lot of trouble here. I'm Five, the man we lost already is Seven, and the two with the President who didn't check in are Six and Eight. That means they might be out of range, or captured, or worse."

The speaker on the Secret Service radio sounded.

"So, Secret Service, you came up three men short on your radio net," the voice with the same strange accent said. "That is correct. Three of your men won't collect their retirement, and we have the President. So far he is safe, well, and he has not been harmed. Later it will be dark. We ask that all of you return to the ranch house where you will be more comfortable. The cook is now preparing a fine meal for you.

"We're not sure how you destroyed our helicopters, but it is of little concern. We have two other plans to leave this area without them. So come in now and we will not harm the President. You have three hours before dark to get here. I suggest that you hurry."

Horowitz jumped as Murdock edged into the small clearing.

"That's my CO, Horowitz, it's okay."

Murdock and the rest of Alpha Squad came in and at once established a perimeter defense around the position. The commander came over to the pair.

"Commander Murdock, this is Mr. Horowitz, with the Secret Service."

The men shook hands. Lam told Murdock about the claim that the President was captured and the two men with him dead.

"Is it possible?" Murdock asked Horowitz.

"The Koreans have at least one of our radios. So they have captured or killed at least one of our men. The President's guards didn't respond to my radio net check. So something is wrong."

"What's the range of your sets?" Murdock asked.

"On flat land about ten miles. Up here it could be a mile depending on the terrain. A ridgeline could block out the signal."

"Think the President just might be out of range and the Korean is bluffing?"

"Could be."

Senior Chief Sadler and Jaybird came in from the perimeter, and Murdock filled them in.

"Could you have blown up their choppers?" Sadler asked Horowitz.

"Sure, if we could have moved in close enough," Horowitz said. "I always carry a fragger on jobs like this."

"So the Koreans don't know that anyone else is here," Murdock said. "That's good. We can give them a few surprises." He looked at the Secret Service man. "Any of your men have long guns?"

"Nothing but the Uzis. We usually work close-up."

"We have the rifles and machine guns if we need them. Now all we need to do is to figure out what to do. DeWitt, we'll leave our mikes open. Cut in whenever you want to. We're having a strategy session."

The woman in the red dress walked up to the group.

"Commander. I'm Beth Arnold, the President's National Security Advisor."

Horowitz broke in. "Commander, this is Major General Beth Arnold of the U.S. Army."

The four SEALs saluted her. She returned a crisp professional salute. "General, I'm Lieutenant Commander Murdock, this is Senior Chief Sadler, Operations Specialist Second Class Lampedusa, and Machinist's Mate First Class Sterling. We always have enlisted men help when planning an operation."

"May I sit in on your session? I've had some experience."

"General, by all means. You've seen the ranch house. We haven't. Where would their strong and weak points be?"

"It's a ranch-style house, long and one-story. The kitchen is on the extreme left end, the large living room and activity rooms in the center, and the bedrooms mostly on the right-hand side. There are twelve bedrooms. They probably have the President in one of them, if they really have him."

"I'd say we have to assume that he's a captive, so we can't use our 20mm rounds on the house," Jaybird said.

"Agreed," Murdock said.

"It's got to be a silent hit," Lam said. "We move up and watch and wait and try to pick them off one at a time, quietly."

"You have suppressed weapons?" the general asked.

"Yes, two of the new Mk 11 from Knight with the twenty-inch barrel and silencer. Then we have other silenced weapons including our MP-5 sub guns."

"The way Lam slipped up on me without a sound, I would have been a dead man if he'd wanted me to be," Horowitz said. "Be sure to use Lam."

"I've heard about SEALs' work before," General Arnold said. "You're the platoon that the CIA and the President use for covert operations, correct?"

"Yes, ma'am," Murdock said.

"Damn glad you're here. Should we send men into both ends of the house, say three on each end, and start working silently toward the center?"

"Good idea, but first we'll have to take out any exterior

guards," Senior Chief Sadler said. "Be good to get two men up there quickly to check it out in what's left of the daylight."

"I agree," DeWitt said on the Motorola. "Lam and Fernandez would be my picks."

"Lam, you and Fernandez get on your horses," Murdock said. "Each of you take the silenced M-11. Move up on each end of the place. Close enough so you can find any exterior guards. Report back by radio. Then hold your positions for our arrival."

Lam lifted his Knight sniper rifle and vanished into the brush.

"That's a roger on this side," DeWitt said on the radio. "I sent Fernandez out. He goes up to about fifty and checks the scene."

"Right," Murdock said. "Be sure nobody in the house can see you, Fernandez and Lam."

General Arnold looked at Murdock. "You have any extra cammies with you?"

"Yes, ma'am, but . . ."

"No buts about it, Commander. Find a man about my size and get his spare shirt and pants. I'm going with you and this damn red dress isn't a combat outfit."

Murdock grinned. "Glad to have you on board, General."

Sadler nodded at Murdock and went to the perimeter. Murdock looked through the trees at the ranch house over seven hundred yards away. "Where would they be keeping the President, if they have him, General?"

"My choice would be the owner's suite. It's larger, has a big window facing the front, and has access only from a hall in back that runs the length of the building."

Murdock turned to Horowitz. "Did the team with the President have a SATCOM with them?"

"Yes. That must be how they called for help. Oh, yes, so now the Koreans may have the SATCOM as well, so we can't use yours. You do have one?"

"That's a roger, Mr. Horowitz. We just lost another trump card. We have to do it on our own."

"Overhead planning for this trip called for two Airborne Ranger Platoons to drop in here in case of any trouble," Horowitz said. "What happened to them?"

"The coast is on a total blackout," Senior Chief Sadler said. "They got snafued up along the coast somewhere when a county sheriff wouldn't let them take off at the city airport. Not sure where they are. They were supposed to arrive the same time we did."

"Back to the planning board," DeWitt said on the radio. "We'll need men in front and in back of the place. You want Bravo to take the back and cut off any of them bugging out?"

"Yes," Murdock said. "But keep your silenced weapons for the kitchen entrance on that end. Use your MP-5's. When the front is clear, send Fernandez around back to check for guards there."

"Right. Three men in there should be enough. Leaves me five to cover the whole back. Can do."

"I know two of my men have MP-5's in their drag bags, which gives us four silenced." Murdock turned to Horowitz. "How many of the North Ks are there?"

"Eighteen. So with the general and me, we match up man for man."

"Can you call in your Uzis? Go ahead and make a net call, and tell your men that they should report to their areas for Plan B, and be there promptly at 1930."

"Won't that tip off the Ks?" the general asked.

"Not really. We'll be moving in long before then. But it might get some of the Secret Service men closer to the buildings wondering what is happening. They heard the Korean demand for surrender. So they'll be cautious."

"I was second in command of our protection unit," Horowitz said. "If I tell them, they'll move. They know the net is compromised. They'll have to figure out what Plan B is. We don't have one."

"At least it will give the Ks something to worry about," DeWitt said. "I like it."

Sadler came back with the cammies and an MP-5 with five magazines. "Best we have, General. These might be a little large, but we can roll up the pants legs."

"This is great, Chief, thanks." She took the gear and walked into the woods.

When she was gone, Murdock frowned. "Let's not get a general shot on our watch. She is to be kept out of harm's way. We keep her safe in every way except tackling her. Agreed?"

The men nodded. "I should take her to the rear to be in our blocking position," DeWitt said. "But I can't get her over here."

Murdock shook his head. "She wouldn't agree to that. She wants to be out front. I'll post her with the front sniper. She can help watch for any targets out there. Might hold her.

"Jaybird, Lam, and I will go in the bedroom end of the place after Lam and Fernandez eliminate any guards out front. Then I want Fernandez to go around to the back and check for any exterior guards. When the front and back are clear, then the two three-man teams move into the house. Any problems or suggestions with this plan?"

"We use only silence MP-5's inside?" Jaybird asked.

"Right, I'll trade my Bull Pup for a Five."

The SEAL radios came on.

"Skipper, I'm about fifty yards from the right end of the place," Lam said. "So far I haven't seen any guards out front or near the right end. They must have somebody here. I'll keep watching."

"Don't go any closer," Murdock said. "Settle down and wait. We have an hour before dusk."

The general came back and grinned. "I haven't had on cammies for over four years. Feels good. Now, does anybody have an extra floppy or a watch cap?"

Murdock reached in his combat vest and pulled out a black knit watch cap. "Will this one do?" he asked.

Major General Arnold chuckled. "Now I remember, you're the Commander Murdock the CNO talks about. Wanted you on his staff, but you turned him down. Takes guts. He said you were right. You're more valuable leading your platoon."

Murdock smiled. "General, I hope you think the same thing when this operation is over. Our man up front said he can't spot any outside guards. I don't like that."

"Seems they should have somebody watching their front and their back," General Arnold said. "Looks like we'll have to play it by ear and count bodies as we go. Right now, eighteen. Wish we could cut that down two or three before we go inside."

Murdock took a deep breath and plunged forward. "General Arnold, one thing we need to get clear. On this mission, I'm in command. On this ground I outrank you. You can come along, but you will follow my orders. Do you agree?"

"Absolutely, Commander. I'm at your service. Just don't leave me back here with the kitchen help. The two girls over there are friendly and nice, but I'd really hate to be stuck here."

"Good. When we set up, I want you up with Lam. When he shifts to the right-hand end to enter, you'll trade your MP-5 for his Knight and be responsible for anything moving out front. You'll have the new Knight sniper rifle. It's semiautomatic, a lot like the SR25. I'd bet you can handle a long gun with no problem."

"I was on the rifle team for five years. Then some skinny, redheaded, flat-chested little corporal beat me out for the last spot on the team. I nearly had her court-martialed."

"Yeah, I bet. General, you'll be firing at seventy-five to a hundred yards. Fish in a barrel for a sharpshooter."

"Skipper, Fernandez here."

"Go, Fernandez."

"I've got one guard. He's in and out of the kitchen. Eating all the time. Has a sub gun but nothing longer. I can take him out whenever you lads get in position. Seems like he's on a definite post here."

"Roger that. We'll wait until dusk and move up. Hit them about 1820. You clear anyone there, then move to the rear. Right?"

"Copy that."

Murdock looked at his watch. It was 1800. "Horowitz, have you ever had any Army training?"

"No, sir. Just the regular training."

"We need a good man to stay here with the other two women. Can you take care of that job?"

"Yes, sir. If that's the best spot for me."

"We need you here. Watch for any Korean infiltrators. The rest of you, let's move up to Lam and Fernandez. Copy that, DeWitt?"

"That's a roger."

"DeWitt, time for you to move the rest of your squad to

the rear of the ranch house. Swing wide, leave Fernandez where he is as sniper, and get the rest of your guys into a blocking position forty yards behind the house if you have cover."

"Roger that, we're moving out."

The Alpha Squad SEALs formed up in a single line, five yards apart with General Arnold in the center, and worked up the slope through the heavy brush and timber. They were completely screened from the ranch house.

Ten minutes later they jumped as a voice called to them. "You guys make enough noise to raise the dead," Lam said as he stepped out from behind a big pine tree three feet from Murdock, who led the line. Lam grinned. "Well, maybe not that much. I'm about twenty yards up there, but the good cover stops here. So far I've spotted two guards. One is walking up and back in front of the place, and another one is shielding the entrance on this right end. Suggest that Fernandez take the front guy from his end. The man seems to move all the way to the kitchen. I think he has the munchies."

Murdock settled the men down in the brush and crawled up to Lam's lookout.

"Oh, yeah, I can see the one on this end," Murdock said. "He's sitting on a chair with a cushion on it. Tough little guy. He's got a long gun of some kind. Maybe an AK-47."

"I'll make sure of him first."

"General Arnold will be up here with you. You take out the guard, and any more, then you move with me. Trade her your Knight for her MP-5. Be sure she has cover here."

"Got it, Cap. We don't want a major general gut-shot on our watch."

They lay there watching the house.

"I haven't seen anybody at the windows," Lam said.

"Fernandez?" Murdock said into the Motorola.

"Go, Cap."

"Have you spotted a second man who works the front and goes over to the kitchen?"

"Got him, Cap. He'll be my first hit when he's here. Then I get the second one. All silent. Roger that."

"We wait until it's almost dark, maybe twenty minutes. You in position, DeWitt?"

"All hunkered down and waiting. Fernandez is at the front sniper station, and I'll take Canzoneri and Franklin with me to the kitchen entrance. Mahanani will use the Knight here in back looking for guards. Give us a countdown from five minutes and I'll get everyone settled in."

"Roger that, DeWitt."

Murdock moved General Arnold and Luke Howard up to Lam's sniper spot. "I want both of you to stay here for any movement out front. Bradford, Ching, Sadler, and Van Dyke, you'll stay spread out about here for a blocking team. Spread out twenty yards apart across the front now, guys. Nothing and nobody gets past you."

"Murdock, I've got Donegan, Victor, and Jefferson in blocking."

They waited. Murdock checked his blockers, then led General Arnold and Howard up near Lam. He found good cover for the two of them five yards behind Lam.

"All set?" Murdock asked the general

"As much as ever. First combat I've seen since Desert Storm. Don't worry, I won't shame you."

Murdock checked his watch.

"DeWitt, you have your five before we move."

"Copy that."

Mahanani checked his view of the rear of the house again. He had seen no guards out back, but there could be one stationary one. DeWitt hurried back to his spot near the kitchen, keeping thirty yards of brush and trees between him and the structure. He met Canzoneri and Franklin, and they planned their run to the kitchen door after the guards were down.

The sun had been behind the far ridges for twenty minutes when dusk dropped in on the ranch house.

"Snipers in front," Murdock said. "It's a go. Your weapons are free."

Lam had been sighting the Knight sniper rifle in on the North Korean at the end of the ranch house. The man had just stood up and stretched. Lam refined his sight and pulled the trigger.

18

Lam's silent shot huffed into the high Sierra night air. The North Korean guard slammed forward, dropped his long gun, and sprawled next to the ranch house. Murdock waited, watching the man through his NVGs. The green image in the night goggles showed the man as still as death.

Lam swung his head to the left and checked the other guard. The one who had been walking his post came almost to the kitchen, then stumbled and fell. Lam squirmed back to the general and traded weapons with her.

"Nineteen rounds left in the magazine," he said. He took the MP-5 and her magazines and moved to the tree that he and Murdock had picked out for their meet. The other two SEALs were there, and Jaybird motioned him forward. They jogged the forty yards to the right-hand entrance and paused a dozen feet away to watch it. They saw no movement.

The dead guard lay where he had fallen. Jaybird sprinted for the door and tried it. Unlocked. He pulled it open slowly. Coleman gas lights were on now inside the house. He could see down a hallway with numerous doors leading off it. Murdock and Lam crowded behind Jaybird. Murdock motioned to the first two doors on the left, pointing to the other two men. He had the doors on the right. He stepped into the hall and waited. No sound, no movement.

Murdock turned the knob on the first door and jolted it open. The room was empty, but clothes were scattered on the unmade bed. He eased down the hall to the second door. He saw Lam and Jaybird shake their heads as they exited their rooms.

They checked the eight doors on the wing and found no

people in any of them, and no dead bodies. When they came to the large living room they waited. DeWitt had to be coming down there somewhere.

On the other end of the ranch house, Ed DeWitt watched the two guards go down from the sniper rifle. One tried to crawl away, but a second round stopped him. DeWitt and his two men rushed to the kitchen door. They opened it and found two cooks there busy with their job of getting a meal.

They looked up in surprise.

"Who the hell are you guys?" the taller of the cooks, with the white chef's hat, asked.

"Navy SEALs. Where are the kidnappers?"

"Hell, got me. Last I saw of them, this one boss gook guy said he wanted a box of sandwiches and six gallons of water. Made them up for him. Must have been an hour ago."

"Any of the staff still here?" DeWitt asked.

"Don't think so. Everybody ran out when the helicopters blew up. We were working and didn't even hear it. Didn't know nothing was wrong until the Chinks came in."

"They're North Koreans."

"Slants, what's the difference? You guys hungry?"

"Later," DeWitt said, and hurried through the kitchen into a hallway that led to a pair of empty but recently used bedrooms, then a big double door.

"Clear it?" Canzoneri asked. DeWitt nodded. He grabbed the door handle and shoved the panel open. Nothing happened. Canzoneri looked around the doorjamb from floor height.

"Can't see anybody," he said.

DeWitt charged into the room, his MP-5 swinging to cover it. There were two rooms and a big window facing the front. Had to be the owner's suite.

"Nobody," DeWitt said. They left the room and moved down a short hall to an empty dining room, then to the large living room.

"Entering the living room area," DeWitt said on his Motorola.

"Copy that," Murdock said. "We're here as well. We came up empty."

"So did we, except for two cooks," DeWitt said. "The Ks

have bugged out." The SEALs moved forward cautiously through the living room and activity room until they met.

"Looks like we're all clear on the ranch house," Murdock said to the Motorola. "You men on blocking, turn around and give us a perimeter while we figure out what to do. Snipers come inside. You too, General Arnold."

Murdock frowned. "First we check out this place and see if they hid anybody here, or if any of them are hiding. Let's do a complete search. Ed, take the kitchen and those rooms down there. Alpha Squad will do the bedrooms down the other way. Let's do it."

Twenty minutes later Lam opened a closet in one of the bedrooms and jumped back. Two dead bodies fell out.

"Skipper, better come take a look. Fourth bedroom from the end."

Murdock checked the bodies. "The man was shot to death, two in the back of his head. An execution. He must be the Secret Service guy. Jaybird, go down and bring back the three civilians we left behind."

The second body was a woman, early thirties. "Probably one of the dining-room servers," Lam said. She had also been shot, Murdock saw, two rounds to the chest. DeWitt checked in by radio. His men had found nothing in their search area.

The SEALs met in the living room. "So do the Ks have the President or don't they?" DeWitt asked.

"We can't tell," Murdock said. "They left. Why? Could be because they had the President, and that's what they came for."

"Where can they go up in this wilderness?" Lam asked. "Unless they have some alternative transport, like a backup chopper somewhere."

"Let's hope not," Canzoneri said. "Then we'll never find them."

"Lam, can you track them in the dark?" Murdock asked his lead scout.

"Should be fifteen or sixteen of them. That will make a good trail. Give me two Maglites and I'll give it a shot."

Horowitz came running in. "You find the President?"

"Afraid not, Mr. Horowitz," DeWitt said.

"Use your radio and bring in all of your men," Murdock

said. "Have them bring any civilians with them. The Koreans have left the area, so it should be safe. Tell them to make themselves known. We have a perimeter set out."

Jaybird took the Secret Service man down the hall to identify the dead man, and soon they heard a scream of protest.

Lam took two flashlights and went to talk to the cooks.

"Yeah," said the taller cook, "they took the box of sandwiches, put them in their packs, and the water jugs, and took off. Was still light then. They headed out the back door here and walked due left down toward Wildcat Canyon. It's about two miles over."

Lam told Murdock what he knew on the net and headed out the door, checking the ground for what should be at least fifteen sets of footprints. Even on a trail he should be able to follow them. In the brush or woods it would be easier.

The Secret Service men and the resort staff began drifting in. There were four more government men, and they brought eight workers along with them. The Secret Service men huddled at one side. Horowitz left them and talked to Murdock.

"We want to use your SATCOM to call our office in D.C. and tell them what's happened and ask for instructions."

Murdock shook his head. "Not a good idea. We don't know what's happened. If we say the President has been kidnapped, it could cause a panic. Let's hold off awhile. Your office can't help us right now. What we need is a company of Marines for a blocking action and a pair of choppers with infrared imagers to show us where the Koreans are. We don't have either and won't get them. We wait on Lam and move out when he tells us to."

The cook DeWitt had talked to came in and grinned when he saw all the people.

"Good, somebody to feed. I have sandwiches and beef stew in the dining room if anyone is interested. There also is plenty of coffee, tea, and soft drinks. I've set up for thirty, is that enough?"

Murdock called in the screening troops and they sat down to eat.

"Great time for a counterattack," General Arnold said.

Murdock sipped his coffee and had another bite of the

tuna-fish sandwich. "They are out of the area, I'm sure. Lam will keep us up to date."

"What can we do until we hear from your tracker?" Horowitz asked.

"Not a hell of a lot except wait," DeWitt said. He looked at Murdock. "Skipper, I checked the North Korean KIAs. No papers, no ID, nothing to indicate who they are or what they are doing."

"Figures," Murdock said, and reached for another sandwich.

Meanwhile, Lam came to a small stream and studied the obvious boot prints on the near side. All seemed to head directly into the water. But did they just cross or go downstream to confuse a tracker? No, they would go straight across. They would have no idea they would be followed at night. He crossed the stream and picked up the trail. Thirty boots tromping along was not hard to follow even at night. He used one light to save the other batteries.

The trail had swung downhill, and in the moonlight through gaps in the timber, Lam could see a meadowlike clearing coming up. He stopped and turned off his light and listened.

Nothing.

He flipped down the Motorola mike from his floppy hat brim. "Lam to Murdock."

"Go."

"Figure I'm about three miles from the ranch. Generally to the southwest, heading at a slant downhill. A clearing is coming up, a big one, like a meadow. Can't see anything yet, or hear anything, but should be there in about ten. I'll keep you posted."

"Copy that."

Lam moved forward, keeping the flashlight close to the ground. He watched for broken plants, mashed-down leaf mold, an occasional broken-off branch. By the time the last man had been through a narrow space, an easy-to-follow trail had been gouged out of the woodsy floor.

The tracker edged up to the fringe of woods around the open space. Yes, a mountain meadow that probably once was a lake. It was depressed in the center and covered ten or twelve square city blocks. Maybe twenty acres. He could see all around the edges of the opening and checked for lights. There were none. He held his breath, closed his eyes, and listened.

Yes, a muted laugh, a few words, all in some foreign language. They were somewhere close by. Why would they stop here? He checked the meadow again. Yes, it was dry, filled with grass. An ideal landing zone. He tried to sniff the faint breeze that blew toward him. There was no scent of oil or grease or even petroleum fuel. If there was a chopper close by, he couldn't detect it. Why would they wait if they had a bird here? They wouldn't. So maybe this was a pickup spot to be used in case of an emergency. They certainly had an emergency.

He backtracked a hundred yards and checked in with Murdock on the Motorola outlining where he was and what he had found.

"I haven't been close to them yet, so I don't know how many of them, and can't tell if the President is with them. Want me to move up or wait for backup?"

"See what else you can find out. Then give us a compass heading so we can come find you. My guess is the quicker we get there the better. They could bug out again."

Lam gave them an approximate compass heading and moved back toward the meadow. This time he stayed in the woods and worked his way fifty yards toward the voices before he angled back toward the opening. The wind shifted and he smelled wood smoke. Yes, they had a camp, so they would be there a while. He worked ahead slower, making sure he made no noise whatsoever that could be heard a dozen feet away.

Ten minutes of snail's-pace moving later, he came over a slight rise and could see the reflection of firelight on the trees. He judged it to be fifty yards ahead. He closed his eyes again and listened. Yes, more voices, high-pitched, excited. They were celebrating? If so, they were a little premature.

Lam checked every three steps looking for exterior guards. He was sure they would have some out, maybe three of them. One was all he had to take care of. He moved to a large pine tree and edged his head around it. He figured he was still thirty yards from the camp.

Movement, just ahead. What? He lifted his NVG and checked. Yes, a man in jungle cammies with a sub gun sitting against a tree ten feet ahead. His chin had lowered to his chest. He could be dozing. Lam worked to his right, moving out of sight of the guard, then forward past him and to the left so he could come up behind the man. It took ten minutes to make the silent trip of forty feet. Then Lam was directly behind the man's tree. He felt on his waist and pulled from his belt a length of piano wire that had been fitted with padded loops on each end. He held the ends and edged around the tree.

In one swift move he jumped beside the Korean guard, swung the loop of wire over his head, and jerked back hard with both hands. The surprised guard had time only to gurgle once as the thin wire sliced through his windpipe, then his jugular vein, and then cut through both his carotid arteries supplying blood to his brain. Blood spurted from the ruptured carotids with each beat of the Korean's heart. The spurts became weaker and weaker, until no blood came out at all. In less than a minute the guard had expired.

Lam let him fall to the ground, cleaned the garrote on the dead man's shirt, and put it back around his waist. He knelt and looked at the camp area. He still could see little. But the way should now be open. He worked ahead silently as a fox.

It took ten minutes to move thirty feet, and then he parted some heavy brush and looked out from ground level. Twenty feet ahead he saw the Koreans' camp. There were two wall tents twenty feet long in a cleared area. Both had lights on inside. He could hear a muted engine that must be powering a generator.

The fire he had seen first glowed between the tents. Four men in jungle cammies sat around it eating off metal trays. The fronts of the tents faced each other. One had a door flap open. The other tent's flap was closed and two armed guards stood in front of it.

If they had the President, he was in that guarded tent. What else would they guard? Yes, they had kidnapped the President. Was there any way Lam could get him out? The back of the tent stood only ten feet from the brush and tall trees.

Silently Lam worked backward and away from the camp. He moved fifty yards and then flipped down the swinging microphone and talked on the net.

"SEALs, I found them. My guess maybe four miles from the ranch house. They are on the edge of a meadow, maybe twenty acres. Somebody there might know where it is. They have a campsite that was built before tonight. Two ten-man tents and a generator for electricity. One of the tents is guarded, so my guess is that the President is inside. I need some backup. Suggest the platoon come on down."

"Copy that, Lam," Murdock said. "We'll ask the locals if they know where that meadow is and if they can guide us there. Be in touch in five and on our way in ten."

"Roger."

Lam found a good spot and lay down. He rested his head on his hands and relaxed. He would hear the platoon if it came within two hundred yards of him. Murdock called back on the net that he had found one of the cowboys who knew of the meadow and would lead them to it. Lam rested for half an hour, then moved back along the trail toward the ranch for five hundred yards. Best to catch the troops away from the target and make their plans.

A half hour later, Lam came upright in a rush. Sounds, muted, the soft noise of someone moving through the woods. He relaxed. The sound came from the trail toward the ranch. He picked out a sturdy pine tree and stood behind it waiting to see if it really was the SEALs.

Lam watched the men approach. It was Murdock out front. Lam stepped out from the tree, waved, and then pointed his finger at them.

"Bang, bang, you're dead," he said.

Murdock stutter-stepped and then got his stride.

"You always surprise me that way, Lam. The cowboy led us to where we could see the meadow and then he went back. It looks like a camp that's been there for some time?"

"Right. Small stream for water, generator, tents, the works. No rancher is going to put a setup like that out in here. The Koreans must have done a lot of planning for this hit."

They walked forward. They talked in whispers.

"Is there any way to get the President out of there before we gun down the place?" Murdock asked.

"I think so," Lam said. "The back of the tent comes within ten feet of the brush. I should be able to get to it, slit the tent open, and get inside unseen. Then take care of any interior guard and hustle the President out the back into the brush, and you guys open fire as soon as we clear."

Murdock nodded. He passed the sign back down the line of SEALs for total quiet, and they marched on.

When they came within thirty yards of the tents, they stopped. Murdock moved the men into positions where they had open fields of fire. They were slightly above the level of the tents and had plenty of targets. Murdock had mandated no 20mm's would be fired. When all the men were in favorable firing spots with cover, Murdock waved Lam forward.

He moved slowly, working on his belly the last ten yards to the fringe of woods just in back of the tent he figured the President would be in. Lam lay there for five minutes listening to the Koreans, watching for any more guards, checking to see if anyone walked behind the President's tent. No one did.

It was time.

Lam edged out of the brush and took four quick steps to the back of the tent. He had his KA-BAR knife out, pushed the sharp point through the canvas head high, and pulled it slowly down. It made a soft slicing sound, and then he had it open to the bottom.

Lam pulled the sides of the tent apart and looked inside.

19

Lam could see little inside the tent. Only a dim candle burned. A cot to one side held some blankets, but he couldn't be sure if anyone lay there. Cautiously he pushed the opening wider and stepped through. Two steps brought him to the bed. No one there. He looked around the tent. The rest of it was nearly empty, no cots or other gear. On a small table he saw a large briefcase, and recognized the Presidential seal on the side. He checked it. The lock had been broken and inside were hundreds of sheets of paper and file folders. Must be important.

He heard voices outside, and stepped quickly to the front of the tent to the side away from where the flap would open. A new voice came in English.

"Hell of a note when a guy can't even take a piss by himself. You sure you went two years to UCLA?"

"Quite certain, Mr. President told them I was a South Korean. Now if you'll just go back in the tent and have a nap, this night will be over before you know it and we'll be on our way again. Our transport will be here a half hour after dawn. So be well rested and ready for travel."

"By then you'll be chatting away with your honored ancestors in hell, or wherever you people go."

"Wishful thinking, Mr. President. Now inside."

The flap opened and a man came through. Lam had never seen the President in person. The man stepped inside, went to the cot, and sat down heavily.

"Where in hell are the Marines when you need them?" he asked out loud. Lam moved without a sound on the canvas floor to the far side of the President and called out softly.

"Don't be alarmed, Mr. President."

President Dunnington's head jerked up and he stared at the man in the shadows of the one candle.

"What in hell?"

"Not the Marines, Mr. President," Lam said softly as he stepped toward the Chief Executive. "Just a few SEALs come to help you out of this mess. Should I carry your briefcase as we go through the back of the tent?"

The President looked at the long slit in the tent and laughed softly. "Oh, yes, that would be good. You with Murdock?"

"Yes, sir."

"Damn good. Let's move."

They stepped through the slit in the tent one at a time, and Lam carried the heavy briefcase. The President ran into the woods, and Lam came right behind him. He stopped the President.

"We have to move slowly and without a sound so they don't know you're gone. We need thirty yards to clear before the rest of the platoon opens fire. Straight ahead, Mr. President."

It seemed to Lam that it took forever before they were thirty yards away from the tent. He saw Murdock on the ground ready to fire, and waved at him.

Murdock pulled down the mike. "Nobody is in the tent on the left. Riddle the other one and get anybody who comes out. Open fire."

Lam helped the President sit down, then pulled the MP-5 off his back and joined in. The MP-5's stuttered out three-round bursts. The 5.56 rounds spurted out of the Bull Pups, and the rest of the weapons rained instant death on the North Koreans. The tent on the right ripped into shreds and fell. Men spewed out of it firing to the rear, but were cut down at once. Lam rushed the President behind a big pine tree, then found a pine himself and fired around it. Two men fell into the campfire and didn't move. A half-dozen tried to run into the brush beyond the small clearing, but were flattened by the withering fire of the automatic rifles and the H & K 21A1 machine gun. When the SEALs saw no one moving, they slowed their firing, and then stopped.

"Donegan, Bradford, make sure," Murdock said. The two SEALs lifted from their cover and moved up to the scene slowly, watching for any movement. Bradford swung to the right and fired three rounds at a North Korean who lifted up with his rifle. The man flopped down and stayed.

Donegan moved closer and then into the clearing. He fired a single shot, and moved on. Bradford fired another single round to put a wounded man out of his misery. SEALs take no prisoners.

"When you're sure of every body, count them," Murdock said.

Lam went back with the President, who still sat behind the tree. "There were fifteen of them with me," President Dunnington said. "Two of them spoke good English. They didn't talk much about why they attacked the ranch. They did say that they would keep me captive until the United States made massive war-crime payments to the North Korean people. They wanted three trillion dollars in trade, goods, credit, and hard cash. Ridiculous. They were the ones who attacked South Korea two years ago, not the other way around."

Murdock and DeWitt went to the clearing and looked for any kind of papers or plans. They found a map on one of the bodies, and some papers in Korean on another. The rest of the men had no identification of any kind, not even dog tags. DeWitt found the SATCOM in the riddled tent. It had taken three slugs and was ruined. He slung it over his shoulder. Maybe they could repair it. They never did find the Secret Service radio.

Murdock went to where he saw Lam, and knelt down in front of the nation's highest elected official.

"Mr. President, do you feel like walking back to the ranch house?"

"Ready right now. You're Murdock? Lieutenant Commander Murdock of SEAL Team Seven, Third Platoon?"

"Yes, sir."

"We've talked several times on the phone. Strange that we meet this way. But I'm grateful. How are my people?"

"My senior chief told me that all of your staff people are fine except for one we can't find, Maria Alvarez."

"I know, I saw that bastard shoot her in the head. I thought he was bluffing. He also killed one of the waitresses. How many North Korean bodies did you count down there? I hope to God that you nailed him."

"There were fifteen dead North Koreans, sir. We had them boxed in, in a cross fire. Not much of a chance anyone could get away."

"Thank God for that. But it won't bring back Maria. She was a good one. They also killed Barney Bronson, who owns the ranch. What about General Arnold?"

"Yes, we found her in the brush. She has on cammies and is packing a rifle. She helped us on the perimeter defense."

"Sounds like her." The President paused. "Well, I'm ready to travel anytime you are. Have you notified my office about this yet?"

"They know you were attacked. We didn't tell them that you were captured. Now we don't have to. We have a SAT-COM that you can use as soon as we get back to the ranch house."

"Move us out, Commander."

"Yes, sir, Mr. President."

They left the camp and the bodies where they lay. Someone would come in the next day or two, bury the bodies, pick up the weapons, and clean up the area so it could revert back to the natural Sierra woodland. In five years no one would be able to find the exact spot where the President had been held captive by a foreign power. It would be better that way.

The hike back to the ranch house took an hour and a half. Murdock and the President were in front, and the SEAL let the nation's leader set the pace.

Back at the ranch house, the President at once called his office on the SATCOM and had a long private talk.

Murdock got the SEALs collected. They had taken no casualties in the firefight. Lillian Bronson, wife of the murdered owner of the ranch, said that they could sleep in the bunkhouse, off to the left of the main house. It turned out to be a dormitory with thirty beds in two big rooms.

Murdock used his SATCOM and called the Quarter Deck in Coronado. They had their ears on.

"Murdock, hoped you would call," Master Chief Petty Officer MacKenzie said. "How is the mission going?"

"Wrapped up, Master Chief. You still blacked out there?"

"On and off, mostly off. Wrapped up? You found the man and he's safe."

"Safe and sound and talking with his office right now. We'll stay here tonight and do any cleanup work we need to tomorrow. Hold the paperwork for me."

"Can do that, Commander. Glad he's all right. When you move, use that chopper you left at the bridge. He's still there and getting hungry. The jet is waiting for you at Sacramento. Keep up the good work, Commander."

"You too, Master Chief. See you tomorrow."

Murdock talked to Mrs. Bronson, and had a car take a big pot of coffee and a dozen sandwiches down to the men at the helicopter near the bridge. There was a good road that went down there and the lady said it would be no problem. Murdock knew the men wouldn't leave the chopper unprotected. They'd sleep beside it all night.

General Arnold came in, still wearing her cammies and watch cap. "I like them," she said when the men with the President looked at her. "We going to have another meeting tonight, or are you wimps so tired you need to go to sleep."

President Dunnington came up and grinned at her comment.

"If they aren't too tired, I am. The SEALs saved all the papers we had been working on. North Korea would have loved to have had them." He looked at Murdock and walked over and shook his hand. "This mission wasn't covert, so I'm going to have a unit citation struck for your platoon. Also I'm giving your man Lampedusa an instant promotion to first class. Figure it out any way you can. The man deserves it big-time. He grabbed me right out from under the noses of fifteen armed killers." The civilians stared at the President. "Yes, I'll tell all of you about it when we have time."

He stopped and looked around the dining room where most of the President's men, the staff, and the Secret Service men had congregated. "I've lost four good people on this trip. Three of my top Secret Service men and Maria Alvarez. The responsible parties have paid with their lives, but that doesn't bring the dead back with us. First order of business tomorrow is to locate our dead and have them flown out by helicopter to Sacramento. I have ordered enough CH-53's into Sacramento from surrounding bases to take everyone out of here by noon. A graves-registration squad will come in with its own transport to take care of the North Koreans. They will not be sent back to their homeland. That team will also retrieve the weapons the terrorists used and tear down and dispose of the camp that was built there." The President looked at Lillian Bronson, who now owned the ranch.

"Lillian, did you and Barney know about that camp?"

"We heard that it was being built. Some man from Sacramento said it would be a boy's camp for underprivileged children."

"Was he Oriental?"

"Yes, he said he was Chinese."

"So they really did a lot of planning," the President said. "How did they know we would be coming here?"

"I can't figure it out, Mr. President. The camp went up in a week just before you arrived. They asked if they could drive across some of our pasture with a truck."

"So, I've got a leak somewhere among my top advisors, or their staffs. I'll work on that." The President turned and looked into the activity room. "Anybody want to shoot a game of nine ball? Pool always relaxes me after I exercise."

Murdock excused himself and went out to the bunkhouse. He'd had enough exercise for one day.

The next morning the breakfast buffet began at 0600 for the staff and cowboys, and lasted until 0930. The SEALs all feasted on their choice of bacon, cheese omelets, breakfast steak, hash browns, pancakes, waffles, fruit salad, eggs to order, and lots of coffee, tea, and hot chocolate.

"Why don't we eat here every day," Jaybird said.

The big cook with the chef's hat put out a fresh tray of crisp bacon. "Hey, SEAL, you can come to my kitchen anytime. I like a big eater," the chef said.

By 0800 the President led six SEALs with two stretchers up the trail where he and the Secret Service men had been attacked. Both agents had been shot once in the forehead.

"They were on us before we knew what happened," the

President said. "They could have killed me as well. Now I'm sure they wish they had."

The SEALs wrapped the bodies in sheets, put them on the stretchers, and took turns carrying them a mile down through the woods and past a small cabin. A man with a dozer blade on a tractor pushed the five burned-out helicopters off the parking lot.

Promptly at 0930 three big CH-53's whupped their way up the mountain, circled, and then all landed on the now-empty parking lot.

They had found Maria Alvarez where she had fallen when the North Koreans executed her. They wrapped her in a sheet and took her to one of the helicopters with the three dead men. One Secret Service man went with the bodies to see that they were flown as soon as possible to Washington, D.C. Mrs. Bronson had found her husband's body, and had had her men put it on the bed in the master bedroom. She would call the sheriff about it later.

"The blackout is lifted at Sacramento," Lillian said to the President. "I just got word on the telephone. Most of the coast is up and working again, and airliners are getting serviced and starting to meet their schedules."

Murdock caught the President's attention. "Sir, is there anything else you need us for?"

The President shook Murdock's hand, then pulled him into a bear hug. He released the hold and stepped back. "Commander, I don't know how to thank you. I tried to promote you, but the CNO said if I did, they would have to bounce you out of the platoon and boot you upstairs somewhere. I don't want that. I might try a promotion order to take effect as soon as you leave the active SEAL platoon. That might work. I appreciate it. The nation is thankful. You're going to get a big blast of publicity about this because I'm turning loose my press secretary on it. You'll have many visitors from the press and TV. Now, to answer your question. Yes, you may be relieved of your duties here and report back to Coronado."

Lillian had been listening. "I agree with what the President has said. I'm just sorry I couldn't talk my husband out of trying to fight off fifteen men with a pistol." She turned away and touched her eyes with a tissue. "At any rate, I have a stake truck that is available to take you and your SEALs down the hill to your helicopter, if that would be all right."

"Yes, that would be fine. And I'm deeply sorry for the loss of your husband."

"Thank you. The truck will be at the bunkhouse when you're ready."

The trip back to San Diego was routine. Electrical power had been fully restored to the entire Western electrical grid, and slowly life returned to near normal. Except at the airports, which had planes and passengers stacked up so far that it might take a week to get things straightened out.

Murdock checked his watch as he kicked off the bus from North Island to the Coronado strand outside the NAVSPECWARGRUP-ONE Quarter Deck. It was just after 1500. He had promised the men they would be through for the day as soon as they cleaned their weapons and took care of their gear.

"Oh, yeah, gonna see my honey tonight," Jaybird yelped. "Got me this hot little number down in Chula Vista . . ."

"Hey, no good woman ever came out of Chula Vista," Bradford shot back. "Creepy, crawling things all over them."

"Hooha yourself, big buddy. You ain't never seen this little gem. She's a keeper. Well, for a couple of months at least."

Mahanani listened to the chatter as he cleaned his weapons, stashed them, and took care of the rest of his equipment, refilling his ammo pouches with the regular supply of rounds. Then he was across the Quarter Deck, in his Buick, and heading for his apartment. He had on his civvies, and a new jet-black driving cap with a short bill like they used to wear in the twenties. He'd heard they were coming back and he liked the way it fit on his head.

His palms were itching for some action, but then he remembered he had been cut off from playing at the casino. Damn them. Sure he owed them a few bucks. Maybe he should make enough drug runs to Tijuana for them to clear his IOU. That would take a lot of trips, like fifteen. He had only made two so far. A dozen more? Sounded good, but he had a strong feeling that before he was through, he'd get nailed by the Border Patrol guys for sure.

He drummed his fingers on the steering wheel as he sat outside his apartment. Hell, it was early. He could do a run to TJ and be back in time to catch a good war movie on TV. He turned, headed across the high Coronado Bay Bridge, and drove to the east to where the Casa Grande Casino flaunted itself near the highway.

He parked in the big lot and thought about it. A risk, sure, everything was a risk. But he'd have a clean car and not overloaded, so no reason the inspectors would challenge him. He'd give it one more try. Maybe this time he'd figure out how to nail these bastards and get them put away. How was he going to work a trap?

He locked the Buick and walked in the front door. This time he turned into the hallway and went directly to the Hammer's office. He pushed inside and saw Harley talking to Martillo.

"Well, the hero comes home," Harley said. "Heard about you SEALs rescuing the President up there in the Sierras."

"Yeah, that's the job. Can I make a run to TJ today?"

"So, Mahanani, how many of the North Koreans did you kill?" Martillo, the Hammer, asked.

"I didn't keep track. You need any goods moved today or not?"

"He doesn't want to talk about it," Harley said. "He's the sensitive type."

"I should have called first. Maybe I can do some good next time," Mahanani said. He turned to leave. Harley moved quickly in front of him.

"Hold it, man. We didn't say we didn't have no goods. Just curious about the big shoot-out." Harley frisked him expertly, found no weapons, but it seemed to Mahanani that he searched for a wire and transmitter as well.

"Clean as a baby's bottom."

"Yeah, you can pick up a load," the Hammer said. "Get down to San Ysidro now and pick up a car and leave it at the TJ garage. Then have a couple of drinks and shop or some fucking thing, and don't go back over the border for at least four hours. The pricks down there are getting leery of over-and-back trips that are too quick."

Mahanani stared at the Hammer for a few seconds, then nodded. "Yeah, I can do that. Another four hundred off my bill, right?"

"Right," Harley said. "I'm keeping track. Remember to be relaxed when you come back across. Don't act nervous or you'll end up in Chino Prison for five to ten. Now go."

Mahanani left the room, marched down the hall, through the lobby, and outside. The fresh air felt good. He couldn't imagine what it would be like to be stuffed into a cell for twenty years. So he had to do everything right this time. Once more. Then he'd figure out how to turn in these bastards without getting both his legs broken and a pair of .22-caliber slugs in the back of his head.

20

San Ysidro, California

Mahanani paced outside the garage. It seemed like it was taking a lot longer this time for them to get the car ready for him to drive. He sat in his Buick and waited. His Buick and the Indian gambling Casino's Buick. How had he ever got into this goddamned fucking gambling problem? It could wash him right out of the Navy if they went to his CO. Murdock would have to write a report and that would do it.

It was another half an hour before the door rolled up and they drove the six-year-old Chevy out of the garage.

"You be good to car," the Mexican mechanic said. "She in good shape. You drive safe."

Jack Mahanani growled a reply and slid into the car. It had the usual camouflage. A child's booster seat in back, a box of tissue, and a box of baby wipes. Scattered soft drink cups from Jack in the Box. Even half of the Sunday newspaper. A woman's blouse lay on the passenger's side.

Mahanani drove. It was a short trip to the border, then through Mexican customs with hardly a slowdown, and into the border city of almost a million people, all scratching to survive. He turned into the right street and saw the garage with the same door open. He'd used it before. Something didn't feel right this time, but he couldn't figure out what. He drove into the garage, walked out the back door, and came around the end of the alley to the street and then to a cantina he'd noticed on the last run. The Tecate beer wasn't bad if it was cold enough. It was.

He spent the next four hours over two beers, then some burritos at a good restaurant. He hoped that they didn't make him sick this time. Then he walked around the tourist-trap areas, turning down fantastic offers of fake Rolex watches and good-looking diamonds. When he went back to the garage through the back door, the one Mexican who could speak any English shook his head.

"Not ready," he said.

Mahanani had not seen where they hid the drugs in the car. He didn't want to know. But now he watched as two men fastened the rear seat back in place in the Chevy. Did they hide the drugs in the seat itself, or a compartment under the floor? He had no idea, and he still didn't want to know. Just knowing it was somewhere in the car was enough.

Chino. He shivered every time he thought of that state prison up by Los Angeles. Maybe he should dump the car this side of the border and walk across? Sure, and get sliced up by the Hammer while two of the big guys were holding him down. They would think he had ripped them off for the five hundred thousand dollars worth of coke. Not a chance he would try that.

"Okay," the Mexican lead man said, and handed Mahanani the keys. The engine started on the first try, and somebody pushed the garage door up. Mahanani drove out of the garage, turned left, and headed for the border.

There was an hour wait to get across. Not unusual. He wished he had a book to read. It would make the time go faster. He inched ahead in line and chose inspection gate ten as his lucky number for the night. It was fully dark by then. Maybe they would be tired, or sleepy, or their drug-sniffing dog might be off his feed.

At last he came up to the inspector, who asked him where he was born.

"Hilo, Hawaii," Mahanani said.

"Yeah? Hey, I've always wanted to get over there. Maybe next year. You have anything to declare?"

"Not a thing. Just a little cantina hopping."

The inspector nodded. His phone rang and he picked it up. He listened for a moment and said something. When he looked back at Mahanani, he frowned.

"Sorry to bother you, but your car has been selected for a random inspection at the secondary lane. Would you pull over there, please? Shouldn't take more than five minutes."

"Randomly selected?" Mahanani's voice was strange, his blood had thinned out to nothing, and his heart hammered in his chest. Maybe he should cut and run? Ram through the barrier and slam down the freeway at 130 miles an hour. Maybe . . .

"Shouldn't take more than five minutes, sir. Now if you would please drive over to the secondary inspection lane. We're a little stacked up tonight."

Mahanani nodded and touched the gas. He steered into a lane where a man motioned to him, and stopped when a second inspector signaled.

"Sir, would you step out of the car?"

Mahanani got out feeling pure terror grip him. Nothing in the SEALs had ever been so frightening. He wasn't sure that his legs would hold him up. To his surprise they did. He was busted. Shit, there was not a fucking thing he could do about it. He stood beside the hood and waited. A handler came up with a dog that sniffed around the sides of the car, then stopped at the back and barked twice.

"Could I have your car keys?" the inspector asked. Mahanani reached inside and took out the ignition key. He noticed there were five keys on the ring like most key rings had. The inspector thanked him and opened the trunk. The dog jumped in and sniffed around, then jumped out and continued on around the car.

"Sorry about that, sir. Queenie thought she smelled something in your trunk. Nothing there."

Mahanani felt like he was going to wet his pants. He took the keys and held them, not sure he could get back in the car and find the ignition. The dog made another circle of the Chevy. Then he and the handler moved to the car behind them. A second inspector had been in the backseat, crawling around, checking under the carpet flaps, and behind the seat and under the cushions. At last he slid out of the car and closed the door.

"You're all set, sir. Just a routine random stop. Sorry for your inconvenience."

Mahanani stepped into the Chevy, fumbled to get the ignition key in the slot, and started the car. An inspector waved him out into the traffic lane, and he accelerated gradually.

He couldn't believe it. He was out and home free. They had checked the car, the dog had done his thing, and they hadn't discovered the drugs. How had the Mexicans done it? He was going to watch them tear this car down and dig out the drugs. He had to know where it was and how they hid it. Most of all, he wanted to know how they had fooled the usually reliable nose of the drug-sniffing dog.

The trip into San Ysidro lasted ten minutes, even in the traffic, and when he pulled up to the garage there, the door was open. He drove in and saw the door drop behind him.

Harley leaned against the Coke machine working on a reefer. He was high already.

"Well, I see our man made it across. No problem?"

"Secondary inspection, the dog and everything. How did it get through?"

Harley chuckled, took a long drag on the reefer, and held the smoke in his lungs until he nearly passed out. Then he exhaled it and grinned.

"Oh, damn, what a good hit. How did you get through? Because this Chevy was clean as a bishop's daughter. There were no drugs in it. You ran a decoy. Yeah, you still get paid. Our contact at the border told us they were checking six-year-old Chevies tonight. Almost every one that comes through gets the secondary inspection. So we sent them a virgin."

Harley laughed. "Hey, Mahanani, you still look a little green around the gills there, boy. You have a real scare down in that secondary lane, I bet. How come you didn't try to make a run for it? We had a driver try that. Turned out he had a piece with him and shot at the guards, and they blew him away before he got twenty feet down the lane."

"Why didn't you tell me it was a dry run. I almost shit my pants down there when that damn dog came up. Then he barked and I knew I was down and out."

"Didn't tell you because it takes all the fun out of it. Hey, it cost me four hundred bucks. I'm entitled to a little fun for that kind of money. Now take your damn Buick and get out of here. If you're still in town in three days, give me a call at the number I gave you before. We should have another load for you, a real one. Now take off."

"Or you're gonna have me beat up again?"

"If I think it might help, damn right. Get out of here. And no gambling. Your water has been shut off."

Mahanani kicked the tire of the Chevy and swore under his breath as he walked out to his faithful Buick. He jumped in and spun gravel and dirt from the rear tires as he slammed out of the small lot to the street and headed for the freeway on-ramp.

"Damn them. Goddamn their fucking eyes. I've got to get them good. Now how in hell do I do that?"

He stopped talking out loud, mindful that there could be a bug in his car. They just might do that. His thoughts raced from one diabolical plan to the next as he drove carefully on his way home. He didn't need a car crash.

Could he do something that would work, that would get him out of his debt, and let him stay in SEALs? Also, he didn't want the drug ring hit men to come after him with Ingrams spitting lead. What he had figured out before still seemed the best. Tip off the DEA about the operation, and let them know both locations, and then have them be there when he brought in a load. At the same time they would have to take down Harley and Martillo out at the Casa Grande Casino east of town. It could be done. The DEA had the troops. Then they would find out if the casino knew anything about the drug mule train. He bet none of the operators or management there knew of this side game that Martillo had. Now, how to contact the DEA?

The good old telephone book. The group would be listed. He'd look up the number and make a call at night when nobody would be in the office. They would have a readout on the calling number, so he would use a public phone far from his house. Pacific Beach, say. Yeah.

At home he looked up the Drug Enforcement Administration number in San Diego in the blue-tinged government-listing pages before the business section of the phone book. It showed four numbers: main, registration information, southwest laboratory, and the San Diego County Integrated Task Force. He picked the last one and wrote it down, then checked it twice and put the slip of paper in his billfold.

Then Mahanani sat down at the kitchen table and wrote out exactly what he would say. He put it down, then made changes and wrote it again. The fourth time through he had it the way he wanted it. It went like this: "Hello, DEA, this is a concerned citizen. I know of a drug mule operation from Tijuana to San Ysidro. I got sucked into it. I can show you the whole operation if you grant me immunity and leave my name out of any report. It involves medium-sized shipments worth about a half-million but working on a regular basis. They are extremely hard to detect by border inspectors. If you're interested, leave a message for me at your number. My handle is the Reverend. I'll call back in two days and ask for the message."

Mahanani read it again, made one small change, and folded the paper and put it in his shirt pocket. When to make the call? He snorted. The sooner the better. He grabbed his car keys, his black cap, and headed for his Buick.

In the Pacific Beach section of San Diego, ten or twelve miles from his apartment, Mahanani found a phone booth where there wasn't a lot of traffic noise and put his coins in the machine. He dialed the number. The phone rang twice and someone picked it up.

"Good evening, this is the DEA county task force."

Mahanani hung up the phone and drove away from the phone. Not quite 2000. He'd try again later. Was the phone manned all night? He went to a movie, then at a different phone in downtown San Diego tried the DEA number again.

"Hello, this is the San Diego County Integrated Narcotic Task Force. No one is here right now, but your call is important to us. Please leave a message as long as you need to. We'll return your call as soon as possible. Leave your name and number after the tone."

The phone buzzed three times, and he took a deep breath and read his statement just as he had written it. Then he wiped sweat from his forehead, hung up the receiver, and hurried to his car. He got in and drove away. The seed was planted. Now he would see what happened.

When he got home, Mahanani saw the red message light blinking on his phone. He pushed the buttons and listened.

"Jack, this is your mother. You're never home. I never can get you when I call. Why don't you have a nice safe nine-to-five job like your brothers so I can call you the way I do them?

"Never mind. I want you to put on your calendar the date of the twenty-fourth. That's a Saturday afternoon three weeks away and I want you to come to our family luau. You missed last year again. Said you were in Europe or Africa or somewhere. You travel so much I can't keep up with you.

"Never mind. The whole family will be there. With your three brothers and their wives and children, we now have fifteen in our extended family. Two more are in the oven but not quite done yet. Now listen, I really want you to come. I have to show these mainlanders just what a real luau is. Yes, we'll have the buried pig this year, a fifty-pounder if I can find one that size. Your brother Mark has contacts with a farmer and he should be able to help us. So call back anytime. Call and tell your old mother that you'll be there. You come on the twenty-third and sleep over in your old room, and you can help us dig the pit. Your father isn't as well as he was last year. The arthritis is the problem.

"Oh, by the way. I'm inviting a nice girl I want you to meet. I know her from church and she's lovely, single, and sings in the choir. Beautiful alto voice and so pretty. I keep hoping that you'll find a girl and settle down and stop all this running around. I know it's dangerous and I really think you've done your share.

"Well, I hoped that you'd come home while I was talking, but I guess not. I just pray that you're not out there somewhere and getting shot at.

"You be good and take care, and be sure to come on the twenty-third to help me dig the pig pit. Good-bye. Now call me, Jack."

Mahanani started to call, then looked at the clock. The talk with his mom would take at least an hour. It was already almost 2300. They had an 0730 call in the morning. He felt drained. That secondary inspection lane at the border had almost wiped him out. He was sure that he had been busted big-time. He could imagine being led off in handcuffs, his mother notified, and him being in jail without bail for weeks.

It would have been the end of his Navy career and he'd be looking at seven to twenty in prison. He couldn't let that happen. The next run he took would be his last. And the end of the casino mule-skinning drug runs. He hoped. If something fouled up somewhere and the DEA didn't nab the whole operation, the ones left would kill him. He knew that.

Mahanani had a long shower and fell into bed. He figured he would never get to sleep. The next thing he knew the alarm went off at 0600.

NAVSPECWARGRUP-ONE
Coronado, California

Blake Murdock had set up a brutal training schedule. His platoon hadn't been really tested for some time and he wanted to see how everyone stood up. There had been no casualties in the Sierras, but that had been a relatively simple operation. If they had a really tough one, he wanted to be sure the men were ready, so they had to stay in shape and razor-sharp all the time.

They started at 0800 with a warm-up, a twelve-mile run from BUD/S to the end of the Coronado Strand and back. Then they checked out two IBSs and launched them through the surf. They got together beyond the breakers and Murdock called to them.

"We're going to shoot the surf, ride in on a breaker the way the surfers do. Just be damn sure you don't let the bow get down and dump us. Surf along the side of the wave if you want to, but then turn and come in with your bow straight for the beach. We'll do this three times. If we dump one of the boats, that squad has to do a makeup. Let's roll."

They headed the fifteen-foot-long Zodiac craft toward the beach. Jaybird watched the swells forming. He would be their caller. He let two swells surge up and go past them without breaking. The third one was larger, carried more water. He watched it, then shouted.

"Paddle hard, now, go, go. We can catch this baby. Flat out, faster, faster."

The small rubber boat surged forward with the six SEALs paddling. Then the powerful moon-driven surge of the swell peaked and began to break. The IBS was in exactly the right spot, and the nose tipped down just a bit as the water broke and the wave curled and hurled the Zodiac down the five-foot mountain of water. Jaybird guided the craft along the side of the wave for twenty feet using his paddle as a rudder. Then, just before the wall of salt water broke over them, Jaybird turned his paddle as a rudder and angled the rushing boat's bow away from the wave. The massive rush of sea-water pounded just behind them and smashed them forward toward the beach. The SEALs in Alpha Squad gave a hoorah, and surfed in on the surging wave of foam until the craft bottomed out on the sandy beach. The SEALs sat there slumped over their paddles a moment gathering their strength.

"Oh, yeah, that was a dandy," Jaybird said.

"Not bad," Murdock said. "Let's get out and launch and do it again."

Both squads made it through three runs at the beach without a wipeout, and they carried the 265-pound rubber ducks back to supply. After depositing the boats, the men formed up in squads in a column of ducks.

"Men, it's time to try out that new CQB down by our explosion pit. You've been watching it being built. It's eighty-percent underground, so there can't be the remotest chance that a round could get loose and go into the highway or out to sea. Absolutely fail-safe. Don't prove me wrong. I lobbied long and hard to get this CQB built here for better access, rather than driving all the way to Nyland. Weapons in hand, normal ammo load, let's chogie. Senior Chief, show us how and lead us out at six minutes to the mile. Let's move."

When they had come out of the water, Murdock had taken a new waterproof pouch off his combat harness and opened it. Inside lay a cell phone. He punched up the master chief's number and let it ring.

"Good morning, this is Navy SEALs Central, how may I help you?"

"Damn, you're grouchy this morning, Master Chief."

"Murdock, sir. How did the waterproofing work?"

"Must be okay, we're talking. What I want to know is

what happened to that order for the underwater personal radios that Motorola promised us?"

"Those sonar/radios that work submerged? Yes, we ordered enough for both your squads. Cost us a bundle, something like twenty-five hundred dollars each."

"If they work they'll be worth it. The demo on them worked fine, but that was two months ago."

"Takes a while, lad, to get things through the proper channels. This is the Navy, you know."

"I'm being reminded. Any fallout from the North Korean fiasco?"

"Lots of it. Our United Nations ambassador has demanded a vote of censure and damage to be paid by North Korea. The U.S. has stopped all food and humanitarian shipments to North Korea. Our seventh fleet is heading for waters off North Korea and it is on full wartime alert."

"About time. They've attacked South Korea without provocation, and now trashed the West Coast in a move to save face. We should cut them off from the rest of the world. Put a tight blockade on all their ports."

"Now, lad, Commander Murdock, sir. That's being a little easy on them. How about a twenty megaton nuke on Pyongyang?"

"True, they deserve it. They killed five people up there in the Sierras, a big bunch on that airliner, three hundred in San Francisco, and probably dozens more due to the blackout. I don't know what the hell else they have planned."

"We'll see in due course, sir. You sound short of breath, lad. Any breathing problems?"

"Just when I'm running ten miles an hour through the sand and trying to carry on a conversation. Do a trace on the order. I want to test out those underwater radios as soon as possible."

"Aye, aye, Commander. Consider them traced."

"I'm running out of breath. I'm out."

"Right, and remember, Commander, you're not twenty-two years old anymore."

Murdock liked the new kill house. It was made of four-by-twelve planks for the walls and the ceiling, with two feet of dirt and sand on top. No round could possibly penetrate

four inches of Douglas fir. It had been dug out so all but the
roof was underground. Ramps led to the front and back
doors. Inside there were four small rooms, each set up with
electronic targets, terrorists, hostages, innocents, and SEALs.
The targets popped up electronically from pressure pads on
the plank floor. The computer had programmed more than
fifty thousand combinations of targets so no run-through was
ever like any other.

Murdock took his turn at the close-quarters-battle house
with Jaybird. They missed a terr in the second room, and
both were shot according to the computer readout. They finished the course, and Jaybird had shot only one hostage. No
scores were kept.

Murdock watched the other men go in, and checked them
when they came out. The consensus was that the new house
was good and would serve them well without the long drive.

"Be good to use this once a week," Ed DeWitt said. "Keep
us sharp."

Murdock's cell phone sang a small tune. He pulled it from
his combat vest and flipped up the cover.

"Murdock."

"Lad, we're in business again. The Old Man wants to see
you pronto. He's sending a Humvee for you and DeWitt. Get
your men back to their quarters and have them ready to
travel. Not sure how many will be going, but we should be
prepared. The Humvee just motored down the highway. He'll
cut through the sand and meet you on the high tide mark."

"What's up?"

"His Lordship didn't confide in me. You know the routine.
It's something that needs to be done quickly, and we get the
call. Oh, speaking of calls, there was one from Washington,
D.C., but she said she would call you tonight. You probably
know who it was."

"Probably, Master Chief. We'll meet the Humvee on the
side of the highway. Be faster that way. Out."

Murdock yelled at DeWitt and Senior Chief Sadler. He
told them what was up. Then he and DeWitt walked through
the soft sand up to the fence and through to the state highway
that connected Imperial Beach with Coronado. Sadler pulled

the men together and began a quick march back to their quarters.

"What in hell?" DeWitt asked.

"Don't know," Murdock said. "I've got a hunch we haven't heard the last of the sneaky North Koreans. This could be something more about them."

21

Commander Dean Masciareli looked up as Murdock and DeWitt entered his office. They both braced at attention.

"At ease," he said. "I just received an order through channels to activate some of the platoon. You may not have heard, but there have been ten forest fires in Oregon and Washington through the Cascade Mountains. All of incendiary origin. One eyewitness to one of the fires has reported that a pair of Orientals wearing cammies and backpacks and carrying rifles started a fire, then hurried away and vanished into the woods. The backpackers said the Orientals didn't see them."

"Are the fires under control?" DeWitt asked.

"Four of them have been put out. Two are out of control and burning in valuable timber. There's been another sighting, and now the National Forestry officials say they have reports of four teams of arsonists loose and on foot that they want to track. They are limited as to manpower, and want some help. Frankly, they want eight men who are expert trackers who can deal with the arsonists if and when they are run down."

"That's where we come in?" Murdock asked.

"Right. I want each of you to pick the three best trackers in your squads and be ready to shove off in thirty minutes. Go light on the ammo, take all of your Bull Pups for long-range work, and be in the parking lot in thirty. That's all. You're dismissed."

The two officers did snappy about-faces and hurried out the door.

"Tracking arsonists?" DeWitt asked as they hurried back to the platoon area.

"Better than a sharp stick in the eye, but not much," Murdock said. "I'm taking Lam, Jaybird, and Bradford. You?"

"I'm thinking. Franklin, Mahanani, and Fernandez. Eight men, but we only have seven Bull Pups."

"Have the other man bring an MP-5. We might need it."

Twenty-five minutes later the eight SEALs, in fresh cammies and dry floppy hats, waited on the parking lot for the bus. They wore their combat vests with the usual gear and carried one GPS device and a SATCOM.

The Gulfstream II that had brought them back from Sacramento had been serviced and restocked and waited for them at North Island. The crew chief was a cute little dark-haired second-class petty officer who checked their seat belts and made sure their gear was stowed safely.

"Good morning, SEALs. You may not know where we're headed. Our pilot tells me he has flight orders to take you to Portland International Airport up in Oregon. From there you'll go by CH-46 to the nearest sighting and get to work."

"Are we all on the same trail?" DeWitt asked.

"That I don't know. Now, settle down, we have some good Navy chow coming for you." She grinned. "Not true. We do have some first-class flight trays that we're waiting for. They are three minutes late, but the pilot says he won't leave until the chow gets here. There will be one meal."

"Flight time?" Murdock asked.

"Commander, that will be about two hours. We're on maximum cruise of five-oh-five miles an hour and the distance is a thousand and ninety miles. Make it two hours and fifteen minutes." She looked at the front of the craft. "Good, the food has arrived. We'll be taking off in five minutes."

She vanished into the front cabin.

"I could get used to this first-class living," Jaybird said.

"The crew chief is not included on the menu," Mahanani said.

"Don't throw boiling pineapple juice on a man's dreams, Hawaiian beach boy."

Two hours later they landed in Portland, and were rushed to a pair of waiting CH-46's with National Forestry markings.

"Two different locations," DeWitt said.

Murdock conferred with a Forestry pilot, then motioned DeWitt and his men into one chopper. He and his Alpha Squad men boarded the other one. The doors closed and both birds took off at the same time. At once they flew in different directions.

Murdock went to the cabin and talked with the pilot.

"Orders are to take you into the Cascades just north of Government Camp," said the pilot. "Lots of good timber up in there. Two fires have been attacked and put out, but there is another one burning and the arsonists are moving slowly east. We hope to land you in front of them so you can net them as they come through."

"Where does the tracking come in?" Murdock asked, talking loudly over the constant roar of the engine and the whupping of the rotor blades.

"If you miss them in the net, you find their tracks and hunt them down. I understand you're good at that."

"We've done some tracking work. How long till we hit the LZ?"

"Fifteen minutes. Not far, but damn rugged territory."

"How high is it in there?"

"You'll be just east of Mt. Hood, which is almost twelve thousand feet. Most of the area you'll be in is around five to six thousand. No snow this time of year, but it gets nippy at night."

Murdock went to the back of the chopper and filled in his three men. He felt naked with only half his squad. If they were lucky there would be no gunfire and it could be wrapped up quickly. Finding a couple of firebugs should be a snap.

The crew chief came back wearing a frown. "Commander, we've just had word that these arsonists you're looking for have at least one rifle and maybe two. They fired on some backpackers who happened past. No one was hit, but the packers got out of that area in a rush. They had a radio and gave the warning. Their position seems to be west of where we have our LZ and the Koreans are moving east."

"Thanks. How long until we hit the LZ?"

"Maybe five minutes. I'm opening one side door. That enough?"

Murdock nodded, and the second Forestry man unlatched and opened the right-hand side door.

Murdock motioned for the men to stand, and they quickly checked each other's equipment. Then they picked up their weapons and stood near the door watching the green on green of the Oregon forest passing by below. Then the chopper took a sudden diving slant to the left, straightened out, and moved slowly ahead. Then the nose came up and the craft settled the last two feet to the turf. The SEALs jumped out of the bird and ran into the woods thirty yards away. The helicopter lifted off and darted back the way it had come.

The SEALs stopped just inside the cover and looked at each other. "What the hell are we supposed to do now?" Jaybird asked.

"Find the bastards," Lam said. "First we need to get to some high ground where we can watch the countryside to the west."

"How we going to see anything with the thick forest cover?" Bradford asked. "These damn Douglas fir, spruce, and cedar are so close together they make a canopy over the ground. Only place we can see through them is where they burned off or were logged over."

Murdock saw a small ridge to the left, and he led the men that way. "So we watch the open spaces. If they're smart or tired, that's where they'll hike. The path of least resistance."

When they made it up the ridge, they found there were six different areas they could see to the west that would provide any hiker with an easier trail than jamming through the brush.

"We watch them," Murdock said. He'd made sure each of the men had a pair of binoculars. The men sat down in the grass and wildflowers and began watching their assigned areas.

"I've got some movement just at the edge of that little

meadow down there. Second from the top," Lam said.

"Yeah, I have it," Bradford said. He paused. "Jeez, look at that, a white-tail doe and a fawn. Sure wish this was deer season."

"Speaking of venison for supper, how many MREs do we have?" Jaybird asked. "I only brought three. We could be out here for days."

"We're only ten miles ahead of the last known fire," Murdock said. "If these guys are any good, they'll do ten miles along these ridges and start another fire."

"What if they start one before then and we see the smoke?"

"We radio the Forestry people on TAC Four and report it. Then we hunker down and go meet the firebugs who must be hightailing it toward us."

Lam scowled and shook his head. "Skipper, it seems like we're making a lot of assumptions. We're planning on what these guys are going to do, and we don't know if they will do any of the four or five things we hope they will do."

"So we sit and wait and watch." Murdock moved his sight line higher. "Hold it. About two fingers over that last open spot, is that smoke?"

"Hell, yes, Skipper," Jaybird chorused. "You get a merit badge for fire-fighting. They expect us to go down there and put out the fire?"

"Not until we report it. Bradford, get it in gear."

Bradford unhooked the eleven-pound SATCOM radio from his back and set up the small dish antenna. He turned it until he picked up the satellite, and then snapped on the switches and dials and gave the handset to Murdock.

"Ready to rumble, Commander."

"Forestry Four, this is Murdock. Over." There was no response. Bradford checked the SATCOM antenna position. He made a small adjustment.

"Forestry Four, this is Murdock. Over."

"Yes, Murdock we hear you. Over."

"We have a smoke. It's almost on a direct line west of us from where the chopper set us down. You have that position."

"Roger that, Murdock how far on that heading?"

"How far, Lam?" Murdock asked.

"Three miles, three and a half."

"Three to three and a half miles, Forestry Four."

"Roger, we're on it with a tanker and a jump crew. We expect the fire-starters to move toward you on that same heading. Over."

"Right, Forestry. We're about ready to go and see if we can meet these gents. Over."

"Extreme caution. They are armed."

"Thanks, Forestry Four. We've got a bit of firepower ourselves. We'll keep you informed. Murdock out."

Bradford turned off the set, folded up the antenna, and stashed it with the SATCOM.

"Let's figure their best route this direction from that smoke, then get down from here and sit and wait for them."

"Moving is good," Bradford said. "My ass was getting sore sitting on that hard ground."

Lam studied the land between them and the smoke. It seemed to come up from behind a ridge about three over. "Could be another ridge in there, but my guess is they would go up the valley where they set the fire, then over the ridge when it petered out and swing back west again."

"Another assumption," Jaybird said.

"That's the best we have," Murdock said. "Lam, we go down to the second ridge from the fire and watch over the top and see where they show up?"

"About the size of it. Second ridge will give us some operating time."

"Got to thinking about the Bull Pup," Bradford said. "If they stick to the trees, an airburst might not be much good. Too many big fir trees to absorb the shrapnel. If they do take the easy route out in the open, the laser might be the ticket." Murdock put them on a fast pace down the slope and up the other side, then down another one and up. They paused on top as they all slithered up to the ridgeline and looked over it down into the third valley.

"No movement," Lam said.

"Not time enough for them to get here," Jaybird said.

"Not many open spots down there for them to utilize either," Murdock said. "So we wait."

Twenty minutes later, Jaybird was the first to see the

movement. "Yeah, I got something. About twenty degrees right of that old lightning-hit snag halfway up the slope."

"Got it," Lam said. He refined the focus on his glasses. "Could be another deer going through the brush," he said.

"Or some gook crashing brush in Pyongyang City Park chasing some slant-eyed little beauty," Bradford said.

All four binoculars zeroed in on the spot.

"More movement to the right," Murdock said. "Could be working toward that rocky open spot more to the right."

They waited. Then Bradford grinned. "Be damned. Two of them, two guys in cammies or I'm a horntailed, fucking cow. Look at them, like they didn't have a worry in the world."

"How far, Lam?" Murdock asked.

"Two thousand yards, maybe more. They just look closer."

"I was figuring about twenty-five hundred. Too far for a Bull Pup shot. Anybody guess where they are headed?"

Jaybird studied the landscape in front of the pair. "They're on the side of that ridge. They go down it to that small valley, work it toward us to get back on their east heading. My guess is they cross the valley in the open and work toward us at about a forty-five-degree angle, and climb the ridge one or two down in front."

"There's that one more small ridge down there between us and that valley," Lam said.

"Oh, yeah. Missed it." Jaybird scowled. "So hey, we just wait until they get down the second one and come up this little one. Then they'll be in range of the Pups."

"If we can catch them away from the trees," Murdock said. "It might not be that easy."

They waited.

"I'm taking up the harmonica," Jaybird said. "No kidding. It's a great little instrument. Heard a guy in an improv club the other night, and he was great. They don't cost much, and I can get a book and learn myself."

"Keep it in the woodshed while you're learning," Bradford said. "My brother tried to learn. Sounded like a damned train whistle that was out of whack."

"Hey, man. I say I'm gonna do something, I'm gonna do

it. Fact is, I bought an instrument couple of nights ago and I've been practicing."

"Just so you didn't bring it with you," Lam said. "We're on a quiet watch here."

A soft wail of four notes on a harmonica answered him.

"Just a test," Jaybird said. "No, I'm not going to practice. I do that alone."

"How long until our friends push over that ridgeline down there?" Murdock asked.

"Another twenty," Lam said. "That's tough going, up and down that way, and they must be bushed."

"How far is that ridge, Jaybird?" Murdock asked.

"Eight hundred yards. Hey, damn, it's in range for a laser, and no real trees up on top. Barren as an old maid's womb."

"My guess was seven-fifty, so we're good. Lam and Jaybird, take the first shots as soon as they come all the way over the ridge. Bradford and I will ride herd. If they don't go down, or scramble for cover, it's our turn. All lasers."

They settled in and waited. All with rounds in the chambers, the safeties off, and sweat starting to ooze out of their foreheads.

"Waiting is always the toughest," Bradford said.

"Not for me," Jaybird said. "I can catch a little nap and wake up refreshed and ready to nail these bastards."

"Look, there's the smoke," Lam said. "Now it's up where we can see it again." A moment later they heard an airplane, and then saw a big tanker lumbering over the ridges. Evidently the pilot spotted the smoke, climbed, and did a series of turns, and then came down at a flat angle and vanished behind a ridge. Seconds later he zoomed up from the other end of the ridge.

"Borate," Murdock said. "Borate bombers. It's a red powder that is a fire-retardant. Things just don't burn where it falls. Washes away in the winter and causes no harm."

"Can they put out a fire that way, without a ground crew?" Jaybird asked.

"If the fire is caught early, and they get lucky. A ground crew will go in and mop it up, but this way they can hit it while it's small. Might take a ground crew six, eight hours to find the flames. And by then half the hill would be on fire."

"Those gooks have used up their twenty minutes," Lam said. "They must be getting tired."

"Hope they don't flake out for a nap," Jaybird said.

"I've got movement midway along that second ridge," Murdock said. The rest saw them then, the two men in cammies, who came to the top of the ridge and stood there a moment.

Two shots blasted from the Bull Pups, 20mm rounds lasered, and were on their way.

"I've got the right-hand guy," Murdock said.

The airbursts exploded in a cracking roar as the big rounds finished their mandatory rotations and went off. Murdock watched his right-hand man through the scope. He had the sights set on him as he sagged, tried to run, doubled over, and fell. He didn't move.

Bradford's man looked around and limped toward the ridgeline. Bradford's weapon went off just before the North Korean got to the ridge top and safety. The big round exploded at his feet, blasting a hundred shards of hot steel into his body, taking off half his face and slamming him backward. He fell half over the ridge with only his feet and legs visible.

"Splash two," Jaybird said.

"Bradford, break out the SATCOM," Murdock said. "Jaybird, use the GPS and have our coordinates ready."

Forestry Four came on the SATCOM on the first call.

"Forestry, we have a splash two of the firebugs. Down and out. They are on a ridge in the open about eight hundred yards from our coordinates on a near-westerly heading." He gave the radioman their coordinates from the GPS.

"Well done, Murdock. We'll have a chopper on its way to pick you up in ten. Take it about twenty to find you. Do you have a good LZ?"

"Tell the crew chief to drop a ladder and pick us off the ridge. We do ladder pickups all the time."

"The pilot won't like the air currents around a ridge, Commander. Isn't there a flat LZ around there?"

"Not without trees all over it. We'll do the ladder pickup out the rear hatch."

"I'll tell him. Commander, we just have a new fire sighted. It's about ten miles from you along a road. It looks like one of the team of North Korean fire-starters may have hijacked a car. When the pilot picks you up, we'll try to get you in front of traffic along that road. It's a gravel-surface secondary, will show a dust trail, and not many cars in there this time of year. We'll keep you informed. We'll contact you through the chopper pilot when you're airborne. Leave your SATCOM on this TAC in case we have a change in plans. Four out."

"Hot damn, a car chase," Jaybird said. "Just what we need to brighten our day."

"What you need to brighten your day is one of my marine oil paintings," Bradford said. "I've got just the one for your den."

"I don't have a den."

"For your living room."

"Don't need no damn painting."

"Thought you might like it. It's a lonesome pelican sitting on a piling staring at a charter fishing boat just pulling in."

"Save me the trouble."

"How is the new art group doing at the studio?" Murdock asked.

Bradford shrugged. "We're paying the rent, and nobody is faking old masters."

"The trial come yet?"

"Nope, her lawyer got it put off again. She's out on bail. I fully expect her to skip out and be gone."

"Hey, did any of you guys see rifles with that pair?" Jaybird asked. "I didn't notice any long guns, no guns at all."

Murdock scanned the scene with his Bull Pup scope. "No weapons show on this side of the ridge. They are in cammies. We'll let the Forestry people and the local coroner figure it out."

The SATCOM speaker came back on. "Murdock, this is Forestry Four. The chopper pilot is from the National Forest Air. He says his orders specifically prohibit any in-air pickups. You'll have to find a flat LZ where the pilot can land. Do you copy?"

"Copy that, Forestry Four," Murdock said. Now where in hell could they find a level LZ up in these ridges?

22

Jaybird snorted. "Chickenshit Forestry pilot. Hell, how far are we from where we landed?"

"About a mile and three ridges," Lam said.

"Probably the closest good LZ we'll find," Murdock said. "Let's haul ass back there and I'll tell Four where we are."

It took them more than a half an hour to climb the ridges, slide down the slopes, and find the small meadow where they had landed before.

Murdock told Forestry Four where they were, and within ten minutes the bird circled and came in for an easy landing. The pilot talked to Murdock.

"Hey, sorry about the change in plans. I've never done a rope pickup in my life. We don't even have the rope ladders on here like you SEALs use. I've seen it done, but we just don't do it. Then too, the wind gusts and currents around a ridgeline are murder to try to hover over. Best this way. Everybody gets to go right on drawing his regular paycheck."

"No sweat. You know where we're going?"

"Right. About six or seven miles to a rugged little dirt trail of a road. Not used much, so any rig on it will be suspect."

"Let's go find them," Murdock said.

The bird took off and lifted over the green Oregon forest, and then angled more east until the pilot found the landmark he wanted. Murdock was in the cabin.

"There's the road," said the pilot. "Open only in the summer."

"No cars."

"Never are many. Let's see if we can find our North Korean brethren." They raced along over the road at two hundred feet. It wound around a mountain, lifted up a long narrow valley, and then over a low pass and down the other side. They both saw the dust trail at the same time.

"Got something," the pilot said. He slanted down to a hundred feet and came up on the slow-moving car quickly, flashed over him, and did a climbing turn and hovered, as Murdock and the pilot watched the car. It slowed, stopped, and a man jumped out with a long gun. The pilot pivoted and raced away, moving from side to side, and then did a sweeping turn.

No shots hit the chopper, and the pilot looked relieved.

"Could be our boys," Murdock said. "Curve in the road ahead and a small hill. Put us down behind it where they can't see us, and we'll stage a surprise party."

The pilot nodded, and four minutes later they were on the ground and the pilot had lifted off and raced away from the spot. The road curved around the small hill and came straight toward them. Lots of cover and concealment. The SEALs split, two on each side of the road.

"We'll let him show his colors first," Murdock said. "Lam, when the rig is fifty feet from you, accidentally show yourself from behind that fir. Move out and then dart back and see if you can draw a shot."

"Damn target practice again, and I'm the target," Lam said.

"You love it, quit bitching," Jaybird said.

The men in the car could see none of the SEALs as it rounded the curve and came straight ahead. Murdock figured it was doing about thirty miles an hour on the rough gravel road. The rig was an older Toyota. Murdock could see two heads in the car, but couldn't make out faces.

At the right time, Lam stumbled out from his tree, then looked at the car and jolted back. A shot sounded from the car, and Murdock figured it was from a pistol. The round came nowhere near Lam. Murdock put a 5.56 round through the right front tire, blowing it out and bringing the car to a stop. Nobody in the car moved, and Murdock guessed the men were talking over their options. The heads had vanished below the dashboard.

To speed their decision, Murdock blew out the other front

tire. A moment later the doors opened and a man came out on each side of the car. Both had their hands up, but each man still held a rifle. Jaybird zeroed in and fired, and hit the man on his side of the car in the thigh, jolting him backward against the Toyota, where he dropped to the ground, his rifle lost in his fall.

The other man darted for the woods, five yards away. Hot lead splashed all around him, and one round clipped his flailing right arm as he pounded for the brush. A moment later he had vanished.

"Your side, Lam, go get him," Murdock ordered on the Motorola. Lam was twenty yards from the man's entry point. He went into the brush where he was, and ten feet inside the timber he paused and listened. He heard the Korean crashing brush to the left. He ran that way, then paused and listened again. The sounds were softer then. Lam spurted ahead, determined not to lose the man. This time he ran flat out through the woods, dodging trees and brush, aiming at the last sound position. Only when he had covered fifty yards did he stop.

Yes, more crashing brush sounds and much closer now. Lam ran ahead again, quickly, not trying to be quiet. He had to run down the man or the Korean would vanish in the heavy timber. Lam adjusted his route a little. The Korean was charging along the side of the valley about fifty yards from the road. Where was he going? The Korean had a rifle. Lam didn't forget that. He stopped and listened again. Still going. Running. How far could this guy run?

The next time Lam stopped to listen, he noticed they were closer to the road, barely in the fringes of the timber. Now as he listened, he could hear no brush crashing. The Korean had stopped. Lam used the Motorola. "Skipper, I'm still with the K. He's near the road and stopped. I don't know what he has in mind, but I can wait him out. My guess he's about thirty, forty yards ahead of me and not moving. I'll keep you posted. Out."

Lam dropped to one knee and stared ahead. He could see the road, and up here it didn't look like a car had been over it in months. There were grass and weeds growing in the center of the lane between where the car wheels rolled. This was wait time. He settled down against a tree and watched ahead where he figured the Korean had to be. He had a hunch about this one. He was smarter than the other one, and wouldn't be easy to sneak up on. So Lam would wait.

Fifteen minutes later he stretched and moved enough to relieve the tired muscles. At first he didn't notice it. Then the hum of a motor came through plainly. A plane or a car? He edged toward the road and saw the dust plume a mile away. The rig was coming this way. Another car on this backwoods roadway? It could even be a car hijacked by another team of Korean firebugs.

Lam found a good OP and edged behind a tree so he could see the road and the trees on both sides. There was no movement by the Korean ahead. How far ahead? Lam brought up the Bull Pup and switched it to 5.56 and waited.

The car came closer. Would the Korean shoot into it to stop it and then try to hijack it? To do that he'd have to leave the woods and expose himself to Lam's rifle. Lam waited. The car seemed to be coming slowly, kicking up dust on the rough gravel road, but not making much speed.

Lam heard movement ahead, small sounds as if the Korean was trying to be silent. He scanned the brush and trees in front of him, but could not see anyone. The sounds stopped.

The car was much closer now, only a hundred yards down the road. It kept coming at the same slow speed.

The crack of a heavy rifle startled Lam, and he jerked his head around to look at the car. A front tire blew out and the car stopped quickly, forty yards down the road from Lam's position.

"You will leave the car at once," a voice bellowed from the brush. Two men in the car got out, frowning.

"Who the hell are you?" the man called.

Another rifle shot, and the questioner slammed backward, hit the side of the car, and fell to the ground. He didn't move.

"Leave the car and run back the way you came," the same voice called with a faint tinge of an accent. The second man looked at his downed companion, then took off running as fast as he could down the gravel road away from death.

Lam waited. Nothing happened for two or three minutes that seemed like a half hour. Then a form lifted from the brush twenty yards ahead and rushed toward the car. He wore cammies and a floppy hat, and carried a rifle. Lam tracked him, then sent a three-round burst of hot lead at him. He saw two of the slugs hit the man, one in the thigh and one in the stomach. The man lurched forward, turned, and tried to return fire, but stumbled and sprawled on the ground, his long rifle trapped under his body. Lam fired twice more on each side of the man, then ran into the road.

"Keep your hands in the open or you're one fucking dead Korean," Lam brayed. The man tried to sit up, pushed with one hand on the roadway, then whipped around his other hand with a pistol in it.

Lam shot him five times, three in the chest and two rounds jolting through his face and into his brain. Lam walked up slowly and looked at the two men. He kicked the pistol out of the Korean's reach, then checked the civilian. He was dead. Lam looked in the car. Two suitcases in the backseat and a bunch of camping gear and a plastic cooler. The keys were in the ignition, which had been turned off. Lam sat in the car and flipped down his Motorola mike.

"Erase that second firebug. He killed a kid trying to take over his car. Another good guy ran down the road."

"See if the Korean has any papers, orders, addresses, money, anything," Murdock said.

"Roger."

Lam went through the firebug's pockets, and found only waterproof matches, three new one-hundred-dollar bills, and two time-delay detonators. He told Murdock.

"Figures. Take a hike up the road and I'll call in the chopper. Then we'll see if we can find that other civilian. Did the shots disable the car?"

"Just blew out one tire. If the kid has a spare he's in business."

"Take your time getting here. No rush. The chopper probably won't be here for a half hour, Forestry Four said."

"That's a roger, see you in about twenty."

Fifteen miles to the west of where Murdock waited for the chopper, Lieutenant Ed DeWitt looked down on the smoke that billowed below. It was still small, and a dozen smoke jumpers had dropped from the sky to try to put it out before it ravaged this foothill to the soaring peak of Mt. Hood.

"How do we know which way the firebugs went when they left the fire?" DeWitt asked. The pilot heard the shouted words and shook his head.

"This pair has been moving west, not east like the others. Maybe they just got confused. The fire was reported an hour ago. We figure the Koreans have traveled about two miles in the heavy timber. It's slow going down there. If they keep on their track, they'll run right into Mt. Hood. My guess is that they will swing to the north to go around the steeper slopes. Stay in the foothills."

Any roads in here?"

"Damn few. Over a few miles is Oregon Highway 35, which goes from Government Camp to Hood River on the Columbia. Not much else. We're eight, ten miles from that highway."

"So where are you dropping us off."

"Wherever you say."

"So we have a couple hundred thousand acres and the bad guys could be anywhere. Not much of a chance. Can you talk to Forestry Radio?"

"Yes." He handed DeWitt the headset and a mike. "Just push the button and call for Forestry Four."

A moment later DeWitt had the head man on the radio.

"We don't have a clue where to set down. Do you know for sure that this team went west and not east?"

"We think so. A light plane reported the fire, and the pilot said he saw two men in cammies running to the west through an old burn."

"Okay, Four. We'll set down near the burn and try to find some tracks. Out."

The pilot did a turn and went back the way they had come. They hit the smoke, and then DeWitt saw the burned-over area. It wasn't all that big. To one side of it was a bulldozed area that had probably been used as a landing zone and head-quarters for firefighters.

"You have a radio?" the pilot asked DeWitt.

"A SATCOM. We can get Forestry Four on TAC Four."

The bird touched down, and DeWitt and his team jumped

to the ground and ran out of the rotor wash. When the chopper had taken off, DeWitt told the men all he knew about their target.

"We try to pick up some tracks in the burn and follow them."

"Let's go to the far side of the burn and check along the edge of it for tracks," Franklin said. DeWitt nodded and they moved that direction. They walked through the edge of the burn toward the west, and DeWitt was surprised at the new growth that had already begun to show where less than a year ago a furious forest fire had burned everything in its path. At the far side of the burn they worked the edges critically. Twice they found deer tracks, and places where birds had nested. Then Mahanani yelped.

"Hey, look at these. Fresh damn boot tracks, a pair of them with the toes pointing east. Looks like they're in a rush. See how the heels are pressed in hard where they landed, and then the toes dig in and kick out some dirt and ash to the rear when they push off hard with their toes."

"Franklin, you're my best tracker. Lead out, let's see if we can follow these puppies."

Franklin moved to the edge of the burn and a few steps into the timber, and stopped. He kept looking for boot impressions, but there were none. Then he remembered what Lam had shown him one day about tracking. He spotted a clump of weeds that had only partly lifted up from where a boot had mashed them down. Now he looked ahead and could see a pattern to the plants where they had been disturbed.

Under a huge oak tree he spotted actual boot impressions in the heavy leaf mold. Farther on he caught where a branch had been broken off, and where leaves had been stripped off a limb. Franklin held up his hand, and the four men stopped and listened.

Nothing.

They moved on. Twice Franklin lost the track. He circled out twenty yards from his last sign and found new tracks heading in the same direction. They moved along the side of a small valley, just inside the tree line. Then Franklin stopped and wrinkled his nose.

"Wood smoke," he said. "Either there's a cabin up here with a fireplace, or our boys have started another fire." He took off running through the fringe of trees and into the valley, which showed only a little brush. Ahead not a quarter of a mile they all saw a small plume of smoke.

They ran faster then, and at last had to stop. Franklin struggled forward at a walk, his Bull Pup down and ready. At the end of the little valley he went up a sharp slope, and when he looked over the top he saw the smoke.

Two men stood near the campfire-sized blaze, and they were pushing it into the brush and trees. Both wore cammies and had long guns. Without hesitation Franklin brought up the Bull Pup, lasered directly on the two men, and fired. The round exploded on a tree just in front of the two men, and one went down screaming. The other one darted behind a tree evidently unhurt.

DeWitt caught up with Franklin, saw the fire and the man down, and the two plunged down the slope toward the fire fifty yards ahead. They raced to the blaze, kicked what they could away from the brush, and stomped out the rest. Both were blackened with soot and smoke when Mahanani and Fernandez hurried up and finished off the fire-fighting duties.

"He went that way," Franklin said, motioning ahead and up the side of a hill. Before the words were out of his mouth, a rifle bullet slapped into a tree a foot from his head and the SEALs dove behind protection.

"I'm on him," Mahanani said, and darted to the side into some brush and then up the slope. He had no idea how to track a man. He'd been watching Lam and now Franklin, but still he wasn't sure. Scuff marks he could find, and broken branches. He'd watch for movement of brush. He gained the top of the hill without getting shot, and peered over the crest.

Nothing but green Oregon timber below and the start of a small stream. He took it by areas, watching one section at a time. Yes, there. Just to the right of the creek, brush moved where someone or some animal had gone through. He put a 20mm round into the brush and as soon as the round fired, he charged down the slope toward the target. He didn't go gracefully or without noise. He crashed brush and dodged trees and came to the spot he had fired at quickly. He found a riddled clump of brush, a tree with some bark blown off, and on the ground some spots of blood.

Now he studied the ground carefully. It was full of grass and weeds and young fir trees a foot high. Twice he found drops of blood and the trail led downstream. Again he crashed forward, unmindful of the danger or the wisdom of such a move. He just wanted to catch up with the little guy and nail his hide to the wall.

The creek took a jog to the right, and around that bend he came to a more open area where the stream picked up water and had carved out a small valley. Near the end of it he saw the man limping along. Smoothly, Mahanani lifted the Pup and lasered a round on the man. The enemy was about seventy-five yards downstream, and the round went off almost at the same time as the report of the weapon.

The North Korean firebug had just taken a step forward. He never completed it. His foot hit the dirt as more than a dozen shards of shrapnel from the 20mm round blasted into his head and shoulders after detonating twenty feet above him. He crumpled to the ground.

Mahanani dropped to his knees and wiped sweat from his forehead. He flipped down the Motorola mike from where it had rotated against his floppy hat.

"Now hear this," Mahanani said. "The second little bastard is now communing with his ancestors. Scratch the other half of this firebug team."

"Copy that," DeWitt said. "Make your way back to where we dropped the first one. We're still making sure that this fire is completely out. We'll wind up the SATCOM and see if we can get a lift out of this forest wonderland."

"Where are they gonna land?" Mahanani asked.

"Probably back at the same spot where they dropped us off. We'll move that way after you get here."

"I'm coming. Not even bothering with getting this guy's weapon as a souvenir."

DeWitt had Fernandez set up the SATCOM. It took three tries before he got the small fold-out dish antenna positioned right so it looked through the trees to find the satellite. On the fourth call they made it to Forestry Four.

"Yes, Four. This is DeWitt. You can cross out that two-man team in here by the old burn where you dropped us. They are down and out. They started another fire, but we got there in time to snuff it as well."

"DeWitt, good work. The State Police nailed one pair of firebugs and a sheriff's detail grabbed another pair. We think that's all of them. No more assignments. You can fly back to Portland now."

"Have the chopper pilot pick us up where he dropped us off by the old burn," DeWitt said.

"Copy that, DeWitt, by the old burn. Should be there in about thirty."

Fernandez turned off the set, folded up the dish antenna, stowed it with the SATCOM, and they moved out toward the burn area.

"Maybe two miles," Mahanani said. "Then I'm due for one of Jaybird's little naps."

It was forty-five minutes before the chopper arrived to pick them up, but DeWitt didn't mind. It gave him time to think about this whole operation. What in hell were the North Koreans trying to do besides cause a little hell? Saving face? How could you save face when your teams were smashed and crushed and captured? He'd never understand the Oriental mind, but he had to keep trying.

Murdock and his men waited at the Portland airport for DeWitt to fly in. The same business jet that had brought them to Portland was serviced and ready to go. The SEALs climbed on board and settled into the airliner seats.

"Now this is more in keeping with my station in life," Jaybird said as he leaned back in the soft seat.

"Your train station just went out of business, chatterbox," Mahanani said. "Now don't bother me while I take a Jaybird kind of nap."

"The big kid learns fast," Jaybird said, and closed his eyes.

Murdock talked with the pilot. In two and a half hours they would be home. Not a bad afternoon's work. He wondered if the North Koreans were done. They had inflicted a lot of damage, killed over two hundred people, set fires, blown up an airliner, caused a horrendous blackout in the Western states that must have cost business firms billions of dollars in lost revenue and services. They'd sent missiles into

San Francisco and hijacked a luxury liner. Besides that, they'd captured and almost made off with the President of the United States. How could they have done all of this? Who coordinated the whole thing and where did they operate from? Not from the North Korean frigate. It was just a player in the game, not the leader.

They had to have a GHQ somewhere. He'd have to think on that. It would be good to be home. Maybe Ardith would drop in. He dozed off thinking about her. Now there was a woman. Oh, yeah. He hoped she'd show up again in San Diego real soon.

23

It was dark when they landed at North Island and went by
van to their quarters on the strand. The men cleaned their
weapons, reloaded their combat vests with the usual ammo
and supplies, and checked out over the Quarter Deck.

Murdock and DeWitt sat in the small office, not quite
ready to give it up for the day.

"Where in hell did these Koreans come from?" DeWitt
asked. "Been wondering if they might have arrived by commercial air. They did a lot of planning for this series of
strikes."

"Been bugging me too, DeWitt. They must have a control
group somewhere, a headquarters. We better find it and wipe
it out or we could have these hit-and-run attacks for months."

Murdock looked at his second in command. "You have a
minute?"

"Sure. Milly doesn't know when to expect me."

"DeWitt, the Navy is wasting your talent here in my platoon. You should have a platoon of your own. I'm putting a
recommendation to Masciareli tomorrow that you get the
next platoon opening here in GRUP-ONE."

Ed frowned slightly. "You don't want me around?"

"I depend on you too much, and you take up the slack.
You deserve a platoon of your own."

"Yeah, and if and when I got it, I'd be out of the loop
with this action platoon. Wouldn't get in on all of the juicy
assignments."

"Sure, and you wouldn't get shot at so often. The average
platoon here in the whole group averages only one action

227

assignment a year. Most of them are no-shoot affairs. Milly will love it and you'll still be with the platoons. Besides, you've had three serious wounds in the past two years. You've done your duty here, more than your duty."

"I want to ask you not to send in that paper, Skipper. I like it here. Keeps my juices running. A transfer, even if it meant my own platoon, is something I'll have to think about. Don't send in the paper until we talk again, okay?"

Murdock watched his best friend. They had been through a lot of hell together these past three years. This was about the reaction he'd figured DeWitt would have.

"Okay. Talk it over with Milly. Now get out of here and go play old married man."

DeWitt grinned. "Hey, thanks for the thought about the letter. I might go for it yet. I'm a long way off from another stripe, but wouldn't hurt to be in a spot where it could happen. I'll let you know."

He left the office, and Murdock put his feet up on the desk and let his mind wander. There had to be some answer to this North Korean affair. What kind of a GHQ would they need? Could a submarine offshore do it? They had two subs that he knew of. Not likely. They'd need an onshore headquarters for good communications and movement. He was going to concentrate on the problem and worry it to death until he had something he could take to the brass. The fucking North Korean brains had to be right there on the coast somewhere.

Jack Mahanani checked his watch as he pulled away from the BUD/S parking lot. It was seven-thirty civilian time. The DEA guys would be home, but the operator might still be on. He drove to Chula Vista just south of San Diego and found a phone booth. He dug the number out of his wallet and dialed it.

"Good evening, this is the DEA task force."

"Hi, this is the Reverend. Do you have a message for me?"

"The Reverend? Oh, yes, just a moment, it's here somewhere. Yes. I have it. We have two of our men who want to talk to you. They told me to set up a time convenient to you and they will be there. They suggested a restaurant might be a good meeting place."

"Good. Tonight at eight-thirty in a place in Pacific Beach called Tony's. I'll meet them at the bar." He hung up quickly before they could trace the call. Then he remembered they for sure would have caller ID on all of their phones, so they would know what phone number the call came from. It wouldn't help them any. He took a deep breath. Was he going to meet with them? Did he really want to set up a raid on these smugglers? Damn right. He had to get out of this smuggling trap and stay alive. He would make the DEA promise him that his name would not be mentioned and that he would get a guarantee of no prosecution for his part. Yes, it could work, if they could nail all of the smugglers working at the casino.

He looked at his watch. Plenty of time to drive to PB. He used to live over there, knew all the best spots. He'd get to Tony's early and have a steak. He could use a good steak about now. Sure, then what did he tell the DEA guys? Hey, I just happen to be a narcotic mule and I wanted to spill my guts to you for immunity? Actually, that was about it.

He'd start with the gambling and the hole he'd dug for himself, and then talk about Harley and that damn Martillo. Yeah, he could make a good case for himself. He wouldn't tell them too much, not even which casino, not right away. There were seven or eight Indian-run casinos in the county by this time. Yes, he could do it.

Halfway into Pacific Beach, a section of San Diego, a water main break closed off the main access and he had to take a five-mile detour. When he got to Tony's and parked, it was five minutes to the meet time. He was sure the DEA guys had arrived early and had two or three other men lurking about.

A man read a newspaper in his car in the faint light coming from the dome. He was a ringer for sure. Mahanani shrugged and walked into the restaurant. He hadn't incriminated himself yet. He wouldn't unless he got a guarantee in writing of total immunity and his name not being used.

He went into the bar and checked the men standing there. There was only one pair of men: both in suits and both looked like cops. He walked up and stood beside them and ordered a beer. One looked at him.

"Are you the Reverend?" he asked.

"Might be. Who are you?"

The man flashed a badge that could have been from any agency.

"I better take a better look at the badge," Mahanani said. The man handed it to him. DEA, the right one. They moved to a booth toward the back and waved the waitress away.

"Now, you said you know about a mule operation." The larger man did the talking. No names were given or asked for.

"Right. I got suckered into it. I was stupid." He told them about the gambling and how he was threatened and how they would go to his commanding officer if he didn't pay up or work for them as a mule out of TJ.

"So, you Navy or Marines?"

"Navy. I would have been booted out of the service."

"What do you want us to do?"

"First I want it in writing that I will not be prosecuted in any way for what I might have done, and I want to be completely anonymous. I want to get out of this without getting killed by the druggers."

"That we can't guarantee, the not-getting-killed part. If your story is good enough, I can get the immunity and we'll never use your name. How about some details?"

"Not until I get that letter from your local office chief on stationery that I won't be prosecuted and my name will be kept out of it."

"The problem is we'll need more than that to get the letter."

"Fine, I'll go to the San Diego Police narc squad."

The men whispered a moment.

"All right, you said TJ to San Ysidro, numerous trips, with coke worth about half a million. What's that, fifty kilos?"

"I don't know. I never saw the drugs going or coming."

"How many trips do they make a week?"

"My guess is five or six, but I can't be sure."

"That's enough. Give me tomorrow. Then tomorrow night

you call in and ask for a message for the Reverend just the way you did this time."

"Okay, but if I don't get the letter, you can forget all about this. I know a little how you guys operate. I know you've probably got pictures of me by now, and that one of your men out front has my license plate. Please don't run it. You don't need to know who I am. If this deal falls through, I'll deny everything, even if one of you is wearing a wire. We do this my way, or you don't get a good-sized smuggling operation iced out of business."

He stood and left before either of them could respond.

Outside, he went to the car where the man was still reading the newspaper and tapped on the window. The man rolled down the window.

"Hey, your two DEA buddies inside said you can close up and go home. The party's over."

Mahanani grinned at the surprise and shock on the agent's face. Then Mahanani laughed and walked up the street to his car. Nobody followed him as he drove away.

Murdock went over and over what they knew about the North Koreans assault on the United States of America. He charted it and evaluated it and grouped the acts and separated them, and in the end came up with nothing. It could have been run by one master control, or six or eight different groups could have been launched, funded, given the know-how and weapons, and told to go and do as much damage as they could. He drove home with the start of a headache.

When he pulled into his parking slot at the apartment, he saw lights on in his second-floor unit. For a moment he tensed. No, if the Ks were coming for him, they wouldn't turn on the lights. Either he had left them on when he left the last time, or someone had come for a visit.

He ran up the steps, pulled open the front door, and found Ardith Manchester a step away. She wore a pure white silk blouse and a sleek, tight-fitting black skirt. Her long blond hair hung over one shoulder and framed her beautiful face.

"Hi, sailor, welcome home," she said with the sly grin that he had loved forever.

He swept her up in his arms and walked her across the

room to the sofa, where he put her down gently, sat beside her, and kissed her soundly.

She came up for air smiling. "Now I know that tourist-class flight was worth it. Master Chief MacKenzie said he thought you'd be home tomorrow."

"He's not always right." He pulled her into his arms so her head rested on his shoulder. "Now, any other reason you flew all the way out here from Washington, D.C.?"

"One small reason, not really important."

"How unimportant is it?" He watched her. She was hiding something. There was a hint of excitement in her voice and her brows were a little too high for normal.

"Nothing we need to talk about really. I was just about to get dinner. I'll change the menu. I see you have some good-looking pork chops in the freezer."

He held her fast. "Ardith, that other unimportant reason why you came?"

"Oh, nothing. Actually it's minor, just a small job offer. Now let's get dinner. Do stuffed pork chops sound okay?"

He held her. "Just a small job offer? A job for a midget, right? Nobody over three feet tall need apply?"

Ardith laughed. "Well, the job is for a normal-sized person, but I'm not sure that I want it. I'm just feeling them out. They talked to me in Washington."

"And they bought your ticket out here?"

"Well, yes. But that's common enough."

"Just some little job offer. So tell me about it."

He let her go, and she pushed back and he saw the sparkle in her eyes, the anticipation spreading over her face.

"It's a highly respected firm in the software industry. Yes, a dot-com, but one that isn't tied to dot-com customers. It's keyed to industry as a whole, and works for many hundreds of different clients in every field."

"And what would you do for them?"

"I'd be the assistant manager of the creative applications department. We take a company's problem, figure out a solution to it, and design and develop the software to take care of the problem. It's so creative and exciting that I can hardly sit still."

"But your background isn't in computers."

"Doesn't have to be. In fact they told me they wanted someone in the creative side who wasn't a computer person. Then I wouldn't be thinking ahead that it couldn't be done, or it would be too expensive or too time-consuming. I get the ideas and build the plans to solve the problem. Somebody else does the design and application work."

"Some little job offer."

"Okay, so I lied. It was worth it to see your expression when I explained it."

"When?"

"I go in to see them tomorrow."

"Now we talk about the other. Do you really want to leave government work? You've been happy back there with all the conniving, backbiting, lying politicians. Your father excluded, of course."

"We've talked about this before. I love my work in D.C., but this seems so much more exciting, so on the edge of the science of business, education. They even do some work for state governments. Do I want to leave? I'm not sure. If this job works out, it would be a tremendous move." She reached up and kissed him tenderly. "Then there is that other reason I want to come out here. But we don't talk about that."

Murdock gently eased her down on the sofa and lay half on top of her. He kissed her nose, then both eyes, and gently brushed her lips with his. "Now, little lady, let's talk about that other reason for you to move out to San Diego."

He kissed her again and she moaned softly. When the kiss ended she stroked his face lovingly.

"Hey, there, cowboy. Do you want dinner sooner or later?"

"I think I'll vote for later. Do you want to call the roll?"

"Then later wins by a landslide." They sat up and both grinned. He cupped one of her breasts and bent and kissed it through the white silk blouse.

"Hey, maybe it would be better if we continued this discussion on the merits of the issue before the Senate in the bedroom."

"I'll vote for that," Murdock said. "We can have dinner any old time."

• • •

Much later, over dinner, Ardith was enthusiastic about the job. That was part of it, he knew. She also glowed as she always did after a good romp in bed.

"It's a firm offer. I can take it or turn it down. One good thing is the salary, a hundred and fifty thousand a year." Her eyes were bright. He could see her anticipation, her delight.

"Wow, that's three times as much as I'm making. Won't that irritate me and make me angry?"

"No, because we'll have a joint account." She said it with a straight face, then laughed and kissed him. "The money is good, I get a stock-option plan, insurance, a matching retirement plan, and I'm in line for manager of the department as soon as the current one retires in about a year."

"No lawyer work?"

"Not a bit. Oh, I'll do some pro bono for one of the shelters or a woman's rape group or some such, but none on the job."

"Sounds like you have it all worked out," he said, his voice neutral, noncommittal.

Ardith studied him. This was a surprise. She thought he'd be enthusiastic, maybe ecstatic. "I did some investigation of the firm," she said. "It's listed everywhere. Most agencies came up with a solid four points for them out of four. Locally, they do a lot of charity work, and are involved with two high schools. Yes, I do think it would be a good career move for me."

Murdock picked her up and hugged her, then spun her around off the floor, one slipper flying off her foot.

"Marvelous, wonderful, great. I just wanted you to be sure. I didn't want to seduce you out here and have you pining away for good old D.C. and the government flap. I'm delighted. Now quit frowning. If you want the job, I'm all for it. How did you find it?"

"They found me actually. A friend of a friend knew they were hunting. She turned them down. Her husband wouldn't let her leave D.C. So she gave them my number and they called, we talked. I gave them a tour of the Senate, and one luncheon led to dinner and then a day later, the firm job offer was faxed from here in town."

He kissed her seriously, and sat her back down at her place

at the table. "Your dinner is getting cold," he said.

After the dishes were stashed in the washer, Murdock brought up his small problem. He told her everything she didn't know about the North Koreans and what they had done, and asked her how to evaluate how they did it. Was it a mass of individuals set loose or a closely controlled campaign?

Ardith made a list as he talked, then went over it. "You say it started with a strange ship near an oil-drilling rig, and then an undersea structure of some kind near the rig. Then all these other elements."

Murdock jumped up and pounded his fist into the air like Tiger Woods when he sank a long put. "I've got it. I know how they did it now. I know where their GHQ is. Now all I have to do is prove to the brass that what I think is true."

24

Murdock sailed into his small office at 0700 and at once began working on his laptop computer. He spelled it out the best he could by putting down the litany of what the North Koreans had done in chronological order. Then he made his conclusions.

"The North Koreans did nothing until we examined their underwater building near the oil-drilling rig near Santa Barbara. Only then did they launch their attacks.

"It seems to me that the underwater unit may be their hidden headquarters that launches and controls their attacks. I think that they use the oil rig for their antennas to keep in touch with their many units.

"It is my suggestion that an immediate investigation be made of the oil-drilling platform, checking for antennas, and that all radio traffic from the rig be monitored.

"I also suggest that we explore the best way to open up that sealed underwater building near the tower, and if we can do that, I feel that we will have stopped the attacks on our shores by the North Koreans."

He went over the two pages three times, made changes and used the spell checker, then printed it out. He made four copies, put two in envelopes and addressed them, then took them at once to the Quarter Deck, where Master Chief MacKenzie looked at the sealed envelopes and lifted his brows.

"Something you're not telling me, lad, sir."

"Aye, that's the lot of it, MacKenzie. And a good thing for now that you're not knowing." Both were deep into Scottish brogues.

"So, I'll deliver this one in person to His Nibs the Commander."

Murdock grinned. "Thanks, Gordon. I'll get back to my important work."

At his desk, the first thing Murdock did was to review the folder that showed a record of wounds received by platoon members. He'd looked up DeWitt's for his chat with him. Now he studied the rest of the medical reports.

Bradford had had three serious wounds, but had bounced back. Franklin also had had three wounds, none serious. Ching had had four wounds, two serious. Lampedusa led the list with six wounds, two serious. It made Murdock consider taking Lam off point and removing him as his chief scout. Lam was the best in the platoon. But should he put the man at risk for another wound? Murdock could remember his own three wounds. The rotator cuff shot in his right shoulder had been the worst.

He added his in-and-out lower-right-arm wound on this mission and checked the rest of the men. None of the others had more than two wounds. Lam was the only one he was concerned about. He'd have a talk with the man and see if he wanted to let someone else take the point.

Then Murdock looked at the package that had come while they were away. He tore it open. Six new underwater, waterproof Motorola personal-communication radios. Yes. Now they could talk to each other while on underwater approaches. It would help them stay together. For now there would be three of the radios in each platoon. The radios used throat mikes that would always be on. Just talk and you broadcast. He read a pamphlet that came with them. Good on land for up to six miles. Underwater, where sound transfer was better, up to eight miles. It said sonar would create static on the sets if the frequencies were anywhere near it. He put that down on his list for a quick trial.

He looked over the platoon roster. So far he didn't need any new men. Only one wound. They had been lucky on this sequence. Were there any of the men who weren't keeping up, who were shirking their workloads or messing up in combat? He went over the list twice and found nobody he wanted to boot back into the black-shoe Navy.

Murdock checked his watch. Nearly 0800. The platoon was due in, and Masciareli usually came in about this time. Just as he thought it, his phone rang. He answered it.

"Dammit, Murdock, you just might have something here," Commander Masciareli boomed through the handset. "With everything else exploding around here, everyone just forgot about that neat little underwater building. I have a call into the admiral right now about launching an investigation into the radio traffic out of that area. Simple job with sniffer plane flying over and monitoring the platform. If that warrants it, we'll move out with the Coast Guard and do a complete electronic inspection of the oil-drilling rig."

"What about the underwater building, Commander?"

"That will be the next step. If the tower shows North Koreans, we'll have you and your men go down and blast a hole into that underwater bunker. Then we'll see what really is going on down there."

"Thank you, Commander. We're ready to help anytime you give us the word."

"Hang loose, Murdock. If I know the admiral, this could all go down in a matter of ten to twelve hours."

DeWitt came in and sat down in the only other chair. He picked the training sked off the wall and looked at it.

Murdock said good-bye and hung up. He handed DeWitt a copy of his letter and went out to see how the men were doing. DeWitt came boiling out after him a minute later.

"You think this might be the key? We were so damn close and we let it slip away?"

"Could be. Masciareli thinks the admiral will move quickly on it, maybe even today. For training today let's keep it at home. We'll do some beach running with full combat gear and weapons, then do the O course again. Hey, come in here. Have I got something to show to you."

DeWitt bellowed in delight when he saw the waterproof personal radios.

"Three for your squad and three for mine. We'll try them this afternoon just off the beach if nothing else pops. You keep one, give your point man one, and pick a man for the third. Oh, I'd like Mahanani to have one as the platoon medic."

"Right, Franklin gets the third. He did a good job tracking for us yesterday. Led us right down the trail. Said he'd been watching Lam."

"Do we have any kind of a wound limit? How many enemy wounds can a SEAL take and still stay in the platoons?"

"Never heard of any limit. Depends on the wounds. That third one was just an in-and-out on my arm. They shouldn't count. Like that one you picked up in the Carib."

"Lam has six wounds."

"Damn, that many? Maybe he shouldn't walk point anymore."

"I'm going to talk to him about it." Murdock looked at DeWitt, but couldn't see any change from yesterday. "You mention the idea to Milly about getting your own platoon?"

DeWitt hooded his eyes and nodded once. "Right, we went over it for about an hour. She's all for it. Said it would get me away from Don Stroh and you and all the combat missions we have. I figured she'd say that."

"But you're just pigheaded enough that you want to go right on getting shot at and shot up and maybe killed."

DeWitt grinned. "Fuck, yes, Commander. Why do you suppose you and I are both still here?" They both laughed and waved at Senior Chief Sadler, who walked in.

"That still doesn't answer my basic question, Lieutenant. I'll expect your answer by tonight."

Sadler didn't try to understand. "All men are present and accounted for, Commander. Everyone on deck."

"Thanks, Sadler. Training begins in thirty. Beach run, then the O course. Get them ready." Sadler turned and left.

DeWitt frowned looking at the new Motorolas. "Did we see if they are set with the same chips so they can talk to our old dry sets?"

Murdock shook his head. He picked up one of the sets, studied it a minute, then turned a small on switch and pushed the earpiece in place. Murdock pointed, and DeWitt went into the squad room and used his dry-land Motorola.

"So, Murdock, can you read me," he said after swinging

the lip mike down from where it rested near his floppy hat brim.

"Just about five by five, Mr. DeWitt. I'd say we have a winner here that will mesh nicely with our other sets."

The phone rang and Murdock picked it up. "Team Seven, Third Platoon, Murdock."

"Murdock, stand by. The admiral sounded like he almost wet his pants when I told him about the antennas. He's sending a fixed-wing sniffer plane up there in ten minutes. It can detect any radio signal from half a watt up to broadband and pinpoint where it's coming from. We should know about the radio transmissions in an hour. Let's say we need to blow a big hole in that concrete bunker down there. Can our big limpet mines do the trick?"

"The heavy ones could, or we could rig them with four pounds of C-5 to boost things along."

"Good, draw the mines now. Make it six, and get the extra C-5 or TNAZ. Get on it. I've sent a CH-46 to North Island to be on standby. My guess is that your platoon will be moving within two hours. Hold training. Get your men ready for a swim."

"That's a roger, Commander."

DeWitt had come back in, and looked questioningly at Murdock. "Masciareli again?"

Murdock told him the situation. "I'll go with Senior Chief Sadler to supply right now and draw those limpets and the TNAZ," DeWitt said. "How do we attach that explosive to the limpets?" He shrugged. "We'll figure that out in the chopper, or back here if we have time. Hey, the Navy can move ass-fast when it wants to." He turned and hurried out the door.

Murdock went into the squad room. "Listen up," he bellowed in his best parade-ground voice. The room quieted immediately. "We're probably going for a swim. Remember that concrete blockhouse we found on the ocean floor up near that oil-drilling platform? There's a chance we may go back up there with a fistful of limpet mines and blow a hole in it. The admiral is on it, sent a sniffer plane up there to check on radio transmissions coming from the oil rig. That could be the GHQ for the North Korean operation."

"Hell, wish we had known that a week ago," Jaybird said.

"So do the rest of us. So, no training today. We could be moving in as little as two hours. Get your wet gear ready. Full wet suits. We also have six new underwater personal radios that work as well submerged as they do on dry land. Three in each squad for now until we can get the rest of our order. Mahanani, Jaybird, Franklin, and Lam check out the new gadgets from the senior chief. I'll be in touch."

"Weapons, sir?" Sadler asked.

Murdock stopped. "The Bull Pups won't be much good seventy-five feet down. How many of those short spear guns do we have, Senior Chief?"

"Last time I looked we had ten."

"Issue five per squad. What about bang sticks?"

"I thought the Navy gave up on them, used them just for shark attacks," Mahanani said.

"The brass might have, but we didn't. How many, Senior Chief?"

"Have to scrape the back of the weapons room, Commander. We've loaned some out that didn't come back. I'd say maybe ten."

"Issue each man without a spear gun a bang stick. Probably a one-shot affair with them. The spear guns have three of the short spears?"

"Yes, sir."

"If this goes down, we'll take on the tower first, so bring weapons. My guess here is to go with all MP-5's. We have enough, Senior Chief?"

"Aye, that we do, Commander."

"So use the modified water-to-land combat vest with your pockets filled with magazines for the Five. Let's get to work."

Murdock went to his equipment locker and checked his gear. The new Draegr was ready. He had one of the short spearguns. They were rubber-tube fired and could be reloaded quickly. He checked his KA-BAR. They had a cutdown version of the combat vest that worked with the wet suits. They would take that to support their MP-5's. They didn't know what they would find on the tower. If the North Koreans there chose to fight, it could get deadly in that cramped space. The civilians working there must know something strange was going on. They must be getting triple pay to stay working. How many civilians would there be? Ten, maybe fifteen to run a rig like that. At least to run it during the day and when any ships came near.

Sadler came up to Murdock. "Wet suits and knives and the bang sticks and spearguns and good old MP-5's. What else are we going to need?"

"We'll have the large limpets to get down there. Rustle up six float bags we can use half filled so we don't go down too fast."

"Aye, aye, sir."

Murdock went back to his office and found himself watching the telephone. He snorted and looked away, pulling out paperwork he should have done two days ago. It would keep him busy the rest of the morning. If they had the rest of the morning.

DeWitt came in grinning. "We brought the limpets in a Humvee parked outside. Supply also gave us some epoxy glue that will stick anything to anything. We've pasted the half-pound blocks of TNAZ around the face of the limpets. Four pounds on each one. We've got to be sure every one of our men is above water before those babies go off."

"Good work on the limpets. Heads out of the water, we can do that. Check your squad. Let's be ready." DeWitt went back to the squad room.

The more Murdock thought about the oil platform and the sunken bunker, the more certain he was that he was right. The North Koreans had been planning the attack even while the SEALs had crawled around the outside of their GHQ. The tower must be where the leaders of the attack lived when not down below organizing and managing the hits on the U.S. He wondered again how many of the American men on the tower were in on the game. They had to have a few oilmen on the rig to keep it drilling, or at least give the appearance of drilling. The SEALs would find out soon. The tower attack would come first—if indeed they were ordered to take out the tower and then the underwater bunker.

At 1000 Murdock called the commander. "Sir, it's been over two hours. Anything from the admiral?"

"Yes, we're working on it. The plane reported massive amounts of radio signals coming from the tower. Some in code, some in Korean voices, some in bursts too fast to intercept. The admiral has ordered a hit on the tower. To be sure we surprise them, your platoon will chopper to Santa Barbara and take a Coast Guard cutter out to the tower. The Coast Guard will move you in close enough to land on it. If there is any weapons fire from the tower, you are authorized to use all of your weapons to capture it. When the tower is in friendly hands, your men will go below and blow the blockhouse."

"When do we fly out of North Island?"

"We had it set for 1300. Just a minute. The other line."

The phone went dead when the commander switched. Murdock hung on, and felt like he had one foot out of a chopper to jump into the ocean and somebody had stopped him and said to wait. When Commander Masciareli came back on the phone, his voice had risen two notes.

"That was the admiral. The spotter plane has found a freighter moving up slowly toward the oil rig. It's a mile away, but definitely headed that way. Freighters usually don't sail that route. We're thinking that the freighter has come to take the North Koreans off the tower and out of the bunker below the water. We don't want to let them get away. He's ordering your men into the choppers as quickly as you can make it. A Coast Guard cutter will stop the freighter and board her for a health inspection. Get your men moving now, Murdock." Commander Masciareli's voice boomed over the handset and held a great deal of satisfaction. He had been in on setting up this mission.

Santa Barbara, California

The sixteen SEALs crowded together in the cabin below-decks on the Coast Guard Cutter *Reliance,* a 210-foot ship with sixty-three men and twelve officers. Just after it pushed off from the Coast Guard dock in Santa Barbara, Murdock talked with the skipper, Lieutenant Wilson.

"Yes, sir, Commander. We have two fifty-caliber machine guns that can do a lot of damage if they provoke us. We should be able to keep their heads down long enough for your team to get on board. We just heard on the radio that our cutter that went out to stop that freighter was fired on. We put two rounds from our twenty-five-millimeter Bushmaster over their bow and they kept going for a mile. A second round just in front of the bow brought the ship to a slow stop. They are about half a mile off the tower. They're now anchored, and our plane has reported there is movement from the tower to the freighter in two boats."

"They must have known we were coming," Murdock said. "First we need to take down the tower. I'd guess they will have riflemen on the tower now as well. Can your cutter stop any boarding of the freighter by those boats?"

"We're doing that. The small boats can't get to the rope ladders the freighter has put overboard. So far the other cutter reports there are about ten men in the boats trying to get to the freighter. Unfortunately, they have rifles as well, and are using them."

"How long until we get to the tower?" Murdock asked.

"Another ten minutes," Lieutenant Wilson said. "We're making eighteen knots. That's our flank speed."

Murdock went below and told the men the situation. "If they fire at us, we'll let the Coast Guard return fire with their Fifties. When we get close enough we'll hose the place down with our MP-5's."

"Civilians?" Donegan asked.

"If they don't have sense enough to hide, some of them might get shot," Murdock said. "They knew they were playing a dangerous game. Some of them might lose."

The cutter came within five hundred yards of the tower and she began to take rifle fire. The two fifty-caliber machine guns on the cutter returned fire and quieted the tower rifles for a while. Then the shooting began again, and Murdock edged up to take a look. "Three hundred yards," he told DeWitt, who was just behind him. "Wish we had brought at least one Bull Pup."

One Coast Guard shooter took a round in the leg. Another man grabbed the machine gun and kept it shooting.

Two hundred yards. Murdock decided. "Alpha Squad on deck and fire at will. Three-round bursts." The eight SEALs scattered around the front of the cutter and chattered out a thundering volume of fire. After all the SEALs had emptied a magazine, they noticed that the firing from the tower had stopped.

"Cease fire," Murdock said on the Motorola. The SEAL guns quieted. At a hundred yards the rifles on the tower fired again. "Commence firing," Murdock said, and the eight weapons blasted another thirty rounds each into the tower, 240 9mm slugs jolting into it, glancing off steel and splattering on more steel. Windows in the top level shattered.

"Bravo Squad, get ready to board the tower. DeWitt, we'll keep up covering fire as your men work up the tower. When you want us to cease fire, call it out."

Bravo Squad crouched behind the superstructure of the cutter as it eased up to the small floating dock at the base of the oil-rig tower. The eight men jumped to the platform and scurried up the steel ladders. Murdock motioned the cutter to back off so his men would have better targets. They then fired at anyone they could see on the tower. Whenever a Korean rifleman lifted over a beam or peered around a doorway, he was met with a dozen rounds of hot lead.

DeWitt scrambled up to the first level and called for the cease-fire. Then he worked up cautiously, through the boring level where the drilling had stopped. On up to the areas above where there would be living quarters, a kitchen, and on levels four and five, the control rooms and offices.

The third level proved to be the hardest. It was a maze of small bedrooms plus a kitchen. DeWitt and Franklin worked up to the first door and kicked it in. A man inside held up his hands.

"Don't shoot, I'm an American. Joe Fisher."

"Joe, we're Navy SEALs. Are there any more Americans on this floor?"

"This is where they keep all of us when we're not pretending to be drilling. About twenty of us. Most of these doors are locked."

"Kick them in," DeWitt told his men. "We have to clear this level before we can move up."

They began smashing in the doors, and found only Americans, who DeWitt ordered to stay put so they didn't get shot by the North Koreans.

"Where are the rest of the Koreans?" DeWitt asked an American.

"Hell, all over the place. Now they mostly are on the levels above. I can show you. Lots of the little bastards. They wouldn't let us off. Made us run the rig whenever anyone came around. Prisoners, hostages is what we were."

"Show us where the Koreans are," DeWitt said. The man nodded, and ran ahead of them down the hall to a stairs and up it. He peered over the top into the fourth level.

"Most of them lived up here, and worked the radios on top and in the bunker they built underwater."

DeWitt pulled him down, lifted up, and looked around quickly, then dropped down. A shot slammed into the steel frame behind the stairs. DeWitt lifted his MP-5 over the top of the stairs and sprayed six rounds into the big room, then jolted upward and scanned the place. A man behind a desk on the far side lifted up and brought a submachine gun to bear on him, but DeWitt drilled him with three rounds before he could fire. They found another man with four slugs in his chest next to a door.

DeWitt ran to the first Korean and kicked away the weapon.

"All gone," the Korean said. "American, you lose." The Korean coughed, screamed once, and died.

The American ran up. "Hey, good, you got him. Next level is where most of the gooks worked. Bunch of radios like I've never seen before."

"They still up there?" Murdock asked.

"Probably not," Fisher said. "I saw them bugging out in those two boats."

DeWitt sent Victor and Jefferson up the stairs to check the next level. A few moments later the radio spoke.

"Clear on this level, Lieutenant," Jefferson said. "But really a lot of radios, all kinds." The rest of the SEALs went up the steps and looked at the communication center jammed with screens and radios.

"Murdock, can you read me?" DeWitt asked on the Motorola.

"Fives, DeWitt. You clear there?"

"Looks clear."

Just then submachine-gun fire erupted from a doorway at the far side of the fifth level. The SEALs dove for the floor. DeWitt felt a burning in his right leg as he pumped a dozen rounds into the offending doorway.

Franklin had fired too, but then stopped. Fernandez kept firing into the doorway as he charged the area. He dodged behind a desk and sent six more rounds into the closet area the doorway opened into. No more firing came from the closet. Fernandez charged it and kicked the closet door open. He fired one shot, then turned.

"We have five KIAs here. I wondered where all that rifle fire came from. They're all wasted."

DeWitt sat up and looked at Franklin. He lay where he'd dropped when the firing began. DeWitt scowled and knelt beside Franklin. He had taken three rounds, two in the chest and one in the forehead. DeWitt swore at himself for assuming the floor was clear until he checked.

"Murdock, we've got a KIA here. Franklin caught one in the forehead. He's gone."

25

Murdock squinted against the bright sun and cursed the whole bloody Navy. "Take care of him, DeWitt. Anyone else wounded?"

"Anybody hit?" DeWitt called on his radio.

"Yeah, I got one in the shoulder, up high," Canzoneri said. "Shouldn't have come up to that damn stairway when I did."

"Murdock, we have two wounded. This platform is clear. A local said the Americans were held hostage. We'll do another search. We put down seven Koreans. Figured there would be more than that on here. Checking again."

"Copy that, DeWitt. First take care of Franklin. He was a good man. I just dropped off two men and one limpet for the freighter. It's four hundred yards away. We'll return to the bunker and go below. You hold the tower."

"Roger that, Murdock." DeWitt turned to his men. "Mahanani, get up here. We need to move Franklin down to the first level. The rest of us will go over this platform with guns in hand and see if there are any more shitheads on board. Mahanani, take a look at Canzoneri's shoulder and then my right leg. Let's move, people."

Howard and Bradford swam toward the freighter while ten feet below the surface, towing the large limpet mine along on its flotation device, which was half-filled. They checked their route once, with faces just breaking the surface, then bored in on the stern of the big freighter.

They hit the metal plates and worked along to the stern, then came back ten yards and planted the limpet two feet below the waterline. Bradford inserted the timer detonator, set it for fifteen minutes, and activated it. He pointed back the way they came, and both swam strongly away from the freighter. They kept two feet underwater, and after five minutes lifted up to the surface and swam for the Coast Guard cutter about a quarter of a mile to the west.

They had almost reached it when they felt a jolting force come through the water, and then a rumbling roar as the TNAZ and the limpet went off in a thundering explosion. The two SEALs gave each other a thumbs-up.

"There is one puppy that's going to have to limp into port close by for some repairs," Howard said. "Before the Coast Guard is done with the operators, they will wish they had never tried this little trick." They gave each other another thumbs-up as they watched the freighter list to port and the stern drop five feet deeper into the water. It wasn't enough to sink her, but it would flood one or two of her watertight compartments and get her moving into port.

Murdock left the two small boats to the other Coast Guard cutter, and sent his cutter back near the tower where the bunker lay below. He still had five limpets. Three should be enough. He took his remaining five men with him, and dropped over the side with three limpets and their timer detonators attached. They lowered them to the bottom, slowly letting air out of the flotation devices around them.

When the SEALs hit the sandy, rocky bottom, Murdock saw that they were slightly off target. Visibility was fifteen feet as they swam toward the tower and found the sunken bunker. Jaybird and Murdock had been talking on their waterproof radios.

"Jaybird, put the three limpets in a row a foot apart. That way they should blow a huge hole."

"Roger that," Jaybird said.

"I'll set the timers," Murdock said. "Before I activate them, I want you and the other men halfway to the top. Go on up and keep your heads out of the water. Going to be a tremendous concussion from down here."

"Copy," Jaybird said. "We have the three limpets positioned as you suggested."

Murdock moved in, checked the placement on the almost

flat roof. No magnetism needed to hold them on the concrete. "Get out of here," Murdock said. The five men swam toward the surface. Murdock gave them five minutes, then set the timers for fifteen minutes, and activated them. He made sure they were activated, then swam for the surface, letting the new rebreather adjust the nitrogen level as he went up. He broke the surface and looked around. Jaybird had the other four men about twenty yards away. They all gave him a thumbs-up and they swam for the cutter, which had closed on them.

On board, Murdock checked his countdown watch. "Three more minutes to blast time," he said.

They counted down the last twenty seconds. When the limpets went off, Murdock felt the concussion through the vessel. The cutter's skipper lifted his brows. "That should wake up somebody down there."

The three explosions came so close together, it seemed like one huge one. Murdock and the five other SEALs fell overboard and swam down toward the bunker. Well before they got there they encountered bits of paper and wood that drifted slowly toward the surface.

"My guess is that we punched a hole," Jaybird said on the new underwater radio. Murdock gave him a thumbs-up and they swam the rest of the way to the bunker. Before they reached it, they met more flotsam heading for the surface. As the water cleared, they saw large bubbles of air rising. Then they were at the bunker.

A four-foot hole that gaped three feet wide showed in the roof of the structure. The six men peered inside, but could see little. Murdock had remembered a flashlight, and pulled it out and shone the beam inside. At first they could see only bubbles and bits of paper. Then a human arm floated upward in a sudden upswelling and vanished over them.

"Spooky," Jaybird said.

Murdock eased over the ragged edge of the concrete, pushed apart rebars, and lowered himself into the structure. He vanished into the gloom. They waited. He came back with a briefcase that was still fastened shut. Jaybird took it and passed it along to Tim Sadler.

Next Murdock brought up a metal box a foot long and

about that wide and two inches thick. Jaybird held on to that one. Then he couldn't stand it any longer, and edged into the hole and dropped down. He swam to where Murdock had just upended a desk so he could open drawers. Jaybird held the flashlight for him and they looked in all the drawers. Nothing of value. They swam round the twenty-foot-long oval room. Near the back they found two bodies. Neither was marked. They'd either drowned or the concussion of the bombs had killed them, Murdock decided.

He and Jaybird checked the rest of the structure and found three more bodies, but nothing more they could take up. They edged out the hole in the ceiling, and Murdock gave the sign to swim back to the surface.

Back on the cutter, they put the box and the briefcase on the deck in the sun and stared at them.

"Maybe we shouldn't open them," Lam said.

"Oh, sure, like they have secrets," Ching said.

Murdock picked up the briefcase, looked at the clasp, and pushed a wet copper button. The leather hasp flipped back, and he pushed the top of the case open. It was full of water. They poured the water into the scuppers and then Murdock took out a mass of wet paper. "In Korean," he said. He put the papers back in the briefcase and filled it with seawater from a hose.

"If we let them dry out, they'll glue themselves together and nobody will be able to get them apart to read. Better this way." He looked at the metal box. He handed it to Jaybird, who looked it over, then found a button on the bottom. He pressed it, and the top eased upward a half inch.

He handed it back to Murdock. When the commander opened the lid, the SEALs gasped. It was half full of gold coins. Murdock picked up one and looked at it.

"Krugerrands," he said. "A full ounce of gold, worth whatever the price is for gold per ounce on the open market."

"Two hundred and fifty-seven dollars last night," Senior Chief Sadler said. "Hey, I've got some investments. I like to keep track of gold."

Murdock handed the box of coins and the briefcase to Sadler. "Keep tabs on these, Senior Chief. We'll turn them into Navy Intelligence as soon as we hit our base. Must be about time for us to head back to the home ranch."

Murdock went into the bridge of the cutter and asked if they could contact the Navy.

"Yes, sir, which part?"

"The commander of the Naval Surface Fleet," Murdock said. It took two radio calls before the admiral came on the line.

"Admiral Lawsome here."

"Admiral, this is Lieutenant Commander Murdock in Santa Barbara."

"Murdock, yes, good of you to call. How goes the operation?"

"Just about wrapped up, Admiral. The tower has been taken down with casualties on both sides. The freighter has suffered an explosion in the stern and will be porting quickly for repairs where it can be inspected. Twelve Korean nationals were captured at sea by a Coast Guard Cutter. The concrete blockhouse near the tower has been penetrated and documents and a box full of gold coins retrieved."

"Anything else of value in the underwater structure?"

"Not that we could find on our first search. A later search may be needed. We counted five bodies in the flooded structure."

"Well done, Commander. This should put an end to the North Korean invasion of our soil. You mentioned casualties. One of ours?"

"Yes, sir, a SEAL, KIA. Yeoman Second Class Colt Franklin, sir. I'm putting him in for a decoration."

"I'll approve it, Commander. When you retrieve your men you should proceed to the Coast Guard station in Santa Barbara where the same CH-46 is waiting for you. This mission is not covert. You will probably be hounded by the press. Let the Navy public affairs officers take care of the press."

"Aye, aye, sir."

"Admiral Lawsome out."

Murdock asked the cutter's captain to pick up their men from the tower, then take them back to the dock. "We thank you for the ride, Lieutenant, and for the support fire with those Fifties. They really helped."

When Murdock got back to the fantail, he found the

SEALs flaked out. Howard and Bradford had returned from the freighter.

Ten minutes later they had picked up DeWitt and his squad from the tower and gently brought Colt Franklin's body on board.

"Let's go home," Murdock said.

Murdock sat at his desk pounding out his after-action report. It wasn't 1500 yet. It had been an interesting morning. He'd lost a good man, and he hated that. DeWitt had picked up another wound. Murdock would deal with him later.

He had two calls from Navy divers who had been assigned to go into the blockhouse underwater and retrieve the Korean bodies. The Navy had also picked up the bodies off the tower and turned them over to a United Nations representative in Los Angeles.

Now he had to cope with the tough part, writing a letter to Franklin's parents in Nebraska. He put it off. DeWitt came in from the medics at Balboa Hospital. The slug had nicked the bone in his upper right leg and he'd been put on light duty for two weeks. Canzoneri's shoulder was smashed up a bit, but should heal in a month.

"I'm writing that letter of recommendation this afternoon to get you a platoon of your own. I know there's an opening, and Masciareli might just go for it. Actually I'm sending it with or without your approval." He studied the SEAL's face. DeWitt frowned for a moment, then took a deep breath. Murdock thought he saw a small wave of relief break over the lieutenant.

"Yeah, I guess. Okay, do it. But I want something in return. I want to write the letter to Franklin's family. I knew the guy fairly well."

"Good, DeWitt. Good. You'll do a better job at it than I would. No more duty this afternoon. I turned the men loose. Why don't you get out of here too? We can talk about a replacement man for your squad tomorrow. I've alerted the master chief. He has a list of men from the other platoons who want a crack at us. We'll look them over tomorrow." He paused and watched DeWitt. The man had lost some of his push, his ready-for-anything attitude. When Franklin got killed right beside him, it must have taken a lot of the gung-ho drive out of the man.

"DeWitt. I'm sorry about Franklin. He was a good man. Why don't you get that shot up leg home and be sure to take your pain pills. You don't have to prove anything to anybody. You've been there, buddy, and you've done that more than ninety-nine percent of anybody in the military. Just relax and come in about noon tomorrow."

DeWitt looked up, and Murdock had never seen such pain in the man's eyes. His face sagged and he nodded. "Yeah, Cap, I just might do that. I can write the letter tomorrow."

Out in the squad room, Mahanani was the last one to leave. He had restocked his medic kit, cleaned the MP-5 three times, and at last closed his locker. Time to go. He had been stalling and he knew it. It was time to get home and call the drug task force and set up a plan with the DEA. Mahanani knew that if anything went wrong in a bust of the druggers, he could very well wind up dead in a basket. He snorted, pushed over the Quarter Deck, and ran for his Buick. It was now or never, and the now might just be deadly and forever.

26

Hospital Corpsman First Class Jack Mahanani ran up the steps to his apartment in Coronado. As he opened the door the telephone rang. He hurried in and picked it up.

"Yes?"

"Is this the Reverend?"

"So you ran my plates. I told you not to do that." He hung up. A moment later the phone rang again. He let it sound four times before he picked it up.

"Clancy's Bar and Grill, Clancy speaking."

"Yeah sure. Mahanani, we know everything about you there is to know. Now don't hang up. I've made a deal for you. You will remain completely anonymous, no name, no testimony, no leak to the press, nothing. All you have to do is give us the names of the guys at the casino, the spots where you pick up and deliver the cars. That's it. Just to be sure we don't get an empty cupboard, we'll want you to make one more run, and that's the one we'll bust."

"No way, Mr. DEA. You bust them on my run and they will know that I tipped you and they'll tell everyone in the ring. If just one of them gets away, I'm dead meat within twelve hours. Not a chance. I'll give you the names, and places. You set up a surveillance on the U.S. side. When you see a man drive in, leave his own car there, and take an older nondescript car out and drive to the border, you know you have a runner."

"Might work, might not. What if it's a decoy?"

"Won't be. I ran a dry load last time out. They knew the inspectors were checking every six-year-old Chevy. They pulled mine over and it came out clean. They won't do another decoy."

"So when are you going to give us the names and addresses?"

"How about tonight? You know where I live. You probably have a man outside my place right now. Radio him to come up to my door and ask politely if I need a ride. Then we meet and drive to San Ysidro."

"We'll need the name of the casino and the guys there who shanghaied you so we can have a team out there waiting for us to make a grab."

"Cool, I can do that. Tonight. When will your man be on my doorstep?"

"In about five minutes. Look, Mahanani, we want to make this as easy as we can for you. We know you're a SEAL and good with weapons. Don't bring anything with you. Not even an ankle hideout. Okay?"

"Roger that. No bang-bang."

"Good. Our man will drive down the Strand and we'll meet in Imperial Beach. You'll have to wait for us. You'll be riding with Hernando. He's a good man and speaks Spanish like a native. We'll see you in about a half hour."

Mahanani said good-bye and hung up the phone. He looked over three small guns in the top dresser drawer. The little .32 automatic would fit nicely in a belt holster in the middle of his back. No, they just might frisk him. The DEA said no guns, so he would not take one. He checked his wallet. Twenty-one dollars in cash. He probably wouldn't spend a dollar.

He went to the bathroom, washed his hands and face, and checked his beard. No worry. By the time he had combed his dark hair, the front doorbell sounded.

When he opened the door he saw a Mexican with a mustache, wearing chinos, a tan shirt outside his pants, dark sunglasses, and a baseball cap. He took off the glasses and held out his hand.

"Jack Mahanani?" he asked in a pleasant voice without a trace of Mexican accent.

"That's right. I understand we're to take a ride."

"*Sí, amigo.* I am Hernando. We take a trip to Imperial

Beach." This time the Mexican accent was solid and sure. He grinned. "Sometimes I do undercover work along the border," he said without the accent. "I can play it either way. Maybe I should have been an actor."

Mahanani locked his front door and they went down the steps to a four-year-old Ford.

"Company car," Hernando said. "I drive one of the new VW Beetles."

They drove in silence past the Hotel Del Coronado, out the Strand, and past the SEALs' headquarters. Hernando waved at the complex. "Seems like they keep you guys busy over there," he said.

"Some days we work, some days we train," Mahanani said. He sat there trying to figure his odds of living through the night. If the raid went down without a hitch, and if they nailed at least five bodies at the casino, he would have a chance. He had decided not to call in and tell Harley that he was home but bushed and couldn't make a run tonight. Maybe he'd give him a call tomorrow afternoon.

Not calling tonight might be enough to throw suspicion on him, and they might not make a run tonight. But he often didn't call in for four or five days. He'd leave it like that. Taking down the guys at the casino would be the hairy part.

They waited near a McDonald's in Imperial Beach for ten minutes before a Mercury Grand Prix pulled up in back of them. Two men got out and crawled into the Ford.

"We wanted a car that wouldn't be conspicuous," the taller of the two agents said. "I'm Daniels and this is Ronkowski. Now what casino and who are we looking for?"

"The Casa Grande Casino, out from El Cajon a ways. The man who first contacted me is Harley. He's a member of the tribe out there. I don't know his last name. Seems like he's always near the front doors. The office man is Martillo."

Hernando looked over at him. "Hammer? They call him the Hammer?"

"Right. He's the guy who sent three of his thugs to pound me around."

"We have heard of Martillo. Rojo Martillo, he's sometimes called. The *rojo* probably comes from the color of blood, which he spills quite often. We know him and three or four of the men he runs with. I wonder how he got a job at the casino."

"He had strong Indian contacts last I knew," Hernando said. He looked at Mahanani. "We ready to drive?"

"Are those the only names you have for us?" Daniels asked.

"Yes. Let's drive. Sometimes the cars take off from San Ysidro before seven o'clock."

"It's only six-fifteen, Mahanani," Daniels said. "You left all of your guns at work and at home, I hope."

"Right. If it comes to a shoot-out, I don't want any part of it."

"From what I hear, your special Platoon Three of Seventh does quite a bit of shooting," Ronkowski said.

"We're professionals doing a job," Mahanani said. "We don't like to mix with amateur drug smugglers." He scowled. "You guys must also know what kind of toothpaste I use and when I go to the john."

"Just about," Daniels said. "We like to know who we're dealing with. We didn't compromise you in any way with the Navy or the SEALs. We know how to gather information without the people knowing they are helping us."

"San Ysidro just ahead," Hernando said.

"Take the off-ramp, then go down two blocks and turn left into Pismo Street," Mahanani said. "The little garage has a rusted-out sign, a fence around it, and a wide driveway."

"Yeah, I see it," Hernando said.

"Just ease past it and go down to the end of the block," Daniels said. "Park so we can see the driveway." They had just parked, facing back toward the garage in front of a taco shop, when Mahanani pointed.

"Okay, that Pontiac just eased into the lot and parked where he's supposed to," Mahanani said. "The driver's getting out of the car."

The SEAL then saw that both backseat riders had out large field glasses and were tracking the man. He walked young, but Mahanani had no idea how old he was.

"Male, Caucasian, maybe thirty, wears glasses," Daniels said. "Blue pants, light blue shirt, might have a tie on. He's just going into the Triple A Auto Repair shop on Pismo

Street. This is in the San Ysidro section of San Diego, about three miles from the Mexican/U.S. border."

Mahanani looked back and saw Daniels lower a small tape recorder. "Helps my memory," he said.

"When do you call the men to the casino?"

"We've had undercover people there for two days."

"How did you know which one?"

"We talked to your cleaning lady. She said she was sure that was the one where you spent a lot of time and money. She showed us napkins and matchbooks and a flyer from the casino."

"Fucking sneaky," Mahanani said.

"Like you SEALs, we do whatever works. We go after the bad guys whole-bore with all our flags flying. Which is why you're here."

"The paper with my pardon on it," Mahanani said. He figured the DEA wouldn't give it up unless they had to. Daniels reached in his jacket pocket and took out an envelope. Mahanani opened the envelope, saw the stationery, and read the letter. He nodded, put in his pocket, and watched the kid walk into the garage door. The big door the cars drove into was closed.

"Don't try to tail him when he drives out," Mahanani said. "Yeah, I know you're experts, but with one or two cars you don't have a chance. There might be two hundred cars all trying to get into Mexico at the same time. The smugglers give the drivers tips on what to watch for in case they think somebody is following them. It's a good ten-minute course and they say it works."

"Somebody is coming out," Hernando said. One of the Mexican men from inside came out the regular door and pretended to pick up trash around the lot, but what he really did was check out the street both ways. The DEA men dropped below the level of the rear seat, and Hernando and Mahanani bent down as well when the man looked their way. After a good check around, the man went back inside the garage.

A moment later the drive-in door lifted and a six-year-old Plymouth eased out of the building and angled toward the driveway and the street.

"Same guy we saw leave the Pontiac," Daniels said. "We may have a go here." Mahanani realized that Daniels had switched to a foot-long handheld radio.

"We're on duty here at Gamble One," the radio speaker said. "I asked somebody where Harley was and she pointed him out to me. Told them I was trying to sell them a new type of soap for their rest rooms. He usually hangs out around the front doors. Once I saw him turn around a guy who looked like a street person. Another time he greeted a well-dressed woman and escorted her through a door marked employees only. Not sure where it goes. We're loose. So far I've lost only about ten dollars on the slots. I've got one with a good view of Harley."

"Stay with it. Could be two or three hours. We can't strike too fast. See what you can find out about three big guys who are used for punishment purposes."

"Roger that, Rover. Will do."

While the radio chattered, Mahanani watched the faded Plymouth sedan drive down the street a block and turn the corner toward Interstate 5.

"How long will he be gone?" Daniels asked, looking at his watch.

"They tell their mules to stay in TJ for at least three hours. The inspectors don't like over-and-back trips, cars that they can remember."

"But the inspectors on the U.S. side don't see the U.S. cars going in on the Mexican border," Ronkowski said.

"You're right, but they still tell their drivers three hours," Mahanani repeated.

"So," Hernando said. "We have time for a leisurely dinner in a good steak house."

The other two DEA men laughed.

"Right, Hernando. You're our chef. You get to hike to the nearest fast-food place and bring back enough fish sandwiches, burgers, and milk shakes for all four of us. Get a move on. I missed lunch today and I'm starved."

"I tried," Hernando said with a grin, and opened the door and closed it silently. He vanished down the street away from the garage to where a strip mall showed.

Three hours and a Big Mac and strawberry shake later,

Mahanani saw the six-year-old Plymouth pull up to the driveway and edge in slowly.

"Same license number," Daniels said, a note of satisfaction creeping into his voice.

"Wait until the rig is inside for at least ten minutes," Mahanani said. "Let them get it opened up to where the drugs are."

"The driver?" Ronkowski asked.

"Up to you. Let him walk or take him down, but do it quietly half a block down."

"Hernando, go now and grab the young man as he drives. We'll need him as a witness." The Mexican man left the car quietly and ran down the street and beyond the garage.

Daniels checked his watch. "Let's go," he said.

"Remember, there's that regular door in front and a door in back that's usually open," Mahanani said. "I'm staying here. There's a phone in the small office and probably a radio somewhere. Most men I've seen there are three." He watched the agents get out of the car. "When do you call the casino?"

"After we find the drugs and make the bust. Then we radio for them to close in. They have eight guys in the place and will do it quietly."

Mahanani nodded at the two DEA men, and they walked quickly down the street the half a block to the garage. He saw one at the front door and the other one vanish. A few moments later the man in front sprang into action.

DEA Agent Daniels took a deep breath, hefted his Glock fourteen-round automatic pistol, pulled the door open, and leaped inside. He heard the back door open at the same time.

Immediately in front of him was the old Plymouth that had been backed in. The rear seat had been taken out and the false floor had been pulled up showing bags of something.

"Hands in the air and don't move, you're all under arrest." One man jolted deeper into the building, which held two other cars being repaired. A second man lifted his hands. The third drew a weapon from his back pocket and snapped a shot at Daniels.

Another pistol barked from the back of the building, and the shooter screeched in pain and anger and crumpled to the floor. He didn't move again. Ronkowski rushed up and put his foot on the shooter's outstretched hand, which still held the pistol.

Daniels ducked behind the Plymouth and looked for the third man. He heard him behind the third car, but couldn't see him. A shot blasted into the sudden stillness of the garage, and Daniels reeled backward with a bullet in his shoulder. He ducked farther behind the car.

"Give yourself up," Ronkowski roared with a heavy voice. "You'll only end up wounded or dead. Throw out your weapon and come out with your hands—"

A shot blasted into his sentence. Ronkowski returned fire, six rounds under both cars toward the sound of the other gun. Nothing happened. Daniels held his right shoulder with his left hand to stop the flow of blood. He tried to raise the Glock, and got it up waist high. He aimed it at the third car and put a round through the rear window. Glass shattered as the panel erupted inward, granulating into small squares. He shot out the driver's-side rear window, and had a flash of the shooter, but he ducked away out of sight.

"No other doors or windows out of this firetrap," Ronkowski said. "We're DEA agents and you're under arrest for narcotics smuggling. Why get yourself dead for the big shots who make all the money? A few years in prison and you'll still be alive and back with your family."

Before Daniels could move again, he saw a figure lunge out from the cover of the third car and charge straight at him, a handgun in front firing. Daniels crouched behind the car's rear fender and after he heard six more shots, he lifted the Glock up and found the shooter four feet away and coming fast. Daniels shot him three times in the chest before he fell against the rear deck of the Plymouth and rolled off on the floor, the pistol sliding out of his hand.

Daniels checked him. "We've got a dead body here, Ronkowski. How's yours?"

"Dead and gone," Ronkowski said. "I've got one smart one here and about a hundred pounds of coke. I'll go bring up the car. This one is handcuffed to the rear door handle."

He came around the door and saw Daniels's bloody shoulder. "I'll get Mahanani in here. He's a medical corpsman and can fix up that shoulder until I get you to the hospital. Time to use the radio. What's the call signal."

"Casa Grande Takedown. Tell them we've got two dead and two prisoners including the driver and the coke. They should pounce on the casino guys."

Five minutes later, Mahanani had found a first-aid kit in the garage and treated the shoulder wound as best he could. "Not enough medicine or bandages in here to do much good, but I've got the blood stopped and your arm tied to your chest. I heard the other guy send in the troops at the casino. Hope to hell they get everyone."

"Where's the nearest emergency room?" Ronkowski asked. Mahanani shook his head.

Ronkowski used a cell phone and dialed 911. "Hi, 911, I'm a DEA agent and we have a wounded man. I'm in San Ysidro. Where's the nearest hospital with an emergency room?"

"Do you wish an ambulance?"

"No, just tell me where I can drive our wounded agent to."

"Just a moment, sir."

Ronkowski frowned.

Daniels scowled. "Ronkowski, you stay here and call for some backup to get the prisoners and the coke. Maybe Mahanani can drive me to the hospital."

"Sir, that would be the Paradise Valley Hospital in National City. That's at 2400 E. Fourth Street in National City. I have an ambulance driver to tell you how to get there from San Ysidro."

Ronkowski repeated the directions from the ambulance driver. It was up Interstate 5 and not far off the freeway. Mahanani memorized the route, then took Daniels out to the DEA car and helped him inside. Hernando had driven the smuggler's car back into the lot, with the driver handcuffed to the steering wheel, and went inside to help Ronkowski.

By the time Mahanani drove to the hospital, there were two DEA men there waiting for them. One took Daniels into Emergency, the other drove Mahanani back to his apartment in Coronado.

"How did it go at the casino?" the SEAL asked on the way back.

The DEA man shook his head. "Can't say a thing about that officially. But I understand you set up this raid. I'd say we came out pretty well."

Mahanani stared at his front door. When the DEA car drove away, he walked over to his Buick, slid in, and drove over the bridge and toward the casino. He had to find out just how deep the drug business went in the casino.

In the parking lot he saw no police cars, no yellow crime-scene tape. He parked and went in the front door. Harley did not grab him. He went straight to the floor manager, and then was taken to the night manager. He was an Indian with a ponytail.

"What's this about," he said. "I'm Long Bow Anderson, and I'm the boss around here at night."

"This has to do with Harley and Martillo."

The manager frowned. "How do you know about that?"

"Check your records. Martillo said I owned the casino six thousand dollars. I want to find out if his records are right."

"Can't be. We don't allow anyone to run a tab here. Against our rules. Cash or nothing. Only way we can do business. We do have a short list of those we have banned from playing here due to behavior. Let me check the computer."

He hit some keys on the computer and evidently read down a list. "Mahanani?"

The SEAL nodded. "Nobody by that name on our meet-greet-and-turn-around list." He hesitated. "You were involved with the highly illegal and totally unknown practices that Martillo had been conducting?"

"I got sucked into part of it, yes."

"Let me assure you that you do not have a debt with us, and that if there are any papers of any kind with your name on them, they will be returned to you. Did you put up any collateral for that phony IOU?"

"The pink slip for my car."

"We'll find it and get it back to you within a week. Is there anything else?"

"Martillo had friends. I don't want them coming after me. Was he taken by the DEA people tonight?"

Long Bow looked uncomfortable. "It was done with almost no disruption of our gaming. Yes, they took Martillo, Harley Thunder, and three other men who had originally been hired as bouncers here but had been discharged sometime ago. We believe that those five were the only criminals using our casino as a front for their illegal activities."

Mahanani grinned and stood. He held out his hand. "Thanks, you've taken a great load off my mind. You've given me my life back again."

He walked out of the office and to the gaming rooms. He started to go in, then stopped. There was no pull, not an appeal of any kind. The whole gambling fever had been washed out of him. Nothing like getting scared shitless to cure the gambling fever, Mahanani decided. He grinned and headed for his apartment in Coronado.

27

The day after they returned from Santa Barbara, Murdock sat in the office with Lieutenant Ed DeWitt and both were grinning.

"I told Milly and she kissed me for about ten minutes. We celebrated in the bedroom for the next two hours and had our cold dinner about ten o'clock. Oh, yeah, Milly is just damn glad that I'm getting rid of Third Platoon duties."

"I'm glad, but I'm pissed off too," Murdock said. "You're going to be impossible to replace, so I'll have to find a clone of you that I can train up to your level of skill and technique and judgment in the field. Gonna be one tough mother to find that kind of a man."

"Yeah, I bet. You must have the master chief lining up a dozen candidates right now."

"Fact is, I haven't. I just put the paperwork through yesterday afternoon. We don't even know if the Old Man will buy you for that vacancy. I'm betting he will, but you can never second-guess the commander."

"In the meantime the fight goes on," DeWitt said. "What's on deck for training today?"

"Haven't even thought about it. We do need a new man for your squad. That's going to take some doing. Be pleased if you'd sit in on the selection even though you're for sure a lame duck of a squad leader."

"Hey, I like the sound of that. I want to get the best man I can to replace Franklin. Never realize how many good things a man does until he's not doing them anymore. I'll check with the master chief. He's probably got a list of young gung-ho candidates for our platoon who are just itching to get shot at."

"Work on that first. We'll do that jogging and O course work we were going to do yesterday."

Jaybird stuck his nose in the door. "Hey, Skipper, no day off after a mission?"

"You call that walk in the park yesterday a mission, Jaybird? Damn but you're getting soft and touchy in your old age. What arc you, twenty-five now?"

"Getting close, Skipper. Don't worry about us troops out there in the hot sun. Hell, this is what we signed on to do, right? To get shot at. My bet is we hit the O course today."

"Jaybird, get your ass out of here, we're busy."

Jaybird gave an exaggerated salute, a snappy about-face, and hurried out the door.

The phone rang and Murdock picked it up. "Team Seven, Third Platoon, Murdock here."

There was a slight pause. Then the voice came soft and totally feminine. "You always sound so brusque and tough when you say that. You going to be home for lunch?"

"How did the interview go yesterday? I got back so late last night I didn't want to wake you."

"Interview? Interview? I had an interview yesterday? Oh, yes, that old thing. It went fine. We'll talk about it over lunch. I have some shrimp I need to do something with. See what I can whip up."

"See you at twelve-ten."

"See you too. Byc."

DeWitt looked up from the training schedule. "Interview? For Ardith? Whoa, you mean she might move out here?"

"She went to a job-offer meeting yesterday, and I was so bummed out when I got back I didn't wake her and ask her about it. This morning I got in early. Yeah, she had a talk with some guys here who chased her down in D.C. and want her brain out here."

"That scare you a little, old buddy? The ball and chain, and all that sort of stuff. Maybe even the center aisle. Get your scare machine wound up a bit? Hey, it isn't so bad. Believe me."

"Yeah, you're an old married man of what, eight months or so? You're the expert."

They both laughed.

"Hell, there aren't any experts on women or on marriage," DeWitt said. "Just have to take the woman one day at a time, and the marriage one second at a time. And that's my expert opinion."

DeWitt chuckled as he headed for the Quarter Deck to talk with the master chief about a replacement for Franklin. Murdock looked at his roster, then at the officers in the other platoons on Team Seven. He didn't see any one man who stood out over the rest. He'd have to look for a JG. He didn't even know some of the men. Others he had come up through the officer ranks with.

He pushed it aside. He would talk with the master chief if and when Masciareli gave him the go-ahead for a transfer of DeWitt to his own platoon. He looked at the in basket on his small desk and decided it was time to bite the bullet and get some of it cleaned up.

Noon came before he was ready. He drove home quickly and ran up the steps to his second-floor apartment. Ardith met him at the door with a huge hug. She wouldn't let him go.

When he carried her into the kitchen, she at last relaxed her grip on him and lifted her head off his shoulder. Her soft blue eyes were so excited she didn't have to say a thing. But it was her day. He waited.

"Did the interview yesterday go well?"

"Yes." Her grin made her look ten years younger, like a high school kid who'd just found out she'd made the cheerleader squad.

"Went well, extremely well. They liked me. I liked what I saw, and I was taken by the people. Casual, relaxed, yet sharp, inventive, and constructive. They showed me through the routine of a job, a client, their problem, how it was worked on until a solution came, and then a unique way to solve the problem with software that we designed."

She led him to the kitchen table and held the chair for him. Murdock sat down feeling strange being waited on this way.

"You made up your mind?" he asked.

"Oh, yes. I'm taking the job. It's going to be glorious. I can let my creativity flow and billow and soar." She watched him closely. Murdock jumped up, knocked the chair over backward, grabbed Ardith, and lifted her off the floor and twirled her around in the small kitchen.

"Great! Just great. I'm as happy as you are that it worked out so well. When do you start?"

"They wanted me to start tomorrow. I told them I had to give two weeks notice and then pack up and move, and I thought maybe we could find a bigger place, more than one bedroom. You never can tell what might happen. And I can use the second bedroom as a home office, and maybe not go in every day, and all of that, and then you might want a den or . . ." She watched him again intently.

He grinned and sat her down at the table. "Hey, don't worry about it. If you want a bigger place, we get a bigger place. We could even think about buying a house, maybe a used one, the new ones cost so damn much, a half million dollars and up."

Ardith shivered. "So much?"

"We'll work it out. For now we'll store most of your stuff and you move in here and then we start looking. Going to be a big change for both of us."

She reached across the table and grabbed his hands. "You are pleased then?"

"If you're this happy, how can I not be happy too? Happy never fills a stomach. What's for lunch?"

"It seems to me I said this once before. But, well, since you didn't have almost anything in the house to eat, I ate the shrimp before you came. So, well. Hey, your lunch is me." Ardith jumped up from the table and ran into the bedroom. She beat Murdock there by only half a step.

SEAL TALK

MILITARY GLOSSARY

Aalvin: Small U.S. two-man submarine.

Admin: Short for administration.

Aegis: Advanced Naval air defense radar system.

AH-1W Super Cobra: Has M179 undernose turret with 20mm Gatling gun.

AK-47: 7.63-round Russian Kalashnikov automatic rifle. Most widely used assault rifle in the world.

AK-74: New, improved version of the Kalashnikov. Fires the 5.45mm round. Has 30-round magazine. Rate of fire: 600 rounds per minute. Many slight variations made for many different nations.

AN/PRC-117D: Radio, also called SATCOM. Works with Milstar satellite in 22,300-mile equatorial orbit for instant worldwide radio, voice, or video communications. Size: 15 inches high, 3 inches wide, 3 inches deep. Weighs 15 pounds. Microphone and voice output. Has encrypter, capable of burst transmissions of less than a second.

AN/PUS-7: Night-vision goggles. Weighs 1.5 pounds.

ANVIS-6: Night-vision goggles on air crewmen's helmets.

APC: Armored Personnel Carrier.

ASROC: Nuclear-tipped antisubmarine rocket torpedoes launched by Navy ships.

Assault Vest: Combat vest with full loadouts of ammo, gear.

ASW: Anti-Submarine Warfare.

Attack Board: Molded plastic with two handgrips with bubble compass on it. Also depth gauge and Cyalume chemical lights with twist knob to regulate amount of light. Used for underwater guidance on long swim.

Aurora: Air Force recon plane. Can circle at 90,000 feet. Can't be seen or heard from ground. Used for thermal imaging.

AWACS: Airborne Warning And Control System. Radar units in high-flying aircraft to scan for planes at any altitude out 200 miles. Controls air-to-air engagements with enemy forces. Planes have a mass of communication and electronic equipment.

Balaclavas: Headgear worn by some SEALs.

Bent Spear: Less serious nuclear violation of safety.

BKA, Bundeskriminant: Germany's federal investigation unit.

Black Talon: Lethal hollow-point ammunition made by Winchester. Outlawed some places.

Blivet: A collapsible fuel container. SEALs sometimes use it.

BLU-43B: Antipersonnel mine used by SEALs.

BLU-96: A fuel-air explosive bomb. It disperses a fuel oil into the air, then explodes the cloud. Many times more powerful than conventional bombs because it doesn't carry its own chemical oxidizers.

BMP-1: Soviet armored fighting vehicle (AFV), low, boxy, crew of 3 and 8 combat troops. Has tracks and a 73mm cannon. Also an AT-3 Sagger antitank missile and coaxial machine gun.

Body Armor: Far too heavy for SEAL use in the water.

Bogey: Pilots' word for an unidentified aircraft.

Boghammar Boat: Long, narrow, low dagger boat; high-speed patrol craft. Swedish make. Iran had 40 of them in 1993.

Boomer: A nuclear-powered missile submarine.

Bought It: A man has been killed. Also "bought the farm."

Bow Cat: The bow catapult on a carrier to launch jets.

Broken Arrow: Any accident with nuclear weapons, or any incident of nuclear material lost, shot down, crashed, stolen, hijacked.

Browning 9mm High Power: A Belgium 9mm pistol, 13 rounds in magazine. First made 1935.

Buddy Line: 6 feet long, ties 2 SEALs together in the water for control and help if needed.

BUD/S: Coronado, California, nickname for SEAL training facility for six months' course.

Bull Pup. Still in testing; new soldier's rifle. SEALs have a dozen of them for regular use. Army gets them in 2005. Has a 5.56 kinetic round, 30-shot clip. Also 20mm high-explosive round and 5-shot magazine. Twenties can be fused for proximity airbursts with use of video camera, laser range finder, and laser targeting. Fuses by number of turns the round needs to reach laser spot. Max range: 1200 yards. Twenty round can also detonate on contact, and has delay fuse. Weapon weighs 14 pounds. SEALs love it. Can in effect "shoot around corners" with the airburst feature.

BUPERS: BUreau of PERSonnel.

C-2A Greyhound: 2-engine turboprop cargo plane that lands on carriers. Also called COD, Carrier Onboard Delivery. Two pilots and engineer. Rear fuselage loading ramp. Cruise speed 300 mph, range 1,000 miles. Will hold 39 combat troops. Lands on CVN carriers at sea.

C-4: Plastic explosive. A claylike explosive that can be molded and shaped. It will burn. Fairly stable.

C-6 Plastique: Plastic explosive. Developed from C-4 and C-5. Is often used in bombs with radio detonator or digital timer.

C-9 Nightingale: Douglas DC-9 fitted as a medical-evacuation transport plane.

C-130 Hercules: Air Force transporter for long haul. 4 engines.

C-141 Starlifter: Airlift transport for cargo, paratroops, evac for long distances. Top speed 566 mph. Range with payload 2,935 miles. Ceiling 41,600 feet.

Caltrops: Small four-pointed spikes used to flatten tires. Used in the Crusades to disable horses.

Camel Back: Used with drinking tube for 70 ounces of water attached to vest.

Cammies: Working camouflaged wear for SEALs. Two different patterns and colors. Jungle and desert.

Cannon Fodder: Old term for soldiers in line of fire destined to die in the grand scheme of warfare.

Capped: Killed, shot, or otherwise snuffed.

CAR-15: The Colt M-4A1. Sliding-stock carbine with grenade launcher under barrel. Knight sound-suppressor. Can have AN/PAQ-4 laser aiming light under the carrying handle. .223 round. 20- or 30-round magazine. Rate of fire: 700 to 1,000 rounds per minute.

Cascade Radiation: U-235 triggers secondary radiation in other dense materials.

Castle Keep: The main tower in any castle.

Cast Off: Leave a dock, port, land. Get lost. Navy: long, then short signal of horn, whistle, or light.

Caving Ladder: Roll-up ladder that can be let down to climb.

CH-46E: Sea Knight chopper. Twin rotors, transport. Can carry 25 combat troops. Has a crew of 3. Cruise speed 154 mph. Range 420 miles.

CH-53D Sea Stallion: Big Chopper. Not used much anymore.

Chaff: A small cloud of thin pieces of metal, such as tinsel, that can be picked up by enemy radar and that can attract a radar-guided missile away from the plane to hit the chaff.

Charlie-Mike: Code words for continue the mission.

Chief to Chief: Bad conduct by EM handled by chiefs so no record shows or is passed up the chain of command.

Chocolate Mountains: Land training center for SEALs near these mountains in the California desert.

Christians In Action: SEAL talk for not-always-friendly CIA.

CIA: Central Intelligence Agency.

CIC: Combat Information Center. The place on a ship where communications and control areas are situated to open and control combat fire.

CINC: Commander IN Chief.

CINCLANT: Navy Commander-IN-Chief, atLANTtic.

CINCPAC: Commander-IN-Chief, PACific.

Class of 1978: Not a single man finished BUD/S training in this class. All-time record.

Claymore: An antipersonnel mine carried by SEALs on many of their missions.

Cluster Bombs: A canister bomb that explodes and spreads small bomblets over a great area. Used against parked aircraft, massed troops, and unarmored vehicles.

CNO: Chief of Naval Operations.

CO-2 Poisoning: During deep dives. Abort dive at once and surface.

COD: Carrier Onboard Delivery plane.

Cold Pack Rations: Food carried by SEALs to use if needed.

Combat Harness: American Body Armor nylon-mesh special-operations vest. 6 2-magazine pouches for drum-fed belts, other pouches for other weapons, waterproof pouch for Motorola.

CONUS: The Continental United States.

Corfams: Dress shoes for SEALs.

Covert Action Staff: A CIA group that handles all covert action by the SEALs.

CQB: Close Quarters Battle house. Training facility near Nyland in the desert training area. Also called the Kill House.

CQB: Close Quarters Battle. A fight that's up close, hand-to-hand, whites-of-his-eyes, blood all over you.

CRRC Bundle: Roll it off plane, sub, boat. The assault boat for 8 SEALs. Also the IBS, Inflatable Boat Small.

Cutting Charge: Lead-sheathed explosive. Triangular strip of high-velocity explosive sheathed in metal. Point of the triangle focuses a shaped-charge effect. Cuts a pencil-line-wide hole to slice a steel girder in half.

CVN: A U.S. aircraft carrier with nuclear power. Largest that we have in fleet.

CYA: Cover Your Ass, protect yourself from friendlies or officers above you and JAG people.

Damfino: Damned if I know. SEAL talk.

DDS: Dry Dock Shelter. A clamshell unit on subs to deliver SEALs and SDVs to a mission.

DEFCON: DEFense CONdition. How serious is the threat?

Delta Forces: Army special forces, much like SEALs.

Desert Cammies: Three-color, desert tan and pale green with streaks of pink. For use on land.

DIA: Defense Intelligence Agency.

Dilos Class Patrol Boat: Greek, 29 feet long, 75 tons displacement.

Dirty Shirt Mess: Officers can eat there in flying suits on board a carrier.

DNS: Doppler Navigation System.

Draegr LAR V: Rebreather that SEALs use. No bubbles.

DREC: Digitally Reconnoiterable Electronic Component. Top-secret computer chip from NSA that lets it decipher any U.S. military electronic code.

E-2C Hawkeye: Navy, carrier-based, Airborne Early Warning craft for long-range early warning and threat-assessment and fighter-direction. Has a 24-foot saucer-like rotodome over the wing. Crew 5, max speed 326 knots, ceiling 30,800 feet, radius 175 nautical miles with 4 hours on station.

E-3A Skywarrior: Old electronic intelligence craft. Replaced by the newer ES-3A.

E-4B NEACP: Called Kneecap. National Emergency Airborne Command Post. A greatly modified Boeing 747 used as a communications base for the President of the United States and other high-ranking officials in an emergency and in wartime.

E & E: SEAL talk for escape and evasion.

EA-6B Prowler: Navy plane with electronic countermeasures. Crew of 4, max speed 566 knots, ceiling 41,200 feet, range with max load 955 nautical miles.

EAR: Enhanced Acoustic Rifle. Fires not bullets, but a high-impact blast of sound that puts the target down and unconscious for up to six hours. Leaves him with almost no aftereffects. Used as a non-lethal weapon. The sound blast will bounce around inside a building, vehicle, or ship and knock out anyone who is within range. Ten shots before the weapon must be electrically charged. Range: about 200 yards.

Easy: The only easy day was yesterday. SEAL talk.

Ejection seat: The seat is powered by a CAD, a shotgun-like shell that is activated when the pilot triggers the ejection. The shell is fired into a solid rocket, sets it off and propels the whole ejection seat and pilot into the air. No electronics are involved.

ELINT: ELectronic INTelligence. Often from satellite in orbit, picture-taker, or other electronic communications.

EMP: ElectroMagnetic Pulse: The result of an E-bomb detonation. One type E-bomb is the Flux Compression Generator or FCG. Can be built for $400 and is relatively simple to make. Emits a rampaging electromagnetic pulse that destroys anything electronic in a 100 mile diameter circle. Blows out and fries all computers, telephone systems, TV broadcasts, radio, streetlights, and sends the area back into the stone age with no communications whatsoever. Stops all cars with electronic ignitions, drops jet planes out of the air including airliners, fighters and bombers, and stalls ships with electronic guidance and steering systems. When such a bomb is detonated the explosion is small but sounds like a giant lightning strike.

EOD: Navy experts in nuclear material and radioactivity who do Explosive Ordnance Disposal.

Equatorial Satellite Pointing Guide: To aim antenna for radio to pick up satellite signals.

ES-3A: Electronic Intelligence (ELINT) intercept craft. The platform for the battle group Passive Horizon Extension System. Stays up for long patrol periods, has comprehensive set of sensors, lands and takes off from a carrier. Has 63 antennas.

ETA: Estimated Time of Arrival.

Executive Order 12333: By President Reagan authorizing Special Warfare units such as the SEALs.

Exfil: Exfiltrate, to get out of an area.

F/A-18 Hornet: Carrier-based interceptor that can change from air-to-air to air-to-ground attack mode while in flight.

Fitrep: Fitness Report.

Flashbang Grenade: Non-lethal grenade that gives off a series of piercing explosive sounds and a series of brilliant strobe-type lights to disable an enemy.

Flotation Bag: To hold equipment, ammo, gear on a wet operation.

Fort Fumble: SEALs' name for the Pentagon.

Forty-mm Rifle Grenade: The M576 multipurpose round, contains 20 large lead balls. SEALs use on Colt M-4A1.

Four-Striper: A Navy captain.

Fox Three: In air warfare, a code phrase showing that a Navy F-14 has launched a Phoenix air-to-air missile.

FUBAR: SEAL talk. Fucked Up Beyond All Repair.

Full Helmet Masks: For high-altitude jumps. Oxygen in mask.

G-3: German-made assault rifle.

Gloves: SEALs wear sage-green, fire-resistant Nomex flight gloves.

GMT: Greenwich Mean Time. Where it's all measured from.

GPS: Global Positioning System. A program with satellites around Earth to pinpoint precisely aircraft, ships, vehicles, and ground troops. Position information is to a plus or minus ten feet. Also can give speed of a plane or ship to one quarter of a mile per hour.

GPSL: A radio antenna with floating wire that pops to the surface. Antenna picks up positioning from the closest 4 global positioning satellites and gives an exact position within 10 feet.

Green Tape: Green sticky ordnance tape that has a hundred uses for a SEAL.

GSG-9: Flashbang grenade developed by Germans. A cardboard tube filled with 5 separate charges timed to burst in rapid succession. Blinding and giving concussion to enemy, leaving targets stunned, easy to kill or capture. Usually non-lethal.

GSG9: Grenzschutzgruppe Nine. Germany's best special warfare unit, counterterrorist group.

Gulfstream II (VCII): Large executive jet used by services for transport of small groups quickly. Crew of 3 and 18 passengers. Maximum cruise speed 581 mph. Maximum range 4,275 miles.

H & K 21A1: Machine gun with 7.62 NATO round. Replaces the older, more fragile M-60 E3. Fires 900 rounds per minute. Range 1,100 meters. All types of NATO rounds, ball, incendiary, tracer.

H & K G-11: Automatic rifle, new type. 4.7mm caseless ammunition. 50-round magazine. The bullet is in a sleeve of solid propellant with a special thin plastic coating around it. Fires 600 rounds per minute. Single-shot, three-round burst, or fully automatic.

H & K MP-5SD: 9mm submachine gun with integral silenced barrel, single-shot, three-shot, or fully automatic. Rate 800 rds/min.

H & K P9S: Heckler & Koch's 9mm Parabellum double-action semiauto pistol with 9-round magazine.

H & K PSG1: 7.62 NATO round. High-precision, bolt-action, sniping rifle. 5- to 20-round magazine. Roller lock delayed blowback breech system. Fully adjustable stock. 6-×-42 telescopic sights. Sound suppressor.

HAHO: High Altitude jump, High Opening. From 30,000 feet, open chute for glide up to 15 miles to ground. Up to 75 minutes in glide. To enter enemy territory or enemy position unheard.

Half-Track: Military vehicle with tracked rear drive and wheels in front, usually armed and armored.

HALO: High Altitude jump, Low Opening. From 30,000 feet. Free fall in 2 minutes to 2,000 feet and open chute. Little forward movement. Get to ground quickly, silently.

Hamburgers: Often called sliders on a Navy carrier.

Handie-Talkie: Small, handheld personal radio. Short range.

HELO: SEAL talk for helicopter.

Herky Bird: C-130 Hercules transport. Most-flown military transport in the world. For cargo or passengers, paratroops, aerial refueling, search and rescue, communications, and as a gunship. Has flown from a Navy carrier deck without use of catapult. Four turboprop engines, max speed 325 knots, range at max payload 2,356 miles.

Hezbollah: Lebanese Shiite Moslem militia. Party of God.

HMMWU: The Humvee, U.S. light utility truck, replaced the honored jeep. Multipurpose wheeled vehicle, 4 × 4, automatic transmission, power steering. Engine: Detroit Diesel 150-hp diesel V-8 air-cooled. Top speed 65 mph. Range 300 miles.

Hotels: SEAL talk for hostages.

Humint: Human Intelligence. Acquired on the ground; a person as opposed to satellite or photo recon.

Hydra-Shock: Lethal hollow-point ammunition made by Federal Cartridge Company. Outlawed in some areas.

Hypothermia: Danger to SEALs. A drop in body temperature that can be fatal.

IBS: Inflatable Boat Small. 12 × 6 feet. Carries 8 men and 1,000 pounds of weapons and gear. Hard to sink. Quiet motor. Used for silent beach, bay, lake landings.

IR Beacon: Infrared beacon. For silent nighttime signaling.

IR Goggles: "Sees" heat instead of light.

Islamic Jihad: Arab holy war.

Isothermal layer: A colder layer of ocean water that deflects sonar rays. Submarines can hide below it, but then are also blind to what's going on above them since their sonar will not penetrate the layer.

IV Pack: Intravenous fluid that you can drink if out of water.

JAG: Judge Advocate General. The Navy's legal investigating arm that is independent of any Navy command.

JNA: Yugoslav National Army.

JP-4: Normal military jet fuel.

JSOC: Joint Special Operations Command.

JSOCCOMCENT: Joint Special Operations Command Center in the Pentagon.

KA-BAR: SEALs' combat, fighting knife.

KATN: Kick Ass and Take Names. SEAL talk, get the mission in gear.

KH-11: Spy satellite, takes pictures of ground, IR photos, etc.

KIA: Killed In Action.

KISS: Keep It Simple, Stupid. SEAL talk for streamlined operations.

Klick: A kilometer of distance. Often used as a mile. From Vietnam era, but still widely used in military.

Krytrons: Complicated, intricate timers used in making nuclear explosive detonators.

KV-57: Encoder for messages, scrambles.

Laser Pistol: The SIW pinpoint of ruby light emitted on any pistol for aiming. Usually a silenced weapon.

Left Behind: In 30 years SEALs have seldom left behind a dead comrade, never a wounded one. Never been taken prisoner.

Let's Get the Hell out of Dodge: SEAL talk for leaving a place, bugging out, hauling ass.

Liaison: Close-connection, cooperating person from one unit or service to another. Military liaison.

Light Sticks: Chemical units that make light after twisting to release chemicals that phosphoresce.

Loot & Shoot: SEAL talk for getting into action on a mission.

LT: Short for lieutenant in SEAL talk.

LZ: Landing Zone.

M1-8: Russian Chopper.

M1A1 M-14: Match rifle upgraded for SEAL snipers.

M-3 Submachine gun: WWII grease gun, .45-caliber. Cheap. Introduced in 1942.

M-16: Automatic U.S. rifle. 5.56 round. Magazine 20 or 30, rate of fire 700 to 950 rds/min. Can attach M203 40mm grenade launcher under barrel.

M-18 Claymore: Antipersonnel mine. A slab of C-4 with 200 small ball bearings. Set off electrically or by trip wire. Can be positioned and aimed. Sprays out a cloud of balls. Kill zone 50 meters.

M60 Machine Gun: Can use 100-round ammo box snapped onto the gun's receiver. Not used much now by SEALs.

M-60E3: Lightweight handheld machine gun. Not used now by the SEALs.

M61A1: The usual 20mm cannon used on many American fighter planes.

M61(j): Machine Pistol. Yugoslav make.

M662: A red flare for signaling.

M-86: Pursuit Deterrent Munitions. Various types of mines, grenades, trip-wire explosives, and other devices in antipersonnel use.

M-203: A 40mm grenade launcher fitted under an M-16 or the M-4A1 Commando. Can fire a variety of grenade types up to 200 yards.

MagSafe: Lethal ammunition that fragments in human body and does not exit. Favored by some police units to cut down on second kill from regular ammunition exiting a body.

Make a Peek: A quick look, usually out of the water, to check your position or tactical situation.

Mark 23 Mod O: Special operations offensive handgun system. Double-action, 12-round magazine. Ambidextrous safety and mag-release catches. Knight screw-on suppressor. Snap-on laser for sighting. .45-caliber. Weighs 4 pounds loaded. 9.5 inches long; with silencer, 16.5 inches long.

Mark II Knife: Navy-issue combat knife.

Mark VIII SDV: Swimmer Delivery Vehicle. A bus, SEAL talk. 21 feet long, beam and draft 4 feet, 6 knots for 6 hours.

Master-at-Arms: Military police commander on board a ship.

MAVRIC Lance: A nuclear alert for stolen nukes or radioactive goods.

MC-130 Combat Talon: A specially equipped Hercules for covert missions in enemy or unfriendly territory.

McMillan M87R: Bolt-action sniper rifle. .50-caliber. 53 inches long. Bipod, fixed 5- or 10-round magazine. Bulbous muzzle brake on end of barrel. Deadly up to a mile. All types .50-caliber ammo.

MGS: Modified Grooming Standards. So SEALs don't all look like military, to enable them to do undercover work in mufti.

MH-53J: Chopper, updated CH053 from Nam days. 200 mph, called the Pave Low III.

MH-60K Black Hawk: Navy chopper. Forward infrared system for low-level night flight. Radar for terra follow/avoidance. Crew of 3, takes 12 troops. Top speed 225 mph. Ceiling 4,000 feet. Range radius 230 miles. Arms: 2 12.7mm machine guns.

MI-15: British domestic intelligence agency.

MI-16: British foreign intelligence and espionage.

MIDEASTFOR: Middle East Force.

MiG: Russian-built fighter, many versions, used in many nations around the world.

Mike Boat: Liberty boat off a large ship.

Mike-Mike: Short for mm, millimeter, as 9 mike-mike.

Milstar: Communications satellite for pickup and bouncing from SATCOM and other radio transmitters. Used by SEALs.

Minigun: In choppers. Can fire 2,000 rounds per minute. Gatling gun-type.

Mitrajez M80: Machine gun from Yugoslavia.

Mocha: Food energy bar SEALs carry in vest pockets.

Mossberg: Pump-action, pistol-grip, 5-round magazine. SEALs use it for close-in work.

Motorola Radio: Personal radio, short range, lip mike, earpiece, belt pack.

MRE: Meals Ready to Eat. Field rations used by most of U.S. Armed Forces and the SEALs as well. Long-lasting.

MSPF: Maritime Special Purpose Force.

Mugger: MUGR, Miniature Underwater Global locator device. Sends up antenna for pickup on positioning satellites. Works under water or above. Gives location within 10 feet.

Mujahideen: A soldier of Allah in Muslim nations.

NAVAIR: NAVy AIR command.

NAVSPECWARGRUP-ONE: Naval Special Warfare Group One based on Coronado, CA. SEALs are in this command.

NAVSPECWARGRUP-TWO: Naval Special Warfare Group Two based at Little Creek, VA.

NCIS: Naval Criminal Investigative Service. A civilian operation not reporting to any Navy authority to make it more responsible and responsive. Replaces the old NIS, Naval Investigation Service, that did report to the closest admiral.

NEST: Nuclear Energy Search Team. Non-military unit that reports at once to any spill, problem, or Broken Arrow to determine the extent of the radiation problem.

NEWBIE: A new man, officer, or commander of an established military unit.

NKSF: North Korean Special Forces.

NLA: Iranian National Liberation Army. About 4,500 men in South Iraq, helped by Iraq for possible use against Iran.

Nomex: The type of material used for flight suits and hoods.

NPIC: National Photographic Interpretation Center in D.C.

NRO: National Reconnaissance Office. To run and coordinate satellite development and operations for the intelligence community.

NSA: National Security Agency.

NSC: National Security Council. Meets in Situation Room, support facility in the Executive Office Building in D.C. Main security group in the nation.

NSVHURAWN: Iranian Marines.

NUCFLASH: An alert for any nuclear problem.

NVG One Eye: Litton single-eyepiece Night-Vision Goggles. Prevents NVG blindness in both eyes if a flare goes off. Scope shows green-tinted field at night.

NVGs: Night-Vision Goggles. One eye or two. Give good night vision in the dark with a greenish view.

OAS: Obstacle Avoidance Sonar. Used on many low-flying attack aircraft.

OIC: Officer In Charge.

Oil Tanker: One is: 885 feet long, 140 foot beam, 121,000 tons, 13 cargo tanks that hold 35.8 million gallons of fuel, oil, or gas. 24 in the crew. This is a regular-sized tanker. Not a supertanker.

OOD: Officer Of the Deck.

Orion P-3: Navy's long-range patrol and antisub aircraft. Some adapted to ELINT roles. Crew of 10. Max speed loaded 473 mph. Ceiling 28,300 feet. Arms: internal weapons bay and 10 external weapons stations for a mix of torpedoes, mines, rockets, and bombs.

Passive Sonar: Listening for engine noise of a ship or sub. It doesn't give away the hunter's presence as an active sonar would.

Pave Low III: A Navy chopper.

PBR: Patrol Boat River. U.S. has many shapes, sizes, and with various types of armament.

PC-170: Patrol Coastal-Class 170-foot SEAL delivery vehicle. Powered by 4 3,350 hp diesel engines, beam of 25 feet and draft of 7.8 feet. Top speed 35 knots, range 2,000 nautical miles. Fixed swimmer platform on stern. Crew of 4 officers and 24 EM, carries 8 SEALs.

Plank Owners: Original men in the start-up of a new military unit.

Polycarbonate material: Bullet-proof glass.

PRF: People's Revolutionary Front. Fictional group in *NUCFLASH,* a SEAL Team Seven book.

Prowl & Growl: SEAL talk for moving into a combat mission.

Quitting Bell: In BUD/S training. Ring it and you quit the SEAL unit. Helmets of men who quit the class are lined up below the bell in Coronado. (Recently they have stopped ringing the bell. Dropouts simply place their helmet below the bell and go.)

RAF: Red Army Faction. A once-powerful German terrorist group, not so active now.

Remington 200: Sniper Rifle. Not used by SEALs now.

Remington 700: Sniper rifle with Starlight Scope. Can extend night vision to 400 meters.

RIB: Rigid Inflatable Boat. 3 sizes, one 10 meters, 40 knots.

Ring Knocker: An Annapolis graduate with the ring.

RIO: Radar Intercept Officer. The officer who sits in the backseat of an F-14 Tomcat off a carrier. The job: find enemy targets in the air and on the sea.

Roger That: A yes, an affirmative, a go answer to a command or statement.

RPG: Rocket Propelled Grenade. Quick and easy, shoulder-fired. Favorite weapon of terrorists, insurgents.

SAS: British Special Air Service. Commandos. Special warfare men. Best that Britain has. Works with SEALs.

SATCOM: Satellite-based communications system for instant contact with anyone anywhere in the world. SEALs rely on it.

SAW: Squad's Automatic Weapon. Usually a machine gun or automatic rifle.

SBS: Special Boat Squadron. On-site Navy unit that transports SEALs to many of their missions. Located across the street from the SEALs' Coronado, California, headquarters.

SD3: Sound-suppression system on the H & K MP5 weapon.

SDV: Swimmer Delivery Vehicle. SEALs use a variety of them.

Seahawk SH-60: Navy chopper for ASW and SAR. Top speed 180 knots, ceiling 13,800 feet, range 503 miles, arms: 2 Mark 46 torpedoes.

SEAL Headgear: Boonie hat, wool balaclava, green scarf, watch cap, bandanna roll.

Second in Command: Also 2IC for short in SEAL talk.

SERE: Survival, Evasion, Resistance, and Escape training.

Shipped for Six: Enlisted for six more years in the Navy.

Shit City: Coronado SEALs' name for Norfolk.

Show Colors: In combat put U.S. flag or other identification on back for easy identification by friendly air or ground units.

Sierra Charlie: SEAL talk for everything on schedule.

Simunition: Canadian product for training that uses paint balls instead of lead for bullets.

Sixteen-Man Platoon: Basic SEAL combat force. Up from 14 men a few years ago.

Sked: SEAL talk for schedule.

Sonobuoy: Small underwater device that detects sounds and transmits them by radio to plane or ship.

Space Blanket: Green foil blanket to keep troops warm. Vacuum-packed and folded to a cigarette-sized package.

SPIE: Special Purpose Insertion and Extraction rig. Essentially a long rope dangled from a chopper with hardware on it that is attached to each SEAL's chest right on his lift harness. Set up to lift six or eight men out of harm's way quickly by a chopper.

Sprayers and Prayers: Not the SEAL way. These men spray bullets all over the place hoping for hits. SEALs do more aimed firing for sure kills.

SS-19: Russian ICBM missile.

STABO: Use harness and lines under chopper to get down to the ground.

STAR: Surface To Air Recovery operation.

Starflash Round: Shotgun round that shoots out sparkling fireballs that ricochet wildly around a room, confusing and terrifying the occupants. Non-lethal.

Stasi: Old-time East German secret police.

Stick: British terminology: 2 4-man SAS teams. 8 men.

Stokes: A kind of Navy stretcher. Open coffin shaped of wire mesh and white canvas for emergency patient transport.

STOL: Short TakeOff and Landing. Aircraft with high-lift wings and vectored-thrust engines to produce extremely short takeoffs and landings.

Sub Gun: Submachine gun, often the suppressed H & K MP5.

Suits: Civilians, usually government officials wearing suits.

Sweat: The more SEALs sweat in peacetime, the less they bleed in war.

Sykes-Fairbairn: A commando fighting knife.

Syrette: Small syringe for field administration often filled with morphine. Can be self-administered.

Tango: SEAL talk for a terrorist.

TDY: Temporary duty assigned outside of normal job designation.

Terr: Another term for terrorist. Shorthand SEAL talk.

Tetrahedral reflectors: Show up on multi-mode radar like tiny suns.

Thermal Imager: Device to detect warmth, as a human body, at night or through light cover.

Thermal Tape: ID for night-vision-goggle user to see. Used on friendlies.

TNAZ: Trinittroaze Tidine. Explosive to replace C-4. 15% stronger than C-4 and 20% lighter.

TO&E: Table showing organization and equipment of a military unit.

Top SEAL Tribute: "You sweet motherfucker, don't you never die!"

Trailing Array: A group of antennas for sonar pickup trailed out of a submarine.

Train: For contact in smoke, no light, fog, etc. Men directly behind each other. Right hand on weapon, left hand on shoulder of man ahead. Squeeze shoulder to signal.

Trident: SEALs' emblem. An eagle with talons clutching a Revolutionary War pistol, and Neptune's trident superimposed on the Navy's traditional anchor.

TRW: A camera's digital record that is sent by SATCOM.

TT33: Tokarev, a Russian pistol.

UAZ: A Soviet 1-ton truck.

UBA Mark XV: Underwater life support with computer to regulate the rebreather's gas mixture.

UGS: Unmanned Ground Sensors. Can be used to explode booby traps and claymore mines.

UNODIR: Unless otherwise directed. The unit will start the operation unless they are told not to.

VBSS: Orders to "visit, board, search, and seize."

Wadi: A gully or ravine, usually in a desert.

White Shirt: Man responsible for safety on carrier deck as he leads around civilians and personnel unfamiliar with the flight deck.

WIA: Wounded In Action.

Zodiac: Also called an IBS, Inflatable Boat Small. 15 × 6 feet, weighs 265 pounds. The "rubber duck" can carry 8 fully equipped SEALs. Can do 18 knots with a range of 65 nautical miles.

Zulu: Means Greenwich Mean Time, GMT. Used in all formal military communications.

SEAL TEAM SEVEN
Keith Douglass
Don't miss the rest of
the explosive series: